The Queen's Wing

JESSICA THORNE

Bookouture

Published by Bookouture in 2018

An imprint of StoryFire Ltd.

Carmelite House
50 Victoria Embankment
London EC4Y 0DZ

www.bookouture.com

ISBN: 978-1-78681-618-4
eBook ISBN: 978-1-78681-617-7

For Pat

Chapter One

The clockwork songbirds create an unnatural musical harmony which soars through the house at Elveden. It never gets old. I could listen to them forever. If I lean back just enough I can see them on their gilded branch, the turn of their heads, the way they bob up and down, how they unfurl their wings – too precise every time to be natural, but still beautiful. No one would think they were crafted from metal and jewels, with a Keltan crystal as their tiny hearts. There's barely a hint of the mechanical about them. They move like real birds should, sing like them as well, but just a touch too perfect, thanks to that piece of a far-away world deep inside them and the work of the craftsmen who live there.

'Belengaria, your report.' Nerysse's voice carries a touch of warning on its edge. She's caught me again. That's the trouble with having the woman who nursed you, raised you and cared for you as a governess as well. Why couldn't I just go to military academy like everyone else my age? Like my brothers.

I know the answer to that. Too well. My father. Or more correctly his family. Because my mother 'hadn't been good enough' for him; because the king said no but they married anyway; because even the daughter of a minor member of the court has to have a governess instead of a real education, no matter how unimportant I actually am. Because Imperial politics trump everything.

The birds fall silent, the little shining traitors, complicit with Nerysse in not allowing me to put this off any longer. There's no way I can turn them on again with Nerysse looking straight at me. I clear my throat. Only to give me time to think, but it works. Sort of.

'Anaran states that the key to any strategy is information. The flow of information dictates the flow of battle. When information is withheld, something vital is missing from the overall plan. Possibly something fatal. He draws a comparison to breath – which is completely over-wrought in my opinion—'

'I asked for a report, not your opinion on the finest strategist Vairian has ever produced, thank you very much, young lady. Continue. On topic if you please.'

'But you know all this, Nerysse. And so do I.'

Nerysse glares at me, her old eyes still sharp and dangerous. She hasn't always been a nursemaid and a governess. She was a flight commander when my mother first took to the skies. It doesn't do to forget things like that.

'Rather the point, don't you think? To find out if you do.'

Infuriating woman. But what choice do I have? I'm stuck here and the only way out is through. 'Information is like air. Cut it off, kill your enemy. Transmit lies and misinformation, poison your enemy. Ration it, control your enemy. With enough of it under your wings, you rise far above your enemy's machinations. Did I miss anything?'

'Well, apart from all the details and the poetry of his words, no.' Nerysse purses her lips and I know I've done it, got it right and put it in the succinct terms she usually goes for. The relief is heaven, but it doesn't last. 'Very well. Write the report.'

It's torture, that's what it is. They should cover it in the Imperial laws.

Thou shalt not make students write reports on Anaran's theories on a perfect flying day.

'After that we can try some aerodynamics and engineering,' says Nerysse, kindly enough.

I try not to make a face. I love to fly, and everything connected with it, but the mathematics involved make my brain hurt. Only my brother Art gets it, boy genius that he is. The other two are as bad as me.

'There's always history,' Nerysse goes on. Is she trying to torment me? Why? 'Or geography. Tell me about the Firstworld and its satellites.'

I squirm in my seat. I can't help myself.

'Or I could just go flying if you'd sign the release paper. Please, Nerysse? Look at those skies this morning. Have you ever seen so perfect a day for it?'

Nerysse glances out of the mullioned window to the azure sky beyond and a look of unexpected pain crosses her face. Damn it, I never think. Or if I do, I think only of myself. Nerysse has been grounded longer than I can remember, her health no longer permitting her to take to the air as once she had. She caught some sort of poison gas when her wing went down. She can't fly now. Not since the last war with the Gravians, the same time I lost my mother.

'Oh go on then,' Nerysse says at last, so softly that I'm not sure I heard the words correctly.

'Really?' I've got to move, before she changes her mind. I try to get up, close my books and shove them unceremoniously into my desk all at once. 'Thank you, Nerysse.'

Her face is still serious, her eyes spearing me. 'But we'll do an extra hour tomorrow in lieu, understand?'

'Yes, absolutely.' Whatever it takes. Tomorrow can take care of itself. It might be grey with rain, or the wind too high. I'll seize the chance of flight time when offered. As I head for the door, my mind is already on soaring above air currents, and the sound of wind in the canvas and brass flying machine I love.

'Forgetting something?'

Nerysse holds up a slip of paper. It already bears her signature and the ink is dry. It's been signed for hours.

It's not often I hug Nerysse these days. But I ought to do it more. 'You're the best!'

Then just in case any other conditions might materialise, I grab the paper and beat a hasty retreat.

*

As I leave the house, a squadron flies overhead, the iridescent glow of their engines rippling the air behind them. I smile as they whir over me, points of darkness against the wide, blue sky. The lead Wasp turns and heads inland, over the dense Forest of Ilnay and on towards Higher Cape. It's so graceful, every manoeuvre like poetry. I'll be there one day, leading my own Wing. It's my promise to myself. Zander got command of a Wing at nineteen. Luc was only eighteen. That's less than a year from now for me, if I can't do it sooner. The Wing follows its leader, the formation perfect.

'Are you just planning to just stand there looking at them?' Shae's voice contains the same laugh I always hear in it. He's leaning against the wall of the spice store, half in shadow, his lean, muscular form coiled and ready for action. He's wearing his uniform, just like always. I can't imagine him out of it.

Except I can. I shouldn't but I can.

The deep green jacket ends where his weapons sit against his hips, gun on one side, a wicked looking hunting knife on the other. I can't imagine him unarmed either. I shouldn't be imagining him at all.

My throat is tight as I force words out. 'I was heading out for a flight. More hours in the sky—'

'The more likely you are to get a commission, I know. Still after that Wing?'

I sketch a bow, to hide what I hope he can't see in my face, and look up at him, grinning. 'Naturally. There's always method in my madness.'

Shae shakes his head and pushes off the wall, striding towards me. He looks so good. More than good. Dangerous, lethal, gorgeous. I can't help but admire that.

'Madness, yes, that's a good word. You missed training this morning.' He stops in front of me, close enough to touch, so unbearably handsome that for a moment I just gaze into his blue eyes. The same blue as the sky. Most Vairians have brown eyes. Blue are rare. I lift myself up on my toes and wish I had the nerve to just lean forward and kiss him.

Instead, I take a step back. If only I wasn't such a coward. I'd probably give him a heart attack if I acted on that impulse. But if I did... if I kissed him... Kissing Shae is something I've thought about for far too long. He's not with anyone – not that I've seen – but there are plenty of people who would do anything for him. Anything. He's six years older than me but that's not that big a difference. Not really. I wish I could just kiss him.

But I can't. Not just like that.

He shakes his head and I wonder, for a mortifying moment if he can read my thoughts, if he knows. If he does, why doesn't he do something about it? But he's never given me any sign. Not even an untoward glance.

'Where are you heading today?' he asks.

I shrug, and look away, hoping to hide the flush on my cheeks. 'Out over the forest, maybe as far as the sea. Where the wind takes me.'

He laughs, a deep, rippling laugh that does interesting things when it travels through me. 'I hope that isn't the flight plan you filed, or Zander will light you up.'

'Zander's an old hen with a clutch of eggs,' I reply, knowing it isn't true. Poor Zander hates being in charge of the flight plans almost as much as he hates being grounded. But he'd gone off on a free-wing once too often and our father wasn't having that. Not of his eldest son. Duty, honour, discipline – that is everything. We may not be particularly royal any more, he says, but we're still in the rolls. Nobility has obligations.

'Make sure to check your coms,' Shae says in firm tones. 'And pack a survival kit. And don't stay out too long, okay?'

Something in his tone makes me pause. It's the uncharacteristic question at the end. Almost a plea. I give him a long look, searching for the problem. 'What's up?'

He rolls his shoulders, a shrug that is so much a part of him, fluid and elegant. 'We picked up some strange transmissions from the outer planets.'

I'm not even going beyond the atmosphere. My Wasp doesn't have the equipment installed. But then I remember the Wing I saw earlier and don't make the flippant reply which springs to mind. A more modern Wing, fully equipped, not a pleasure craft like mine. 'Seriously?'

'Seriously. It could be nothing, but special ops are checking it out.' He's special ops himself so he should know. I don't ask how. 'Make sure that kit is in place.'

I nod. The survival kit is always in my Wasp. Father had drummed it into each of us from the moment we first took to the air. Before, really. Mother would have expected no less. Yolande Astol didn't plan on joining a noble house, but then she probably didn't plan on falling in love with my father, Marcus Merryn, the youngest and least important grandson of a king. She was a pilot. She just wanted to fly. I understand that.

Shae follows me to the airfield. It's a whirl of activity, pilots and mechanics everywhere. The wide-open space contrasts starkly with the densely packed, low huts, all in their drab grey and green. Vairian military style never goes out of fashion here. We were built on war. We live and breathe it. Twenty-five years ago the Gravians tried to invade. The ensuing war lasted ten years and only came to an end with my people entering into an alliance with the Empire to stand against the threat. We'd been outsiders before that, mercenaries at most. For the last fifteen years, we've helped the Empress bring stability and calm to this part of the galaxy. But we're still at the vanguard of her battles. And at the edge of Gravian space. We are always prepared.

Shae checks my flying machine himself in the end, despite the assurances of the various mechanics who have already looked it over. He isn't a flyer. Shae comes from a long line of infantry and he's proud of it, but he's spent enough time around the airfields and my family that he knows what to look for. There's no point in arguing. He'd just ignore any protests anyway. He's done this before. And I know it'll be in perfect order because that's how I keep it. Always. The Wasp is an older model, originally Zander's. If I look after her, she'll look after me. And much like my eldest brother, she needs a *lot* of looking after. They're worth it.

Much like Shae, I think, watching the way he peers at the gears, looking for wear and tear. Warmth spreads through me. My feelings for him shouldn't matter, but somehow they do. So very much. Once again, I imagine telling him, picture his confusion and probably his laughter. That's what always stops me. I couldn't bear it if I was wrong, if he laughed. Even if he didn't, I'm from a noble line, kin to the royal family, which means links to a dozen other noble houses on other worlds, and even the Imperial line itself somewhere way back on the Firstworld. They're not there anymore, of course. No one lives on the Firstworld, or so I'm told. It's a dead planet, used-up and broken. The Empress has her seat of power on Cuore, the city planet, and that's far away from here, in the heart of the whole system. *A spider in the centre of her web*, my father sometimes calls her, when he thinks no one is listening.

I know what Shae would say if I told him how I felt, if he didn't laugh, even if he felt the way I do. He's just a soldier, and even if I didn't have any great part to play in the grand scheme of things, few people would be able to overlook that. My mother was just a pilot and look at the trouble that caused her.

I'm nobility and Shae isn't.

But if he loved me… every time I almost convince myself that he doesn't even see me as a girl, he does something – sometimes just the smallest thing – and my heart soars like my Wasp.

The gentle touch of his finger on my nose brings me back to reality and I almost jump back a yard. He shouldn't do that, not when I've been thinking those thoughts again. But he does and it makes me quiver inside. The fact the finger belongs to a hand trained to fight and kill from the earliest age doesn't upset me. He's a warrior. I love that about him. I respect it too. But he doesn't have to treat me like a child.

'Maybe you shouldn't go.'

I fix him with my hardest glare, the one my brothers know not to engage with. 'You really didn't just say that, did you? I mean, you'd *never* say something like that to me, would you?'

Shae gives a brief laugh and pulls my goggles down over my eyes, surrendering. 'Don't do anything stupid.' It's a warning, but one only half serious. He knows me too.

I examine his strong, sculpted face, and put on my gravest expression. 'I promise. I'll be back in no time, you'll see. Maybe even in one piece.'

I climb into the narrow body of the Wasp wishing it would carry two. What would it be like to just fly away with Shae and never return? What would it take to convince him to come with me, to forsake duty and honour and all the things that define our lives as Vairians and fly off to the farthest horizon?

*

The engine of the Wasp is a low hum in my ears, pure music, a sound which vibrates along my veins with my blood. Hours of freedom, hours where no one tells me what to do or where to be, or drills me on politics or history... hours of the song of my Wasp and the open air around me.

'Born to fly,' I'd told my brothers on more than one occasion. Having tried to best me in the air, one after the other they all had to concede it now.

Born to fly isn't strictly true, of course. I'd been born, if anything, to be a very minor game piece in the interstellar games of houses and bloodlines, married to someone the Empire or my family deemed suitable or at least convenient. I've never been one for living under illusions. I can still hope however. My main hope is that I am just not that important.

Lucky for me I'm not my second cousins, with so much riding on their marriages that they barely have any time to themselves at all. They'll marry royal houses, travel to other planets and found dynasties, be placed in the highest position –that's the lot of a prince or princess. I hear they've already chosen some off-worlder for my cousin Elyssa. At worst, I'll probably be married off to a minor noble and that will be the end of my political usefulness. If I'm lucky, he'll be my own age, or close to it, and respect me enough to be bearable. And Vairian, I hope. Oh ancestors, I hope so. Someone who would understand my need to fight, and to fly.

I don't know when I first realised that I love Shae. It seems like I've always loved him. How could I not? He looks at me and my stomach does that tight, twisting thing that makes my breath catch.

How would I ever explain that to my father? He ought to understand. He married for love after all. Surely I should be allowed to do the same?

But what if Shae doesn't feel the same way? What if he only sees me as... I don't know – a child, a duty... what then?

I'm too much of a coward to find out.

Here in the air, I can pretend that things are different, that I live to pilot machines of brass and canvas on the currents of the air, to take other mechanisms out beyond the stars, for feats of adventure and daring, for another life.

One that cannot be.

The radio crackles inside my ear, jerking me out of my thoughts.

'My Lady, this is Control, over.'

Reluctantly, I key up the coms. My Lady, indeed. I don't know who's on coms but I'll let him know what I think about that when I get back.

'Bel here, Control. Over.'

The noise of some kind of brief scuffle at the other end makes me glance down and then Zander's voice barks over the radio instead.

'It's me. Get home now. Right now. There's been... an accident. Do you read me, over?'

An accident? My hands tighten on the controls. This doesn't sound good. It also doesn't sound like my brother. His voice strains for control, the tone unusually terse. He never talks to me that way, even if he is the eldest of us. Never.

'Roger. Heading home immediately. Zander? What happened? Is it Father? One of the boys?'

'Negative. We're all fine. We need radio silence now, Bel. Over and out.'

'Roger,' I whisper, unsure if I have keyed the coms or not this time. 'Over and out.'

My shaking finger slides off the control and I bank the Wasp around. I have a sinking feeling in my stomach, a sickness that isn't right. None of this feels right.

Adjusting the canvas by intuition more than design, I fly on in silence, scanning the distant horizon and the rolling tree canopy below. My instincts hum with the knowledge of a threat. An accident, he'd said. But even I know that most 'accidents' on Vairian are nothing of the kind. A Gravian hand is generally to be found when you look beneath the surface. Our ancient enemies. They haven't gone anywhere, not really, despite their defeat. They strike – hard and heartless – and then melt back into hyperspace, ghosts in the ether.

At the end of that bitter war, fifteen years ago, my mother led the Third Wing in defence of the Vairian skies – the Glorious Third. We've all heard about them, all our lives. The story never gets old. Not for me. After a lifetime, maybe I should put it behind me. Warriors die in battle. That's the way of the world. It doesn't make me feel any better though. It's only months since the latest Gravian attack. They've grown cunning, more dangerous. And I want to take them on. If I was anyone else, from any other family, I would have joined the academy at fifteen, but they can't stop me forever. Even the chance to spill Gravian blood makes my pulse quicken. I can feel it in my throat, hammering away. It isn't fear. I won't let it be fear.

A flash of light on metal in the trees below is the only warning I get. I imagine I hear the whine as the weapon charges. I manage to jerk left as the pulse of a plasma rifle turns the air beside my right wing iridescent.

'Clear!' I crow, not that they can hear me. 'You'll have to be quicker than—'

The whole Wasp bucks beneath me. It feels like being kicked in the chest by a pack mule. The Wasp's engine whines, gives a splutter and stalls. My flying machine drops from the sky.

I punch the controls, frantically trying to start her up again, turning the engine which only clunks and gutters painfully. There's precious little gliding in a Wasp but I manage to get the machine under control before it goes into a full spin.

It's like trying to fly a brick.

Further weapons fire lights up the air behind me. I keep the Wasp steady, tracking the ground ahead for the safest place to put down. All trees. This isn't going to be easy. Or in any way pretty.

Transmit position – the instructions drilled into my memory replay now, my mother's voice, calm and reassuring, persistent. *Transmit position in an emergency just as fast as you can. Get the Wasp down in one piece. Take the survival pack and weapons and get clear in case of an explosion.*

Training takes over. It's effortless. I move before I think.

'Base, come in, this is Bel. I'm going down. Repeat, going down. Co-ordinates—'

Zander's voice cuts me off. 'Negative!' he yells. 'It's an open channel. Negative on the co-ordinates. Over.'

What? This is madness. I'm crashing, Zander. I'm going to die.

'Under attack!' I protest, my voice tight. 'Wasp is dead. Over.'

'You know what to do! We'll come for you. Repeat, we'll—'

The impact with the canopy shakes the whole ship and throws me upwards. I hit the roof hard and slam down again, tumbling with the Wasp, crashing through branches, the screams of torn canvas, metal and wood drowning out my own, deafening me. My head slams into the controls and the sudden pain is blinding. With an almighty, bone shaking crash, we land, my broken Wasp and I, and all is horribly still.

The radio hisses. Something has done for it. My vision blurs as I try to look around. I blink furiously to clear it. As I attempt to move, icy pain shoots through my shoulder and my stomach heaves. Damn it, I'm hurt. And concussed, probably. And my Wasp is in bits.

I can't think about this now. I'm a sitting duck. I have to get out.

It hurts so much that twice I think I'm going to pass out. But I push myself out of the Wasp and tumble onto the forest floor.

My goggles are cracked but the world of the shattered Wasp seems even worse when I push them out of the way and drop them. There's blood on them too. *Don't think about it. Not now. Keep moving.* But my face throbs and there's sticky stuff covering the side of my head… *more blood…*

Survival gear, my training tells me adamantly, forcing me to ignore pain and damage. They don't matter. Only one thing does. Getting out of this alive.

Oh, and weapons. Yes, weapons too.

Weapons are terribly important when anyone is trying to kill you.

A laugh bubbles up in my throat, born more from panic than humour. *Is this shock? Feels like shock.*

I roll out on to the churned earth and then reach inside the broken machine, feeling around for both the slim pack of supplies and my rapier. The pistol at my side is loaded at least, but I have no extra charge packs.

It'll have to be enough. It's all I have.

*

I hear them before I see them. Grunts, Gravian ground troops, crashing through the forest towards my downed Wasp. They're wearing heavy body-armour that makes them look like beetles, but inside they're pale and fleshy. I've read the files, looked at footage, seen them dead. I know the weaknesses in their armour, where to hit to wound, or to kill. As they move forward they take no precautions to conceal themselves, or to check ahead. They probably think I'm dead or injured, or that I'm too stupid to get out or maybe even that I'm no threat at all.

They don't know me then. I'll show them a threat.

Flicking the catch on the pistol, I aim with care, my thumb resting on the charge button, my trigger finger primed. I'm focused now. Totally in the moment, fixed on them. The whine of the charge might alert them but it's still fast. I'm fast.

If only I had a plasma rifle. One of those huge, solid ones Shae carries. Or a grenade launcher. That would be better. I'm good with them. And they do a hell of a lot of damage. I scored higher than anyone on the training field with one.

How many? The pistol will only take out one before they attack me. Logically, it has to be a last resort. But if they spot me, if they come for me… They have a nasty reputation when it comes to prisoners. Those that are ever found anyway.

No way I'm letting them take me.

Some would tell me to turn the pistol on myself, to die unsullied, with my pride intact. Because that helps, doesn't it? No.

Better a dead one of them than a dead one of me.

I know this forest. It's my home. I can blend in and wait for them to go. I have all the time in the world. It isn't far to get back to Elveden and home. If I climbed a tree I could probably see the willowy towers and red roofs of my home.

But my head is aching and the blood is getting in my eyes. I'm worried I may pass out.

A flash of metal in the face of the nearest makes my breath lodge in my throat. Not just Grunts then, but Mechas too. That's the other thing they do with prisoners, or at least those who fall in battle – turn them into man-machines with next to no will of their own. Only programming. A mesh of dead flesh and machinery which does exactly what it's told.

'Report. Find me something.'

The hiss of the lead Gravian's voice sends my skin shivering. It's thin and tinny, coming over a radio. Their leader isn't even here with his troops, but directing them from afar. He shot down my Wasp. He's trying to kill me.

'Where is she? I want that girl.'

The Grunts mutter among themselves but the Mechas say nothing. They're his eyes and ears here. I don't know if they can speak. Maybe they take their tongues out too? Do the dead speak and, if so, what would they say? I don't want to know.

My finger itches to fire. To see at least one of them go down spasming in agony. But if I do that the rest would be on me in no time. I have to wait, silent and still. The weapon is my last resort.

They search my Wasp, tearing out equipment and discussing it as if it is no more than a heap of junk.

Anger builds in my chest, burning and hard as steel.

A whisper of air brushes against my cheek and hands seize me, one over my mouth and the other on my weapon. I struggle instinctively, draw in a breath of alarm but don't waste it in a scream. I kick back and bring my elbow down for a stomach jab.

My captor twists slightly, evading me with no effort at all. Only one man moves that way, could have approached so silently in the first place. He taught me almost everything I know about hand-to-hand combat and strategy. No one can match him for stealth.

I relax in his embrace, thanking my ancestors. I'll go and light candles for each and every one of them, even if it takes a week.

Shae doesn't say a word, but releases me once he realises I won't cry out and give us away. As if I would. He gestures over his shoulder and signals a withdrawal. We move like forest cats, ghosts amongst the trees.

Other Vairian warriors appear out of the undergrowth, infantry and artillery mostly, with a couple of trackers leading the way. My sudden relief at no longer being alone rocks me. My head swims again, leaving me sick and dizzy, and at the same time elated. Shae came for me. My treacherous heart beats a little faster.

Once clear of the Gravians and their Mechas, Shae pulls me to a halt and examines me from head to toe, trusting his own eyes before anything I might say at the moment. Because I'd tell him I'm fine, that there's nothing I can't handle, that I'd head back there now on my own without a qualm and take them all on by myself. All lies of course, but he doesn't know that. And he never will.

'You're unharmed?' he says at last. His voice sounds gruffer than usual. His eyes search my face. I can see my reflection in them. My head throbs and there's blood down the side of my face. I look like shit.

'Yes, Captain,' I reply, unable to hide the loopy grin, which makes his expression harden still further. 'Did you think I couldn't cope?'

Giddy with relief to be alive, I'm a cocky idiot.

Normally he'd tell me that. Normally he wouldn't hesitate. I've known Shae since I was five. He was a war orphan, taken in by my family and raised with us until he joined the academy. He's only home between furloughs, before he heads off again into the various Imperial battlefronts. Valiant, disciplined, lethal – he's the perfect Vairian soldier. There is no one like him. No one in all the world. While my brothers had laughed, put frogs in my hair and thrashed me in every training game until adolescence – when I'd shown them what turning the tables actually meant, and maybe broken two fingers in Zander's right hand (never proven) – Shae has always been on my side. He doesn't joke now. It's more than serious. It's terrifying.

'No time for games, Lady Belengaria. Matters have changed.'

Lady Belengaria? I blink as the phrase sinks in. Shae never uses my title, let alone my full name. We agreed that years ago. Bel and Shae. Simple as that. It saves time.

'What's happened?'

Shae wraps my arm in his and leads me forward, his troops still flanking us, some scouting ahead. They're on high alert, as we move carefully away from the crash site. All the while he keeps his voice pitched low so that even I, walking right beside him, have to lean in close to listen. It's almost as if he doesn't want to say it out loud. Doesn't want the others to hear. But I can tell from the way they stiffen, that they already know.

'A small group of Gravians attacked the palace at Higher Cape. They're dead. All of them.'

I stare at him. The Cape? That's insane. It's the capital. A million people live there. The Cape is well protected, secure. Of course the Gravians are all dead. What were they thinking trying that? 'Good.'

'No, Bel. The Royal Family are dead. The family, their cousins… *your* cousins. Obliterated. We took care of the strike force, secured our defences, but the planet is in chaos. Your father stepped forward and he has restored order. He and your brothers are engaged at all incursion points but here. A unit broke off and headed this way so we realised they must have picked up your transmissions. Traced you. Targeted you.'

'A fluke, surely. I'm not worth a ransom or…'

But I knew what I had heard.

I want that girl, the Gravian had said. He'd specifically sent them for me. He'd known who I was. He had to. They had come after me.

'That shot could have blown you out of the air.' He squeezes my arm tighter and speaks through clenched teeth.

I force myself to breathe. 'But it didn't, Shae. I avoided it. Well, mostly.'

'You don't understand. The council has declared your father King. He's next in line as Veron's grandson. Which makes you a royal heir now. A direct royal heir.'

The urge to laugh at the absurdity of it is hard to fight. This is insane. 'This is some sort of joke, isn't it? Did Zander put you up to it? Or Art. I bet it was—'

But it isn't. Not a joke. Not a mistake. Not… not anything. The creeping dread worms its way through me. Shae would never make a joke like this. The Royal Family, and by extension, my family, the poor relations, are everything to him.

'It's no joke, my princess.'

I stiffen. 'Shae, don't call me that.'

'But it's true. You're our princess and the only one we have. Your father is king, Zander is heir apparent and the others princes in their own right. Now, we need to get you home. They targeted you, as surely as they targeted the palace. This was designed to throw us into chaos. To wipe out our royal line.'

'Home,' I echo, feeling as if I'm balanced on the edge of a precipice, where icy winds might snatch me away at any moment. It isn't possible. The king... I only met him twice, once when my mother died. He had been kind to a small grieving girl. But Great Uncle Edris, Galen and the girls... my cousins – vacuous and irritating, sure. But family all the same. So beautiful. So talented... so...

Now they're all dead. And the king's sisters. Their children, all the other royal relatives who thought my father married beneath him.

They're all dead. All the bitter, jealous, overbearing, stupid, fragile...

I inhale an uneven breath. It almost turns into a sob. But I can't sob. I can't cry. I can't do anything like that because it would be weak and I'd shame my whole family.

My family... Oh ancestors...

Focus. Think. The reasons. The strategy.

Chaos doesn't cover it. The Gravians must want to knock Vairian off its axis with a single blow, and make us powerless in the Imperial game. The royal family are the link to the Empire.

And what'll the Empress say? Is the Imperial fleet on the way to aid us already? Or to take charge? Half the fleet are Vairian by birth or by training. They *have* to come. And what remote planets, interstellar paths or stations will be left undefended when they do? That must be it. A small group to attack us and the rest of them... where will they go next?

And now my family are all that stands to stop my world falling into chaos and setting the stage for their next war.

'It's not possible,' I breathe. 'There must be someone else with a stronger claim. There must be. There were at least fifteen people between my father and the throne. Edris, his son Galen, the royal princes, and—'

'They had a molecular bomb,' Shae says in a quiet voice which silences me. I know what that means. But still, he goes on. 'Genome coded. The royal court, the royal city, the military hierarchy... the whole Cape, everything is gone. Rubble and ashes. It took seconds and no one got out.'

I can't cope. I close my eyes, letting the enormity of that sweep through me, making sure to stop before it unleashes a grief I can't control. Faces flare in my mind's eye. So many faces. A million people. Maybe more.

'How did they plant it?' I eventually ask. Such bombs can't be dropped from the sky.

'We're not sure yet. Suicide squad?' His grip turns gentle again. More comforting. I want to pull him closer, to wrap myself in his arms, but I can't. Not with his men watching. And I suspect he wouldn't let me anyway. Not now. I'm not just Bel any more. 'Come. We must get you to safety.'

The Gravians are still searching for me. Their leader, his cold voice, his orders, rise in the back of my brain but I push that away, refusing to allow it in. 'And leave them there? I don't think so.'

Shae nods to one of the others – Petra Kel, isn't it? In battlegear it's impossible to tell – who bends their head, speaking into their coms. Blaster fire erupts behind them. Short-lived. A few brief cries ring out before the great silence of the forest is restored. The stench of burning flesh and body armour lingers afterwards, the charming effects of the super-heated plasma.

'They're taken care of,' says Shae.

And I realise, I've just given my first royal command.

Chapter Two

The battle is over by the time our land transports reach the capital, as my shabby old home of Elveden has been newly designated. I gaze out of the narrow window. Wasps like mine and larger airships circle overhead. I can see Falcons in the higher atmosphere, the real fighters of the air force. Everything is primed, on edge.

On the way, once the field medic had pronounced my head wound minor and I'd cleaned up most of the blood, I dug my tablet out of the backpack. Miraculously, it wasn't broken in the crash, but when I start looking at the news it gives me, I almost wish it had been. Smoking black holes dot the terraces of Higher Cape and the hospital is still burning. The towers of the university are broken. The hulk of a Gravian airship juts from the side of the academy like an obscene new extension. The palace is nothing but rubble.

Images of Higher Cape, of the Peoples' Gardens and the Meeting Square, of the palace where my family, however distant, had lived flicker through my tears like old, degraded film reels. All gone now. Ruins and ashes. Vairian's place in the Empire is a military one. We aren't known for much else, though there are people of all kinds and skills on our world. Elveden is known for its cuisine and the fine wines the vineyards produce, but it's nothing to the gourmet world of Felenar, or the wines produced on Telenon, famed throughout the Empire. It's never bothered me before now. We are an old race, one with a thousand years of our own history from the planet's initial colonisation. We only joined the Empire when we could do nothing else and not as a full member planet. We are largely autonomous. It's an alliance rather than a fealty. At least it is supposed to be. In name. My line stretches back that far, a lineage and genealogy that few save the Empress can claim, not that it had ever mattered to me before now. What's the point? Vairian people are practical, no-nonsense, pragmatic. Soldiers.

But Higher Cape was beautiful.

Now, I have an unfamiliar moment of doubt. With my world crippled, the eyes of the Empire upon it, what will the Gravians do? Where will they strike next in their quest for resources? Another world, one less protected? Or will they be back to finish us off? What will the Empress do? Will she press for closer alliance? For an actual union which would make us all hers?

Vairian needs to get back on its feet as quickly as possible. It doesn't have time to mourn.

The house is in chaos. People hurry to and fro, everywhere, the entire place a hive of activity such as I have never seen before. Too small to be a palace, too cramped for true efficiency, it had always seemed too big for our family with most of my brothers deployed or at the academy. Now I can barely find a square foot of space where I'm not in someone's way.

Zander yells into the shining brass funnel of a central communicator, his eyes blazing. The screens before him scroll with information, almost too fast to read. It doesn't faze him.

'Absolutely not! Not an inch, Luc. The Imperial fleet is already approaching the outer system, weapons hot. They can face us and our allies if they want. We'll blow them from the sky, drive them into the sun. No mercy. No more than they showed at the Cape. If they want to give an unconditional surrender then we'll discuss it. Until then throw all you have at them.'

I'd been looking forward to seeing my eldest brother, but now take a step backwards, startled by this stranger with his face.

'Don't mind him,' the youngest of my brothers, Art, says, as he steps past me. The tablet in his hand is just as busy as the larger screens. He moves his fingers over it rapidly, still talking to me as he works. 'He's mad because he isn't on the frontline any more and Luc's getting all the glory up with the Falcons.'

Zander slams down the receiver and sweeps across the room to snatch me off my feet in a huge hug. I want to hate him for it, but I can't. I had no idea how much I needed this.

'Thank the ancestors you're okay. I should have known you'd hardly have a scratch on you. Sorry about your Wasp, little sister.'

I shake my head when he sets me down again.

'It's just a flyer.' My eyes sting. I didn't expect this. Just a flyer, but I *learned to fly* in that machine. She had been mine, even if she had been Zander's first. And he'd loved her too. 'I'm sorry I lost her. I should have been able to dodge them, to—'

Zander shushes me, his voice gentling. 'Past now. Move on. Father's been asking for you. Don't take up too much of his time though. Oh, and you'll have to swear an oath – a formality of course, but it is required.'

'What sort of oath?'

He ruffles my hair with his broad hand and I almost forget to squirm and wriggle away from him. He's only a couple of years older than me, but you wouldn't know it from the way he acts. 'Always with the questions, Bel. An oath of allegiance. He's King now. You'll have to *actually* obey him rather than just promising to and then running off to do your own thing. You'd better go and clean up before you see him. Nerysse is waiting for you in your rooms. Show me, Art. What did you find?'

There's nothing I can do but obey. Orders, that's what they were. Zander just gave me orders. I stare at him as he and Art bend their heads together in deep debate. He's Crown Prince now. Or will be, if they can find a crown. What does that make me?

*

The first thing I notice on entering my chamber is that it is covered with clothes. It looks as if my wardrobe exploded.

No, not my wardrobe. Someone else's. There are all manner of gowns, spread over every available surface. I stop dead, mouth open, confronted with lace, silk, buttons, corsets, bustles and all the impracticalities I've so far managed to avoid for a flyer's uniform, or a simple shift dress if I must.

'Don't stand there making fish faces,' Nerysse snaps, stepping out from behind the screen with another voluminous ball of silk. 'All of these have been sent over. We need to decide on a suitable gown and get you into it.'

I can only stare at the woman who had been nurse and governess to me these last ten years. The woman who should know better.

'I... what?'

'You. Strip.' Nerysse pauses, glaring at Shae who is still shadowing me everywhere. I hadn't noticed. He is standing at the doorway, returning the expression with equal force. I guess now I know where he learned it from. Same place as me, and we're looking right at her. 'And you, outside. Lock the door if you must. No one comes in. Or goes out,' she adds with ominous intent.

'Her Highness needs a guard with her.'

Her Highness? I cast him a stricken look, which he ignores.

Nerysse doesn't appear to notice. 'Not at all times, surely. Be off with you, Captain Finn.'

'I'll fetch Petra.' He steps outside, summoning the female guard on his coms even as he takes up what is clearly a sentry position outside before Nerysse slams the door behind him.

'Nerysse, what's going on?'

'You've no choice in the matter so don't argue. Your father's orders. I'm to make a princess of you and quickly. Now get out of those rags. The audience is in only a few hours and you're the one chance he has to dazzle.'

'But… but he has the boys…'

'*Boys,*' she says as if I'd suggested he use goats. 'For this he needs you.'

She circles me like a predator, lifting my hair up, twisting it into a chignon, and tuts in that dismissive way.

'Nerysse, please, he knows I don't – I can't wear such clothes and fly.'

That elicits a short sniff. 'You're not going to be flying for much longer, child. You're going to be married.'

My heart skitters in my chest, a hollow, agonised thump. *No. Not this. Please.*

'He wouldn't!'

Nerysse squeezes my shoulders. It's mean to be a gesture of support but it feels like being crushed. 'I think you'll find otherwise. Things have changed, Bel, my dear.'

'No!' I pull myself out of Nerysse's reach and fling open the door, darting past Shae before he can stop me. And I run. I run as fast as I possibly can.

*

The door to my father's study stands slightly ajar. As I approach, I hear voices – my father, and someone else. The stranger's accent is musical, his voice deep and lyric. But the voice isn't the problem. It's the words.

'Of course, if the Rondet consider her suitable, there will still be barriers. She's not the most demure of women.'

My father sounds irritated. 'To marry a Vairian means to make a partnership, not acquire a bauble, Prince Jondar, as I'm sure you already know. Your world will have to leave such expectations behind.'

'Is there another in her life?'

'No. Childhood friends and silly crushes. She's young still.'

'Then there remains only to test her virginity.'

'Her *what*?' Father's voice explodes. I step back, almost tripping over my own feet and draw in a shocked breath. I've never heard him so enraged. As I move, I bump into Shae, who has come to a halt behind me, silent and strong. I look up at his face, bewildered, and he frowns. But he lets me listen, lets me hear this ridiculous, awful conversation and I wish he wouldn't.

Prince Jondar, whoever he is, doesn't appear to realise the danger he's in. 'If she is to marry the Anthaem, we must be assured of it. The Rondet will no doubt demand it.'

Father's voice sounds cold as winter in the mountains. 'Your religious council can demand what they want. I repeat, *she is a child*.'

There is a measured pause, all manners and etiquette rolled up in a moment of silence. Then the prince speaks again, choosing his words with the greatest care.

'Children grow up, your Majesty. Far more quickly than we realise. It is but a formality, an ancient tradition, one of many she will need to learn.'

'She has been protected and chaperoned at all times. I will hear no more of this particular madness. The agreement was with the late king. King Veron, Crown Prince Galen and Princess Elyssa might have agreed but I didn't. It is only through deference to the Empress that we honour it now. If you wish to renege, speak up and we will have an end to it. This union is the will of the Empress, not ours. Bel has not been raised to this. There has been no time to prepare her.'

Blood drains from my face, dizzying, nauseating. Some tiny part of me hoped – prayed – he was talking about one of my cousins, someone who had miraculously survived, especially with the description of 'child'. But my cousins are dead. *Our only princess*, that's what Shae said. And my father needs allies...

Father's voice goes on. 'She will be more than suitable. If you want a simpering puppet, look elsewhere.'

I step back further, not sure I can take any more of this, not wanting to hear it any longer. He can't be doing this to me. Not my father. I'd imagined introductions, stupid arranged meetings between families, and a long slow time to get to know my future husband, to get used to the idea. But this... it's so fast. So final.

How has this even been arranged? We've barely got subspace coms operational again since the attack. It's madness. Utter madness. Like I've fallen into a nightmare and can't wake up. Where am I even being packed off to? Before I have time to think it through, I push the door wide open and march inside. I'm so angry, thought isn't part of the equation.

'Were you even going to tell me? Was I going to have any say in this *at all*?'

It's a mistake. I know the moment I see Father's face. His skin goes white, his eyes narrowing to focus on my muddy flight jacket and trousers, on my mussed hair, on the dried blood I've failed to wash off completely. For a moment his gaze softens with both affection and disappointment. It's worse than his anger and dismay. Suddenly I wish the ground could open and swallow me up.

I've just made a colossal mistake.

'This must be the princess,' says Jondar and I spin around to face him, expecting an overbearing, overweight popinjay. He's nothing of the sort. He's so much worse.

As tall as any of my brothers, sleek and elegant, dressed in a tailored suit and Imperial purple cravat, Jondar – *Prince* Jondar, I belatedly remind myself – gives me the bow of a dancer or a swordsman. His dark hair falls over his eyes momentarily, giving him a rakish look, and when he stands up, the full impact of his face strikes me. Handsome, yes and more – well-bred and elegant, a classical sculpture from the court of the Empress herself. He'd fit in perfectly there, at the centre of Cuore, the pinnacle of human civilisation and culture, where all the most beautiful and intelligent people gravitate. Or at least, that's what everyone says. It's a world so far from Vairian that I actually have no idea of the distance involved. The seat of Empire is light years away.

Something kicks in, some sort of new form of survival instinct, and I drop into a curtsey, the effect spoiled by the flight trousers rather than full skirts. It's the bow of equals, however, a bow of politeness and respect. That's all.

'Prince Jondar.'

He smiles, an expression which make his looks even more devastating. 'Princess Belengaria, how… charming.'

The tone says otherwise. It's like a punch to the guts. I feel like I've been out rolling in something unmentionable and then arrived in for dinner. Worse, I feel like a wayward child.

My father's hand falls on my shoulder. His firm grip is reassuring. 'You came straight from the transport? You should have at least taken a moment, my dear. You've been through so much. The prince is here in embassy for his brother-in-law, the Anthaem, Conleith of Anthaeus, widower of their former Anthaem, Matilde of Anthaeus. He was lately betrothed to your second cousin Elyssa but... well... circumstances have changed.'

My chest tightens in that painfully annoying way it keeps on doing. Mention of Elyssa. She loved to sing, to dance. She smiled. She was older than me, accomplished and courtly. But Elyssa is dead. All of them are dead. Everything has changed. I draw in a centring breath and meet my father's gaze. A rueful smile twitches the corner of his mouth as his eyes flicker with compassion. Just for an instant. He's hating this too. All of it.

It doesn't stop him doing it though. It's his duty and duty is everything.

Anthaeus... I know this. I know about Anthaeus. It's where the birds came from, my mechanical birds. Anthaeus is even further away than Cuore, right on the outer edge of the galaxy, an isolated world, full of wonders and mystery, but perilously close to the far end of Gravian space and secretive to the point of obsession. Even the reports from the Imperial College have next to nothing to say about Anthaeus.

'Had you waited for a full briefing, Bel, before *gracing* us with your company, I would have told you all. With the encouragement of the Empress, Conleith seeks your hand in marriage. Along with military support and guard convoys for trade, naturally. Luckily for us, Jondar was delayed in transit when the attack occurred and had not reached Higher Cape. He diverted here. Matters are moving quickly, but nothing has yet been decided. We *will* be sure that it favours us as well. And you, my dear.'

I sound like an afterthought, but he doesn't mean that. I hope.

He squeezes my shoulder again – a warning, a reassurance – and I glance at Jondar, keeping my face as calm as I can. Nothing could stop the flush that creeps up my cheeks.

'I... I see. Father.'

He ushers me to the door, stepping outside with me, and pulling it closed behind us. Shae straightens, staring into the middle distance, unseeing, unhearing. The perfect soldier.

Did he hear it too? I want to ask but don't dare. Not in front of my father. And even then, I'm not sure I would. I don't know what to do.

'Nothing is settled,' my father says in a hushed whisper. 'And if you keep up this behaviour it never will be. We need this, Bel. Now more than ever. We need to give an appearance of being in control or we lose everything. The Empress will bring in regents or worse, declare us a vassal world which is as good as invading us at our weakest. Even now, Jondar might just decide you're too outspoken for his people to bear.'

Elyssa would never have stormed into a meeting, that's for sure. Elyssa would never embarrass her father in this way. Elyssa would have happily swanned off to whatever far-off wilderness required and married their ancient widower king without a word of complaint. Elyssa, Elyssa... poor dead Elyssa, reduced to ashes with Higher Cape. I hang my head again and Father pulls me into his embrace. 'This is a negotiation, Bel. The Empire is orchestrating this, the hand of the Empress herself. We need the riches of Anthaeus and they need the protection we can offer. *And* be sure the Empress will have her share. This is *her* will. I promise, you will be heard if it's within my power. But not now. Not with this man in earshot.'

'I'm sorry,' I say. 'I didn't think.'

'You need to start thinking, and start thinking fast. We're in the game now, Bel, and can't afford to be caught unawares. You see how quickly it all moves? The hand of the Empress, just as I said. The Gravians have been picking off the weakest worlds and pillaging their natural resources. Their world is dying so they've no choice but to plunder those near them. We've been stopping them. They want to hurt us, to stop us helping anyone else. We may not have much, Bel, but we can fight. That's our art, our gift. It's how we survive. The Anthaese are in an even worse position, for all their wealth and influence. They're isolated. The larger of their moons, Kelta, was overrun less than a year ago, their outpost there destroyed and they had no defence. Now Gravia threatens their world. This attack doesn't just affect Vairian, it's widespread, and it's calculated. Word of incursions came from Melia and Verdeyne too, all key points. Destroying Higher Cape and our ruling class was designed to take us out of the greater battle, and by extension cripple the Empire militarily, but we can't allow that. If we unite, we stand a chance. Only if we unite. Understand?' I nod and he almost smiles. Almost. 'Good. Now go and get cleaned up for dinner. Our guest will be joining us. And tell your brothers too. I want them respectable. Jondar is used to Imperial manners and Anthaese grace. They already think we're savages so they don't need further confirmation.' He touches my face and I wince, remembering the head wound. 'Go to the infirmary first.'

My father straightens up and makes eye contact with Shae. His mouth hardens and he beckons the captain to his side. The conversation is brief, their voices very low. I can't hear, don't want to listen. My mind is reeling and really I just want to throw up. Finally Shae comes sharply to attention. His face is blank.

'Captain Finn will head up your personal guard unit,' my father states. 'Do what he says.' And he steps back to the door. As he opens it, I watch him, the hard line of his shoulders go rigid as if they bear a great weight. And I feel like a child indeed. A selfish, spoiled brat. My family needs allies and security.

And so do the people of Anthaeus, especially with the Gravians poised to fall on them like ravening beasts.

If I'm to be part of the price, how could I even think of making things more difficult?

Shae follows me to my chambers like a shadow, never saying a word.

Chapter Three

Two hours later, dressed in a gown that's twice as wide as I am and which doesn't cover my shoulders at all, my hair trussed in ways that will probably give me a headache for a week, and my waist squeezed by a wholly unnecessary corset, I leave Nerysse at the door of my chambers and begin my slow descent to the officers' mess which has now been designated the banqueting hall. Mother's emerald necklace hangs heavy around my neck. It's the one piece of jewellery of any worth my family still owns. It probably constitutes the crown jewels now. That Father sent it up for me to wear says more about the importance of the situation than I'm comfortable with.

'There now.' My governess appraises me like a drill sergeant with new recruits. 'You are dazzling.'

Dazzling... well, I can only try. I think of how beautiful my mother looked whether she wore a ball gown or a flight jacket. I stop at the top of the sweeping staircase while my name is announced. I've been trained in such formalities, though nobody took it very seriously and I hadn't exactly paid much attention. More of a joke than anything else. I can still hear my brothers laughing about it in the back of my mind, in some dusty forgotten place where all was joy.

Some joke now though.

I swallow hard, struggling to remember the etiquette and manners that Nerysse had tried to drum into my head as my governess. And then my name rings out, more like a title. It sounds beautiful, like someone else's name, like I'm a pretender to my own position. *Princess Belengaria of House Merryn of Vairian, Duchess of Elveden, Countess of Duneen.* It takes all my courage, especially when every eye in the crowd below turns to focus on me.

Then I see Shae and I can't run, not if he's watching me. I can't get out of this, no matter how much I want to.

He stands just beside the foot of the stairs, in his finest dress uniform – green as the forest, golden buttons gleaming – and he looks up at me, his face impassive, his eyes burning. Although the sword at his side is ornate, it's still a weapon and he treats it as such. Its edge is as sharp as any workaday blade. I also spot the familiar bump of a blaster in its holster on his other hip.

I haven't found a moment to talk to him. Not about my father's orders. Not about anything that's happened. I want to, desperately, but I don't have the first idea what to say. Even if there was a moment. He's a soldier, not a nursemaid. The last thing he'll want to do is follow me around a ball. I fix my eyes on him and him alone. A crease forms above the bridge of his nose and he watches me just as closely. If I'm going to get through this, I'm going to do it looking at him.

I swallow hard and begin the descent. If Shae is there, I'll be all right. No matter what happens.

But no sooner do my feet touch the ground beside him, Prince Jondar steps up, giving a graceful bow. I almost shy back, and Shae's hand almost draws his weapon but both of us stop ourselves. It takes every effort.

'Princess, how delightful. You honour us.' Before I know what's happening, he slips my arm around his and leads me away. I'm aware that Shae follows, silent and unobtrusive. I can feel his gaze on me. At least he's still there. At least I have that much.

'Allow me to introduce Lady Elara, of House Mericuse.' Jondar doesn't smile when he says it and I catch something in the way he speaks, an antagonism, reservations. The woman matching the title turns to regard me with cold, assiduous eyes. She's beautiful by anyone's standards, a full head taller than me, golden-haired and perfectly presented. Certainly, the men flock around her, Zander included. I shoot him a look but he just grins at me, unrepentant. It would take more than my disapproval to put him off a woman so classically beautiful.

'Your Highness.' Lady Elara sweeps into the most graceful curtsey I've ever seen. She flows through the movement, elegant as a superbly tuned piece of machinery. I only incline my head, remembering my position just in time before I attempt a clumsy imitation which would make a fool of me. I'm Elara's superior in every way. Supposedly. It doesn't feel likely but that's the general idea. I'm a princess. I have to remember that, as difficult as it will be. Elara's eyes glitter, predatory, and I know she can see right through me. 'I met your cousin, Princess Elyssa. A charming girl and a terrible loss. I was to be her chief lady-in-waiting.' She lifts a gem-studded fan trimmed with ethereal lace so it flutters before her like a butterfly. 'Your kinsmen have been regaling me with tales of your flying abilities.' I almost smile, a brief surge of elation running through me which is shattered by the tone of the words which followed. 'How... adventurous.'

Elara's smile doesn't reach her eyes. I struggle to recover myself, but it's Zander who comes to my rescue. I wish he wouldn't, because he can't say anything helpful.

'In Vairian, Lady Elara, our women take as active a role as our men. I'm sure Elyssa told you that. Our mother for example had a natural affinity for flight and combat. She was a war hero, a leader of men and women, and a martyr to our freedom. I believe Bel will one day outshine even her.'

The unexpected praise starts a glow inside me but I can see the guests don't care about women on Vairian, or flight and combat, or our mother. I really don't think they care about what I might do in the future. They've already decided. To them Vairians are just barbarians. Every one of us.

'How remarkable,' replies Elara. She casts about the room with another devastating smile, easily returned by her adoring companions. My breath catches in my throat. It's so easy for her, isn't it? She knows how to do this far better than I ever will. Zander catches my gaze and gives one of those infuriating smirks. It's the one thing that saves me, my brother and that expression. He doesn't melt before her. I don't think I've ever been so proud of him. It's good to be reassured he isn't a total idiot. Then, she speaks again. 'And have you been in combat, Princess Belengaria?'

Damn her and her superiority. 'Yes.' I lift my chin as I answer. *Well, I have been shot at. That has to count Maybe I never got to shoot back but...* For a moment I sway on my feet as the screams of my Wasp, the wind rushing by me, the crushing impact replay in my mind.

Something flickers in Elara's gaze. Interest? 'Really? Have you killed?'

I remember the soldiers in the forest, the gunshots ringing out. I didn't kill them, but they'd died because of me nonetheless, because they'd threatened me. And Shae had been there. But I would have, if I'd needed to, if I had no choice.

When I don't answer, Elara makes a small humming noise in the rear of her perfectly slender throat, and returns her gaze to Zander, smiling at him.

'I suppose we all have people for that sort of thing.'

I glance around for Shae. He's standing not far behind me, his face stony as ever, his hands folded behind his back. His brow furrows for a moment, questioning me, as we make eye-contact but he doesn't come any closer.

'Your bodyguard, Princess Belengaria?' asks Elara. I turn my attention back to the woman, inwardly cringing when I see the arch look of interest in her eyes. Shae's a handsome man, a dangerous man, just the type of man who I suppose would fascinate a bored courtier. And I've just all but pointed him out to her. 'How efficient he looks.'

'If I may,' Jondar interrupts before I can think of any sort of retort which is fitting for 'polite' company. 'I'd very much like to introduce you to the new Anthaese Ambassador here on Vairian.'

I allow myself to be led away. Fact is, if I stay I'm liable to punch Elara right in her perfect face. Shae follows us, ignoring everyone else in the room, no matter how prettily they smile at him.

Before we reach the ambassador, another fanfare rings out. I turn, along with everyone else, to look up the staircase. The man who stands there looks regal, indomitable and like a stranger. But he isn't.

My father descends the stairs in silence. He doesn't need an introduction it seems. There can be no doubt to the assembled throng who he is, that he is now King Marcus of Vairian. Before we'd made our alliance with the Empire, before the Gravians set their sights on us, there had been a king of Vairian. Before the Empire, before the colony worlds joined together for protection, there had been a king of Vairian. When the first colonists settled on this world, they had selected him from among the best of their warriors, hundreds of years ago. He'd worn a crown like this —a narrow strip of gold, simple and unadorned in any way — which says it all. It's as practical and as impressive as the man who wears it. A soldier's crown.

Tears well in my eyes, blurring what I can see. My father has never wanted this. I blink them away, determined not to shame him now. I'll be strong if he will. I won't let him down. I'll be a princess if he must take on the burden of kingship in such a time of war.

He reaches the chair on a raised dais, that is now the designated throne. All so very makeshift and practical, and so very Vairian. If we don't have it we'll make our own, we'll make do, we'll find our way through the shadows to the dawn. So a simple strip of gold replaces the lost crown, a chair replaces a throne, and the names change, making them what is needed now instead. And a simple man becomes a king. Whether he wants to be or not.

He raises his hand. There isn't really a need, for there is no noise, no whispers or mutterings. All attention is fixed upon him.

'My friends, we are delighted you are here this evening. These are extraordinary times and much has been rushed through that should never be rushed through. But for the sake of necessity, I ask you to put away the need for formalities. Tonight, in the new spirit of cooperation, my daughter becomes betrothed to the Anthaem, Conleith of Anthaeus.'

My breath catches in my throat. I can't breathe, can't do anything. Just have to stand there while they all turn to look at me. It was decided then, without any input from me, without giving me a choice or a say as he'd promised. He just decided.

I swallow on the chunk of air lodged in my airway, pushing down bile and rage. This is what he meant. Put aside not just formalities, but choice, and free will. Because they don't matter, not as much as Vairian. Desperately, I seek out Shae, but he stands as still as a statue, his eyes fixed on the middle distance. He refuses to look at me. *Oh ancestors, why won't he look at me?*

Applause breaks out around me, stuttering and a little unsure. Jondar smiles and begins to clap as well, bowing before me. But I can't move. I can feel it now, the sense of everything spiralling out of control. My life – the only life I've ever wanted –slips between my fingers, draining away leaving me with a sick feeling of dread and a future full of doubts.

I'm lost. I'm on my own.

Chapter Four

The Adeline is an Imperial star liner, and the most impressive ship I've ever seen. From bow to stern her lines are sleek and elegant. She'd been built in space, Zander told me, and didn't have the restrictions of ships which need to escape atmosphere. The Adeline isn't built for any sort of landfall. She lives among the stars. They call it threading, navigating hyperspace at extreme speeds, entirely outside of normal space. The mathematics involved defeats me, but Zander says it's more a case of instinct anyway.

Zander talks about the ship with loving detail, about all the places it usually visits, places that might belong in a fairy tale, places I've always dreamed of going. In another life. People pay the equivalent of a life's earnings to travel in her. Places I'll never go, places I don't want to hear about as my world gets smaller and my dreams are swallowed up.

I listen all the same, trying to remain patient and to keep from fidgeting, not because I need his explanation again, but because I want to hear Zander's voice. To revel in the feeling of easy conversation with my own family while I still can.

The little shuttle wheels around the exterior of the Adeline, heading for the hanger underneath. The light of Vairian's sun glints off the exterior, polished and flawless, giving the impression of a massive, armoured whale in orbit around my world. I study the gemlike portals studding the side, and the crystalline domes of the observation decks, which look like two eyes.

A little further off, escort vessels gather, ready to form the convoy that will take us out of orbit. Smaller, but bristling with weapons, like a pack of hunting hounds, ready to head off.

Then the shuttle flies beneath the liner and into the hanger, a gaping mouth which swallows us down. In the belly of the leviathan.

My stomach dips and loops with excitement, or with the effect of the change in gravity and I fight to sit still, to focus as Shae and the security party assigned to me are focused. I can be a warrior in this, like this, a warrior before a battle. I haven't even met this so-called husband yet, and won't until I reach Anthaeus. The Anthaem doesn't ever, under any circumstances, leave his planet. What in all the worlds they think would happen if he did, I haven't been able to work out. The files I studied imply it's a belief of the Anthaese, something linked to their unique worldview. But they don't have any details. Perhaps nobody really knows the reason. For such a highly cultured civilisation they all seem dreadfully superstitious when it comes to their ruler and religious council… or whatever the Rondet are.

The information in the files about the Anthaem himself – it made me nervous. The title itself, along with all the rank and privilege, brings with it a link to his land that is both mystical and unusual. The Imperial reports sound sceptical but they don't debunk it. The Anthaem is a king, but he is never called that. He's more like a religious figurehead, but not that either because the Rondet take that role. Something changes in the Anthaem once he or she takes on that mantle, something the Anthaese people believe binds the ruler to their world, to the land itself.

And they guard the knowledge of what exactly that something is. Jealously.

It's fascinating stuff. Or it would be if they didn't write it in the driest language known to mankind. I think it's intentional, like you need to be completely motivated to make it through even one report, let alone a whole file of them.

The Anthaem rules at the behest of the religious council, the Rondet, and there are no details as to who makes up their number, how they are elected or chosen. They live in seclusion, far from the city and larger settlements at a secret religious site – and on a world the size of Anthaeus with its tiny population, that is isolated indeed. There are no pictures of the Rondet. Not a single one, ever. And while I found a few images of the former Anthaem, Matilde, I'm not sure which of the various men surrounding her is her husband and heir, Conleith. Apparently they weren't married for long before she tragically succumbed to some kind of cancer. Their succession isn't hereditary – they're chosen, usually by their predecessor and the Rondet.

I study Matilde's face, her bright blue eyes full of intelligence and humour. She was beautiful, no doubting that. Older than me. Which means her consort, now the Anthaem, must be older too.

And I have to marry into this, marry some old man. It doesn't make any sense. I'm never going to fit in. Not with the Anthaese, and certainly not with the mysterious Rondet. They're expecting the royal princess Elyssa. But instead, fate hands them me. I saw for myself Lady Elara's horror at that prospect.

If they reject me, I could go home. I haven't even left Vairian and already the homesickness is unbearable. I'm half tempted to sabotage the whole thing. I have a dreadful feeling I won't need to try very hard.

Lights sparkle into being along the gangway; leading-lights, little points of firefly brightness to guide us onto the landing deck. I push aside an uneasy feeling of having been let down. I don't know. Maybe

I thought my world, my home, would have caused some kind of delay or trouble, some way to conspire to keep me here. But it seems now that Vairian is as eager to be rid of me as everybody else.

*

The great ship rumbles into life. Not a roar, not anything resembling a feeling of flying. Just a deep rooted sensation in the floor on which I stand, something that couldn't be muffled by the deep pile of the crimson carpets. It felt like standing on something that breathes slowly in and out, and that somewhere, deep beneath me a giant heart is beating an implacable rhythm.

Fanciful, of course. It's a machine, like any other. But even my Wasp had somehow felt alive to me. Ships are always referred to as 'she' – a holdover from the Firstworld – but it feels right. Something like the Adeline can't be simply mechanics with a Thread Drive at the centre. I press my hands against the polished wood panels lining the wall. The Liner is the top of her class, no expense spared. My quarters are easily comparable to the state rooms in Higher Cape, each chamber more ornate than the last. The Anthaem is determined to impress me, it seems. Or more likely, my family. The Empire is watching us. Every step of the way. We can't forget that either. My father won't be seen as slacking in any way when it comes to his part of this bargain.

For it is just a bargain. I have to remember that. He doesn't want me – not *me*. The Anthaem wants the protection an alliance with Vairian, and by extension the Empire, can offer, the Vairian-trained soldiers who will come with me, part of a warrior race. He wants it as much as my people need the riches of Anthaeus to rebuild. Higher Cape is gone. All those pretty staterooms, all the towers that gleamed in the sunset like burnished copper... Wiped out by a Gravian super-weapon.

I have to remember that as well. And help to save Anthaeus from the same fate.

And the Empress…? I can't even fathom how her mind works. She wants stability, I know that. She wants to extend her Empire, and she's willing to take as long as needs be to do that. The stories about her say she's immortal, although she appears to age and die like everyone else, appointing a successor to her place before she does. Always a young woman, always an Empress. I'm not even sure she's human really. A world either applies to join in union with her Empire, or is wooed in some way, a use found for each one and a reward offered for service. For Vairian, it's military honours, mutual defence and aid, of course. She's sent a lot of aid our way since our war with the Gravians ended. But then, she's embroiled us in a lot of other wars too. I know she wants the riches of Anthaeus, the same as the Gravians. She's just willing to go about it in a more roundabout way.

By using me.

As I step into my quarters, I catch my breath in surprise.

All along the far wall of the chamber, windows show us the stars racing by. They're framed in gilt, intricately wrought patterns of leaves and flowers. Mirrors reflect the light and the darkness outside. There's a sitting room, and beyond that, a bedroom and bathroom. Each room flows from one to the next, each trying to outdo the previous in splendour.

'Is it acceptable, Princess Belengaria?' asks Jondar with a note of satisfaction already in his voice. 'The ship has the latest in viewing screens.' He waves a hand in front of one of the mirrors and it shimmers, the reflection draining away to reveal various news and entertainment feeds blinking away at us. 'There's encyclopaedic information on a variety of subjects, including a dossier we compiled on Anthaeus for you and a full schedule of events on board ship and when we arrive.' His hands move with a quick and practiced grace, showing me where everything is on the screen, flicking open the files he mentions. I'm suddenly hungry to start examining everything but I don't want to show it. Especially not to him.

So this is for my benefit. Or rather to show me what the future looks like, and what they can do for me. The peasant princess from the backwater world is sure to be cowed by such a display, is that what he thinks?

I grind my teeth together but manage to smile. Barely. 'I'm sure we'll manage, Prince Jondar. How long is the voyage in total?'

'Once we reach the interstellar lanes it's about thirty-seven hours. The threading capabilities of the Adeline are second to none. But I'm certain that we can come up with enough amusements to pass the time. Many of the Anthaem's court came with us to greet you and accompany you home.'

'Vairian is my home.' I say it without thinking, distracted by the stars outside.

Jondar frowns. He wasn't expecting that. 'Your new home, then.'

My face flares hot with mortification. I shouldn't have said that, and Jondar's immediate correction rankles. Shae steps a little closer to me, almost bristling as well. He's got his blaster at the ready. He probably shouldn't but when did Shae let that stop him? The other members of the bodyguard unit – Petra Kel, Thom Rahleigh, Dan Penn and Jessam Hix – look distinctly uncomfortable. They're aware of the implications as much as I am. They're aren't stupid. They wouldn't be here if they were.

A communicator light flashes at Jondar's belt. He checks the panel on his wrist and his features go studiously blank.

Before I can say another word, he gives a deep bow. 'And now if you will excuse me I have preparations to make. Dinner will be served in two hours in the banqueting hall. I look forward to seeing you there.'

He doesn't quite meet my eyes as he leaves.

Shae nods to his men who quickly examine the room, checking every corner and under every item of furniture while Petra guards the door. I wait – they won't let me do anything at all to help – and Nerysse mutters under her breath, irritated by the delay. But she doesn't argue either. She knows it's necessary.

'All clear,' Dan reports to their captain.

There's a brand new collection of rich and opulent objects in my quarters. 'Wedding gifts,' says Nerysse, holding up a slim amber bottle 'Look, it's an ice wine from Telenon. They let the grapes freeze but just the outer surface. It takes great skill to make it and each vineyard can manage fewer than a hundred bottles every three years or so.' Always a teacher, all the details ready at the tip of her tongue.

'You have it if you want, Nerysse,' I tell her.

'But it's from one of the Anthaese nobility. Lady Elara—'

Elara? I bet it's as bitter as she is. 'Well, it shouldn't go to waste then, should it?' I push the bottle into her hand. Nerysse glows with delight, sets it aside for now and then turns on the others. 'Outside, all of you. The princess needs to get ready for her banquet.'

He said two hours. Like I need two hours to get dressed? I glance at Nerysse and realise I might be lucky if it's that quick.

Dan gives me a sympathetic grin as he ushers the other guards outside. He closes the door firmly behind him.

'I wish you'd all stop calling me that,' I mutter. It's useless but I continue to try.

Shae looks thoroughly unrepentant, as usual. 'It's what you are now, Bel. I thought we'd been through this.'

'*You* went through it. I wasn't even present for that discussion.' Nerysse ignores us, already unpacking, taking out gown after gown, each one more ornate and hideous than the last. They are all new, provided by the Anthaese. I wonder if they've chosen the ugliest on purpose.

I leave her to it and head for the bedroom, aware that Shae follows. He stands in the doorway, like a rock, unfeeling, betraying nothing. I sit down heavily on the bed and wish I was home again so I could slam some doors, or better yet, sneak out to my Wasp and fly away.

Oh ancestors, I wish I could just fly away.

No such option here.

'I'll let you get ready,' Shae says in those solemn tones of his. He doesn't smile at me any more. It's like a spike in my chest, realising that. He doesn't smile. When did that happen? We'd been friends, I had hoped more than friends and now…

Now I'm a princess and his job is to keep me alive. And that's all. It's more important than any might-have-beens.

*

Dinner on board is a sumptuous and flamboyant affair, course after course of delicacies and delights, but I'm more interested in the view from the huge picture windows all around the stateroom. The stars flash by them as the star liner threads through the interstellar path, navigating the empty places between, moving faster than possible with regular engines. Blurs of light and colour swirl like abstract artwork. Most of the guests aren't even looking but I can't tear my eyes from the beauty all around us. We're flying through it all, like a swan, effortless in the sky.

The courses keep coming, each more elaborate than the last. There's too much food, far too much for one person to eat.

Finally, when the evening draws to a close and I can escape, Shae walks me back to my quarters.

I change out of the gown and try to make myself go to sleep. But I fail. Instead, I stare at the blurred stars outside until Nerysse comes in to dim the windows and shut them out. Without asking.

When Nerysse retires to her own room, I wrap myself in a silken robe and slip out silently.

Shae stands in the corridor outside, leaning against the wall in such a familiar pose it hurts to see him there. His eyes narrow to slits. 'And where do you think you're going, Princess?'

'The observation deck.'

For a moment I think he'll argue, that he'll send me to my room like some kind of naughty child. I'd hate him if he did that. Especially now. But thankfully, Shae just gives that same solemn nod and falls into step beside me.

'You're angry.'

He doesn't have any trouble keeping up with my determined stride. Not with those long legs. That just makes me angrier. 'Of course I am. I don't want to be here.'

'Who does?'

I look at him, surprised, but can't see anything in his face to alarm me. If anything he looks slightly depressed. 'You don't?'

'Never been a fan of deep space, too many things can go wrong. Give me a good face-to-face battle instead.'

'A battle.' I shake my head, laughing even though I don't want to. 'Because nothing can go wrong in battle, right?'

He flashes that rare grin at me. 'Not when *I'm* fighting.' For a moment I believe it. He's seen combat in four different sectors of the Empire, on worlds I couldn't even imagine. Shae can do anything. That's what I have always thought, after all. But he can't get me out of this. Not this time.

'I don't want this battle, Shae. I don't want to be married to someone I've never met. I don't even want to be a princess.'

And the grin is gone, his face stoic again. 'No more than your father wanted to be king. But here we are. And if it's a battle, well then, you're Vairian. Face it, Bel.'

'We don't all have to be warriors just because we're from Vairian. I wanted to be a pilot. I wanted—'

His voice isn't harsh, but it is not to be argued with. I know that tone.

'Well you can't be. So all you do is face it. That's all any of us can do with life when it defies our wishes. Face it down and put it in its place.' We stop at the door to the observation dome and Shae opens it for me, but doesn't step inside, as if he senses I need to be alone.

'I think that's the most you've said to me since this began.' I smile, my nerves and temper making it wobbly, but it is a real smile. I'd hoped that now we were alone he would finally be himself again, and he'd almost sounded like it. Just for a second. While he was chiding me. Or being honest with me. Or whatever that was. I miss him so much. I want to grab him and kiss him. I want him to do that to me. But we can't. The moment passes. He doesn't move. He looks at me, and then turns his gaze deliberately away.

'I'll be right here if you need me,' he says.

The words sound as if something lingers just beneath them. But he won't say it, whatever it might be. I step away from him and gaze upwards, first closing my eyes to drive away tears, then opening them to focus on the view instead.

The pale light of a distant dwarf star is the only illumination in the observation room, blurred by speed and the effects of the thread path along which we travel. My footsteps echo across the mosaic floor, but I look up, out into the endless reaches of space. I'd never in all my imaginings thought it would be as peaceful as this. Or so beautiful. Like flying at night over still water, like catching a breeze and gliding high over the Deringer Sea by moonlight. I stretch out my arms on either side, tilt my head back so all I can see is the dome and try to feel it again. Stars fly by me, a rainbow of gas clouds, planets gleaming like gemstones in the night. And so many bright stars.

A discreet cough makes me jump. I spin towards the noise, my face heating again. I've got to stop being so transparent. It's infuriating.

Prince Jondar must have come in by another door, although from where I don't know. He wears a silk robe over his night clothes, but he doesn't look as if he has been sleeping any more than I have. If anything he looks wide awake. His gaze trails over my figure in the form-hugging nightdress Nerysse selected and I pull my dressing gown tight around me. But his eyes don't linger.

'I thought I was alone.' You would think that would be pointed enough to get rid of him, but he doesn't retreat. Not one for subtleties, Jondar. Or very, very good at ignoring them.

A slow smile curls the corner of his expressive mouth. 'So I guessed. Trouble sleeping?'

I give a flat stare and turn my back on him. 'Not at all.'

His low chuckle echoes around the empty room and tells me he's moved closer. Damn it. 'Ah, that's more like a princess at last.'

'You want me to act like a bitch?'

'A princess,' he corrects me, all patience and calm. 'Like Lady Elara.'

I snort air from both nostrils. How's that for the behaviour of a princess? 'I'll repeat my previous question then.'

Jondar sighs, a little impatient now, a little – well, if it was anyone else I'd say *dismayed*. 'Elara knows how to survive the games of our court. Not to mention the Imperial court where the games can be deadly indeed. She didn't intend to denigrate you personally. She'll be an asset to you in the court, I promise.' Really? He was standing right there when we met. Wasn't he paying attention?

'She gives a good impression of it then.'

His hand cups my shoulder, warm and gentle, much in the manner one of my brothers would. A shiver of surprise races through me. Too intimate. Too much. I turn around ready to drop him where he stands but he pulls back, and to my surprise I see wariness in his eyes. He looks worried. He looks ashamed. Just for a moment.

'Elara wanted to embarrass me,' he confides after a moment. 'She seeks status and I denied her access to that. I'm afraid she used you as an opportunity to do that. It was petty, but please don't judge her for it.'

'What did you do to her?'

The wry amusement he puts on his face is a mask over something else. She couldn't be sure what though – Loss? Pain? Or both? 'I didn't ask her to marry me.'

I'd expected something more damning. 'Why not?'

'Because I don't love her.'

For a moment I don't know what to say. Even he's afforded the choice I'm denied? That just makes my life complete. 'I'm not sure who is luckier then.'

Jondar dips his head and I think he might say more. Maybe he'll attempt to comfort me. I ball up my fists, ready to hit him if he tries anything.

When he does look at me again, however, his expression is as cold and austere as ever.

'We'll arrive in Anthaese space tomorrow at twelve shiptime and rendezvous with the transport shuttle to take us to the planet. The Anthaem has arranged a reception party in the transport. It will make for a less public first meeting, an opportunity before the crowds descend. It's a great honour and a token of the high esteem in which he holds you.'

Jondar looks at me, waiting for something. He seems more cheerful at the thought of a private first meeting. Perhaps he thinks I will feel the same way.

'I thought the Anthaem never leaves the planet.'

A sardonic smile cracks through his austerity again. 'Visiting a ship in orbit is hardly the same as leaving the planet. If his feet aren't planted on Anthaese soil for a few hours, the world won't come to an end.'

The reports hadn't seemed so sure. Why do they want a private meeting anyway? Not for my benefit, surely? Maybe he's worried about what he's getting in his new wife. Maybe he wants to see me before anything is made public, so he can just pack me off home if I'm too horrendous an option to contemplate. *Maybe...*

I can't say any of that to Jondar, though. I can't say anything. I have to hide what I feel, what I think. I have to get rid of him.

'Of course.' The diplomatic answer. 'The Anthaem is too kind.'

I sweep past Jondar in as regal a fashion as I can muster and Shae appears in the doorway, steel-eyed with anger. More than just anger. When he takes in Jondar's presence something in his eyes flares white-hot.

'Your Highness,' he begins, his voice tight. He hadn't seen him enter then, either. Oh Shae, that was a slip-up. I didn't think it possible. 'What did—?'

'I'm coming back now,' I reply, in no mood for reprimands. I don't need to appear like an even greater fool right now. I've had enough. 'You can lock me in if you must.'

As I reach the doorway, Jondar's voice makes me pause.

'Belengaria?'

He says my name so carefully that at first I think it can't be him. I look back, glare at him, still angry. Ancestors, it feels good to be angry, to let it out.

'The Anthaem is a good man. He… he means so much to… to his people. This marriage is an enormous step, a controversial one. Many of our people do not welcome anything that might resemble an Imperially sanctioned alliance. Our enemies and friends alike have issued many threats. He needs strong and loyal friends at his side.'

I keep my expression smooth as glass, though inside my emotions whirl. Strength I can understand, but loyalty is earned. Jondar is implying more than that. Not through what he says but it's there in his voice, in the depths of his eyes. Devotion. Love.

Does he expect me to love Conleith before I've even met him? Does he hope to persuade me? Or is he trying to express something more?

'I've given my word, Prince Jondar.' I gentle my voice just a little. 'If you doubt me then you don't know the Vairians.'

*

Dan and Jessam are on duty outside my quarters when we return.

The room is too quiet. From the moment we stop outside the door and Jessam opens it, I know something is wrong. So wrong.

Dark, a silence so deep it swallows me up. All the windows are dimmed, opaque instead of transparent, shutting out the stars, muffling everything in darkness, just as I left it. There is no light at all. I wonder where Nerysse is. A shape moves in front of me, one made entirely of hard muscles bristling with controlled alarm. Shae.

He senses it too.

With a couple of nods, he deploys his men and they fan out. Jessam enters first, turning up the dowsed lamps.

Nerysse lies in the middle of the scarlet rug she had so admired. I swallow a cry. One glance and I know she's dead. Histrionics will gain us nothing.

But… it's Nerysse.

Beside her hand lies a glass, a little liquid still in it, pooling on the carpet. The bottle of ice-wine stands open on the table. Too late, I remembered what I said.

I'd told her to have it. She must have come in for a nightcap.

I fed her poison as surely as if I poured it myself.

And then another thought, far more horrible. She died alone. With no one to help her.

A noise somewhere between a sob and a hiccough bursts into the silence.

Shae turns, his eyes wide in alarm. Shamed and horrified, I slap my hand over my mouth to stop it happening again, but the trembling in my shoulders still gives me away.

'Jessam, inform Prince Jondar of what has happened and that we will investigate. Tell him to find the princess another room at once. And check out his choice with a micro-scanner, understood?'

Jessam gives a curt bow and bolts from the room.

Shae approaches the body. I'm frozen to the spot, unable to move. Petrified. But he's all calm efficiency, even though Nerysse had all but raised him too. He kneels down, leans over her to smell her breath, checks her pulse and the clammy pallor of her skin. He takes in everything. Because he needs to know everything.

'Looks like poison,' says Dan.

Shae grunts and a flicker of annoyance passes over his face. No one would notice unless they knew him as well as I do. 'Yes, it does. That doesn't necessarily mean it is though. I want her blood tested for toxins and that wine too. Let's start there. And Dan, keep this a Vairian matter. She's one of ours, as is Bel. No need for Jondar and the Anthaese to get involved.'

'It's his ship, Captain,' Petra tells him. Her voice is solemn but firm. And she's right, of course. 'And the princess is under his care.'

'She's still our princess, for now anyway. Who are they going to argue with? See to it. I want full jurisdiction firmly established from the start. Someone just tried to kill Bel. I will not let this pass.'

A wave of exhaustion sweeps over me, and the shock follows, grief that I haven't even begun to experience looms like a wave about to crash. And I can't tear my eyes off Nerysse. Not even when one of my guards covers her with a sheet.

Chapter Five

It isn't until the shouting wakes me, that I realised I must have cried myself to sleep. My eyes ache and a dull pounding headache has lodged in the base of my brain. I sit up, blinking in the darkness in an unfamiliar cabin. Another one.

Nerysse is dead. And it's my fault.

I freeze, breathing hard. The shouting goes on, but cut with other voices.

Shae. That's Shae, his tone cold and formal but determined, slicing through the roars.

And Jondar. Just as single-mindedly quiet in his anger.

So who's actually shouting?

I push myself up, horrified to find my legs shaking. With grim determination, I force myself to be strong, not to panic or to think of Nerysse. Not now.

Petra sits by the door, but leaps to her feet as I appear. 'Highness. I'll tell them to keep it down.'

I shake my head. 'I think we're beyond that, don't you?'

She presses her hand to the panel and the door slides open, bathing us in light. I blink at the group of men outside, all of them armed, all of them angry.

Dan, Jessam and Thom have their weapons in their hands, but so do four of Jondar's men. It's not going to help anything and a firefight with the Anthaese would be a diplomatic nightmare but that doesn't appear to have occurred to anyone. Shae's arms are folded across his chest, his gaze unswerving, locked on Jondar's face. The prince stands as if perfectly relaxed, but his eyes blaze. His arms hang by his side, his hands in fists. The tension makes my skin tighten on my bones.

They all fall silent and look at me, as if I'm somehow intruding on them. Oh yes, I'm the interloper here. If they'd done this at home, my father would have had them on duty mucking out stables and changing the filthiest sump from every one of the Wings.

And me?

I'm exhausted, and miserable. I've had enough. I don't have the energy to be grace personified, even if I had the ability in the first place.

I remember my mother walking in on us, years ago, when Zander had painted Luc in something green and glowing and was just getting started on Art too. I was an innocent bystander – well, almost – but that didn't matter. She had a look, one which bored through every one of us. One which didn't stand for any lies or dissembling. I use it now. I even manage something like her voice. 'What is going on out here?'

'Princess, I will handle—' Shae starts to say but Jondar steps up beside me, cutting him off.

'This outrage will be dealt with immediately. I have my best people on it, Princess.'

Shae glares at him. 'For all we know one of your "best people" gave her the wine to begin with.'

'Enough,' I tell him. 'This solves nothing, Captain.' Shae snaps to attention, before he seems to know it's me, like he's hearing a ghost, a voice from the past. His glare turns on me, mixed with disbelief. I know he's angry – with Jondar and now with me – and I don't believe he's thinking straight. That's a shock in itself. He's always so cool and firm.

I know how I must look, bedraggled, exhausted. Not like a princess at all. I'm so tired I can't muster the strength to raise my voice. But for some reason that doesn't matter. They both fall silent, intent only on me. This is new. Maybe I'm a commander after all. Or might be. Maybe there's more of my mother in me than I thought. I take a breath to steady myself. What else would she have done? Thought it through, that's what. Figured it out. Above all, she'd take charge.

So I need to take charge, while I have the chance. 'The wine was a gift. From whom?'

'The Lady Elara,' Jondar replies and he reddens. 'But really—'

'Then we need to talk to Elara first. Where is she?'

Both men look at the floor, at the walls, at anywhere but my face.

'She's confined to quarters, your Highness,' says Shae at last. 'All passengers are. We saw to that at once.'

Have I just discovered the source of the shouting then? Because while Shae has the remit to protect me, that probably didn't include locking Anthaese nobility in their quarters. I cast him a reproving glance and he just looks bewildered. He's not used to this. I've always done what he says, or at least backed him up. Guilt twinges in my chest but I push it away ruthlessly. I don't have time for this. It isn't about him. It isn't about either of them.

'Do you think it's possible that Elara masterminded this?' I ask, keeping my voice calm and even, non-threatening.

It's a blunt question, but this is a time for bluntness. Jondar shakes his head at once, his instinctive reaction, and probably, I think, a correct one.

'I need to speak to her,' I tell him. It isn't a request.

To give him his due, Jondar looks more than a little worried at the prospect. Vairian justice is famous. Back at home, I would be well within my rights to demand a duel, which Elara – who I bet has never lifted anything sharper than a dinner knife – couldn't hope to win. But there's something else in his eyes. A genuine concern. Maybe for me. Maybe for what I may be thinking. Somehow I doubt it's for her. 'Elara would never be involved in this. Her credentials are impeccable, your Highness.'

'Then let us go and talk to her. And we'll find out.'

*

Jondar knocks on the door before opening it and I wince. What is he trying to do? Warn her we're coming? Clearly, the Anthaese have no idea how to deal with this sort of thing. I glance at Shae, who, if possible, looks even angrier. *On edge, and therefore useless*, my father would say. He's better than this. Or he ought to be.

Anger is no help to anyone in this situation. Besides, it's my companion who's dead. Nerysse, who had only ever been kind and motherly, my companion. My friend. Shae grew up with her caring for him too. She looked after many of the war orphans who became wards of our family.

Incredibly, Shae's faring worse than I am. Grief is a passion too, and Vairians are always passionate.

'Stay here,' I tell him.

'Princess—'

'Shae.' I put just enough warning in my voice and to my surprise he steps away, his jaw tightening. But he doesn't argue. I follow Jondar inside.

Elara looks terrible. The perfectly arranged hair is in disarray, her face tearstained and blotchy, smeared with cosmetics, her eyes swollen and bloodshot. I take a moment to examine her in silence, a deliberate tactic of dominance, keeping my face impassive and unreadable. I wait.

And it doesn't take long.

'I didn't do anything,' Elara wails, wringing her hands together. 'I gave you the wine, it's true, but I didn't know anything about poison. Why would I want to do that? Jondar, tell her. Please, tell her. Don't let those savages take me. I didn't do anything.'

Savages. Charming. That's what I can expect of the Anthaese nobility. But on the other hand, given the way my guards are glaring through the doorway perhaps Elara is right to be afraid.

But if she's acting now, she's missed her calling. She's a mistress of the art.

'Where did you get the wine?'

'*Where*? I don't know. I spoke to my secretary and he sourced it.' She even sounds indignant, just for a moment, just what I'd expect from her and then her face crumples again. She begins to sob again, hiccoughing through her words. 'I just… I just wanted something… nice to…'

Nice… for me… I doubt that. She wanted something impressive, expensive, something to put me in my place and show her power.

'Where's the secretary?' I ask, but Jondar is already speaking into the little wrist communicator he wears. He looks up, meeting my gaze without wavering.

'Everyone's confined to quarters. He should be here. Or nearby. She never has her servants too far from her. Hang on.'

The voice that comes back is tinny and garbled, but I can make out enough.

'*Cabin 410, interior, right beside you.*'

Right beside us. I'm ready to call out an order, but Shae is already moving. All of them are, my guards, Jondar's people. It's chaotic. Even Elara surges up from the bed in alarm as the door on the other side of the corridor bursts open and plasma fire erupts in the hallway.

Something hard and unyielding crashes into me, and I fall beneath a body. Jondar's body, I realise after a moment. He pins me to the ground, shielding me.

I shove at him and it's like pushing a boulder. What the hell does he think he's doing? Protecting me? For another moment there's just noise, muffled and terrible and then it stops.

Everything is silent. Everything. At last he rises and I can breathe again. I scramble to my feet, cast the prince a withering glare and rush towards the door, furious with him, with all of them.

'Get back!' Shae yells. 'Secure that room. Thom, is he down? Thom?'

There's a body sprawled on the floor of the narrow cabin opposite, his arms flung out on either side and two plasma rifles beside him.

Her secretary, I suppose. Very, very dead.

Fantastic.

Silence settles on us like a thick blanket in summertime. I clear my throat.

'You know, we could have asked him questions?' I tell Shae in scathing tones. My mother's voice again. 'Just a few. Just the pertinent ones. But now we can't.'

Shae scowls, unrepentant. 'What did you expect? That we'd just let you stand there asking all those questions while he shot you?'

I turn my glare on him. Because he's right. But so am I, damn it. This way everyone loses.

Except whoever wants me dead. For now anyway. A commander would ask questions, find out the answers. Whatever it took. That's what I must do. Concentrate, focus. Get them working right now and find out who's behind this.

'Search the room. His belongings. Get his personal logins and his coms history. Everything.' Giving orders comes easily enough as it turns out. It certainly gives me something to do since they won't let me do anything more.

And that's when I remember Jondar. He's staring at me, his face so pale it might have been comical in other circumstances. But it isn't. Not really.

'Prince Jondar? With your permission?'

'My… my permission, Princess Belengaria?' He looks lost. And Elara is still wailing, her voice worse than a siren, which isn't helping. He doesn't know what to do so he's looking to me instead. I seize it.

'Your permission to search the assassin's cabin and possessions. Your permission to continue.' I'm not actually in charge here. I can't really take charge either. Not officially.

He shakes himself, like someone coming out of a nightmare and anger bubbles up in his gaze. Ah yes, that's more like it. But what did I see before it?

'Permission granted, Princess. Olden, Fent, help them.' Two of his guards give a sharp bow and Shae barks out instructions to them too. I don't move, just level my patience at him. That's my weapon. Jondar folds almost as quickly as Elara. 'This should never have been possible. We are not a violent people, your Highness. To carry such weapons, to turn them on another.'

No, not the Anthaese. Violence isn't their way. That's what the Vairians are for. Poisoned wine, on the other hand… I swallow down some comments which would only make matters worse.

'These things happen in war, Prince Jondar,' I tell him. 'And the Gravians are at war with us all.' Elara subsides to a pained sobbing now, a heap of beautiful clothing and rattled nerves. 'Could we find her a medic with some sedatives?'

'Yes, of course.' He speaks into the wrist communicator again, reeling off a short report and requesting the medic, who arrives minutes later and ushers Elara away. Two security guards go with her.

'Are all your voyages so eventful?' I ask Jondar.

He heaves out a breath. 'Not usually.' His com pings at him and he checks it, his face hardening. 'We're almost ready to drop out into Anthaese space. The royal shuttle from the planet is due to meet us in orbit and the Anthaem will be on board. I should let you prepare yourself and your wardrobe.'

So soon. For a moment I'd felt useful, helpful, able. Now... now it's over. I've just been kidding myself that they'd let me get involved with the investigation. And how in the name of all my forefathers am I supposed to get into one of those ridiculous gowns by myself? But I can't say that to him. No, I'll have to find something simple. Hopefully something of my own has managed to stow away amid the piles of lace.

I think of Nerysse and bile rises in my throat. She would have helped me, would have guided me in so many ways. She'd memorised all their court customs, all my duties and schedules. I never even properly looked at them because I'd been so sure that she'd take care of everything. And now... now she's dead. I'll never see her again. Never find out who was really behind this. I'll never know.

I clench my fists so hard my nails dig painfully into my palms and I push down grief and the spiralling panic with it. Lock it all away.

Politics wait for no one. Not me. Not an investigation. Not the dead. The ship powers on towards Anthaeus and my husband-to-be.

'Very well.' I stand tall, wind my spine with steel and promise myself I'll get through this. I have to. Without Nerysse.

Chapter Six

'What about this one?' I snarl, holding up a sea of green silk with flowers and enough bunting to deck out a conferring ceremony for an entire company of Vairian officers.

'How are you even meant to get that on?' asks Petra, peering at it. 'Let alone do it up. Or walk. Do these Anthaese women do nothing all day but sit and preen?'

I can't say how much I envy her sleek body armour and practical uniform. I toss the dress aside and try again. It's so unfair.

'I can go and get some help if you want?' Petra offers at length.

'You can go and do something more useful.' I shouldn't snap, but don't really care right now. Petra just shrugs. She doesn't care either. She's used to being shouted at. Usually 'Argh!', 'Don't kill me!' or general inarticulate pleading. She hears it a lot. That's Corporal Petra Kel.

'I'll check the door again, will I? Just in case? Did you ever read that dossier?'

'I tried. It's impenetrable.'

She picks up the tablet and begins flicking through it. 'They have your days mapped out like a new recruit.'

'Just give me the highlights, Petra.'

'Preening all morning, being paraded around like a prize pony until lunch, eating very little while people bore you—'

'Fine. Very helpful. Thanks.'

'You're not getting married right away, anyway. You've a week to settle in. There's all sorts of presentations – to the nobility first, then to the Rondet. That's their religious council?'

'They're like… a cross between a priesthood and an oracle, I think? They live in seclusion and no one knows anything about them.'

She scratches her nose. 'Well, it says here there are four of them and they only appear in public on the most important occasions, such as the selection of the Consort to the Anthaem. That's you.'

The next dress is pink. It would be better tossed out of the airlock, into space. 'They have the final say?'

'Looks like it. And then the wedding—'

'*If* I pass the test.'

'You will. The wedding is ten days after that. So… yeah, you have about twenty days.'

Twenty days. That's all. Fewer if the Rondet say I'm not suitable, which might be the best thing for all concerned.

'They don't hang around, do they?'

Petra shrugs and puts the tablet down again. 'It makes sense. They need this sorted as quickly as possible. It's for the best. Just throw yourself into it.'

Easy for her to say. Throw myself into a marriage. Not the greatest advice if you think about it. And it is a marriage. I understood that part of the dossier well enough. While I'll have my own rooms as long as I want them, I'm expected to be his wife. His actual wife. In *every way*.

I must pull out every stupid gown in the cases but at last I find it. Carefully folded and packed in tissue, a relic from a bygone age – a dress which is fifteen years out of date. But that doesn't matter.

It belonged to my mother.

I sit with it for a long time, staring at the sleek grey silk, the intricate embroidery on the edges that somehow manages to be simple as well. I remember her wearing it, drifting through the garden, an elegant birdlike creature, ready to fly away in an instant.

And she did. Within days she was gone forever.

Nerysse must have packed it, in spite of all the new gowns the Anthaese provided. I don't know why, but I've never felt so grateful for anything.

Not only is it perfect, it's a touch of home, of my lost mother and a life I have to give up. But I don't have to stop being myself. I can be the woman my mother would be proud of. And that isn't an Anthaese.

I'm not one of them. Never will be and they will never let me forget it. This is a marriage of convenience, of politics and alliances.

So be it.

'Princess?' Petra is watching me carefully. She hasn't said a word all this time. The tablet sits on the occasional table once more.

'I'm fine.' My voice doesn't even shake when I say it.

I'll give them a Vairian Queen if that's what they want. Although… no, the Anthaese will never want a Vairian Queen. But like it or not, that's what they are getting.

Like it or not. That is what I'll be.

I dress, I brush my hair until it shines, and leave it loose down my back. It feels like the ultimate rebellion.

Which is really quite sad, when you think about it.

An understated knock on the door alerts me to Shae's arrival. Can't just use the coms like anyone else, not my bodyguard. I smile but Petra rolls her eyes to heaven. She knows him too.

'Enter,' I say.

The door slides open with a hiss. 'Are you ready? We have—' His voice twists to silence. Shae stares at me with eyes that seem to take up half his face. His mouth is still open.

'I'm ready.'

He closes his mouth, swallows hard. 'Yes, your Highness.'

'Shae?' I step towards him, confused and then stop. Petra's watching us. Someone is always watching us.

Shae takes a step away, then remembers himself and comes to attention, all hard lean lines and unyielding formality. 'The launch is here. We're ready to escort you to the reception and then we'll head planetside.'

Planetside. Wonderful. And the reception means that I'll be meeting my future husband. Now. Or as near to now that it doesn't matter. I'm trying not to shake. Or at least, trying not to show it. I can't. I have to be strong.

Petra steps outside, joining the men who she proceeds to tease about their overlarge eyes and the way they seem glued to my dress.

'Well,' she says in a low warning voice. 'It had *better* be the dress. Eyes front, you two.' The door closes behind her.

I can't stop staring at Shae, his features closed and careful. I've loved him all my life, or as long as I can remember loving anyone. I looked up to him, admired him, wanted to be just like him and then, one day, I'd just wanted to be with him. Wanted him to look at me the way I looked at him.

He did for a moment. Just a moment when he walked in. But he won't again.

Especially not now. Duty wouldn't allow it.

I'm his princess. I'll shortly become another man's wife.

'We should go.'

I'm ready to sweep by him, but Shae reaches out a hand and catches my arm. His touch is firm, but not painful. It stops me in my tracks and sends shivers of electricity through me.

'You look beautiful, Bel. Like a queen. Like your mother.' He hesitates, but he doesn't let me go. His touch gentles, his fingers moving, almost a caress. 'She would be proud.'

'Shae, I…' But what can I say? We're standing too close, barely touching and it's far more intimate than any other contact I've ever felt. For a moment I think he might lean forward and kiss me. I lift my face towards him, part my lips. Shae's gaze softens, and I can see the same reactions flowing through him, taunting him and tempting him to do the one thing I've always wanted him to. His eyelids lower and he opens his mouth a little. He moves closer. His breath touches my skin, a sigh of regret.

It's just a moment. Too fast, too brief. And gone.

'You'll be the greatest queen they've ever known. Even if they don't see it yet. You're Vairian, Bel, and you look every inch of it right now. Don't forget it.'

And he releases me, standing to full and formal attention once more.

'Thank you,' I whisper, and the words have never felt more like a lie. I don't feel grateful for even a second. I feel like crying, locking myself away and weeping until I can weep no more. But I can't do that.

Anyone else could. Any person, on any world, from any other walk of life… except me. I'm not even a person any more. I'm a princess. And soon enough I'll be the queen. Belengaria of Anthaeus. And Bel will be no more.

*

Jondar waits by the entrance to the landing bay reception room, pacing back and forth, but the moment he sees me approach he straightens.

Handsome in his dress uniform, which had more braid on it than a priestess on a festival day, he looks so different from the man I saw the night before, or the harried commander I'd been with this morning. He wears so many faces I keep forgetting what he is. He's a prince, the brother of the late Anthaem.

Now he looks it.

I spot a few faces I recognise from the various receptions, audiences and dinners. There's no sign of Elara and for that I'm grateful. But I can't miss a number of the sharpened glances from some of the noblewoman's friends. They could hide daggers beneath those glares and I bet they'll be slow to forgive whether Elara was involved in the assassination attempt or not. For now though, I've enough concerns of my own and no fear of attack. My Vairian bodyguards flank me, impressive and lethal. No gold on them, no decorations or fancy uniforms. They're all in body armour, black and unreflective.

And I feel the lack of it as if I was naked.

The gown I wear might be beautiful but it leaves me vulnerable and I feel that in a way I've never felt it before. I study my bodyguards. Petra, sleek as a hunting cat, beautiful in the way predators are beautiful; the broad-shouldered reliability of Thom; Dan's determination and ready smile; Jessam's quick wits, his eyes taking in everything. And Shae. I have to try not to think too much about Shae. They're my guards. I have to rely on them now, not daydream about them… about him…

I focus instead on Jondar and the men standing with him, all similarly garbed in finery. The reception party no doubt and among them…

I can't see the king – *the Anthaem*, I correct myself. They don't call him a king – but then, I've barely looked at the images they sent me and wouldn't have been able to pick him out anyway. I don't see anyone who looks familiar now – young, old, tall, short, fair and dark. Definitely no one who resembles a king, even if he isn't called that.

'Your Highness.' Jondar bows, that graceful, elegant bow again but I don't feel that he's mocking me this time. The others follow suit. 'You look radiant.'

Even though I'm not wearing one of the Anthaese gowns? How shocking. I suppress a smirk. To make a comment would be churlish in response to a compliment. Nerysse would never forgive me. I bite down on the things I want to say. Instead, I dip my head in acknowledgement.

'You must forgive my lateness, Prince Jondar. The recent tragedy—'

He takes my hands, and to my surprise, squeezes them, imparting some measure of comfort I hadn't expected. His skin is warm, his touch soft, but I can feel the tell-tale callouses of a swordsman. Interesting. 'Of course. No apology is needed. You will have a full report on our findings as soon as it is available.'

'The man who died, Elara's secretary—'

'A relatively new employee. She's cooperating fully but I firmly believe she was simply a means to an end. Her credentials were thoroughly checked for months before she was chosen as Princess Elyssa's prospective lady-in-waiting. Her former secretary retired suddenly due to ill-health. The replacement seems to have been a member of a house which recently made some poor trade decisions. It might have caused him to resent the Anthaem.'

'Or someone might have paid him off.'

'Indeed, your Highness. I will make sure every angle is investigated. Now, if I may present you to our Anthaem?'

I knew this was coming but now, right now, my stomach clenches in anticipation and fear. Jondar's touch tightens a little, not uncomfortably so, just firm. But I know he's noticed my reaction. Maybe he's trying to help, to be reassuring. He's not.

I look past the prince, expecting to see someone older, one of the blurred faces from my memory of the images, or someone, anyone who might be a king. No one. Although… my eyes alight on one young man with fair hair. Wasn't he in one of the photos in the dossier, next to Anthaem Matilde? He stares at me, no more so than anyone else, his green eyes curious. He stands at the rear of the group, hardly noticed by the others. Young, only a few years older than me, and handsome after a fashion. Not my type but none of the Anthaese so far could be described as my type. There's something delicate about them, like birds. I think suddenly of my clockwork birds with Keltan crystals. He has green eyes like they did, very bright, very clear, green as the leaves of the Vairian forests on a cloudless day. And he smiles, he alone of all of them. He looks right at me and smiles.

I glance back to Jondar, looking for some sort of clue as to who the Anthaem is.

And that's when it happens.

The floor lurches and bucks, throwing me from my feet and everything around me into chaos. The roar of an explosion rips through the air. Screams follow, and shouts of alarm, warning, command, Shae's voice among them.

I look around wildly for him. Is he okay? Ancestors, he has to be okay.

Jondar shouts commands and questions into his coms, struggling up from his knees. Every guard in the place draws weapons.

Beneath us, the engines of the ship make a spluttering, grinding sound and alarms begin to whoop through the air.

Every nerve-ending in me sparks with panic. This is bad. This is extraordinarily bad.

The blond man leaps to the side, already running when all around are still recovering. He doesn't look back, doesn't look for help. The next thing I know he vanishes down a service hatch. A saboteur? Making his escape? There's a sign over the hatch, words which made my chest tighten – Engine Room, Emergency Access, Crew Only. Is he heading down there to finish the job? No one else has noticed. He's getting away.

Without a moment's hesitation, without a thought of warning Shae or Jondar, or anyone else, I throw myself after him.

*

The Adeline lurches again as I climb down the ladder into the engine room. I almost lose my grip, swinging precariously. I'm not sure how far down I've gone – three decks? Four? – but I know it when I reach the engine room. The smell assaults me first, acrid and harsh, tingling in my nostrils, making them flare in alarm when all I want is to seal them up. He went this way, the blond, green-eyed man. He ran the moment the first explosion happened with barely a moment's hesitation. Like he'd seen it. Like he'd known what was happening right away. No one else had seen him, but I can't ignore it, I can't let him get away.

There's oil on the floor, a slick of black with an iridescent multicultural sheen. All around me the ship shudders and groans, like a great beast in its death throes.

This isn't good. This really isn't good. Healthy ships don't make sounds like that. She's dying around me. I know it.

The engine room is deserted. I edge my way between hulking banks of generators, the huge cogs jerking in erratic, unnatural patterns. There's a smell like burning oil and twisting metal. The whole spaceship is a machine in pain. She isn't just dying. She's dying in agony. And if she goes, she'll take us all with her.

I stop, staring at the pressure gage. I don't know anything about engines this size and all I know about flyers is how to fly them, but a shaking needle that far into the red can't be good. I reach out, as I've seen Luc do a thousand times, and tap the glass. If anything the needle just edges higher.

There has to be someone here, an engine crew with a chief and a team who know the nuances of each and every valve and cog. All big ships work that way.

I round the main fuel pumps and find them. Bodies lie strewn on the floor, blood dripping down through the grates to the hidden parts of the engine below, pooling around rivets and metal plates.

Dead. I don't need to check. Staring eyes, gaping wounds, they tell me everything.

'Princess?' Shae's voice echoes in strange ways through the metal chamber, and in the confines of my head, over the shock buzzing in my ears. Distant, hollow, lost in the labyrinth of equipment, I can't even tell which direction his voice comes from. He must have followed me, even when I thought he hadn't been watching.

'I'm here,' I call, before realising that in such a maze that is probably no help at all.

Another voice answers me, down at my feet, so close I jump back, bracing for an attack.

'Quick, hand me the Harrington number five.'

I thought they were all dead. Turning around, my skirt swirling around my ankles, I try to find the source. Two legs poke out from beneath a large block of oil-slicked machinery. They shift as their owner squirms towards me and a grimy hand appears, holding a wrench. I catch a glimpse of his shirt sleeves, rolled up to the elbows and ruined by oil.

'Quickly,' he says in a calm and determined voice. 'I think I've got this, but I need the Harrington five.'

I cast around for tools and find an array spread out on the floor beside his feet.

'I don't know what—' No, that won't help anyone. Not now. 'Describe it.'

He waggles the wrench he's holding at me. 'Like this, but twice as big.'

'Got it!' I snatch up the larger wrench and pass it to him, taking the smaller one first. The hand and half the leg length vanish under the engine block again. I bend down, trying to see who he is and what he's doing. It's dark as night under there. How can he even see to work?

'Do you need light?'

'No time. Pretty much… working by feel.' His voice is a little breathless. Not scared. Definitely not scared. If anything I'd say he sounds excited. 'Good, yes. That's it.' His voice lowers and he sounds like he's speaking to a child or a wild animal. He's so gentle. His voice ripples through me, stirs something in me I didn't know was there. 'Yes, come on now. Just a little more – there! That's it.'

The machinery gives a great sigh, and the engine room shudders again. The beast, shaking something off. Steam billows out of a vent above me and oil squirts from the block, splattering down my bodice and skirt. I gasp in surprise but don't have time to think about it.

'Can you see the Bentley?' the engineer calls out. 'A spike with a crystal tip, like the nib of a pen.'

I try to wipe some of the mess off but only succeed in smearing it further into the fabric. And over both hands. And into my hair. I don't have time for this. Where's the Bentley? And then I realise…

Oh ancestors, this was my mother's dress, my one last piece of home. Nerysse will kill me!

The thought almost stops my breath. Nerysse—

I'm frozen, shaking. I can't move. My eyes sting and my throat is tight. All the air is sucked from me. I can't breathe.

'The Bentley?' he repeats, a little more urgently this time. But that voice, his voice, it works magic. 'We aren't done yet. If I can't seal this off the whole thing will seize up and blow.'

He's right. Focus, Bel. Get this done. Now.

'Right. The Bentley.' I snatch up the tool, guessing which one from the description and pass it to him, kneeling down in oil to peer underneath again. Not that I can make anything out this time either. 'The rest of the engine crew are dead. What happened?'

'I only just got down here myself. Found them. The threading engine was about to blow. It still might.' He shoves the Harrington into my hand. His whole body stiffens and he braces his legs between floor and engine, grunting as he tries to turn something I can't see. Muscles strain. He's strong, but is he strong enough?

'Can I help?'

'No, I've got it. I think I... damnation... no, wait. I've... there we are.'

With a series of juddering clanks, the machine's groans subside. The grinding of metal changes and becomes the soft music of perfectly balanced machinery. He's done it. He's actually done it. The relief makes my legs go wobbly.

Strong arms seize me, pulling me away from the machine. I spit out a curse in shock. My guards fan out around us, checking the bodies, while Jondar's security take up perimeter positions.

'What were you thinking?' Shae scolds me like an old mother hen. He doesn't release me. He's too upset. You'd have to know him to see it. Or at least I hope so. 'Are you hurt? Did you—?'

I shake myself free. 'I'm fine. Nothing happened.' I glance down at my front, at the oil and the dirt on my hands, at my hair hanging down like weeds around my smudged face.

The engineer pushes his way out, his job done, and four weapons power up and train on him in an instant. He's younger than I thought, no more than a couple of years older than me. But he's the same blond man I had seen, the one who I had followed. He wears what had once been a fine shirt and waistcoat. The tailored brocade frock coat is the pile of material and braid on the floor beside them, soaking in oil, blood and liquid from the sump. His back and side are soaked, fine material clinging to his skin. I can make out lithe muscles, the planes and angles of his torso. The chain of a pocket watch gleams in the dim light. His hair isn't just blond, but a rich rose gold, almost metallic, streaked now with black and matted against his skull at the back, and his face is finely sculpted, handsome and intelligent.

His eyes move from one weapon to the next, as if he's examining them, mentally defining their form and function, without a trace of fear. Eyes the colour of the emeralds in my mother's necklace, buried in amongst my clothes.

'Forgive me for being brusque,' he says, rising with grace, or perhaps it's just extreme care. One wrong word at the moment and they'll blame him for the deaths and the sabotage. Vairian justice will be swift as ever, especially if they think I was in danger. Shae has never hesitated in my defence. I recall the Gravian Grunts in the forest at home. And right now I am not even sure he is thinking. Not really thinking. He's angry and he's scared and that makes him doubly dangerous. The engineer doesn't appear to notice the danger. He gives a brief bow, oblivious to the threat confronting him. 'I'm Con,' he tells me and frowns, taking in my appearance beneath the oil and smudges. Can he see my fears? Or Shae's anger? Does he understand the knife's edge on which he balances?

'Bel.' I keep my voice low. At least I got that in before anyone informs him of my full title. It might be the last time I meet someone in a normal fashion, just two people, so that I could be a flyer for one last time. I drop to a polite curtsey.

His face shows confusion and amusement mixed. And a hint of stress.

'You saved the ship,' I tell him.

'Well, as we're on it, that seemed like a good idea.'

To my surprise, I laugh. It comes out of nowhere. I'd almost forgotten how. It's a bark of unexpected humour and it's too loud in the confines of the engine room. It bounces around, echoing off the walls, inappropriate and disrespectful in here. 'The engineering crew?' I glance at Shae, who stands there, still as stone. He responds only with a brief shake of his head. He isn't finding anything funny. And really, there's nothing funny here at all.

'Sabotage and murder,' Con murmurs, and he shakes his head, the humour gone now. 'Someone really didn't want this ship to reach Anthaeus.'

'Well, not in one piece,' I add, the enormity of that sinking in. We're barely in Anthaese orbit and already there have been two attempts on my life. The first claimed Nerysse. The second killed five innocent men and could have killed us all. If not for Con. I owe him. 'How can I thank you?'

I think of all those Vairian stories, of warriors doing great deeds, of boons granted. If he asks for a kiss, would I grant it? It might be the last chance before I'm married off to the Anthaem. Kings – even if they aren't called king – aren't renowned for their looks or charm.

Or their intelligence. Or even as easy going a manner as Con displays. Calm efficiency and dry humour. It's strangely attractive, not anything I've ever considered before. The warriors of Vairian fairy tales were more about heroics and valour. They'd be more likely to leap from an exploding spaceship than patiently take the time fix it.

To my surprise, and more than a little amusement, Con blushes. Can he read my thoughts? That sends my cheeks flaming as well. What had I been thinking? I'm not some brainless girl, to be mooning over anyone. I'm Vairian. I'm a princess.

Shae makes a noise, a deep-throated growl. I almost forgot he's there. I glance his way, both irritated at his belated reminder and intrigued as to what had finally made him notice.

Another voice breaks through the tense silence.

'There you are!' Jondar slides down the ladder to the engine room so quickly I half hope he'll fall on his face. No one should be as graceful as him. It isn't fair. But he sounds frantic. 'Have you lost your mind? What if something had happened to you?'

I gape at him. Concern? Well, maybe he is human after all. But then, if he lost me, there'd probably be hell to pay for him. I'm about to say that nothing happened to me, that I'm here with Shae and a bunch of armed men ready to kill on sight, but Jondar doesn't spare me so much as a glance. He bears down on Con, all dark rage born from genuine fear.

Con doesn't flinch or look in any way afraid, as anyone should with an irate prince and this many weapons in an enclosed space. Bored maybe. Fed up.

'I'm fine,' says my engineer placidly enough. 'Whoever it was had gone by the time I got here. He killed them, rigged the engine and fled. We need to arrange for their funerals, pay compensation to the families and see that—'

Jondar's voice rings off the metal walls of the engine room.

'You didn't even wait for a guard, Con! If they had still been here, that could have been you as well.'

I know that look. My father used to wear it when my mother wouldn't listen to his pleas to stay out of the firefights. He uses it for Zander too, when he won't listen to reason. It's frustration, anger, terror. All born of love.

Con means everything to him.

The reality and hidden meanings of the situation slam into me. I want to glance at Shae and see if he's noticed it as well, but don't dare. Con's completely oblivious. That's plain to see. Right now, he's also annoyed.

'But it wasn't, Jon. And if I'd waited another moment I couldn't have stopped it. Only for Bel coming down here and helping, I couldn't have managed it anyway.'

'You are the Anthaem!' he yells. '*Our Anthaem*, Conleith. You have to remember that.'

'Matilde never hesitated to act, Jondar. Your sister—'

'Matilde is dead—'Jondar breaks off, swearing in a rapid undertone. They aren't words I haven't heard before but from his mouth they seem kind of blasphemous. Con shakes his head.

'You shouldn't talk like that in front of our honoured guests, Jon.'

And then what Jondar actually said finally sinks in.

Instincts kick in, as if Nerysse is in my mind screaming of propriety and etiquette and too shocked to argue, I draw in a breath and sweep into a full, formal curtsey, bowing my head to the man I have promised to marry. Where I find the grace, I don't know, but I make myself do it anyway.

'Oh no, Bel! Please!' He sounds dismayed and I look up to find his hand reaching out towards me. 'Not now, Bel. Please, let's just go and get cleaned up and changed. Let's not—' He gives me a forlorn look and I wonder if he'd been more comfortable as Con the engineer, before I knew his real identity. Or maybe it was better when he didn't know mine, when I'd been no more than a faceless helper. Rather than his future wife.

'Very well, your Majesty.' I must look a state. Not that I would care, but a gnawing sense of shame works its way higher inside me. He was expecting a princess, a representative of the Empire. Not a skinny, gangly girl covered in oil, standing in an engine room. Much as I'd been expecting a king.

Problem is, I rather liked the engineer.

Chapter Seven

The warmer air in the shuttle ruffles my hair as I board it, stepping through the airlock with guards in front and behind me. No one is taking a chance. There's no sign of the assassin. Whoever it was has simply vanished. I realise they plan to investigate it. More investigations. And I have so many other things that should be my priorities right now. I'm exhausted and overwhelmed, but I'm trying to smile, trying to be brave, trying so hard.

The royal shuttle is sleek and polished, as beautiful as the Adeline but smaller, of course, and with a different aesthetic. A wine and gold canopy shades the lights overhead, and the polished mahogany finish shines like something rare and precious. Brass fittings gleam in the same way the light glints off water. The ornamentation reminds me of leaves chasing each other along the surfaces.

As we board, a crewman in an elaborate tailored uniform trills out a series of notes on a small silver pipe – piping us aboard, I realise after a moment, with all the ceremony of the highest Vairian military – and Con takes my hand. Someone has found him a different coat, but the cuffs hang over his hands a little, and the shoulders are a touch too broad. He's lucky that's all. They've done a good job on my hair and face at least – some of Anthaese court and their maids being drafted in to help. I'd been forced to sit there while they prodded and poked me, talked about me as if I wasn't there. Even Petra had looked aghast. The gown they had chosen to replace my ruined Vairian dress is pea green, clings too tightly to my waist making it difficult to breathe and is more like wearing furniture than clothing. I hate it more than I've ever hated anything. I'm sure they've done it on purpose. And there's nothing I can do about it. I just have to endure it and let them see that they can't get to me this way. It just makes me angry.

'Welcome.' Con's voice is soft but distant. He scans the portholes, gazing at the planet beneath, a green and blue globe like a jewel in the night. Such intense longing fills his eyes. I swallow hard and try to see whatever he sees beneath us on Anthaeus, but it eludes me. It's just a planet. The oceans are vast, much larger than those of Vairian but the same blue. The land varies grey to green, jutting from the sea – forests here, cliffs there, mountains beyond it. I can see no sign of vast city-complexes such as you'd find on Cuore. No deserts or wasteland either. Anthaeus is lush and rich, made up of jewel-like colours, a beautiful world, no doubt, but not my home. Con's hand tightens slightly on mine when it trembles.

'It will be fine, Princess. I promise. Anthaeus will welcome you and love you.'

I haven't seen much evidence of this so far.

Another knot forms in my throat. There are words I should be saying, agreeing perhaps, or returning the sentiment, but I can't form them in my mind, let alone with my lips. Shae steps up alongside me, and I glance towards him. He's gazing at the approaching land too but his gaze is entirely different – hard, clinical, assessing the terrain. He's looking for threats, dangers and why not? What have we seen so far that could be considered welcoming?

Two assassination attempts on the journey here alone. Perhaps linked, perhaps not. I'd prefer to say they were Gravian in origin, but

Elara's secretary was Anthaese. So it seems I have enemies down there as well. Maybe he was paid off, but maybe it's too easy to think the Gravians are behind everything. There are also many Anthaese who don't want me here. I'm sure of it.

The landing is fluid and perfect, effortless, and I breathe deeply as fresh air floods the compartment. The shuttle taxies until it pulls alongside an elaborately decorated platform, hung with garlands and silver bells which ring in the breeze. Music plays as we step out, the harmonies soaring, carried by the same breeze as the bells. Children throw flower petals in the air, which float around us. A carriage stands by, drawn by three mechanical horses, their gleaming brass bodies inlaid with mother-of-pearl. I've heard of such things, but never seen them. Just the little songbirds at home. Nothing like this size. Beneath the exterior I can see the little cogs and springs, the delicate movement of machinery and harmonic design which make Anthaese craftsmen famous the galaxy over. Their skill isn't the only reason the Empire courts them – the natural resources of this world alone make it tempting – but the things they build, the way they change everything…

Con's watching me closely. He's seen my interest. I hardly hid it.

'Would you like a closer look?' he asks.

'Yes. They're amazing.'

A smile flickers over his lips, the first genuine smile I've seen him wear since the engine room. It's fleeting, gone as swiftly as it appears.

'No time, your Majesty.' Jondar steps in front of us before we can move, a timepiece in his hand. 'We need to move the procession along. We're late already.'

Con's expression remains carefully schooled to calmness, but his eyes harden. 'Yes, having someone try to kill us really puts a dint in the timetables. Can I not show my fiancée a little of our treasures?'

'Con,' Jondar's voice is a soft growl, all velvet wrapped around a fist. He didn't quite glare at me, but I feel his displeasure too. Like this is all my fault. I bite the inside of my lower lip to keep from saying something. It won't end well if I do.

'Fine,' the Anthaem sighs, and it is clearly not fine at all. His disappointment is palpable. But a moment later, he's apologising to me. 'I'm so sorry. Later, Bel, I promise. But for now we need to be seen and fêted. Can you stand it?'

'Your Majesty?' I'm surprised by the question. It sounds as if he has no more time for this than I do. Do we really have a choice? I didn't think so.

Jondar is calling the shots here, which is strange given that Con is the Anthaem. I wonder what sort of influence the prince has over my husband-to-be. Did he hold the same status when his sister ruled and just carry on as if he were royalty himself? But he *is* royalty, I suppose. He's a prince. Con was chosen as heir rather than born to it. And Jondar seems to run everything…

'Your Highness,' Con replies – an empty reply and I can tell he knows that. As he escorts me to the carriage, I'm sure he's grinning but I resist looking up at his face in case I appear some kind of simpering idiot. Shae is following behind, the others have fanned out on either side. Con's guards shadow them. No one appears to be very trusting. Hardly surprising given our journey so far. I focus on our transport instead. The frame itself is a metal I don't recognise, carrying the same strange sheen like a rainbow in its polished surface. Inside it's lined with cream velvet, the seats soft and plump. I take my place beside him, feeling ridiculously out of place in such a fairy-tale contraption.

Con bows his head, and laces his fingers together. 'There's a certain protocol to everything,' he says. 'And pomp. Ceremony, you understand?

My people tend to insist on that. They like to see us. And to see us as... well, like this...'

I swallow hard on the lump that has suddenly appeared in my throat. This is to be my life now, and he doesn't sound any more thrilled about it than I am. I should reply. I've been quiet too long. The problem is, it's surprisingly easy to talk to him, and I hadn't expected that. I don't know him at all. I desperately need to be careful here. 'Of course, your Majesty.'

He sighs. 'Must we be so formal? It was easier before we knew, wasn't it?'

I smile without meaning to. I probably shouldn't but he's right. It certainly was easier before but I don't know how to tell him that. It implies I'm disappointed now. And I really shouldn't be. At least he isn't ancient. At least he seems kind. 'I suppose so.' I swallow hard, wet my lips. I have to make an effort. 'Conleith?'

'Con, please.' His startling green eyes are trained on me now.

'Con then,' I concede. To be honest, I wish Shae were here. I don't know what to say. I don't like being here on my own. Or with him. Or whatever. Nerysse would have known what to do, would have drilled me, prepared me, but now... I'm on my own, no matter that I'm sitting beside my future husband.

My future husband. It's insane. I don't even know him. We have nothing in common. But at least... at least he's... I glance at him again. He's waiting for something. *Why is he being so nice?*

'You had a question?'

I scramble for one quickly.

'What's our itinerary?'

He studies my face as if he guesses that I just made that up on the spot. 'They didn't tell you?'

I should have read the dossier myself. Or at least questioned Petra a bit more closely. 'They tell me very little, or so it seems.'

Con gives a brief and bitter laugh. 'Yes, I know that feeling.' He reaches up and rakes his fingers through his hair in a movement that's painfully reminiscent of Shae. I tear my gaze away, looking for him. He's getting into a transport behind us, along with Jessam. The others must be elsewhere. I feel curiously alone. Even though I'm not. 'We'll ride through the city, up to the palace. It's the Citadel... you can see it up there.'

He points out of the window beside him and above the huddle of buildings, I can see tall, slender towers, with a pearly sheen to them. When the sun strikes them, they gleam like spun sugar confections from distant Melia.

As Con moves, a roar goes up from the gathered crowd. He waves with a practiced grace and casts me a wry look as the cheers grow even louder. 'They like waving. Would you?'

What else can I do? This is why I'm here, after all. As the carriage begins to move forward – as smooth and fluid as if it's gliding on magnetic rails like the monorail had in Higher Cape – I lift my hand and the people start to shout for me too, calling out my name and cheering.

It's strange. I'm not sure if I like it or not. Perhaps both. There's something unnerving about it. Like looking at a creature which at any second could turn on me.

'We aren't a huge colony, not like the planet-states in your Empire, but we do love a spectacle. On Cuore, in the Imperial city, I believe they have processions every day, and different forms depending on the hour. We make must a poor comparison for you.'

'I've never been to Cuore.' And I have no wish to go there, though I don't tell him that. No one is meant to say that. We've all heard stories about the heart of the Empire, the city of a thousand festivals, where the Empress rules and her court play their many games, each one more dangerous than the last. 'And this is... beautiful.'

I don't know what else to say to him. Con shifts in his seat, and I wonder if he is just as uncomfortable as I am. This can't be easy for him either. He was expecting Elyssa. He must have made preparations for her. I look out the window again, wave my hand occasionally. I'd expected to hate the differences I saw, but the city that passes by me is fascinating. There are many things that are familiar – a baker's shop is a baker's shop the universe over. But the pale trees that line the street are strange to me. On Vairian, the trees are a thousand shades of green and the streets of our cities are wide and regimented. Here the streets wind in and out of each other, twisting together to form squares and plazas, formal parks and market spaces. I'm keenly aware of Con. There's not a lot of space in this carriage, not really. I can feel the warmth from his skin. If I relax, I'll end up with my thigh resting against his and that's a bit too much right now. I sit up tall and straight, uncomfortably rigid, and study Limasyll. I really ought to talk to him but I can't think of what to say.

People have climbed the trees that overlook the road in search of a better view and I grin, imagining how Shae and my guards are probably reacting to that level of security threat right now. This is a city that grew rather than was designed in a formal, structured way like my home had been. The buildings are haphazard, piled one upon the other, leaning over, dotted with balconies bedecked with flowers. And they are ancient. Some of them older than any buildings I have ever seen.

'How old is Limasyll?' I ask. It's a way of making conversation. Luckily Con takes the thread I offer and runs with it. He's as awkward as I am, I'm sure of that now.

'Thousands of years old. There was a city here when Cuore was a village, did you know that? Not *our* city, of course. We came only three hundred and sixty-two years ago, settlers from the central worlds, those who had no wish to be part of the ever-expanding Empire. There were others here before us, long gone when we arrived. Elders or ancients, we call them, the ancient Anthaese. They were… gifted.' A smile traces his lips again, and the warmth of affection infiltrates his words. I could get used to that smile. 'We get our talents from them, but really what we do is a pale shadow compared to some of the artefacts we've found. Our archaeological dig up by Montserratt alone—'

I listen, bemused, as he talks of a people he never met, a people who were gone hundreds of years before his people came to this world from the planets that now form the Empire, as if they are old friends, teachers and guides. He speaks of architecture, engineering, the design of the clockwork trinkets and elegant machines for which Anthaeus is famous. It brings to mind my little metal birds, the communication devices that are used across the Empire, the video and data files on the crystals without which modern life would be impossible, or so it seems now. All Anthaese in design, in origin and powered by crystals from Kelta. And Con doesn't even claim the credit. It comes from their ancients, if he is to be believed, the people who were here before. The current inhabitants of Anthaeus merely rediscovered many of their secrets. Tinkering, he calls it, as if it was something crude or simple and didn't produce wonders.

The road twists around and the citadel looms over us now.

'Of course, we've come up with a great number of new inventions ourselves, but I still think their designs inspire us. Without the springboard they provided, the leap of invention that was already here for us, we would never have come so far. When the Gravians overran

Kelta, we lost access to the crystals that form in abundance there, the power source for so much of our work. That's why it's so important that we negotiate the moon's return to Anthaeus. At the very least we need to repatriate people trapped there.'

'Why didn't you evacuate them?'

'We didn't have time.' Con's tone turns more subdued. 'The first thing we knew was a communication blackout with Kelta. It was at the time Matilde… the time the former Anthaem was dying so our eyes were focused here, not on the moon.' He hesitates, and I know he's thinking about her now. I wait, letting him have the time he needs to master his memories. 'And then… then it was too late. We have an army, Princess Belengaria. There were armed forces on Kelta. We never heard from them, or from those we sent in to rescue them. Those few who made it out…'

His words fail and he looks away from me, out into the cheering crowds, at the petals still raining from on high, at this beautiful city full of life and strangeness. I wonder if it's mention of his wife or the loss of the moon that has rattled him. Or both. Neither are easy subjects. I can imagine the tales told by those who made it off Gravian-occupied Kelta. Labour camps, certainly. Disappearances. Mechas. All those precious crystals torn from the earth because that was the reason for the invasion anyway – the power source to so much of the machinery that everyone used every day, and the key element in the communications network, found in abundance on Kelta. And any other natural resources which were of value to them. Anthaeus had relied on its position, its trade connections and its independence to protect itself. Its very neutrality was supposed to keep it safe.

And with Kelta that hadn't worked. The Gravians had picked their moment and walked right in. They took whatever they wanted.

I glance up at the wide blue sky. Perfect flying day. No sign of the moon now, not in daylight. Kelta is further off than the moons of Vairian, which can sometimes be seen in daylight like ghosts, hanging in the sky. But they are lifeless places.

As Kelta might be now. Or as good as.

I can't work out anything to say to him now so I stare out of the window, lowering my gaze from the sky to the people, and I lift my hand in a wave which sends the watchers wild. Most of them. Some eyes in the crowd feel less than friendly. That's only to be expected. Many don't want me here. I know that. I'm not a fool. They are a people whose ancestors fled the Empire, and here I am, representing it whether I like that or not. Behind this glittering façade I wonder how welcome I really am. Is there graffiti calling for an Anthaese bride instead of Vairian one? For the barbarian princess to be sent home? Do they wonder if the Anthaem is leading them through alliance into subjugation? Are there whispers in Con's hierarchy? I'm no princess, not really. Just a soldier, as I try to keep telling everyone, just a flyer. Or at least I wish I was. I don't belong here.

*

The palace of Limasyll is more than half garden. I know, because I've meticulously studied the view from the balcony outside my quarters. I haven't had much else to do since we arrived three days ago. They're letting me rest and supposedly grow accustomed to life here. I'm exhausted, to tell the truth, so I appreciate the time to sleep. It's peaceful, looking down on the gardens below. It's so quiet – difficult to imagine we're in the centre of a city. Roses spill out beneath me, tumbling over balustrades and clambering up the walls. The balcony is curved, the mosaic tiling swirling around in soft browns and creams, patterned with animals and plants picked out in the tiny squares. The walls shimmer in the sunlight. The central tower overlooks it all, topped with a dome made of multi-coloured glass panels. And the palace of Limasyll is a delight to behold.

But the gardens are what fascinate me, arranged in tiers, each one its own balcony overflowing with greenery and life. All these terraces lead down into the deep valley which holds the central gardens in the heart of the citadel. I'm not sure how far down it actually goes, though I catch a glimpse of a series of lakes and streams at the bottom. They reflect the clear sky overhead.

There are arches and ornately decorated pillars covered with lines of some script I can't read, which sometimes looks like flowers or trailing vines carved into the stone, so perfectly rendered that they might have been real. There are pictures too, domes and suns, trees which knot together to form intricate patterns and something that bears a distinct resemblance to a dragon, although there's something more insectile about them, more like a dragonfly from home. The Empire has many legends of such creatures, thought to be lucky – or unlucky – if crossed. I wonder if the Anthaese have similar tales. They're from the oldest times, from the Firstworld itself, carried out among the stars by her children so many years ago.

Bedecked in finery Vairians could only dream of, the people of Anthaeus wander along colonnaded avenues or in the shade of the arcades that line the gardens. Beautiful and delicate as saplings the columns soar up to delicate and intricate capitals made of strands of stone like spider webs. Even I can appreciate the architectural prowess that must have made them.

And it's old. So old. Patched up and repaired by modern methods perhaps, teeming with human life that moved into the ruins after the first civilisation disappeared.

My bedroom is filled with sunlight during the day, but the heavy velvet curtains block out even the brightest moon at night. Soft breezes waft through the arched windows. The four-poster bed is soft as down. As well as the bedroom, there is a dressing room, a bathroom and a study with screens, tablets and tech built into the mirrors and behind panels. You could throw a dinner for about twenty-five in the receiving room if you moved in a big enough table. All of it just for me. Shae and my guards are stationed in the next rooms, and there are servants' quarters too. If I chose to live here and never visit the rest of the palace, I'd never want for space or attendants.

The same lines and the same eye for luxury created this place as outfitted my cabin on the starship and the rooms I've been given here. Modern technology blends with the older, elaborate decoration, perfectly integrated as if it had always been there. An Anthaese aesthetic, perhaps? This dedication to making everything beautiful, even the most functional. Or, as Con said, something left behind by another race long since vanished from this world, and put to use by those who had colonised it. Adopted. But still so strange.

I find it beautiful in a way quite different to the lush green expanses of Vairian forests and prairies I know, the stark ridges of the mountains, the rolling surface of the blue-green oceans. The dossier doesn't do it justice – finally seeing it stirs something visceral inside me. In the luxuriant gardens some of the flowers are bigger than I am, their bright colours punctuating the verdant green like an exclamation mark. Scents linger everywhere – heady, exotic, calming – an array of combinations. It's so full of life and beauty, everywhere.

So far life on Anthaese has been introductions, small receptions, and a lot of time sitting around. But it has become clear that something is missing. The wide terrace outside my quarters offers a perfect training space, so this morning I ask Shae to gather my guard for drills. He doesn't object, which is something, but he doesn't look too happy about it either. He doesn't look happy about much of anything any more. I fall into rank, relishing the anonymity of standing among them dressed in non-descript clothes, with my hair tied back in as simple a style as possible.

My gaggle of maids gather a little way off, watching. They were outraged when I dismissed them this morning to sort out my own clothes. Even more so when I appeared like this. Their eyes are wide, shocked at this unseemly foreign behaviour, but soon their attention wanders to the guards – to Dan and Thom in particular, whose good looks always attract appreciative eyes – as the troop move into the warm-up, the salutations to the ancestors, the first and second forms. The exercises focus the mind and hone the body. We did them every morning at home, when things were simpler, easier. I close my eyes and imagine it's just like that again, that this sunshine on my skin is Vairian.

Shae leads us, his eyes distant, his voice so very calm, a voice used to command, with so familiar a cadence on the so familiar words. It's easy to follow him. My body flows from one position to the next. Through the third and fourth forms, the movement becomes quicker until by the fifth – engagement – we move like dancers and fighters both, no longer concentrating solely on our own bodies but synchronising with the others, on the movement as a whole. We might be a dance troop, had the steps not had the potential to kill. I spar with Shae, backed up by Jessam, relying on his bulk which compliments my speed. A step, a kick, a twist, a hand grasped for balance and momentum, it's fast and determined. I don't have a moment to think about all the other things worrying me. I swing around Jessam and knock Shae aside, almost taking him down. My companion shouts and dives over me as I duck, and he finishes the job. Shae folds back, not falling but retreating, with a grim smile on his face.

'Good,' he says. 'Petra you're up next. Dan, ready as second.' He gives me a stiff bow which I return but he doesn't acknowledge that. Good is all I'm going to get then, and even that has to be shared with Jessam. My partner grimaces comically and I swallow down a laugh.

Shae would take us both if this had been a battle. His whole demeanour says that. I watch him with the others, noticing details and nuances which tell me more than he ever would. He's playing with us.

As we finish, with a prayer to the ancestors, a celebration of those who honed us as warriors, I finally notice that the small group of maids has become quite a gathering, watching with open mouths and wide eyes. Too late to do anything about that now. Another thing to mark the Vairian contingent out as different. But then again, why should I care? It's a training routine but it's also part of my life, part of each one of us and all our ancestors. So many Vairians were orphaned in the war. It's a unifying exercise. It's important to each of us in different ways. If the events so far have taught me anything, we're going to be different no matter what and I have no intention of changing myself, or demanding my people do so, just to fit in here.

Petra offers me a towel and some water which I take gratefully.

'Wasn't expecting an audience.' She's noticed it too then.

'We're just new.'

'Always wanted to be a circus attraction, didn't you?' The other woman gives a gruff laugh, staring at them until they look away. 'Do you think they do anything for exercise? All that endless wandering about perhaps? Or does the scandal they hunt for in the simplest things take care of it for them?'

I laugh but Shae's voice brings us to attention.

'When you're both finished gossiping…?' he says. There's something smug about him now. I'm not sure I like it. He's up to something. 'We all have duties to attend to.'

They do. I don't. Other than at functions, I've barely seen Con. I don't know if he's too busy or it's another random Anthaese tradition I've failed to understand. Three days so far and I've seen him at one dinner with between fifty and a hundred others, at two lunches and at a concert where between the music and the well-wishers, we couldn't talk at all. Mostly we smile politely and awkwardly at each other and avoid eye contact. It's not going well.

I lean on the stone rail that hugs the edge of the terrace and drink my water, gazing down at the gardens and wondering who could have built such a place. Not the settlers, though they took its beauty and made it their own. It's all too old for that, more than even Con had implied. Thousands of years old. The doors are strangely wide, the windows round. Everything is made of curves and swirls. Barely a straight line to be found. The dossier, however, contains few facts about the lost culture Con told me about. Whoever they were, they're extinct, millennia gone, yet their buildings remain intact. Not many of them, but those that do are beautiful and delicate. The rest of the land is wild, filled with every natural resource one could wish for. With the empty buildings waiting, the colonists just moved in. Three hundred or so years ago the human colonisation of Anthaeus had been little more than a walk in a very ornate park. They had come here seeking refuge and found paradise. And more.

'Your Highness?' a discreet voice interrupts my thoughts and almost makes me jump out of my skin.

Lady Elara stands behind me. I stare at her as if the woman has sprouted an extra head. What is she doing here? I'm hardly aware, until I hear the crunch, that I've just crushed the water bottle.

Elara shifts, uncomfortable. 'Your Highness, I formally present myself as your lady-in-waiting.'

As far as I'm concerned, she still isn't making any sense. I touch the com I now wear on my wrist, a jewelled bracelet that really is the latest tech available. A gift from the Anthaem, Jondar told me when he delivered it. More than the latest tech. It's the finest Anthaese craftsmanship, beautiful and ingenious. I've never seen anything this delicate. And I thank my ancestors for it right now.

'Shae? I need you here.'

He's there in moments, Thom and Dan beside him, all looking perfectly refreshed, dressed in their day uniform as if they hadn't been sweating earlier. And I'm still in the training gear, my skin feeling sticky and shining too much next to the cool, polished beauty of the Lady of House Mericuse. I look like I've been labouring in the fields and it sets my teeth on edge.

'Lady Elara,' Shae greets her cordially. 'You're early.'

'Would you care to explain this?' I snap.

'Well, you *do* need a lady-in-waiting.'

I wait for some kind of revelation, but nothing happens. Pieces click into place so slowly it's painful.

'*Elara?*'

'Yes, your Highness?' She sounds hopeful, so pathetically different from the woman who had been so cruel and cynical. What in all the worlds am I meant to do with her?

'You, stay here,' I tell her. 'Shae, come with me. *Now.*'

I lead him into my receiving room, the outermost of my private chambers, and close the door firmly behind us. I fling the towel towards the dressing room door, hard enough that it hits the wall with a slap.

'Why are the words "*Elara*" and "*lady-in-waiting*" creeping into the same sentence?'

Shae gives me that ridiculously handsome grin which means he has caught me out, proved himself more clever than I. He loves that. It has always irritated the hell out of me. The urge to slap him is strong. Not that there would be a point. He'd intercept my blow before it got anywhere near him. This is why he looked so smug.

'You need a lady-in-waiting.'

'No, I don't.'

'Yes, you do. You need someone to help you navigate this court. An ally. She's perfect.'

My head swims and I pinch the bridge of my nose in an attempt to centre myself. Is he insane? Has a blow to the head knocked his brain out? I didn't think any of us actually managed to hit him during training but maybe I missed it. Maybe they ganged up on him while I wasn't watching.

'Perfect because she's a total bitch or because her servant tried to kill me? And of course we still don't have an answer on who attempted to sabotage the Adeline. Which one? Clarify for me.'

Shae shake his head slowly, deliberately, as if I am being painfully stupid and he's being so very patient. 'She was in custody when the ship was sabotaged. And your would-be assassin manipulated his way into her employ. She's clean. A bit naïve perhaps, but that's all. She won't make that mistake again. She was chosen for Elyssa, and passed *every* security check. She wants to clear her name. She'll be so loyal to you that she'll do anything for you. She needs you to show that you trust her, or she will never have any standing in this court again. And she would rather die than lose her position. So you see, it's perfect.'

My mind reels. 'Who came up with that? Jondar?'

It had to be Jondar. Too bloody clever for his own good. Devious enough to put Elara firmly in her place. He'd love this.

'Me, actually.' Shae sounds a little affronted that I thought of the prince before him.

I stare at him, shocked. I'm not even sure where to go with this. 'Shae,' I chide him and try to turn it into a joke. Because jokes are easier. Much easier than blowing up at him. 'Since when were you so nasty?'

He shrugs, somewhat placated and a slow smile tugs at his sensuous mouth. I haven't stopped dreaming about that mouth. Perhaps I never will. But I'm so angry with him now I'm going to try.

'Whatever works.'

'And the fact that I don't want her anywhere near me has no bearing on this?'

'None at all. Look, Bel, we don't have time to get someone from home, or run these sort of security checks on someone else suitable. Even if we did, there's no one else with the connections and the intel that woman possesses. This court is her thing. She's worked it all her life. Trust me on this. It's perfect. I'll be here the whole time. Just a com-link away. Petra's posted on the balcony and Thom is on the corridor outside. You know that, Bel. We are with you all the time.'

Perfect. Right. And my feelings don't matter. But then, they hadn't since this whole nightmare began. If my feelings mattered none of us would be here at all.

We are with you all the time. That's what he said. If only that was actually true.

'Fine.' I sigh, even though it's not, and another weight falls to rest on my shoulders. It's just another thing to endure and he's right. Damn him. 'Fine. But if she does try to murder me, I'll make you very sorry.'

Shae casts me an arch look, that shows more of his old sense of humour than I have seen in a while. 'Not if she succeeds, Bel.'

'Oh, if she succeeds, Shae, I plan to come back from the dead to prove the point.'

There's a fraught moment and then he laughs. Such an easy, uncomplicated laugh that I almost forget where we are and what's happening. And he'd called me Bel again. Almost like old times. I missed that. I can't help but join in.

He's still grinning when he leaves. All a huge joke to him, apparently. Wonderful.

Chapter Eight

Elara wastes no time while I wash and dress. Her first act is a declaration of war against my wardrobe as she tears through every gown that had been brought from the ship, discarding most of them and sending messages to a dozen dressmakers in language that would have made my father grind his teeth. Not that I mind. I've been wishing I could do something similar myself.

'Who ordered these?' She shakes something that looks like a scarf with miniature cannon balls attached to the end. They clang together and rattle as she drops the whole thing to the floor. Who? I have no idea. It might make a decent weapon, at a push.

Petra and I stand close by and watch the noblewoman rampage through the clothes, corsetry and accessories. The maids assigned to me have the look of frightened rabbits faced with a snake.

Elara doesn't appear to notice. 'Jondar probably got some maiden aunt to choose half of this. You'd think they were *trying* to sabotage you.' She glares pointedly at the maids as she tosses another offending article in the pile to be immediately exiled and continues her litany. 'Out of date, last year's style, never *in* style, hideous colours, and... oh ancients, really?'

I'm beginning to suspect the Lady of House Mericuse is actually having the time of her life, but that doesn't make me warm to her. Petra toys with the hilt of her belt-knife meaningfully. I suppress a smile. At least I have someone on my side. That's something.

Elara emerges again, holding the gown I was wearing when the liner was sabotaged, oil still staining the front. 'Now this—' Elara begins.

No. She isn't insulting that. Not in a million years. Something white hot and terrible flares up inside me.

'*That* is mine,' I interrupt firmly. 'It was my mother's.'

Elara gazes full into my face and smiles more gently than ever before. '*This* is perfect. But we need to get it properly cleaned and repaired. I want the dressmakers to see it though, to base their designs on it.'

'But it's a Vairian dress.'

'Yes, it's Vairian, and as you're so fond of pointing out, so are you. Let's combine the best of the two cultures.'

My face twitches with the suspicions that twist inside me. 'Are you still talking about dresses?'

'I'm talking about everything. Your appearance, your style, your comfort. Every eye will be upon you, your Highness. I think to try to hide the Vairian in you is a mistake. You're here for a reason. Why should my people forget that?'

Thom gives a rare grunt of approval. He's meant to be guarding the door, rather than paying attention to what's going on. But all the same, it's hard not to appreciate the Lady Elara in full flight. I'm finding it fascinating, despite myself.

Elara smiles artfully at him, instantly flirty and charming. 'At least someone agrees. And here I thought your interests lay elsewhere, Corporal Rahleigh?'

To my amusement, the young guard turns the shade of a beetroot and averts his gaze. 'My Lady,' he mutters.

Petra snorts derisively and Elara pales, her shoulders stiffening. She's afraid of Petra. Doesn't know how to handle her. Or me, probably. She finds men easier. The brief, easy moment vanishes like morning mist. But maybe there's hope here after all. Maybe she's not *so* bad.

Measurements are taken, designs drawn up, some ready-made gowns bought and, miracle of miracles I even manage to get a couple of outfits ordered that look closer to my flying gear than court attire. I don't know when I'll get to wear them, but at least I'll have them. At the end of the day, I'm exhausted, but Elara is at last content.

'Your court presentation is in a week's time. We'll have the first of the bespoke outfits in the next two days even if they have to work through the night.' My presentation to the court is a formality really, the first time I will appear before all of the Anthaese nobility, my introduction. I'm met some of them, it's true, but not like this. It's terrifying.

'But the dressmakers don't have to—'

'Believe me, they want to. They'll be vying for it. To design the formal presentation gown for the Princess of Vairian to the Anthaem?'

'And so once I'm presented… then the marriage will be decided?'

'Oh no, your Highness. Only the Rondet will decide.'

The Rondet. Right. The religious leadership that no one has any information on. *They* get to decide my fate. Because of course they do.

'Who are the Rondet, Elara?'

She falls silent for a moment, fusses with some of the clothing as if she's tidying things up. I wait, watching her. She genuinely does seem to want to help me, to make this go as smoothly as possible.

'They're… they're his closest advisors of course. And they're special. They don't live among us. I… I really can't tell you more.'

I frown at her flustered answer. 'Can't or won't?'

She shrugs her shoulders. Being Elara, even that action is as elegant as the movement of the finest dancer. I'd look like a docker if I tried. But her face falls.

'I can't, I'm afraid. I've only ever seen them at the Rondet gathering and only from a distance. They're very beautiful, I can tell you that. And strange. Few are so honoured as to have an audience directly with them. I wish I could help, your Highness. I have some information that may help. On our heritage and customs in relation to them and... I can draw up some more dossiers for you?'

I suppose that will have to do. I don't doubt that she's telling me the truth – I suspect Elara would give anything to know more about the mysterious Rondet. But her words give me something, and that's a comfort. 'Thank you. So I'll see them the day after the presentation? I suppose I'll need a gown for that as well.'

She grins brightly, delighted to be back on a safer subject. 'Of course. I'll line up our best designers and get them to work. I won't let you down, I promise. They really will be fighting to design for you. I know some dressmakers who would stab out the eyes of their rivals for a chance. Now, you should get as much sleep as you can. The days are longer here than on your homeworld and you'll need your rest for all that lies ahead. I'll draw up a schedule of tomorrow's appointments for you before I retire.'

She has the servants draw a bath, lay out my nightgown and a robe and promises – or is it a threat? – to be back in an hour.

Once she leaves, dismissing the servants with her, I can finally breathe again. Thom secures the room, and with a curt nod lets himself and Petra out. It seems terribly quiet all of a sudden. I press the communicator on my wrist. 'Shae?'

I say it quietly, not really sure if he'll be there, if he'll answer. I should never have doubted him.

'Your Highness? Is everything well?'

'What have you got me into?'

He opens the door and stands there in the honeyed evening light. One look at Shae's lean countenance makes my chest tighten. I want nothing more than to throw myself into his arms. My body refuses to move.

It's probably just as well.

'Aren't you meant to be bathing?' he says.

I want to make a joke, something glib and artful, but the words die in my throat. 'Anything in from home?'

A brief frown flickers over his forehead, casting his eyes into shadow. 'No. Do you want me to contact them? Arrange a transmission?'

Of course I do. I've never felt so homesick. I long to laugh with my brothers or even hear their incessant teasing and one-upmanship. What have they been doing since I left? How is our father?

But it would be a waste of resources, I can't do that. 'Never mind.'

I shouldn't feel this desperately lonely. It's just homesickness. It will pass. After all, I'm not a child. I'm seventeen. I need to get used to this world, this life. And fast.

'Bel?' He steps inside, closing the door behind him. And suddenly it's worse. So much worse. I can't quite breathe properly so I turn away, trying to hide it. He isn't fooled. Of course he isn't. His gentleness unnerves me, sets my nerves on edge. He's worried. He cares about me. 'Are you okay?'

'Sure.' My voice sounds thin and twisted even to me. Panic spirals through me, faster and faster.

'Is there anything I can do? Tell me.'

Oh, there is. But I can never tell him. 'No, I should... I should bathe. She'll be back here soon.'

His tone darkens. 'Did she do something?'

I shake my head. Poor Elara. That will always be the first question anyone asks now. Even though I do believe she's genuinely trying to help. Even though she has found charities and recycling centres for all the clothes, prestigious employment for the dressmakers, even though she is doing everything within her power to make amends for something that wasn't even her fault. That question will always be there.

'No, nothing. I'm sorry. I shouldn't have called you in.' That at least is true. So very true. I should not have called him at all. 'I just wanted to talk to someone. You know? With a friend.'

I look back at him and a ghost of a smile finds its way to his lips. 'I'll be here. I promise. Whenever you need me. Always.'

Before I can answer, he crosses to me and pulls me into an embrace, warm and comforting. I stiffen and then wilt, shocked and at the same time utterly relieved. I've dreamed of this. Just this. And more. I breathe in his scent, soak up his warmth, feel him all around me. It's bliss. More than I could have dreamed of.

And yet it isn't enough.

I fight against the sob of despair welling up inside me, dig my fingernails into the fabric of his uniform.

As quickly as he had moved to hold me, he steps away. Awkward, uncomfortable. Like he has read my mind again and can't bear to touch me a moment longer. His face speaks of confusion, and even of longing for a moment, I'm sure of it. And then the formal mask slips back into place. A shroud of misery closes around me. I've messed it all up again. I knew I would. I shouldn't have called him in. I shouldn't think these thoughts. Dream those dreams. I'm an idiot.

'I should go,' Shae tells me. 'Elara will be back – I'll send Petra with her – and you should…' His eyes dart to the bathroom and he swallows hard, his Adam's Apple moving in his sculpted throat. I wouldn't have believed it if I hadn't been looking right at him. He looks completely flustered at the thought of me bathing. Of me naked. 'I should leave you to it.'

I've never seen Shae retreat from anything or anyone. I certainly never thought I'd see him retreat from me.

I stare at the door as it closes behind him, trying to work out what just happened.

Just like that, I'm alone.

*

The week before my presentation to the court goes by with frightening speed. Morning training sessions continue but get shorter and less intimate as more of the Anthaese turn out to watch. It's like being a zoological attraction. Everywhere I go people stop and stare, eyes following my movements, judging me. All the time. It feels like I'm on display, constantly. Not that I go very far. Looming over me, the prospect of the Anthaese court and my presentation hang like a death shroud. I'm unprepared for it, for everything about it, but it still approaches, relentless, implacable, each passing day bringing it closer. I don't know how to stop it and so by the time I actually have a moment to think about it, it's far too late and I'm dressed, pampered and preened and almost ready to be presented to the Anthaese court like some sort of prize that's been won. I would have worn the opals Nerysse had so admired but Elara reminds me that I can't show any particular favours and if I wear one gift I'd have to wear them all. I'd clank as I walked. I can't even remember who sent them. The thought of Nerysse comes unexpectedly and with it a wave of grief I have to hide. I can't show weakness. I don't know why but I can't. If I break down now, I'll never get through this.

'Does that include the daggers?' I like the daggers. Beautiful pieces, the finest steel, perfectly balanced. They'd come from Zander.

Elara gives me a withering look. 'No, your Highness. No daggers.'

I grimace, but she doesn't seem to notice. Or if she does, she's tactful enough to ignore it.

In the end, Elara picks out a heavy gold necklace from the Anthaese treasury and I wear it like an extremely expensive collar. Sapphires flash at my throat and make me think of Shae's eyes. The image really doesn't help.

All along the colonnaded walkway from my quarters to the central palace, I breathe in the heady scent of jasmine and passionflower. The music drifts on the same breeze, but as I pass beneath an arched entranceway into the tower I can't hear it any more. Out of the sunlight the hallway we enter is strangely cold and quiet.

We climb the sweep of stairs, a spiralling helix carved of white stone. There are only guards visible, the royal guard of Anthaeus more impressive than I'd imagined them. My own escort surround me, Shae at the fore, in a dress uniform for the first time since we left Vairian. It suits him, suits his looks and his hardness. Makes him look every inch the hero I know him to be. He ought to be celebrated as such, not exiled here to guard me.

And yet, I know if anyone asked him, he'd say there is nowhere else he wants to be.

It makes me feel oddly guilty, and oddly grateful. But I'm not entirely sure if it's true. I don't know what Shae wants any more. After that moment in my room, I don't know whether he wants to be here with me or not.

At the top of the staircase I step out onto a second floor landing above the enormous reception room and for a moment try to catch my bearings. What is the point in climbing up all those steps only to climb down again? But as I look over a sea of people, all dressed in their most elaborate finery, I understand. To make an entrance. The stairs before me are a single, graceful curve rather than the tight spiral of the first and they are carpeted in crimson. As I stand there, silent, taking in the beauty of this room, the high windows letting light stream down, the arched doorways leading out into more of the verdant gardens, listening to the hum of music, voices and laughter rising up to meet me, the room goes quiet.

The herald announces me, that strange litany of names that don't seem to fit me, and yet are bound up with my life and my future. I descend the staircase, trying to shake off the weight of inevitability.

This is why I'm here.

This is no romantic event. No fairy tale. I'm a game piece on a vast board. I'm not even a real wife, if you think about it. A political marriage, an alliance, and a promise. With his only daughter on Anthaeus, my father and all of Vairian will see it protected. And by extension the might of the Empire will follow.

If they accept me, and the Empire I represent.

Amid the terror of walking into a room with so many eyes upon me, so many hopes pinned on me, I have that moment of painful clarity.

It isn't Bel entering the throne room, it is Belengaria, Princess of Vairian. I can hide behind that mask and it will shield me as effectively as any armour. I hope.

Against some things, like the weapons of the court. Weapons which scare me a lot more than knives or firearms right at the moment.

The assembled throng bows before me. At the far end, on a raised dais, Con stands waiting. He even smiles. A quiet, sure smile, that I know is meant for me alone. Who else is looking at him right now?

Somehow that makes it easier to walk the length of the room, crossing the elaborately decorative marble inlays, beneath the high dome with its delicate stucco plasterwork and coloured glass panels. I step up onto the dais and join him there.

'Greeting to you, Belengaria,' he says in a clear, ringing voice that somehow fills the room. 'I welcome you as our honoured guest.'

He takes my hand, raises it to his lips as he bows. His kiss is the gentlest brush against my skin. I had expected this whole thing to be perfunctory – kings aren't meant to bow, are they? – but there is no doubting the sincerity of his movements. His eyes shine, amused. He squeezes my fingers ever so slightly, a gesture of encouragement, and then leads me to the seat beside his own. We're strangely isolated up here, away from the courtiers who are talking amongst themselves. The music starts again and I shift in my seat, unsure of what I should say to him. I'd hoped for time alone to get to know him, but not like this. Alone, but surrounded. Con clears his throat as if to say something, but when I look up, he seems to think twice about it and blushes. Everything about this is painfully awkward and I feel my chest tighten. I force myself to breathe and look away.

I focus instead on the crowd as the music plays on, studying faces, noting who stands with whom, where loyalties lie or appeared to lie.

And then I see him. There's a Gravian in the middle of the crowd. Out of place, like a nightmare, screaming into the centre of my attention and setting off every instinctive alarm. Pale face, ridged and almost reptilian amid the smooth golden tones of the Anthaese. It isn't possible. What is he doing there? He's just standing there, like he belongs. One of their aristocracy, clearly, judging not just from his clothes and presence, but by his very demeanour, the way he stands, the disdain with which he watches the crowd. And me. He's looking right at me now. His skin is pale as parchment, a stark contrast to the black silks and velvets he wears. His features are delicate and finely sculpted, probably by design. They alter everything that doesn't please them. Technology, genetics, torture, surgery, whatever it takes. And if they can't alter it they destroy it. Even his white hair could have been elaborately carved from alabaster instead of being in its natural state. His eyes are the worst. Cold and flat as grey stones.

He blinks, the second eyelids staying closed a fraction of a second longer than the outer ones.

Steel fires up the length of my spine. No one else seems to react and I wonder for an instant if I'm hallucinating. But no, he turns and speaks to an Anthaese man at his side. They actually laugh.

Why is he here? Now? In the middle of all these people. Laughing.

'Princess?' Con's voice is quiet and assured, but tinged with a note of concern. 'Are you well? Do you need anything?'

He's seen my appalled expression. So have many others, I'm sure.

I keep my tone as low and lean towards him. 'No, but… there's a Gravian over there.'

He doesn't seem surprised. 'The Gravian ambassador, yes. He's often here, usually with demands.' There's almost a laugh in his voice.

Is he trying to make a joke of it?

'No one warned me.'

'Warned you? We have many visitors. There's a delegation from Camarth over there to the left.' He subtly gestures towards three figures in heavy robes which cover them entirely. Religious caste then, from a world I'd studied with Nerysse a year ago but never thought to see the inhabitants, not in real life. 'And from Melia, there.'

'But a *Gravian*, your Majesty—'

'*Con*, please.' There's actual pain in the words.

He's going to pick a battle of names now? I don't bite. This is too important. I can't believe he's being this naive about Gravians. They aren't to be trusted. Not ever. Vairian children learn this in the cradle.

'Whatever. The war between our two worlds lasted twenty-five years. No family in Vairian is unscathed. Not to mention that Gravians lately destroyed the majority of my relatives and tried to shoot me from the sky just as they did my mother. Aren't they still occupying Kelta? And he's just... standing there?'

A flicker passes over his face and his eyes harden again. He knows my history – he *has* to know – but perhaps never thought it through before this moment. His tone becomes conciliatory. 'I should have warned you. I apologise.'

But it isn't about me. It's about the monster standing in the middle of his ballroom as if he belongs there, as if he doesn't worship death and have plans to pillage every world with a terrifying efficiency.

'They shouldn't be here.'

'And how are we to arrange a peaceful resolution to this conflict without engaging in dialogue?' He shakes his head, as if speaking to a child, which just makes the heat in my face rise higher. I want to leave but it would cause a diplomatic disaster if I did. Probably not as bad as if I punched him in the face though. Him or the Gravian. 'We have to talk to them, Bel.'

I stare at him, unable to believe the words. The light catches his face, just the line of his cheekbone and gilds it. For a moment it looks as though he has tiny golden scales there. It's hypnotic but the illusion fades an instant later.

I shake myself and anger rushes back along my veins to drive out a flicker of wonder.

'Vairian and Gravian don't engage in dialogue, *Con*.'

'But the Anthaese do.' He sits back, the discussion apparently over. I clench my teeth, my eyes searching for Shae. How dare he dismiss me like that? Shae is already staring at the Gravian ambassador with murder in his eyes. Thom and Dan have positioned themselves to cover me. Just in case. Every eventuality thought of. And as for Jessam, he's at the foot of the dais, his hand resting on the butt of his weapon with feigned nonchalance. Petra stalks along the top of the stairs like a jungle cat, covering the whole room, glaring down at the crowd. They know. They understand the danger.

They came to Higher Cape for peace talks at first. And our people went to Gravian space. They met on neutral worlds with hope of a settlement. And what followed was years of war, of countless lives lost.

They don't want peace. They want resources. They want sacrifices to their bloody goddess. They want bodies to create Mechas. They hate us. We're not like them and they hate us. There's no logic to it, no reason. No chance at peace.

I wish for weapons again. Apparently it's fine for my guards to carry them, but not for me. Great. I'll just remember to have Shae carry a spare piece he can throw to me if it comes to a firefight. The Anthaese are too trusting by half. Way too trusting. And right now there's nothing I can do except sit here and wait.

Various people are presented to me. I haven't a hope of remembering the names, they go by so quickly. I don't even know if there's a particular order or how the hierarchy works. In reverse or something? By family?

And if I'm honest, I'm only partly paying attention. I can't tear my eyes off that pale, flat face and the way he's watching me.

Finally Jondar kneels before me, accompanied by a younger man who had to be related judging by his similar looks.

'Prince Jondar and Prince Kendal of House Henndale,' the herald duly announces.

Jondar's brother then. He's my age, I'm sure of it, but looks as soft and pampered as a toddler. He has the same sort of pout as well. He doesn't approve of me, that much is clear. I can tell by the fixed stare past my shoulder, the way he holds his jaw so tight. I make a mental note to watch him carefully and to quiz Elara later.

But Kendal doesn't pay more than a moment's attention to me. He glares at Con instead.

'I wish to say something, if I may, your Majesty?' From his belligerent tone it's less a question and more like a threat. From the look of acute embarrassment and anger on Jondar's face it's patently obvious that this had not been planned and yet had been dreaded. Too late now. I almost feel sorry for him.

Con's eyes narrow and his mouth hardens a little. There's a tense pause and then Con waves a hand to let him continue. The smug look on Kendal's thin face is not attractive. He's that sort of man then, who will rely on others not wanting to cause a scene and use it to his advantage. I've met the kind before.

'My *sister*,' – the word carries such weight, such implications and he wields it like a weapon – 'the late Anthaem, believed that all should be given fair hearing in the matters of our world. And yet, here we are leaping blindly into an Imperial alliance before giving full weight to the *other* alliance offered by the Gravians.'

His voice wobbles as he speaks, passion some might say, fear, the less charitable. I dig my fingernails into the arms of the chair.

'We have no offer of alliance from the Gravians,' Jondar cuts in.

'Ah but we do,' his brother continues, as if he is pulling off some great practical joke. He revels in it, this moment of triumph over them both. His eyes sparkle with cruel delight. 'I have secured it myself. Ambassador Choltus, if you please, join us.'

There's a wave of panicked uproar as the whole room reacts. You don't just invite a member of a notably aggressive race to step up close to royalty. It just isn't done. Protocol, manners and all those things aside, security takes precedence. This is madness. Stupidity. I tense, unable to mask it this time. Kendal smirks at me. Ancestors, it's clear that he's a nasty piece of work.

The scramble of Con's guards would have been comical if the matter was not so serious. I curse my lack of weapons once more, cast a desperate glance at Shae, who flicks aside his coat to reveal – just for a split second – another gun. A tiny thing, but it will be effective enough at close range. He knows me better than I know myself. He palms it as he draws it from the holster, without attracting attention to himself, the fingers of his other hand flashing a signal I know.

Stand ready.

A strange calm settles over me. If the Gravian attacks I can protect Con from here. And myself. I hope. Shae just has to throw the gun. I won't hesitate.

Ambassador Choltus pays us no heed, ignores the Anthaese who scurry out of his path, ignores the guards who are muttering furiously into com links, and the Vairians poised like cats about to pounce. He's Gravian. He doesn't care what we think. He walks up to the dais like he owns the world, but doesn't mount it. He isn't stupid or suicidal.

Arrogant though. He bows to Con, but only as far as he must. It's not quite an insult. He merely inclines his head in my direction. It's more a way of indicating me, and dismissing me, than actually acknowledging me.

'Your Majesty, this proposed marriage is a ploy by the Empress to gain your world and all its precious resources for her own,' the ambassador says.

A shock of recognition shudders through me. I know that voice, recognise it. It rings through my nightmares, where I hid in the undergrowth and waited for them to come for me.

Bring me that girl.

It's the same voice that had rattled over the radio in the forest at home, the same man. The one who had ordered me shot out of the sky.

And now it has a name – *Choltus*.

He's looking at me now, a look that brands me unclean and makes me feel it. His colourless eyes drag over me, dismissing me again as if I'm of no more interest than the carpet beneath his feet.

'This girl is but a child of a lesser noble of Vairian, which itself is nothing but an outskirt world of little importance to the Empire, filled with bloodthirsty barbarians. Their chief family are dead and the Empress has set her pawns up in their stead. You are being duped, Anthaem.'

'Ambassador,' Con replies. The tone is gentle enough, but there's an underlying steel I hadn't expected. 'I understand many questions remain about the recent attack on Vairian which the Gravian High Council has not yet answered.'

The Ambassador bares his teeth in what I suppose is a smile. Or a threat. 'Unproven accusations, your Majesty, by a prejudiced people. Even the Empress has made no statement on the matter because she does not trust their word.'

I ball my fists at my side. I can't believe what I'm hearing and yet no one else seems to be reacting to it.

If the royal family of Vairian are dead, who would want them killed but the Gravians? The words boil up inside me but I can't say any of this. Con has to handle the situation. It would shame him, disgrace me, make me look like the very backwater fool Choltus has just described if I succumbed to an outburst now. Perhaps that's what he wants. To show me up. To cause an outrage.

And Con just sits there. I glare at him but he doesn't appear to notice. He *must do something*. I squirm in my seat and force myself to keep quiet. The effort makes my stomach twist painfully. I have to think. I need to think.

I glance to my guards. I can read nothing from Shae's face. *Be ready*, I warn myself. The moment he moves, the moment he strikes, I must be ready.

'This is neither the time nor the place, Ambassador.' Con uses his calm, measured voice like an expert orator, and it surprises me. How does he sound so controlled, so in command of this nightmare situation?

'Majesty,' Choltus draws out the word so much it sounds mocking. 'The Gravians have offered to share technology and strength of arms for the right to mine here. We have been most generous. We do not try to dupe you with some…' He looks at me then and I wish he hadn't. His eyes seem to strip me bare and find me abhorrent. '…*chit* for sale.'

There's a moment of shocked silence. And icy cold drenches me and my throat tightens.

'Enough,' Con's tone doesn't appear to change, but something does. He seems firmer all of a sudden, and unexpectedly colder. As if he has already emotionally withdrawn from the conversation. Is this anger? This strange, quiet intensity?

'You are here by invitation, Ambassador, to represent your home-world, not to discuss our current political situation. But since you insist on bringing up politics, there is still the matter of Kelta.'

In the silence that follows I don't even dare breathe, I just stare at Con. Has he just made a terrible mistake? Or does he want a public spectacle, to force such an issue now, in front of everyone?

'Kelta is a traditional colony of the Gravians, your Majesty.'

Con's fingers tighten on the arms of his throne. Almost impercep-tible. It's only that I'm sitting right beside him. Maybe there's steel in this Anthaem after all.

'And yet, the oldest antiquities there are of Anthaese patrimony. Not to mention its orbit around our world, far from yours. Our people were the only inhabitants for the last several hundred years. No, Ambas-sador, Gravian claims to Kelta are spurious and we all know that. Let us dispense with such tales. We have danced around this subject and your prevarications have made negotiations impossible. Tell me now, are your forces ready to withdraw?' Choltus gives no answer and Con lifts his chin. Maybe the Gravian didn't expect him to go there, today of all days, to make his own demands. Perhaps he thought with me beside him, the Anthaem would be distracted. Thankfully, I'm not that distracting. I don't know what he hoped to accomplish.

Con knows he can rely on the support of his people – it must be the reason why he's dragged this discussion into the open, in front of the entire court. If I managed to understand anything in the dossier on Anthaeus, it was that the people idolise the Anthaem. And the evidence I've seen since I came here shows how much they adore Con. They'd do anything for him. Imagine the power the Gravians could exert if they had control of Con? What did Choltus want allying himself with Kendal?

Embarrassment all round perhaps, wrongfooting us on so important a day, or maybe he thought Con would make a mistake and give him what he wanted.

If so, he underestimated the Anthaem, and so did I. Con smiles, a thin, cold smile and I hope he never turns that on me. It's worse than a knife.

He dismisses Choltus curtly. 'With the blessings of the Rondet, this marriage will proceed.'

'I wish you joy of it then.' The Ambassador doesn't bother to hide his sneer. 'However misguided it may be. I stated my objections to this farce from the first. I have petitioned you and so have many of your own people. The High Council of Gravia will not stand witness to it and has issued a declaration of objection to all known worlds. And now, with regret, I must remove myself from your court.'

He gives only a perfunctory bow and then sweeps away again, followed by Prince Kendal who protests and apologises to him like a slighted lover, ignoring his own people. The voices burst like a wave on the shore the moment his party leaves the hall – shocked, outraged, afraid. Anthaeus, with all its manners and protocol, has never seen the like.

I can't keep staring at Con, but it's hard to tear my gaze away. One thought keeps going through my mind. *He wanted this.* I don't know what he's doing, but he wanted this confrontation for some reason.

Jondar looks ready to strangle his brother if there hadn't been so many witnesses. Chances are, he might just do it anyway. There are some who look ready to help. I force myself to breathe, to stop the trembling in my hands and greet the remaining people as courteously as Con, who doesn't seem affected in the slightest. He's the picture of grace and calm. I'm not sure how he manages, but I won't let myself and my people down by doing any less.

But I think of that cold look, that mask on Con's face, that bland smile, and I shiver.

*

After the presentation, there's another banquet.

'They like to eat,' I mutter to Shae as we make our way into the banqueting room.

'They like to talk,' he grunts in reply. 'Thought that would never end.'

'The Gravian was in some interesting company. He and Kendal left together, didn't they? Have they actually quit the court?'

'It looks that way,' he assures me. 'And it will mean trouble. They don't make idle threats. I don't know what your Anthaem is up to. Stay alert. There was more than one person dancing around Prince Kendal and the Gravian. I'll crosscheck their names with you later. Elara and Jondar can help.'

I have to tell him. Shae needs to know what I know. We reach the top of the room, where the main table is raised on a dais, overlooking the rest. The roof is painted a deep indigo with small golden stars picking out the shapes of all the constellations. A fine damask tablecloth covers the table and it is extravagantly laid with silver and delicate china.

I stop before stepping up onto the raised area and take his hand as if I need help climbing the single step. I lean in close and whisper.

'It was him, Shae. Back home, in the forest. He was in charge of the group that came after me.'

He freezes for just a moment, every muscle taut. 'The ambassador?'

'Ambassador Choltus. Yes.'

He glances up, checking who could hear, who might talk. But he doesn't doubt me or question if I'm remembering correctly. For that I'm grateful. He stays calm, controlled, not willing to let anyone else see the flicker of concern in his eyes. 'I see. We'll look into it, Princess. You have my word.' And just like that he changes the subject and leads me to my seat. 'How do you find the Anthaem?'

Funny he should say that. Con joins us a moment later and I never get a chance to answer. The Anthaem smiles, but he's locked in conversation with Jondar.

I barely have a chance to talk to Con even now I'm here at his side. Hardly a full conversation. Only enough to have my views completely dismissed when it came to Choltus. Every time I look his way, he's deep in discussion or listening intently to someone else. Finding time with him could be the real stumbling block in this so-called marriage. That is if he is willing to talk to me at all, or hear my dubious opinions. It'll hardly be the partnership a marriage should be. Especially a royal marriage.

Or maybe that's all a royal marriage is. Because honestly, what do I know about marriages, royal or otherwise?

Everything, even talking to the rather elderly and eminent priest from Cuore on my left hand side, suddenly seems so much more difficult. I poke at the roast beef in a rich Melian red wine sauce, and push some of the vegetables around on the plate.

Con laughs at something I didn't catch and then gets to his feet. Everyone there follows suit but as I try to stand alongside him, his hand touches my shoulder, pushing me ever so gently back into the seat. It's unobtrusive, and the gesture might have looked fraternal to anyone else. It makes my skin tingle where he touches me, an unexpected intimacy. I don't know what to make of it.

Silence falls over the vast banqueting room, the rustling of clothes, tinkling of glasses and hum of conversation dying away instantly.

'Honoured guests.' Con's voice carries well. He speaks so quietly when it's just the two of us, I never thought his public speaking voice would be so riveting. Out of sight of anyone else, against his hip, his hand clenches into a fist. He's fighting nerves, the same way I do. I stare at his hand, trying to will him the strength he needs. His face is handsome in the golden lights which gave his skin that same peculiar illusion of gilded scales for a moment once again. I can't take my eyes off him. 'Tomorrow we make our way to the Rondet, in celebration and hope. We will present to them her highness Princess Belengaria of Vairian, Duchess of Elveden and Countess of Duneen, in the sure belief they will find her more than worthy.' He smiles down at me, and to my surprise I see that he's blushing slightly. His lips almost fumble with the next words, and he stalls, looks away, swallowing hard before he continues. 'I ask you all to raise your glasses in toast to our future, our alliance with Vairian and the Empire, and Princess Belengaria.'

A chorus of voices rings out. 'Princess Belengaria.'

A cold weight sinks to the pit of my stomach. Tomorrow. No one had bothered to tell me that. Tomorrow, it will all be decided. Whether I like it or not.

*

I pace back and forth across the elegantly decorated tiles, watching the material of my skirts sweep across castles, forests, birds and lizards. I stayed as long as I could at the banqueting table but it was easy enough to make my excuses and leave. There was wine flowing like a mountain spring. I doubt many of them would miss me. I stop in the centre of the balcony, staring down at the circular centre, where four creatures like dragons intertwine. Each has two pairs of transparent wings, picked out in crystal, and huge gemstone eyes. They shimmer. The artwork is beautiful, so delicate I can imagine them leaping off the floor and taking flight. But how are they here? Did the old Anthaese have legends like those of Vairian? Like those of the Firstworld?

'Princess? You asked for me?' Con's voice makes me start and turn away from my fancies like a guilty child. He doesn't look like he's had much to drink, which is a relief. This would be so much more difficult without sobriety.

'Yes.' And now he's here I don't quite know how to say this.

He smiles down at the decorated floor. 'Pretty isn't it? It's a folktale from Montserratt where the—'

'Con,' I interrupt him. I don't have time for a folktale now and Con sounds like he's liable to spin it out for an hour or more. Shocking, given his usual reticence. He has that air of enthusiasm which usually goes into intricate details and hand waving. But this is more important. I need him to listen. 'He tried to kill me.'

Con goes perfectly still and his eyes narrow to slivers of emerald. 'Who?'

'The ambassador, the Gravian ambassador, Choltus. Back at home, when Higher Cape fell. He—'

I see the change in his expression. He's not listening. He's not even listening to me. 'Bel, there is no proof that he was involved.'

'No proof but my word!' I snap, marching right up to him. He doesn't back off. He ought to because I'm angry, but he doesn't. He just stands there, watching my fury. 'I remember his voice, Con. They killed millions of my people. They wiped out our capital, along with all the royal family, blood of my blood.'

'The Empire sent us copies of the reports on the incident. They haven't found enough evidence that it was an official Gravian government action.'

'Then who was it?'

'A radical offshoot. A terror organisation. Those who won't accept peace.'

'No Gravian accepts peace. They wanted Vairian. They wanted the riches in our soil and our stones, the lumber from our trees and the oil beneath our seas. They probably even wanted the water itself. They would have taken everything. They bring only death and destruction.'

He steps back from me at last, his hands held out before him in a gesture of peace. 'Bel, please…'

I slap his hands away from me. 'I heard him, after I crashed. I hid in the trees and I heard him. I'll never forget that voice. He wanted *me*, Con – as a hostage, as a captive maybe, I don't know. Dead, more likely. But his voice…'

Bring me that girl.

As if I was no more than a commodity. A bargaining chip. The memory steals my words. I shudder and Con's hands brushes my arms. He holds me, gently, carefully, as if I might break. No one has ever held me like this before.

'Sit down. You look pale.'

I shake myself free, my newly polished nails digging into my palms. I can't show weakness now. He has to believe me. 'It's called anger.'

'Maybe the voice just sounded the same. His accent or something. You were stressed and afraid, in hiding and you'd just been in a crash—'

Stressed… right… And as for *afraid*… 'I'm a Vairian soldier, Con. Are you saying all Gravians sound the same? You know better than that. I'm trained to listen, to commit things to memory for later reports, to—'

'Bel!' His shout shocks me to silence. Con freezes, his own face surprised that he has raised his voice so much. 'Bel,' he tries again, more softly, almost apologetic. 'Even if it was him, it happened on Vairian, not Anthaeus, far outside my jurisdiction… What can I do?'

He's right, curse it. I fold my arms tightly across my chest and turn away, hating it. Hating him just a bit right now. But he's right. What can he do? Arrest an ambassador on my say-so? One already at the centre of a diplomatic disaster and after the way Con spoke to him, cornered him? No. That's madness.

But it doesn't make me like it any more. In fact, I hate admitting it.

I glare at him, willing him to understand that this is far from over and that I will remember every word. If he's going to be my husband, he needs to understand that he can't just dismiss me. He's vastly underestimating the Gravians. He doesn't understand them at all. And he isn't listening.

'You could have believed me,' I whisper, and walk away, back to my quarters. I'm unsure if he follows or not. I can't bring myself to look back.

Chapter Nine

An airship takes us from Limasyll the following morning. In a few hours I'll be taken to see the mysterious Rondet and my fate will be decided. A small party, apparently, although almost thirty people travel with us and I still don't get a moment alone to talk to him. Maybe he's terrified I'll make another scene. Or make him raise his voice again. Or that I'll ask difficult questions. Jondar is there of course, and Elara. My bodyguards are my constant shadow, and Shae is the grimmest of them all. He keeps his distance though, watching those present like a hawk. Con has fewer guards, and they aren't a patch on mine. But to be fair they are still dedicated. I have to respect that.

The ship lifts off and while most people choose to go into the cabin, to sip fine wine and eat delicate canapés, I stand on the outer deck and let the wind stream past me. I'm flying again, although the experience is entirely different. I cling to the rail, close my eyes and smile as the breeze ruffles my hair and makes my skin tingle, feeling alive for the first time since my Wasp fell from the sky.

We fly over farmland and forest, then thick forest. The mountains jut from the lush green below, and lakes, resembling molten silver, reflect us as we pass. No towns or cities, not that I can see. The land beneath is as lush and overgrown as the gardens of the palace. Where do they all live? There are few settlements and I catch glimpses of houses amid trees, surrounded by vast tracts of land. There are few inhabitants compared to the size of the area. Unlike the Vairians, the Anthaese live in their two main cities, or in almost complete isolation. I don't know why. More things to find out, more questions to ask, if I ever get the chance. These are things I should know, if I'm to live here, if I'm to help Con rule here. I have so much to learn.

It is a beautiful world though. I can see why no one would want to leave it.

All too soon, the airship begins to descend towards an open area on the edge of the thick jungle. A sparkling dome rises from amid the trees and we pass it as we come in to land.

A smooth landing, flawlessly executed. I'll have to compliment the captain later. Hopefully that's the right thing to do. Who knows?

A path leads through the trees. It's lined with lights and garlands of flowers. There are people among the trees too, watching us as we process down the gangplank. Con gives me an encouraging smile and takes my arm. Gentle music plays and groups of Anthaese converse, sipping cool drinks and eating tiny delicate canapes. Most of the group who came with us peel off here, but Con and I are still not alone.

'Don't be nervous,' he says as we walk towards the treeline. 'Just be yourself.'

'I'm not.' My voice sounds far more confident than I feel. 'Nervous, I mean.' I'm also not *myself*. Not since I lost my Wasp in the forest and my world turned upside-down. But that isn't something I can share with Con. Not yet. Perhaps not ever.

'I just mean, it can be a bit overwhelming at times. Matilde always—'

'I'm sure I'll be fine.' I don't want to think of his former wife just now. I don't actually want to think about her ever. I know that everything I am, everything I do, will be compared to her. And I can never live up to her legacy, never be part of Anthaeus the way she was. I'm about to tell him that but as we reach the end of the path, I can't find words any more. The sight before me steals my breath with wonder.

The dome of the Rondet is – like everything else in the Anthaese culture – beautiful, delicate, impossible. Hidden away in dense forest, miles away from anywhere else. I pass through the entrance and look up, wondering at it. A dome of coloured glass, ornately edged with scrolled metalwork representations of vines and leaves, as if natural things had been transformed into metal rather than metal shaped into an imitation. The dome is filled with plants too. Everywhere I look green and gold life rolls and unfurls. The scent of a thousand flowers, the heady atmosphere of living things is everywhere. In the centre is a crystal. Huge, beautiful, bursting up from the ground like a living thing. I hastily smooth my expression. The tones and clarity identify it as similar to a Keltan crystal, but this is Anthaeus. What is a Keltan crystal doing here? It's embedded deep in the earth, I can see that. It looks like it's in its natural setting, but maybe it was brought here? But I've never heard tell of a crystal this size anywhere. No wonder they hold this place sacred and restrict entrance. The things that crystal could power… the amount of power it could potentially put out… the Empire would pay a fortune for it. The Gravians would… well, they wouldn't pay, that was certain. But they'd want it. Oh ancestors, how they'd want it.

And he's showing it to me as if it doesn't matter.

Or maybe he's not showing me the crystal at all.

Four people sit on a circle of grass beneath the crystal, as if they are simply enjoying a picnic, fantastically dressed figures, human but not quite, not entirely. You'd never actually mistake them for human. Not really. It's like looking at a human with something else projected over the top. Their skin bears the tell-tale sheen that is curiously metallic in the light within the dome. I think of the golden tone of Con's skin, and glance at him, seeing the change at once. In this strange light he seems to intensify, as if he is made of gold and gems. I've never seen the alien in him so clearly before this moment, but they say all Anthaese have some old race blood in them. I'm not sure how. There was no one here when human settlers arrived. An ancient, but dominant gene picked up by the very first colonists perhaps? Or something absorbed from the water or the land itself? It's like the Rondet exists to deliberately point it out and shock me. Just by being there, standing in this place, in this light. Compared to them all, I'm awkwardly plain. It's not a good situation to be in.

'Please take a seat, Belengaria,' says one of the women. Pearls are threaded through her white hair and a belt of iron links joined with leather rests low on her hips. Other than that she wears green which highlights the copper tones of her skin and the cool glow of her green eyes.

I glance back. Con and Jondar stand nervously by the entrance. I can see Shae and Petra beyond them. There's no one else. These are the only witnesses. While the obvious importance of this is not lost on me, it's a relief.

There are no chairs. Are they waiting to see what I'll do? Wincing at the thought of the disapproval I immediately expect from the Anthaese nobility, I settle myself on the grass like a child, the same way they are. No one says a word, or passes comment.

Spread out between them is a delicate tea service made of near-transparent porcelain, so thin I can see the liquid through it when the light hits it just right. It's decorated with hand painted dragon images – those insect-like dragons, or dragon-like insects again – made of swirled paint strokes by an inspired hand. One of the Rondet pours the fragrant liquid with elaborate ceremony, a protracted stream of liquid from the spout to the cup. It draws me in, beautiful, elegant, long fingers on fine porcelain, the curl of steam, the perfume that accompanies every moment.

The copper woman hands me a cup and gives a brief smile made somewhat feral by her sharp teeth. I inhale the steam and then realise they are all waiting for me to drink.

It's like tasting love – mild at first, warm and comforting, but with an underlying sensation that everything is about to spiral out of control.

'Tell me, Belengaria,' says the oldest man there. At least I assume he's the oldest. Everything about him is white and silver, but his skin is as smooth and flawless as the others, almost opal. Almost human, but not quite – like the image of a human projected onto something else, almost disguising the otherly nature of what lies beneath, but not quite managing it. A chimera combining the most beautiful of both species. 'What is the primary duty of a queen?'

I swallow, thinking of all the things Elara had said, all those wretched books on etiquette and propriety, all the customs and petty rituals I've endured each morning since coming here. They burn at the back of my throat, each one lacking.

Instead, I clear my throat. 'Your teachings say—'

Someone makes a dismissive hiss, the male who has not spoken so far, and the copper woman touches my arm with her long fingers, her skin so cool. 'He didn't ask what our teachings say. We know them. He wants to know *your* thoughts.'

I catch my lower lip between my teeth. Another thing I shouldn't do. This is all going wrong. They'll refuse me and send me home in disgrace. I will have let down the whole Empire. True, I would at least be home again, something I want more than anything, but the consequence for my family could be terrible. If the Empress is displeased…

And they need us. They really need us. And so does the Empress. *Focus, Bel. Try to concentrate and don't mess this up.*

I think of my mother, of what she'd done for our people, what she would have done, for my family, for my father. Then, now, any time she was asked. My mother... who had given everything...

'I think... I think a queen's duty is to her people. To support the king and offer love in all things...' Why had I used '*love*'? I don't *love* Con. 'And... and to be the voice of conscience and care, to make him rest when he needs it and will not do so, or... or to stand up for injustice. She's the voice of his people, speaking for them to him when he can't hear. And when he's wrong... when he's wrong she tells him. She stands her ground and doesn't back down. She's the strong arm in his defence, and in theirs. Even if it's from him.'

Con is listening to me, I know that. And I briefly wonder is he thinking of our conversation last night, when he didn't believe me.

I remember my mother's death, fighting for a village no one else cared about, saving lives and holding back the invaders so her husband could fetch reinforcements from Higher Cape. And when they ordered her back to base, when they'd told her to stand down, when my father had begged her... The way she'd led the Third against the orbital assault carrier and taken it out before it could reach striking range. Her last message to her family...

Look after them for me, Marcus. Because those they've taken have no one but me now. And my children still have you.

She hadn't been a queen. Not in name. But she'd acted like one.

'She's the kingdom's heart,' I whisper and then remember where I am. My face heats as I realise every eye is upon me and every ear listens intently to my mangled words.

Silence greets me. The copper woman is staring at the roof with an indulgent smile on her lips while one of the others, a woman with sapphire eyes and skin like burnished gold, pours more tea. She's dressed in blue and cream and she doesn't look at me at all. White and silver wears a distracted look, his eyes fix on something I can't see, far, far away. The bronze tones of the final member of the Rondet glow in the sunlight. I fidget under his unyielding gaze.

The silence stretches out into a kind of agony. And not just for me.

'Maestre Aeron?' Jondar says. 'With respect, she has answered.'

I hadn't even seen him approach, but his voice makes me jump inside. Con stands at his side, silent and hesitant, his green eyes very large in his pale face. Similar eyes to those of the Maestre. So bright a green they seem to be alight from within. He looks worried. Really worried.

'Yes,' replies the leader of the Rondet. No doubt that is his role in this. His expression is austere and cold, hard as the stones, and he is staring at me. 'Despite my many years, I have the faculty of hearing still, young Jondar.'

To my surprise, Jondar blanches and bows his head. My lips twitch, but I keep control of myself. Later, I promise myself, later I will laugh myself silly. In private. Or maybe with Shae.

One day I might laugh about it with Con too. Now there's a thought. But not today. Not yet. Maybe not ever.

'All the same, she has answered.' The copper woman's voice interrupts my thoughts. 'And deserves to hear our response in turn.'

'Indeed, Maestra Rhenna.' Aeron smiles. So strange an expression, beautiful. The same wolfish grin Con had worn when he'd stood there in the engine room having saved them all, when he had just been the engineer. For a moment I wonder if they are related. They have to be. But before I can linger on that, he goes on. 'She has answered, and answered well.' He gives a deliberate look to the others who bow their heads. 'Very well. We accept her.'

It should make my heart soar.

'Announce it,' Con tells Jondar, who marches off towards the distant onlookers.

The cheer that goes up around us is a sound of joy. Instead the world seems to drop out from under my feet. It's real, all in this moment, suddenly, terribly real. I'm never going home. I'm tied here. I'm going to be married to Con.

My last way out just slammed shut.

Chapter Ten

Limasyllian Court life moves on its well-oiled rails, an elegant and ancient machine which whirls around me, incorporating me into its rhythms and cycles whether I want it or not. I wake early by inclination and the long experience of a military household, which means I find I have time to myself at first, until the servants adjust to my routine. There's usually a bath. I take that alone but it took two days to get that idea into everyone's heads. After that, my Vairian guards usually keep me company and we train. Sometimes I see Con for lunch, but more often than not he's called away to deal with something or other. A dignitary or honoured guest often joins us when he is there. So we still don't actually get to talk. I wonder if he's avoiding another confrontation?

Or just avoiding me.

The afternoons are another series of engagements, and I'm hurried from one to the next. Elara makes sure I have a schedule and the information to prepare. Dinners are a lavish affair and I'm constantly in awe of the way Con manages to keep smiling. Well, not smiling exactly. He keeps his face in this sort of neutral pleasant expression which wouldn't offend anyone. Like a mask.

Sometimes there is music in the evening. Sometimes a play. Sometimes inane conversation and studied politeness.

It's possible I'm depressed. I'm certainly numb. I don't care any more.

It's been a week since the Rondet sealed my fate.

'You're letting the court take command of you,' Petra complains. I stare at the range of dresses Elara has picked out for me to wear this afternoon. I need to choose one. I'm overwhelmed, anxiety of the potential mis-steps making me afraid to make any decisions at all.

'But I don't know what to do. All these traditions and everything.'

'Well, ask someone. Get one of them to teach you about life in this wretched court. You have to do something or they're going to swallow you whole. What do you think Elara is here for? *Accessorising?*'

She has a point, something which I'm reluctant to admit. Elara has been making me lists and handing me dossiers from day one and is a mine of information if I just paid attention and asked her. I'm embarrassed I hadn't thought of it myself. I should have. Ask. Get a brief. Clear, distinct, functional. A soldier's solution.

Hugging isn't something Vairian warriors do so when I fling my arms around Petra's neck and squeeze tight, she stiffens in shock. But after a moment she relaxes and slowly returns the embrace. She's my own age, after all, give or take a year. Being here is hard for her too. It has to be.

'It's okay,' she murmurs, and something warm inside me blossoms to new life. 'It's going to be okay.'

Thankfully, Elara's dressmakers have delivered a series of gowns in the Vairian style and I'm comfortable in their fluid and easy lines. I'm seeing more and more of them around the court too. Even Elara wore one last night, a deep blue that suits her to perfection. Her taste is, as always, impeccable.

I choose a green and gold one, embroidered with butterflies and stars. There's a concert after dinner, a new piece of music composed in my honour. What I've done to deserve that I don't know. Thankfully I won't have to sit through a banquet beforehand, just a small intimate dinner in the library, Elara informed me and I knew hope for a moment. Just fifteen guests, she added and my heart fell.

Before that I have a dress fitting. For the wedding dress. I'm desperately trying not to think about that.

Limasyll's library is in the heart of the palace, the second and third floor of the enormous domed tower. Con has a study on the upper floor, I've discovered. Not that I've managed to go there. It must be huge. At least he has a space of his own.

My quarters in the west wing are connected to the central palace by a series of balconies and walkways which lead into the tower through the gallery. I walk its length with Thom and Petra flanking me and a flurry of female attendants following behind. Courtiers watch me as I pass by. And portrait after portrait examines me with just as calculating an eye. Anthaems and their consorts, their families and children, notable courtiers and who on earth knows what, gaze blindly down and judge me. I can feel their disapproval.

At the far end of the gallery, a single portrait, larger than I am, dominates the room. Candles have been lit all around it, and little offerings of flowers tied in ribbons have been laid out before it.

Con stands there, looking up at the face of his former wife with a rapt expression. His hands are clasped behind his back and his own bodyguards stand at a discreet distance.

I wait, unsure of protocol. I hadn't expected to encounter him until dinner, and certainly not in what appears to be so private a moment. The truth is I hardly ever see him. Our royal duties often take us to other parts of the palace, or in his case away from it entirely. There are certainly times he isn't anywhere to be found and no one will tell me where he is. The preparations for the wedding are supposed to be consuming my time, but I'm fully convinced they are going to drive me insane first. It's only six days away. Less than a week. Besides which, it's not really like they need my involvement. Like life at the court, it's happening whether I help or not. And when Con is here, he's often in talks or sequestered away in his study at the top of this glass domed Great Tower. I wonder what he does up there. I wish... I wish I had somewhere to hide as well.

Con turns, looking more startled than annoyed. I don't know if he heard me or sensed me. I didn't make a sound. It's like someone whispered in his ear that I was there, like someone else warned him. Someone I can't see. He stares for a moment, his green eyes very bright as his gaze falls on me.

'Princess Belengaria, how lovely to see you.'

'And you, your Majesty.'

An awkward silence follows as I desperately try to think of something else to say but can't find a single thing. I suspect Con is doing the very same thing which doesn't make it any easier. We stare at each other, and I feel my face getting hotter and hotter while the ground is dropping out from underneath me again. In just a few days this man will be my husband. I'll have to be able to talk to him about something, won't I? Anything at all. Something.

I look past him to the portrait of the Anthaem Matilde. She had been a handsome woman, tall, stately, and here she is beautifully depicted. Her hair is a deep, rich gold. She has startling blue eyes, made more so by the golden tones of her skin, an Anthaese trait it seems. They remind me of the other female member of the Rondet with her sapphire eyes. And though Matilde had been older than Con, it doesn't show here. Maybe the painter had been flattering her, or maybe it had been painted in her youth. It hardly matters. From the candles and offerings, it could be a shrine and I have no doubt how much the former Anthaem is still loved.

By her husband, by her people. By everyone.

'Matilde,' Con says in a soft voice. 'She didn't look like that, not really. She was never so serious. And she hated formality.'

I feel a sudden surge of sympathy for her. I understand that feeling. At the same time I don't want to. I don't want to understand Matilde.

'Did you know her well before you… you know…'

'Married?' He shakes his head. 'Not really. I was young and she was busy. I had no idea how busy until she was gone and I was Anthaem instead of consort. She was kind, distant though. Respectful to everyone. And she cared so much about our people.'

'Like you.' The words are out before I can stop them. Well, he does care, doesn't he? And he is kind and… oh, ancestors… I should just stay permanently silent.

I blush even more fiercely. But so does Con.

From somewhere behind me I hear hushed whispers. Comments from the courtiers who have suddenly appeared, from those who followed us. Con and I are never going to be able to just talk, are we? Normal people can, but not us. I'm going to marry someone I will never have a private conversation with.

Con lifts his chin. He looks just a little proud, a little bashful. 'I try to live up to her example.'

As if on cue, at the perfect moment to interrupt, Jondar approaches from the far end of the gallery. 'Ah, there you are, Con. Your Highness.' He gives me a brief bow. I return it, noting that he never uses my name in front of Con. I'm a rank to him, not a person. And I'm fairly certain he resents me – my relationship with Con, not that I actually have one, my future, everything. Do I blame him? Not really, but I wish he wouldn't take it out on me. 'We're needed in the council chamber, Con, and the princess is wanted for a wedding dress fitting.'

Con. He calls him Con, the easy use of a familiar name instead of a title. The Anthaem to everyone else, but to his face, always Con. He's the only one who does. Although Con asked me to do the same. I'm not sure I'm brave enough yet. Not in front of everyone. I'm not sure what Jondar would do if I did. Throw a fit of some kind probably. He's so protective of him, the Anthaem, patrolling his every second. Sometimes I think he keeps us apart deliberately but I can't work out why.

The world of the court whirls on around me, forcing me on to the rails where it wants me to be. Jondar is its chief conductor, master of the well-oiled machine. There are times, fair or not, when I hate him for that. I wonder if he regrets bringing me here? I'm not what anyone was expecting. I'm not good enough. I'm never going to be Matilde. I glance at the portrait again and wish I hadn't.

'Of course,' Con replies. 'The Martial Council is meeting, and then I have to see an envoy from the Frisain system, isn't it? We have time, Jondar.'

'We need to prepare. There's much to discuss in the—'

'You have a martial council?' I ask, wishing I was on it. That would be something at least. Rather than being a clothes horse.

'This way, your Highness.' Elara sweeps by Jondar with an imperious gesture. I never even saw her coming but clearly she's been tracking me from the moment I gave her the slip. I sigh and turn to go, but Con catches my arm, stopping me. His touch makes me start. My skin shivers in response.

'I… I look forward to our life together, Bel. I really do. We can do so much for Anthaeus, the two of us.'

And with that, he is gone, leaving me staring after him with my mouth open in a most un-princessy way. What did that mean? It sounded like he was giving a public address.

I don't even get a chance to process what just happened before Elara ushers me on to yet another pointless dress fitting.

'I didn't know he had a martial council,' I mutter to Thom and Petra as we walk. 'Did you?'

'Of course he does,' says Thom. I don't say that it isn't actually an answer to my question. He'd deliberately avoid getting into that discussion. Unfortunately, when no one fills the silence, he goes on talking. 'The captain's going to be on it as of today. That's where they're all off to, an investiture for him.'

'Shae?' I try not to sound startled but fail miserably. He hadn't told me. Well, of course Shae should be on it. He's the experienced combat veteran, a career military officer, a brilliant strategist, trained from childhood, born to the life the same as his father before him. They're lucky to have him.

I might be the daughter of warriors but what have I ever done? Other than crash a Wasp and get rescued. By Shae, naturally.

But I could have been asked to be on a martial council, couldn't I? I mean, even as a gesture. I'm Vairian. The Vairian Princess. And Shae... Shae didn't even tell me.

I march onwards, grinding my teeth, aware now that my guards are hanging back from me slightly.

'Oh well done,' Petra mutters to Thom. 'That helps *everyone*.'

*

The corset tightens still further and spots blossom in front of my eyes. If they do it any more I'll begin to suspect some kind of secret torture club has me at its mercy. I blink and the Minor Receiving Room come back into focus. Imagine having a special room just for meeting people? Let alone a minor, less important one. It's not part of my chambers, but a more general space somewhere in the rabbit warren near the south gate of the citadel. To be honest I have no idea how we got here and no idea of the route back. The arched windows on either side are huge and flood the room with that thick, golden Anthaese light. Beyond it, the gardens beckon. If I make a run for it, I'm sure I could get through it and out onto the lawns below before they can stop me. I'd probably be able to navigate my way out there. But I can't move, can I? Besides there are far too many people, milling around, in the way. So many they would definitely thwart my escape. So I stand still. Waiting. Swathes of shimmering silver material drop over my head and I have to battle my way out through the top of the bodice. As it settles around my torso and waist, the chosen designer wanders around me in a circle, tutting like a sergeant major at inspection of raw recruits.

Silver bridal gowns are an Anthaese tradition, apparently, especially when it comes to royal weddings. I'm not entirely sure what to make of it, but there seems to be no point in arguing. In truth, does it really matter? I'm to be married no matter what colour or style of dress I wear.

I suppress the urge to cringe as the designer makes some caustic comments to her assistant who jots them down. It isn't as if any of this is my fault. Indeed, I have next to no say in it at all and maybe it is better that way. I am of little more importance to them than the mannequin they'd hauled the voluminous costume off when I arrived. 'You highness doesn't quite have the colouring we are used to,' the designer says, leaning right in to inspect my face, studying my dark complexion. Would it matter if I punch her? It wouldn't be a diplomatic incident this time. Might take some explaining, but really, I'm clearly being provoked. My guards would definitely vouch for me.

'Her highness is flawless.' Elara all but growls, much to my surprise. 'It is far more likely that it is your silks that are washed out from having been left in the sun. Hmm...' She picks up a length of material, and runs it through her fingers, judging it by touch, by experience. It is found wanting. She lets it drop with a sigh which the silk echoes. 'Perhaps Ferrault might have a better selection after all. He imports his silks directly from Verdeyne. There's still plenty of time. He works so quickly.'

The designer's eyes narrow and the line of her mouth hardens still further. When she smiles, she shows her teeth.

'Ferrault? Well, if you feel that's best, Lady Elara, but he has a diminishing reputation.'

'And this commission will *create* a reputation where there was formerly none at all.' Elara fusses ever so expertly with my long black hair, sweeping it up from my neck. I see myself in the mirror, examining the exotic creature displayed there. I look so different. My long neck becomes elegant under Elara's hands, my colouring so different from everyone else in the room that I'm suddenly transformed. I see it in the mirror, and in their eyes. I am something else, rare and beautiful. I breathe out a sigh in surprise and Elara smiles. 'Yes. A reputation. It could be good *or* bad. Shall we carry on, or would you rather leave and save us all the trouble?'

The designer takes a step away and gives what even I recognise as a rather curt bow. Elara makes a very faint, self-satisfied snort under her breath that no one but me would have heard and steps away too, smoothing down the sleek skirts she wears.

She's terrifying, really.

There is a hierarchy even among the dress designer's attendants. Various assistants look to particular women for direction. A seamstress proceeds to pull out and inspect every skirt and petticoat in the gown, checking the hems and pointing out imperfections to her assistants, who rapidly set to work re-pinning them. She has to have the eye of a flight engineer for precision. They work swiftly and silently while the other women present either assist or inspect with a critical eye. Petra paces by the door, occasionally scowling at them. She hates this, I know. As much as I do. And it's taking hours. But the male guards can't be in the room while I undress and dress. Anthaese protocol forbids it. Even with a screen, or so I have been told by Elara in the sternest terms possible. So Petra is all I have.

'It's no different from countless other times,' I assure my guard during a brief moment when I am not technically needed.

'Except for the amount of sharp things to hand.'

'Naturally. They'll prick me to death with pins.'

Petra doesn't laugh.

I thank my ancestors for Petra on a daily if not an hourly basis, but this dress fitting is a torture too far. I might just as well not be there in truth. The mannequin could do the job. When I point this out I'm met by a stony silence so great I think I've broken some kind of religious taboo. Even Elara looks appalled and she's meant to be on my side, isn't she? But no, not when it comes to this nonsense. I have to be here for this fitting and that is that. There is no escape.

I amuse myself by watching the women on the periphery, the assistants who never get to approach the material of the gown, who hand out pins, thread, or chalk as required and wait silently, anticipating every need. One of them rummages in a basket of equipment, some of which would look right at home in a torture chamber. She pulls out an enormous pair of shears, their blades gleaming razor sharp in the sunlight that streams through the window.

What does she think they'll be cutting? The others labour on, oblivious as she comes closer. No one is looking for her, no hands are held out in mute demand at her approach. Indeed she isn't looking at anyone in particular like the others do. She doesn't make eye-contact with anyone, but moves quietly, deliberate but unobtrusive.

I stiffen as the girl passes in front of me but nothing happens. The room is full of people, but the only trained soldier is at the other side of it. I try to shake the feeling that mounts inside me, a dull suspicious dread.

She stands beside Elara now, and contrasted with the noblewoman's golden mane, expertly teased and dressed, she is plain and beneath notice, her hair mousy brown, in a functional bun. The shears dangle almost forgotten from her hand, a hand covered with a tracery of tiny white scars. There are similar scars on her neck, so fine and delicate that I'm second-guessing myself that they are there at all. She doesn't handle the shears as if they are a weapon, but there's something off.

Perhaps this is my imagination running away with me.

But she doesn't handle them the way the dressmakers would either, no matter how lowly her position. The others carry the tools of their trade around as if they are sacred relics. But this one...

And then someone finally notices her.

'What in the world are you *doing*?' the designer snaps. 'Get back over there and put those *down*.'

The mousy haired girl transforms in an instant, moving like a creature possessed. She casts aside the meek and awkward persona of an underling, revealing the fluid lines of a killer. The shears snap wide open into a double ended, razor sharp blade. A weapon, without doubt. She dives towards me. Instinct kicks in. I twist free of the others. They scatter around me, crying out in alarm. The gown hampers me as I move but I push that knowledge aside, ducking under the flash of the blades. Elara screams, the sound loud and piercing, and before I know what is happening she throws herself right in front of me.

Blood splatters everywhere, scarlet on the silver, on my face, blinding me. I grab a fistful of material to wipe my eyes. I need to see. I've got to see. Petra launches into an attack, my guard and the assassin circling each other with me in the centre, like a mouse between two cats, pinned there. Elara lies at my feet, sobbing and cradling her arm. Alive though, thank the ancestors. I drop down again, crouching over her protectively. She's hurt, that much is clear and it's severe. There is blood everywhere, an arterial wound. I grab a strip of discarded cloth and wind it tightly around Elara's arm.

'Hold it,' I bark at one of the seamstresses. 'Don't let go or you'll kill her.' White-faced, the other woman seizes Elara's arm in hands strong and sure from her work, clamping down on the wound to staunch the flow of blood. Good. That's good. But I'm still a target.

A pair of tiny scissors catches my gaze. They're long bladed and slim, the entire thing fashioned in the shape of a heron, an elaborately decorated bit of whimsy. The blades make the long beak, its point very sharp, but it's no bigger than my hand. I grab it from the ground where it had been dropped in the panic. It's all I can get to.

'The alarm has been raised,' Petra says calmly enough, still moving, still looking for an opening. The assassin doesn't give her one. 'Give this up. You've nowhere to go and you've failed.'

'Have I?' She bares her teeth and darts at Petra who moves to block her. I stifle a cry as the assassin twists aside. It's a feint. The shears slice across Petra's stomach and she doubles over them, an expression of shock masking her suddenly pale face.

No. Oh ancestors, no. Petra starts to fall.

The assassin slips by my falling bodyguard, and bears down on me, triumph blossoming on her scarred face.

I don't think, don't hesitate. To do that is to die. I fling the bird scissors underhand at my assailant as hard as I can. The way I'd trained with a throwing blade, the way Zander had taught me. It's more muscle memory than planned. The scissors shoot forward like a dart and slam straight into her right eye, all the way up to the finger holds.

The assassin jerks backwards, as if her feet have been pulled out from under her and she goes down hard, with a sickening thud.

Someone screams over and over, a fierce high voice like feedback in my brain. I rise slowly, my hair falling over my face. I push it back, smearing it with the blood on my hands.

Con and Shae burst through the doorway, their guards spilling in around them. I stalk forward to where the assassin twitches on the ground. I need to look into the girl's face and know that she really is dead. And she is. Her body just hasn't caught up with the news yet.

Shae reaches me first. He grabs my arms in his strong grip, turns me around and away from my victim. My attacker. That... that girl. She's so small, so thin. She looks pathetic now.

'Are you hurt? Did she hurt you?' He looks frantic, so consumed by panic he didn't even realise how many people were looking at us. He shakes me gently. 'Bel, talk to me!'

Bel. Not Princess. Bel.

I pull away from him, aware of the surprise on his face, quickly masked as he remembers, as he catches sight of Con hastening to join us. I shake aside their concern. I'm not hurt. Why can't they see that?

Then I glance down and see the blood. I'd been aware of it of course, but not how it looked on me. Everywhere. Someone is yelling for a medic and I struggle to find my voice.

'She infiltrated the dressmaker's assistants. Used those—' I nod to the shears which lie on the ground by the limp hand of the woman who had wielded them. 'Petra tried to stop her but—'

Petra! I suck in a breath and look around for my friend.

'Here, your Highness.' There's a ragged edge to Petra's voice. She sits on the ground, with Jessam beside her, acting the field medic. 'Just a flesh wound and shame. It's my fault, Captain. I should have paid closer attention.'

Shae shakes his head and I have no doubt as to where he assigns the blame. Not with Petra. She's doing enough of that herself. No, Shae doesn't blame her. He wasn't here. Petra did all within her power, took a blade to protect me, but that girl had been so fast. So frighteningly fast.

It doesn't matter to Petra either. She looks devastated, even as the medical staff arrive, swarming around her. She gazes up at Shae, her remorse written large on her face. As far as Petra is concerned, she has failed, and Shae has seen her failure. I want to tell her that it isn't true, but I know that Petra would never forgive me if I did.

Thom helps the sobbing Elara to her feet, assisted by Prince Jondar. The two men hesitate, standing there with her like dancers unsure of a move. Elara wilts between them. Her arm is still bleeding profusely and Jondar demands a medic attend her too.

'*Bel?*' Con's voice is like steel slicing through the chaos around me. His green gaze is cold and the sunlight gilds his skin again. He looks appalled, and part of me can't blame him. What must I look like now? A savage indeed.

'I had no choice.' I try to explain. He looks angrier than I've ever imagined he could become. 'I realise we could have questioned her—'

The voice of the designer rises over us all, high and hysterical, a siren of outrage. 'She killed her with a pair of embroidery scissors!' Like's that the sin here. I used embroidery scissors. She goes on, babbling out the words to one of the guards, trembling from head to foot. 'Just threw them, right into her eye and killed her stone dead.'

It sounds terrible when you say it like that. It sound terrifying.

Did I really do that?

The hardness vanishes from Con's features. He looks sick. And worse, he looks afraid. 'She didn't hurt you?' I shake my head, bewildered. He hesitates, as if afraid I'll break if he gets too close. Or perhaps attack. 'You did what you had to do. You survived.' He turns to the guards with him. 'Find out what we can from the body and question all her colleagues.' Then his attention is back on me. Focused, desperate.

He holds out his hands to me.

And here I am, covered in blood and wearing a ruined bridal gown. That's more than just unlucky by anyone's traditions.

'I'm sorry,' I whisper. 'The dress...'

'Doesn't matter. You're unharmed? You're sure she didn't hurt you?'

I shake my head and let Con take my hands, draw me away from the carnage and I try not to look at Shae or the others.

'I'm fine,' I murmur, feeling lost and bewildered at all this attention. I just want to wash and change. I want out of this cursed gown and to stand under a stream of hot water until I wash even the memories away.

But some memories can't be rinsed down the drain, no matter how hard I try. I suspect what I've seen here today will join them.

'I'll escort her Highness to her chambers,' says Con. 'Shae, Jondar, I want a full report on this immediately. Every last detail. Do we have an understanding?'

Chapter Eleven

The rumours and stories are flying in no time at all. The pictures are the worst. I'm not sure how it happened but someone managed to capture an image of me, blood-soaked in my ruined bridal gown, and it spread like wildfire, an instant viral sensation all across the news networks and interstellar media. Screens on Anthaeus are built into mirrors and elaborate frames, and seeing myself there, like the portraits in the gallery, is disquieting. I'm the complete opposite of Matilde, a monster beside her saint. The reports aren't kind, or even understanding. Just scandalous. Vairian barbarity is something to set the ever virtuous heart trembling. They need our protection but they don't want us nearby. Too dangerous. Just look.

THE BLOODY BRIDE, one proclaims. MARRIAGE MADE IN BLOOD, says another. And even IS THIS WHAT ANTHAEUS CAN EXPECT WITH A VAIRIAN QUEEN? The pictures used just corroborate the tales they spin.

Yes, I'm the monster. Wonderful.

But the official autopsy reports, which arrive the very next day, detail how the assassin had been riddled with Mecha implants, and are more worrying by far. She'd looked so human, and so young. The medics called in to perform the examination assured Shae and Jondar that not a single faculty was unenhanced. She'd moved so fast because she'd been engineered to do so.

She was a Mecha which didn't look anything like a Mecha. Not until she'd moved.

I think of the tracery of scars on her skin. I don't know how they make them –Vairian military have captured their machines, studied the schematics and dissected other Mechas to learn about them, but all the actual science is beyond me. I just know it must have hurt so much.

The news reports don't dwell on those details either. I'm not so very surprised. Mecha means Gravian. No one wants to point the finger. The Empire doesn't want another war on its doorstep.

No one says it because everyone fears it too much. Better to report a Vairian killed another woman than tell them what really happened, that I overcame a bio-enhanced Mecha sent by an enemy force to assassinate me.

They don't want the truth. No one does.

Shae keeps himself busy, coordinating my day, tightening security. Con is similarly absent, busy with affairs of state or locked away in his tower. Jondar appears more frequently however, and Elara, once recovered, arranges for Ferrault to deliver a different silver gown, which by a miracle, doesn't require a personal fitting session at all. Two days have passed. It feels like a lifetime.

Petra recovers quickly, but the watch is doubled. If that's a punishment for failure or a slight on her abilities to guard me, Petra never lets on. One of the others is always with her now, no matter what the propriety of Anthaese court might think.

It irritates me to a level I can't describe. I killed the assassin myself and still end up surrounded all the time, locked up like an expensive doll. I want to scream with frustration. What do I have to do to prove I can take care of myself?

'That's hardly the point,' Shae says, when I yell it at him the following evening in the private garden behind my chambers, surrounded by white roses and a heavily scented jasmine that trail everywhere.

'Then what is?'

'That you should never have been in that position to begin with. Jondar's mortified. Con's enraged. And we've a lot of damage control to make up. It does the image no good.'

'The image,' I scoff.

'Yes.' He's so quiet, it isn't like him.

I fall still, looking at him closely, perhaps for the first time since we arrived on Anthaeus. Strain shows in lines beside his brilliant eyes, in the shadows under them. I reach out to touch his arm, half afraid he'll pull away. But he doesn't and that's even worse. I squeeze his sleeve, which is like squeezing a fabric-wrapped rock.

'Shae?' I whisper his name, not even sure what I want to ask.

Shae closes his eyes, the lines between his eyebrows turning to furrows.

'Please, don't.'

'What?' My hand falls away from him, too nervous to keep touching him.

His voice emerges, but it hardly sounds like his voice. He's shaking all over and the words just spill out. 'Don't say anything. I saw you. I saw the blood, all over you. So much blood and I thought—'

I understand at last, I think. 'That you'd failed to protect me.'

His eyes snap open, fierce and gleaming, eyes I know as well as my own. I see him now, the Shae I've known since childhood. The Shae I love. And he's furious.

More than that, I realise in the same instant. This is a Shae I've never seen before. He's terrified. He's desperate. His hands close on mine and his grip is so tight I think he might crush my fingers. But I don't care. I can't even think of that. All I can do is look at him, at the fire in his eyes.

'That I'd *lost* you!'

Before I can say anything or recover from the shock, he pushes himself to his feet and stalks away. He quivers with anger, with despair. In another moment he'll be out of sight and I fear he'll keep going, that I'll never see him again.

But he doesn't leave. He stops a few yards from me, staring at the entrance to the garden. Con is there, flanked by Thom and Dan who had been on duty by the gate. They couldn't exactly stop the Anthaem, could they? Right now, I wish they had at least tried.

'Your Majesty,' Shae says, as if nothing has happened. As if he hadn't just sounded like I'd ripped out his heart and stomped it into the ground.

'Captain.' Con's tone is carefully measured too, wary. Did he hear us? Or is he just angry, as Shae had said. Angry with everything, with the situation, with the systematic failures that almost killed me. To be fair, I'm the one who should be angry here, if it's just about that. 'I came to see the princess. How is she?'

I smooth down my skirts as I get up and resist the urge to tell them both that I'm right here and I can answer for myself. Instead, I interject 'I'm well, your Majesty.'

He tries to smile. It's a strangely nervous expression on his handsome face. 'May I sit with you a while?'

Now?

Of course now. Why not now? It's the perfect moment – just when I need to talk to Shae rather than Con. But I can't refuse him.

Shae gives away nothing at all. What had he meant? Was it just that he had failed in his duty, and almost lost his charge to an assassin? Of course it was. What else could Shae mean? He's Shae and by the ancestors he won't allow it mean anything more. No matter what I want from life. I'm never going to get it.

Con is studying me, his green eyes intent and far too intelligent. He takes in everything, and, I suspect, understands more than I wish. It's unnerving.

Shae dismisses himself, stalking off before I have a chance to say a word. What could I say now anyway? Con watches him go.

'That man is too hard on himself.'

'He's too hard on everyone.' I catch the bitter tone in my voice and wince inwardly. That's not fair and I know it. But I'm not sure I feel like being fair right now. It's true, all the same.

I sit down again, deflated.

'I'm sorry I haven't been more attentive to you,' he says, clearly choosing his words with care. 'I've been buried in my work these last few weeks since you arrived. There's a new solar cell we've been developing and the prototype is tricky to balance. But it could really revolutionise the industry.'

Solar cells? Why is he going on about solar cells?

Con lingers by the roses, and picks one, a perfect white bloom. He turns, examining it closely, and sits beside me.

'They told me you were hurt after all?' *When I'd told him I wasn't.* It's almost an accusation.

I shrug. 'A couple of bruises. Nothing more.'

The Anthaem gives a soft hum, his eyes still fixed on the rose. 'We examined the girl. I'm sure they've told you. I made sure Shae had all the details. The results were… well… I've never seen such a Mecha. Everything was enhanced, every sense, every nerve, every faculty.'

'I know. I read the report.' Read every detail. I couldn't stop, even when I wished I could. I'd insisted Shae give it to me, even though I knew how reluctant he was to do it. I couldn't let this just be something that someone else dealt with, something I listened to. I had to know.

'Good... good, you should know everything. There was more. We didn't put it all in the official reports because people would be...' His voice trails off as if he's reluctant to go on.

'Would be what?'

Con takes a deep breath and closes his hand around the rose. 'I attended the autopsy, to be sure. They must have taken her apart to do it. Cut her to her core, removed her organs, tempered her nerves and twisted steel around her tendons. Her eyes were ocular implants merely disguised as eyes, and there were nodes in her brain, to control and signal back, to relay information and images. There was an uplink directly to the nets and they posted the images first. That's how they got up online so fast. They were watching you, Bel.'

'The Bloody Bride images? Who... who was watching me?'

If he hears my soft whisper, he doesn't respond to it. 'But that's almost irrelevant when you consider what they did to her.'

'What do you mean?'

'Normally Mechas are created from the dead, or the near dead. Not in this case, so I'm told. She was alive – and probably conscious – the whole time.'

I let that sink in. They took her apart, put her back together, knitted her full of implants and metal, microchips and the ancestors alone knew what. Alive. They'd kept her alive.

'Who was she?'

He shakes his head. 'A seamstress' assistant. Nothing more interesting than that. She just happened to work for the wrong person. Her name was Eleena Maspe, a Limasyllian. She was nineteen.'

I hold up my hand to stop him. I don't want to know more. I should want to know, but I don't. She'd been kidnapped, reprogrammed and she must have known everything. Every step of the way. Monstrous doesn't begin to describe it.

'Who did it? Who, Con?'

He closes his eyes, his mouth a tight, hard line. The tension chisels his face and the blood drains from it. He looks like one of the sculptures that dot the gardens and terraces. Except that they look peaceful, calm. He, on the other hand, looks like someone in pain.

The words, when he says them, tear like gravel on his throat. 'The Gravians.'

I swallow back my initial response, wait carefully, composing myself because I'm not sure what I might say... or scream. I knew it. I knew from the moment I heard the Ambassador's voice. I knew and Con wouldn't listen.

'The Gravians? Are you sure?'

'The parts, the skill, the transmission coordinates... it all points to them. I *should* have listened to you, Bel. I apologise.'

Now? Now he apologises?

I didn't expect that. He's the Anthaem. None of the Vairians would have done it, for fear it would have made them look weak. I can't imagine Zander, or my father apologising so humbly. And as for Shae... no, never.

My throat tightens and I reach out to Con's hand, the one closed around the rose. His skin feels cold beneath my fingers, the tendons tight as wires, but as I touch him, he relaxes and opens his eyes once more.

'It doesn't matter. I'm fine,' I say.

His fist unfurls and he offers me the rose, unharmed.

*

The last thing I expect is a communiqué from home. The signals tends to be erratic and unreliable, distances and enemy interference taking their toll on communications. But as I sit down to lunch the following afternoon, I open my daily dossier expecting the usual reports and notes on things I should already know in order to live on Anthaeus, to find the message.

His Royal Highness, Crown Prince Lysander Merryn of Vairian, Duke of the Lost Cape and heir apparent takes the greatest pleasure in accepting the invitation to the wedding of the Anthaem, Conleith, to his beloved sister Princess Belengaria Merryn, Duchess of Elveden, Countess of Duneen. Due to circumstances beyond his control he is unable to stay more than the day of the wedding itself, and will continue on by command of the Empress herself to the Imperial seat of Cuore, to await her pleasure.

It's both the most exciting and the most worrying thing I have ever read. Did Con invite him? I wasn't expecting a family representative. I didn't think anyone else had thought of it. It must have been Con. The rush of gratitude is quickly halted by the implications of the second half of the message.

'What is it, your Highness?' asks Jessam. He's on duty this morning, Thom with him standing by the door.

'Zander's coming to the wedding.'

'But that's good news, isn't it?' He grins. They idolise my brother almost as much as they do Shae. He's a hero, a warrior, everything they aspire to be.

'Yes.' And it is. But the second part of the message, the part he'd been sure to put in there makes me nervous. He's being summoned to Cuore. A knock at the door makes me look up and Con enters the room, his guards and attendants flocking around him. I get to my feet in greeting and he responds with an elegant bow.

'Princess Belengaria. I heard the news you received from home.'

I force myself to pack my concerns away, to smile as if it was the greatest news ever and there was no hidden meaning at all.

'Yes. Wonderful news. Even if it's only for a day.'

Con smiles, a bright, genuine smile. 'I've heard many stories about your brother's heroism. It will be an honour to meet him.'

I'm not sure what to say in response. That awkward silence settles between the two of us again, a long and drawn-out moment where we look at one another and struggle to find words amid the formality surrounding us. I shift from one foot to the other, grateful no one can see it under the green brocade gown I wear this morning. I'm wearing my hair down, in a more natural style I managed to persuade my maids to try. At least this didn't make my head hurt by midday. Perhaps they're being kinder because of the whole almost-assassinated thing. Or perhaps they're scared of me now.

Con doesn't look any more comfortable than I am. So many people around us, so many eyes and ears, so many agendas. There's no way, it seems, that we can just talk to each other. And yet we're going to be married. How is this ever going to work? Will there be someone supervising us on the wedding night as well?

I trip over that thought, something that hadn't occurred to me before. And it really should have. I'm going to be married to him. That implies… well, everything. Sharing a bed. An heir.

My skin grows hot and my clothes too tight. I hadn't thought about that at all. I find him attractive, it's true. But…

'Bel?' Con's voice is still gentle, concerned. 'Are you feeling well? Here, sit down.'

Oh ancestors, he knows what I'm thinking.

He's there, guiding me into my chair. His touch makes my skin warm. Why does it do that? Ancestors, this is just embarrassing. 'I'm sorry.'

'You've a lot to deal with right now. I'm sorry; I didn't think it would be such a shock.'

'A shock?' Zander, I realise. He's talking about Zander. And his summons to Cuore. 'Why would the Empress summon him?'

'It could be nothing. Nothing at all. Perhaps just to get to know your family. That's the most likely reason, isn't it?'

'I suppose so.'

He squeezes my hand, a gesture of encouragement, but in his eyes I see something else there too. A warning? Yes, I'm sure of it. A warning. We're being watched all the time, naturally. By everyone. And people talk. Some of them make reports, and not necessarily to the people who we might want to know our business. We are all aware of that.

'Of course. The Empress has heard the stories about your brother as well, no doubt. She probably wants to see for herself if they are true. Lysander, and Lucius are war heroes. They've led assault forces, rescue missions, driven back a dozen Gravian incursions across the galaxy. Their names are known everywhere.' And he laughs. So artless a laugh and yet I know it's by design. I don't think I can hold it against him though. He's trying to make me feel better. And protect me, I think. And his knowledge of my brothers makes me feel proud.

He turns his attention from me, to the room and smiles.

'A moment, if you please, ladies and gentlemen,' he says in a louder voice. 'A groom may have a moment with his bride alone. I'm sure we're quite safe from one another.'

He makes it a joke, and everyone laughs as they leave the room. I wish I could emulate that easy tone of command that makes people *want* to do what he asks. Despite the fact that several people there might not think he's safe at all with just me. The Bloody Bride. I might attack him with a spoon.

Con pulls up a chair and sits opposite me. Suddenly, all is seriousness and the relief evaporates like morning mist. 'We won't have long. A moment is all in truth.'

'Is Zander in trouble?'

He shakes his head but he doesn't look so sure. 'The pictures that leaked from here did none of us any favours, especially not your brother. He made some statements asking why you weren't better protected. He sent me a message too, but the Empire intercepted it. Or at least I believe so. What came through was corrupted.'

Corrupted, or censored?

I can imagine what he might have said. I only hope he'd at least taken a moment before sending it. But I doubt it. It was probably just as well Con hadn't been able to read it. But I worry who else might have.

'There's more, isn't there?'

'Nothing to worry about, I'm sure. There's been a lot of noise on the communication systems. A lot of movement, ships going missing in the spaceways or altering course without cause, troop movements. And threats. Tensions are high. The Gravians are posturing, and have issued protests to the Empress. She's ignoring them, of course. And Lysander...' He doesn't have to finish that one.

I wince. 'Let me guess, he spoke in anger.'

Con's mouth quirks into a grin. 'Oh yes. He threatened to come here not for the wedding but to take you home before our ineptitude got you murdered or we made a pact with the Gravians. Misinformation, it seems, reached him about our intentions. But that has been taken care of. The Imperial Council weren't even going to let him attend in case he did something rash. And the Empress was furious with him. Although some suspect she's intrigued by him as well, by all of you. Your family rules Vairian now but you're an unknown quantity to the court.'

'Then why even send me here?'

His smile is sad and he looks away. 'Because we needed you. You know that, don't you? Anyway, don't fret about your brother. As things stand now, I believe they're just limiting his attendance at the wedding to teach him a lesson.'

'And no doubt my father agreed. He must be mortified.' I picture them, seeing those pictures of me, of the blood. The combination of fear and anger must have been potent indeed. My family must have been sick with worry, with rage. I can picture them, Zander furious, Luc summoning his squad and Art designing countless stratagems to rescue me, and our father, trying to hold it all together, to keep control of them while at the same time desperate for information and assurances. I wonder if he called on my mother's ghost to watch over me. Nothing would surprise me. If positions had been reversed I'd turn over mountains to reach them. 'About what happened, Con... I'm so sorry.'

'For saving your own life?' He takes my hands again, his grip firm and reassuring. 'Never, never apologise for that.'

I swallow hard. It's like a lump of ice in my throat. Panic bubbles up beneath it, something I really can't control.

'I'm not sure I can do this, Con. I mean, I'll try. I'll do my duty, but I'm not sure… I'm not made for this life. I'm not…'

'Shhh…' He presses his fingers to my lips, silencing me with gentleness. 'No one is. We'll get through it.'

'But… *the Bloody Bride*?'

He laughs. He actually laughs. 'Better than what they called me when I married Matilde. The Boy King. A ready-made son. Her toy boy. At least it makes you sound… formidable.'

I hadn't seen it like that. It must have hurt, to be dismissed in such a way. 'Was she much older than you?'

'Not so much. But enough. Matilde knew she was dying for some time. There wasn't that sort of pressure, so she was choosing an heir in choosing a husband.'

'What about her brothers?'

The pad of his thumb brushes the back of my hand, running over my knuckles and sending a shiver of warmth through me again. He's so tender and he doesn't even seem to notice it. 'The Anthaem isn't a hereditary monarchy. Jondar didn't want the crown. And Kendal's even younger than me and tends to be a hothead. As you probably saw. She doubted his judgement.'

Kendal had more than proved that point. The thought of him in charge of Anthaeus, allied with the Gravians, makes me shudder. What could someone like that do to this lush and beautiful world? What would he let them do? They devoured planets and left wastelands in their wakes.

She was wise, Matilde.

'Let me show you something,' says Con, interrupting my thought. 'Just you and I.'

*

It isn't just the two of us, of course. Not at first. Con summons an airship, not the huge one we had used before when travelling to the Rondet, but smaller, more compact and clearly faster. It's a military vessel, but an Anthaese one rather than a Vairian one, which means I run my hands across polished mahogany and gleaming chrome, sit on red velvet upholstery and wonder why there is a need to decorate the interior quite so elaborately. The engines rumble to life and Con sits beside me. Five of his guards join us, along with Thom and Petra who looked distinctly uncomfortable. They hadn't been able to contact Shae and had been forced to leave messages with the others.

I don't care. I'm out of the palace and the further we get away from it, Con seems more able to shed hangers-on. If Shae hadn't been avoiding me he'd know that.

'Can I… can I see the cockpit?' I ask.

'Of course.' He gets up at once and waves all the guards back down as they go to follow. 'No room up there for all of us. We'll be fine.'

They don't look happy about it but he's right. We squeeze up behind the pilot, a neat, business-like woman with red hair and a wicked smile. I like her already. Her co-pilot steps back to let me take his seat and I slide into it as if I belong there.

Which I do. It's like putting on an old flight suit. The controls are universal – beautifully decorated of course, but instantly recognisable to me. I can't help but smile.

'Do you want to take the controls, your Highness?' she asks.

My heart does a little jump inside my chest. Do I want to fly? Do I want to breathe?

'Please,' I say and like that, it's done. I'm flying the ship. My heart sings for me with every minute.

I think I smile the entire time. The pilot, Ellish, navigates but I soon realise we're taking the same route as we did before – south, out over the vast forests towards the Rondet dome. The transport isn't as responsive as a Wasp – how could it be? – but it's a good ship, powerful and fluid in motion. It doesn't give the same sense of being part of the machine, but I don't care. Ellish is justly proud of it. We talk a little, about her experience, her training. She asks about the Wasp and I try to describe it, not terribly well. We even laugh together while Con just watches, taking everything in. I'm keenly aware of him standing behind me, turning away anyone else who tries to join us. And I know he's doing this for me, to give me this one thing.

I catch an air current that speeds us along, and the tailwind is perfect. With a faster ship and perfect conditions it takes just over an hour instead of the three of the previous trip. Hopefully my piloting skills help too.

Ellish takes back command in order to land, and we disembark without pomp and ceremony. The wide space in front of the dome is filled only with birdsong today. The Rondet dome itself is empty. Con takes out a bottle of wine and two glasses from the basket one of his men carries for us and promptly dismisses them all. They fan out, securing the perimeter while Con leads me inside.

Thom and Petra hesitate at the entrance, ready to follow me but suddenly unsure when Con turns on them.

'This is a sacred site,' he says. 'I'm afraid you'll have to stay outside.' They don't look ready to obey. I roll my eyes.

'I'm fine,' I tell them, knowing they won't actually obey him if I say nothing and that there could be a breach of etiquette at any moment. To be honest they might not even obey me. 'Wait here.'

Thom makes to protest anyway, but Petra nods.

'You take your time with your fiancé, your Highness. We'll keep watch here.'

She leans in and whispers something in Thom's ear. To my surprise, Thom blushes and then nods as well. I glare at my only female guard, wondering what on earth she could have said, dreading the answer. Petra knows me too well. And knows things I don't, I suppose. I'll quiz her later on, even though I probably don't want to know. Con is to be my husband. Some things are understood. Even if I don't entirely understand them all myself.

I follow Con into the centre of the Rondet, below the great dome, where the crystal glitters with broken light, more beautiful than ever. But he doesn't stop and sit down on the grass. He turns to the left and heads down a small incline, into a secluded clearing and up to a wall of rock.

'Are we alone?' he asks. There's no one else here. Not even the Rondet themselves. I wonder where they are. There's no sign of any kind of housing or shelter apart from the dome itself.

'Yes.'

He presses his hand against the stone, his fingers spread wide.

'You have to ask,' he tells me. 'To request entry, you see? But they've never refused me.'

The rock slides to one side with a creaking groan and I bite back a gasp of surprise. For a moment I just stare, trying to figure out how it's done. I can't see any tech. It's like magic. If I believed in magic. Beyond it is a passageway, lit by the eerie glow of phosphorescent rocks dotted along its walls. Each one is faceted and polished, worked by loving hands.

'Coming?'

I hesitate. 'Are you sure? Is it safe?'

Con smiles. 'Yes. Perfectly safe. I promise.'

I take a step forward, hesitate as I think of Shae's face if he could see me right now, or indeed his face when he realises he has no idea where I am. Has he started tearing the palace apart yet? Has he called out the guard? Even if he got word that I'm here, if he came, would he find us? But I'm here with Con, my almost-husband, so that has to be all right, doesn't it?

'Shouldn't we... shouldn't we tell someone where we're—'

Con raises his eyebrows and he grins again. 'They don't know about this place. Few people do and they aren't allowed to enter. This is a sacred place, I didn't make that up. It was our secret – Matilde's and mine. And now yours. Please, Bel.' He holds out his hand. What can I say?

I wrap my fingers around his, feeling the warmth of his skin, the hint of calluses that came not from a weapon but from tools. How strange. How wonderful.

'If you're sure...'

'Of course I am. Trust me.'

That's when I realise that I really do trust him. It's something of a shock if I'm honest. How has he won me over so quickly? It doesn't seem possible, but here I am, following him down the secret passage below the meeting place of the Rondet like a besotted girl. I need to fathom this new feeling, but I can't seem to think right. No more than I can let go of his hand.

The silence goes on until I begin to feel awkward.

'Matilde showed you this?'

'Yes, not long after we were married.'

He says it so calmly, he has to be masking some kind of emotions. But then, Con rarely seems to show emotions at all. Not really. He's pleasant, kind, courteous. The only time I've seen him show passion of any kind was when I was attacked or when he was underneath that engine, barking out orders like a drill sergeant. He should have been scared, or at least worried, but he'd been nothing of the kind. He'd been enjoying himself. Facing certain death and enjoying himself.

Deep inside, beneath that calm exterior, lurks something of a daredevil which doesn't get out very much. That just makes it even more volatile.

But I don't ask about that. 'Did you love her?'

I instantly regret my question.

He stumbles and pulls his hand free to catch himself. At least, that's what he means it to look like, what he wants me to think. While he doesn't show emotions as openly as a Vairian, he certainly feels them. The mask slips back into place a second later.

But I saw it. Such grief.

'Yes.' He says it simply enough. 'I did, very much. She was kind to me. And I was very young.'

He falls silent again and I can't think of anything else to say. I didn't mean to hurt him. But bringing up Matilde was a mistake and I ought to know that by now.

Why do I still do it? Why can't I just leave things alone?

But she's like a ghost, lingering behind the two of us, always perfect, always there.

Even when it's just us, we are never really alone.

Chapter Twelve

Symbols and images similar to those I saw in Limasyll decorate the walls of the passage. I study them as I pass – dragons, spirals, diamonds and sunbursts – trying to avoid speaking so I won't say something else gut-wrenchingly embarrassing. I definitely won't be bringing up his late wife again. Before long the narrow path widens out into a domed chamber, the walls curved and smooth. Light streams in from the crystal overhead. It's faceted like the glowing rocks, creating a rainbow of colours in the stone room beneath.

'It's the crystal at the meeting place,' I say, staring up in wonder. 'We're underneath it?'

'Yes. The light from the garden travels down here. It's a magnificent piece of engineering.'

'It's beautiful.'

His gentle expression suits him. A smile ghosts over his lips.

'That's what I said.' I give him a stern look. He may have meant it but he didn't actually say it. Or maybe, as far as Con's concerned, he had. He looks completely unrepentant, 'I'm glad you like it.'

I return his smile. The look on his face is infectious.

'But what is this place?'

The room itself is round, unadorned except for the squiggly symbols I'm starting to recognise as ancient Anthaese. They run in lines around the walls, across the floor and ceiling. No pictures in here, just the writing. I wonder if anyone can read it. I bet if anyone can, it's Con but I don't say it. He'll think I'm flattering him or something.

'It's a... a meeting place, the same as the space above. But more private, more personal. And it's...' He paces away, turns and purses his lips. Whatever he's about to say he's worried about how I'll react. Interesting. 'It's a sacred place, or so we believe.'

A sacred place... He said that before. It's so important to him. Does he think I'll make fun of that? Of his beliefs? I'd never do that. I look up at the crystal. It's so big. Only a tiny portion of it is visible above ground. Traces of it run through the stone, right down into the chamber.

'Con, if there are crystals that size in Anthaeus, why do you need Kelta?'

He pauses as if trying to come up with an answer to a question he doesn't seem to understand.

'I have people on Kelta,' he says grimly. Or at least he *had* people on Kelta. The Gravians have them now, and I doubt there's much left of them which could be described as 'people', but I can't say that to him. 'And as for the crystals here, they're more like a network, or veins... It's easier to show you.'

Con presses his hand against the smooth rock like he did to get in here in the first place and it ripples beneath his touch. I stare. This is impossible but there it is, movement in the stone as if someone has tossed a pebble in a pond. All the grey slides away from a panel beside him, like water flowing down glass, washing away steam, and all I can do is stare.

A figure lies inside the rock, asleep or entombed in crystal similar to the one above. It isn't human. Not even close. It isn't like anything I've ever seen. Like some kind of great insect or lizard, cocooned within a diamond. Faceted eyes gaze sightlessly upwards and its body is mostly enfolded in multiple iridescent wings like a cloak. The face is elegant, tapering to a long pointed chin, and it's strangely beautiful. Metallic glints highlight the skin, beneath the paper-like wrappings that I now see cover it. It reminds me of the hints of something alien I have seen in the skin of the Rondet, the glimmers I sometimes see in Con's skin. It reminds me of the creatures in the carvings and paintings that decorate the walls everywhere. The things I have taken to calling dragons...

I wait for an explanation.

'Maestre Aeron,' Con says. That's the name of one of the group I'd spoken to, the leader of the Rondet. I examine the creature again, daring it to be true, dreading somehow that it is.

'But...' I begin, and stop. I'd thought at the time he'd seemed alien, less than real. But this? Actually alien? 'The others too?'

Con moves further along the wall and presses his hand to another smooth place. Another panel slides away to reveal a similar creature, this time more copper than gold. 'Maestra Rhenna.'

Who had been so kind. Tears well up in my eyes, unexpected and unwelcome. They look dead. How can this be Rhenna?

'But... the people in the dome... they were human. Well, kind of human.'

I see him smile, his face reflected in the crystal surface, but I can't turn around. I can't tear my eyes off the alien lifeform in front of me. 'They're... projections. It makes it more comfortable for many people.'

Projections? But they held things. They seemed so real. They gave me tea. 'How?'

He makes a sound, half a laugh. 'I asked the very same thing. Matilde didn't know either. Their technology is embedded in the earth around us. The crystals, the veins of them, amplify—'

'Con, I don't understand. Are they real or not?'

'Of course they're real. They try so hard to make the image perfect, but elements of their true nature seep through.'

I press my hand against the crystal panel, entranced. So they aren't human. But they are real. 'Who... who are they?'

'The Rondet. They're ancient Anthaese, the beings who were here before us. The race who lived here before us. This was their world long before it was ours. Normally, they don't appear. It takes all their energy. Most of the time, they sleep.'

They are the original Anthaese, the ancients who the slim files I read before coming here had mentioned, who had built the palace at Limasyll and precious little else. But it had been implied they were long extinct. The Empire doesn't allow colonists to settle on planets with existing indigenous races. It never has. That was the foundation of the very first interplanetary agreement. They might co-exist, with the agreement of the other races, but there can be no settlement. That would be tantamount to an invasion and that's the sort of thing the Gravians do. Instead, alien worlds are invited into the Empire, although they rarely come. And uninhabited worlds are far more numerous anyway...

I struggle to breathe, to quell all the questions clamouring up inside me and ask instead the right ones. I fail. They all come out at once. Tangled together.

'How... I mean... why... Con?'

He reaches out to me but I shy back from him, and my elbow connects sharply with the panel separating me from Aeron. A clanging noise fills the chamber. It echoes like a bell.

'Please...' The tenderness in Con's voice quells some of the rising hysteria. 'Please, just listen—'

'To what?' I draw my arms like a vest around my chest as if they'll offer some kind of protection against this madness.

'They're our friends. Always have been. They built many of the structures here, the palace, much of the city. Although not as much as I would have expected. I think they dwelt more underground than above. We've found traces, like this place, hints. Other doors I can't get through. Not yet. And their carvings... so beautiful, so precise, pictures as documents, plans and designs. They were artists and engineers, scientists and philosophers. Dreamers.'

'But the files say they're extinct.'

'No. Just dormant. But only these few. We have their permission to be here, their agreement. They asked that we keep their existence secret. The first exploratory group woke them, in a way, when the colonists first came here. Not physically but... look, here, I'll show you.'

He closes his eyes, like a child attempting to concentrate very hard on something important. 'Maestre Aeron, if you will?'

There's a moment when the air trembles. I take another startled breath and a voice sounds, not around us, but in us. Inside my head.

'*Greetings Conleith and Belengaria. How goes your day?*'

I let the air out of my lungs, all in one rush. 'How are you doing that?'

'Not me. It's Aeron.'

'*Indeed it is. What a delight. Con has shared our secret with you, young queen. Rhenna, awake. Your favourite is here.*'

The air shakes again and then another voice comes, a lighter touch in my mind, sprinkled with delight. My knees give out and I slide to the floor as Rhenna speaks to me as well.

'*How wonderful. We had not thought to speak again so soon. But here you are and my heart is gladdened.*'

Con sits down beside me, takes my unresisting hand in his, as if it's the most natural thing in the world, as if we're both just sitting together under perfectly normal circumstances. In the dark, underground, surrounded by hibernating aliens.

'You see? They're friends, Bel.'

Friends. He's happy to let alien minds into his and call them friends? Is that what changed him and so many of the humans who settled on Anthaeus, leaving those little marks on his skin and that strange look in his eyes? Not environmental factors, but this odd communion. But he says it's a secret. All the Anthaese can't possibly know about this, not if he won't even let the guards see.

And then something else occurs to me. 'Can they read my mind?'

'No. Only that which you wish to share. It's a form of communication. Tell them something, something new. Locked away here in their dreams they rarely see anything new.'

There's a soft chuckle. It shudders through me. Rhenna, I'm sure of it. It carries an echo of a cat's purr.

'You give us new things all the time, Con. New ideas, new ways of thinking, new creations. He is a wonder, Bel. Truly.'

My grip on his hand tightens, even if I don't mean to do it.

'Like what?'

'Memories of your home maybe? They've never left Anthaeus, so memories of another world would be a gift beyond price. Things you loved there. You could tell me too, they'll show me. Nothing you don't want to show, but... Try something simple. What was the best gift you ever got? Your favourite hobby? Was there a place you loved to visit? Trust me. It will all be new to them.'

The best gift? The thought springs to my mind in an instant, vivid and complete. The day Zander gave me the Wasp. The first time I flew it on my own. I close my eyes, losing myself in the memory and letting it loose. The wind in my hair, the creak of cables and canvas all around me, the sound of its gears and cogs a sweet music. Take-off had stirred a host of jewel-bright dragonflies from the surface of the lake beside my house and they'd followed me, blue, green and purple iridescent points around the Wasp. I soared in the little flying machine, much further and higher than I should have. The remembered sense of freedom is a palpable thing. It makes my heart race again. To touch it so clearly, after years, is both wonderful and unnerving. All I care about is flying. It completes me. It makes my soul feel whole.

And knowing it's gone… knowing I'll never feel that again… the grief spears through me.

'I had no idea,' whispers Con, his voice a little broken. His thumb carefully strokes my fingers, as if to touch me any more than that might shatter me. And perhaps it would. I open my eyes to find my cheeks wet with tears. 'You gave up that feeling to come here?'

I hadn't been thinking that and yet it's there as well, riddled throughout every memory. I don't expect to fly again. Not now, not here, as a queen. They'll never allow it.

Except today I'd stolen a few moments, and I'd flown us here. It isn't the same but it is something.

Is that all I have to look forward to now? Stolen moments that will never be quite as good as the real thing.

'*So beautiful,*' Aeron murmurs. '*To soar like that, to be so free.*'

'But you have wings of your own,' I tell them.

'*Do we?*' Rhenna laughs, an oddly forlorn sound. '*It has been so long that I can't recall.*'

Other voices whisper at the edge of my mind, the other members of the Rondet awakening, experiencing what I share.

'Hush,' Con says, to them, I realise. Not me. 'Gently now. You'll scare her.'

At his admonition they grow quieter and I look into the depths of his eyes, seeing flecks of gold amid the green. Just a little alien I'd first thought. And now they seem so much more so.

'*Flying was important to you, Belengaria,*' says Aeron. '*A liberation.*'

'My mother flew,' I reply. I feel the need to defend my feelings by explaining them. I'm not sure why. 'She was a warrior. She loved the air as well.'

A memory of her flickers through me, her embrace, her kiss, her laugh. The way I always felt safe with her. Until she was gone.

'*And died protecting you all. I see. And your brothers? Do they also love to fly?*'

'Oh yes, but not as much as me.'

'"*Born to fly,*"' says Rhenna. '*You are a revelation, my dear queen. Can you share more? Can you show us your land from the air? We might remember it, if landmarks have not changed too much. If once we flew.*'

'My land isn't...' How do I explain another world, the vast distance and void between our worlds? 'It isn't easy to...'

'*Another world?*' Aeron chuckles, though it's a gentle sound. I think I've heard it in Con's voice too, or an echo of it. '*We have seen other worlds in our time, though we cannot leave our own now. But we have seen countless worlds in the minds of others. Show us yours. Please.*'

I shrug, uncertain but willing to try. The clarity of my memories is no doubt linked to this odd communion, but the lure of it is great. I miss home so very much and the memories feel so real, it's almost like being there.

'Close your eyes again.' Con draws me in against him. The warmth of his body encircles me, comforting me.

'Won't they be looking for us? Duties to perform, things to do? Jondar will have a fit.'

He smiles again and I'm sure I sounded more bitter than I had intended.

'Always. Jondar likes things to run smoothly. But our duty to the Rondet outranks all the petty things that the rest of the day holds. This is our agreement with them and Jondar understands that. We share our experiences and they share their wisdom; our dreams are exchanged for their memories. We share as much as we will, or can, and they guide us. It works well, as a system. Has done since the first colonists found them. They know this world and have an affinity for it we'll never attain. But their long sleep—'

'*Oh not that. It's boring,*' Rhenna interrupts. '*Uninspiring. Dull.*'

Con laughs at her and opens the wine, pouring it into our glasses. He hands one to me. 'Here. They enjoy tasting the wine as we taste it.'

I drink and feel Rhenna purr with delight. 'You entertain them?' I ask.

'We do.' He slips his arm back around my shoulders. I tense but this is what I wanted, wasn't it? To get to know him, to spend time with him. I force myself to relax, to allow myself to enjoy this. I let my head rest against his chest. It's intimate, but carefully restrained. And so very comforting amid all this strangeness. 'And they help us, teach us, inspire us. Most of my people don't know, or feel it as a religious experience, a sense of the numinous. For me – for us – it's different. They are someone to confide in, someone to trust.'

'All right,' I say, and close my eyes, picturing again soaring over the forests and lakes, of circling the spires of Higher Cape and catching updrafts off the Cliffs of Orm. I remember racing Zander and winning by the skin of my teeth thanks to a lucky current I managed to spot, that he, the fool, missed. The sweet victory of it. I share it all with the Rondet and Con, trying to deaden the keen sense of loss and regret, the pain of separation from home and family and the realisation again, that as queen I will no longer be permitted to do it.

I dive and loop, the Wasp responding perfectly to me. But then it always did. It's so real, so perfectly real that I lose myself in it. I fly everywhere I can remember, navigating through my memory, the sound of wind, canvas, metal and balsa wood like music swallowing me up, the hum of the engine like the heart of an insect whirring away.

I have no idea how much time passes as I sit there, dreaming of lost dreams alongside alien dreamers. It might have been minutes or hours. Con wakes me gradually, a more subdued man than the one who had cheerfully led me down to the chamber.

'We should get back.'

He helps me to my feet but releases me at once. The intimacy is gone, as if it had never been there.

I chew on a corner of my lip, suddenly unsure. 'Con? Did I do something wrong?'

'Not at all.' But he doesn't smile again. He turns away, heading towards the passage and the outside world.

It needs a different approach. 'Rhenna?' I whisper, hoping he can't hear me. 'Can I speak to you? Just to you?'

'*I will speak to you alone, Bel.*' Rhenna's voice fills with amusement, undercut with laughter and knowing. '*And it is private. Just between the two of us.*'

Con's shoulder-blades are tense, wary. I send out the thought. *What did I do?*

'*Con never realised what you gave up to be his. That is all. For Con it was an honour. For you, a sacrifice.*'

'*But he gave up things too, he had to.*'

'*Yes. But he had not realised that either. He was young, had many dreams, but they never seemed real. Not like yours. Be gentle with our Anthaem, little one. He has a heart only newly mending.*'

'Please, Bel, your bodyguards will be worried,' Con interrupts, still not turning to face me. Another sharp tone has entered his voice. He's angry, upset, but he doesn't know how to deal with it.

My bodyguards. The thought comes out so sharp and strong that I can't shield it, not from anyone. Shae will be so angry—

Con stiffens, the muscles across his back tightening, his shoulders squaring. And he still doesn't look at me. If I thought he was upset before—

He knows. I'm absolutely certain he knows. Because for all my freedom in the skies, for all those dreams of joy I had shared, when I was not alone in the skies of Vairian, I had been with Shae. He was my companion, my friend, the man I'd loved, dreamed of, wished for. It had always been Shae.

And now Con knows that too.

*

I can't sleep. I toss and turn in my bed until I've twisted the sheets to such a state that they are useless. There are only two days left to our wedding and my fiancé knows… well, whatever it is he thinks he knows. Eventually, I admit defeat and get up, pulling on a robe. Jessam and Petra are on duty outside, and when I step from my room they stand to attention.

'Stop it,' I grumble. 'Get some rest. I need fresh air, that's all.'

There isn't a hope. Not after everything that's happened. They follow me silently. With a resigned sigh, I walk along the edge of the terrace.

Some of the flowers are night blooming, their scent relaxing and on any other night, they might have helped. But it's useless tonight.

The palace gardens are still and silent. I lean on the balustrade, wishing there was something I could do. And then I hear them. Voices drift up from the lower level. I know them at once. Con and Shae. They're having a conversation, or at least Con – ever the diplomat – is trying.

'If I'm out of line, tell me, but she had no choice but to come here.'

'It's Bel's duty and honour to be here.' Shae's gruff reply doesn't surprise me. I'd expect nothing less. 'Ask her.'

'And I'm sure that is what she would say. Her father, her duty, the Imperial command and all that. But I wanted to ask you. She cares about you, Shae. Very much.'

I wait for an answer to drift towards me, feeling my face heating in the cool night's air. The one that reaches me is devastating.

His voice sounds hollow. 'Your Majesty is reading too much into our relationship. We met as children, it is true. I've been a family friend for many years, but she's just a girl… No, not just a girl, she is the Royal Princess of Vairian and I am sworn to protect her, to give my life for her if needs be. And I would do that. In a heartbeat. But she… she's nothing more to me.'

The words stab inside me. I wince and bite the inside of my lip to keep silent. My face feels so hot in the chill of the night's air.

'Shae, please…'

'She is going to be your wife, Anthaem. That is the end of it.' There's no denying the venom in Shae's voice now. A bitter silence closes over them.

Con clears his throat, awkward and uncomfortable. 'I see.' And I know he does. Far too much. He understands things better than we do. 'I hope… I hope you and I can be friends, Captain Finn.'

Silence follows that, cold and terrible. And finally Shae answers. 'Anthaem Conleith, I will serve you, obey you, protect you unless it puts Bel in danger, but...whatever we are, your Majesty, we are never likely to be friends. There's too much between us, isn't there?'

No answer comes, just the sound of booted feet moving away at Shae's familiar swift pace. I imagine Con just standing there, speechless. Has anyone ever spoken to him like that? So brutally honest? That's Shae down to the core. It doesn't make it any easier to bear when it isn't directed at me.

I breathe out a broken sigh. As I straighten and push off the stone wall, I see Petra and Jessam watching me with care. So they've heard everything as well.

Oh, of course they have. They always do. Perfect. That's just perfect.

'Bel...' Petra begins, her tone ready to be reasonable, to calm and comfort, to offer explanations. She knows Shae too. Probably as well as I do. *Maybe better*, a vicious little voice inside me whispers. I don't want to hear any of it, not her suspicions or mine.

'I'm going back to my room. No one is to disturb me. Do you understand?' I don't wait for an answer.

Shae doesn't care. I hear that loud and clear. I'm nothing to him but a duty, a silly girl, something to guard. I've been such a fool. And not just recently. For years. A stupid, besotted fool.

Chapter Thirteen

The night before a royal wedding the Anthaem hosts a masked ball. It's a great tradition, every invitation the highest honour. I'm somewhat grateful there will be a mask because I have dark rings under my eyes thanks to last night. After I went back to my bed, I didn't sleep. Just kept turning everything over and over in my mind like an idiot. Even with a whole day supposedly to rest and prepare, I'm exhausted. I wait patiently while Elara fusses over my dress and make-up, each option more elaborate than the last. Finally however, she settles on an owl mask, made from silk and feathers, studded around the eyeholes with winking garnets. My dress is the same colour as the gems, a deep blood red, trimmed with gold. They wind gold braid through my hair and loop a necklace of rubies around my neck. The little matching earrings look like drops of blood.

'I'm not sure,' I murmur, thinking of the assassination attempt and the subsequent reports, those viral images of me. 'You don't think it sends the wrong message?'

Clearly the thought has occurred to Elara as well. She, on the other hand, loves it. 'If they're going to make up stupid titles for you, you might as well own it.'

The Bloody Bride, dressed as a bird of prey – why not?

Petra snorts out a brief laugh of approval. 'She has a point. Imagine their faces when you enter.'

They grin at each other, delighted with themselves. And that, it seems, is that.

There's no further news of Zander and sadly no sign of an earlier arrival. The ship departed Vairian on schedule, the reports told me, and yet I couldn't shake off a nagging concern for him. I'd hoped he'd be here by now. I'd hoped to see him. Trust him to be late.

Dancing is already underway when I'm finally allowed to enter. It's another tradition that the bride arrives in disguise with the ball already at its height. Some sort of semi-legendary event is the impetus apparently. Who knows? It has always been done that way, Jondar informed me firmly. To be honest I've almost got to the point of not listening any more, just nodding, smiling and doing whatever I'm told. It's easier than listening to all the endless explanations. I enter without fanfare. So that's a relief.

Probably the last time that'll ever happen though. And it's not exactly hard to guess who I am. Petra, wearing no mask, is still by my side, but I have no choice there either. Even less with my bodyguards than with the court. All the same, it's nice to pretend.

That's all this is really. Pretence.

A man wearing elaborately tailored clothes and a mask of a tiger dances with me first. I think it might be Jondar until, with a wicked smile he asks me for news of Vairian. It's the way he says it, poisoned with loathing and I recognise the younger Prince Kendal.

'The colour suits you,' he says with a sneer as we part. His eyes rove over me from behind the mask and I suppress a shudder. 'You should wear more of it.'

He's gone before I can react, leaving me feeling the need to wash. I hate him for it.

My next dance partner hardly speaks at all, except to wish me well on my wedding day. Like I have much to do with it.

'You don't seem happy, Princess,' my third partner tells me, from behind a gilded mask in the form of a lion.

'Don't I?' I ask, taken rather aback. He's the first to notice.

'I'm told brides often are happy?' There's a teasing note to his voice that is rather attractive. I peer at him a little more closely, trying to place his voice, his eyes, the line of his jaw. In answer, he twirls me around so I don't have a hope. I laugh, unable to help myself.

When I face him again, I see that he's smiling, even if I can't see all of the smile. His eyes show me, the way they crinkle behind the mask, but shadows mask their colour.

'Happy the man who has your heart,' he says. His voice is wistful and soft, unfamiliar. 'He'd do well to deserve it. Live well, Princess.'

Live well. If I can. That'll be the trick. And no one has to win my heart, do they? My heart has been bought and sold, or rather I have, all of me. This is about duty, not love. My heart doesn't come in to it. That has been made more than clear to me.

He pulls me closer as the music winds towards its end and his touch reminds me for a moment of Shae, of the way he holds me when protecting me, and in my dreams. The shock of it steals my voice. He holds me against him for just a moment. A moment too long.

'If I had the chance to win your heart,' he whispers. 'Just one chance, I'd never let you go. But it's too late already, isn't it?'

They are words I've longed to hear from Shae all my life.

The song finishes and he steps away, leaving me bereft. And shocked.

He's gone as quickly as he had appeared, my beautiful lion, hidden in the swathes of people. Another partner finds me, an Imperial Ambassador from Melia who tells me who he is from the first even though that isn't the point. How typical of a servant of the Empress. The hierarchy of the Empire doesn't play games and wants everyone to know exactly who they are from the first. How else can they impress?

I don't see the lion again, not even in passing. But it must have been Shae. He disguised his voice somehow. Who else would say that?

The more I look for him, with or without a mask, the more he evades me. There are other masks, similar but not the same.

And then I find him.

He stands at the garden doors, without a mask now, watching me with eyes that seem to be on fire. He wears his dress uniform. I can't remember what he was wearing when we danced – I had been too dazzled – but it had to have been him. Who else would talk to me like that? Who else would say such things?

When he turns to walk outside, what else could I do but follow?

*

Shae walks ahead of me too fast, his head bowed and I have to run to catch up with him, across the terrace and down the steps. He stops at the gates leading to the garden. Ornate imitations of vines made of gold run riot over the bars, tumble down either side like real growing things. Shae watches me, stepping away as I stretch out my hand to him, evading me. Instead I rest it on the cold metal. It's real and solid when my whole reality feels like a cruel joke.

'Did you mean it?' I ask. 'Don't run away from me.'

He stops abruptly, indignation all over his face. 'I'm not running away from you.'

Liar. 'Did you mean what you said?'

'What I said when?' Shae stiffens, a flash of guilt crossing his face. 'They told me you were listening last night. No matter what I said, I'll always be here.'

I give half a laugh. A full one is beyond me. Between what he'd said last night, and what he'd said inside, I'm just too confused. 'I know. That's part of the problem.'

A long silence follows. When I glance at him, his face is hidden in shadows. I can't hope to read his expression. 'Then I'll reassign myself.'

Reassign? He'd *go*? Is that what this is all about? He's planning to leave me?

'No! You can't.'

'But if I stay—'

'I don't care. You can't go.' I'm selfish. Stupid. But I couldn't bear to see him go. He can't leave. He's all I have now. 'I need you.'

He moves like a predatory animal, one second so still, primed and in the next he holds me against him. His body is hard, but warm. He presses me back against the gate, his arm above my head, the other blocking my escape to the right. Slowly, so slowly, he pushes the mask up above my brow so he can see me. His face is so close, his breath on my skin, his body cradling mine. In only a brief moment he could kiss me. I couldn't do anything to stop him, and don't want to. It's madness but I don't want it to stop. My body hums with need, breath and blood dammed up in the moment before and without a care for the after. All I can think is finally. *Finally!*

His lips brush mine, so soft, so warm. I'm so stunned that I can't even react for a moment and he pulls back, studying me. It's the briefest kiss. It's everything.

He strokes my hair with a gentle touch and his face softens as he drinks me in with his bright blue eyes. No one else on Vairian has eyes that colour, eyes like his.

I don't wait, can't wait. I kiss him again, just in case he'll come to his senses, that his sense of duty will suddenly make a reappearance. I press my hands to his chest, slide them up to his shoulder and his neck, trying to consummate every sensation I've ever dreamed of. I can feel the raw strength of him, the tense and primed muscles, restrained by his will alone. His hair is like silk between my fingers.

'We could run,' I whisper, my lips fumbling against his. I can't move away from his mouth. I might lose him forever. 'Get a ship, passage to one of the outer planets. Far beyond the Empress and her machinations. We could just go and leave this mess far behind us.'

The thought of being free from the court – from the snide looks and my constant failings, from Con's benign distance – is so tempting. More tempting in the form of Shae. Why shouldn't we? It's a chance at happiness. I don't care about being a princess, about Anthaeus, about anything…

Except… I do. I care for Con. I feel it now, like a blade twisting in my chest. Even as I think it. How could I even imagine doing that to Con?

When I look up into Shae's face, I know he sees it too, written in the depths of my eyes. I could never lie to him. I draw in a shaky breath. My fiancé, my husband-to-be… I've already hurt him. And he's been hurt too many times. He loved Matilde and lost her. He should have had Elyssa who knew all about royal duty. He deserves a wife who truly loves him but then he gets me. I have to consider his feelings now. Even though it's no love match, even though the union is political, hardly a marriage at all. It isn't what my parents had shared. But there had been more to their marriage than love and passion alone. Loyalty, duty, respect. Things I owe Con, if only for his kindness.

Why does that feel like a lie? The surprise makes my breath catch in my throat. Con… the thought of him, the memory of his touch, his closeness, the gentle way he speaks to me, the time he takes to explain things to me when he can *find* the time. Not like a teacher but like an equal, as if there can be no doubt that I would understand it, as if he fully expects my input and participation. His touch, tender and yet… passionate? It isn't just kindness. How had I not noticed that before?

I stare at Shae, thinking only of Con, and any hope of life with him dwindles.

'You can't,' he says. 'Can you?'

I watch the fire of hope die in Shae's eyes and hate myself for it. Hate him too, just for a moment, for making me think it and then making me realise the truth. For making me do that to him.

'I'm sorry, Shae.'

He pushes himself away so violently, I think he might turn and hit something, a wall or a tree, something he could break himself against – not me, I never think he'd hit me. But instead he carefully reins in his anger, struggling to win back his perfect discipline.

'You have nothing to be sorry for, *Princess Belengaria*.' The way he says my title sounds like an accusation. 'It is a matter of duty.' I wince but hide the pain inside. Better he doesn't see. It's the only way I can protect myself. Make sure that none of them can see. Not even Shae. Especially not Shae.

This has been a mistake. Dreams like that are for children and I can't afford them any more. I'm never going to have a future with Shae. Whether I want one or not.

'We should re-join the ball,' I say in formal tones.

He gives a curt nod. The whole way back we don't speak again. I leave him at the door and try not to run as I enter the ballroom. I just want to keep going, to get the hell out of there and escape back to my rooms. But the ball itself betrays me. The midnight bell chimes and people everywhere begin to take off their masks. My lion stands on the main staircase with Jondar and a number of other Anthaese nobles.

My first thought is surprise that it isn't Shae. He's still behind me. I should have known. The clothes, his manner, the fact he didn't have a mask outside... The child in me just wanted it to be Shae and almost made me believe it. Shae is outside in the darkness, broken-hearted and cold.

And I know, with a bitter assurance, I know who he is. The lion.

Con takes off the mask, his eyes fixed on me and only me. He tries to smile, the smile I had thought I recognised as Shae's and, ashamed of myself, I turn away, fleeing the ball. It's only when I reach my apartments that I realise that my mask is still pushed up on top of my head. I wrench it off and flung it across the room. It cracks as it hits the wall and my composure breaks with it.

Someone knocks on the door.

'Princess?' It's Dan. He must have followed me, probably with Petra. I'd heard nothing.

'I'm here,' I call, amazed at how sure my voice sounds. 'I'm fine. I need to sleep.'

There's a brief pause. I imagine my guards exchanging a look, the way they always do. They know. How could they not know? They know everything. They have been trained to use their eyes, to reason and strategise. They watch me night and day, know every facet of my life. They know bloody everything.

'Yes, my Princess,' Dan speaks more gently than I could have imagined. 'Sleep well.'

My eyes burn and my throat tightens as if a noose has closed on it. Trying to silence my sobs, I sink on to my bed and pray for the morning to never come.

Chapter Fourteen

My prayers are not answered. Only a fool would have believed they would be, but then I proved myself a fool many times over last night, so what do I know? My ancestors have abandoned me here. Maybe they can't hear me on an alien world. Maybe... maybe I've disgraced them and they no longer care.

What would my mother say to this, to see me behaving this way? She'd be furious, I'm sure of it. She'd tell me to get up, to do my duty, to make the best of things. I've never hated her before. Not even for a moment. Now I loathe her memory, everything she stood for, all that honour and discipline. It flows through my veins and I know it comes from her. I can't deny it.

My wedding day dawns, clear and bright, with the sound of songbirds outside the window. Mocking me. Not my clockwork birds, which had been so much a part of my youth. These are the real birds they were based upon. And I hate them too. Two months ago, if I'd heard of Anthaeus I hadn't paid it any mind. And now, a month after arriving here, I'm going to be married to the Anthaem.

My maids bring a light breakfast, a tisane for a hangover as if balls are always followed by such tender reparations. Overindulgence is not my problem. There is nothing that could repair what I did last night. To Shae and to Con. To myself. Nothing can make it right.

Elara appears shortly afterwards with a thousand things to do.

And from that moment on everything takes on a life of its own, the great machine of court set on its tracks and rumbling on, hurtling towards my wedding with me as a helpless passenger.

What does it matter now? I made my choice last night. I told Shae as much and watched hope and love die in him, smothered by duty. The duty I reminded him of by my declaration. Duty is everything and I know that. I've always known that.

Where is he? I wonder, while they primp me, decorating me from head to foot.

There's been no word of Zander either – or at least none that has reached me. Glitches in the interstellar signals, I'm told when I ask. Problems with solar flares, in the space lanes, or something in the air. When I get any sort of answer at all. I'm sure now that I'm the least important person in this affair. Hardly surprising. But it would be nice if someone thought to tell the bride whether her brother has shown up. I don't ask again, afraid of looking needy or scared. I just lock all my worries inside me, lift my chin and carry on. A soldier. I have to be brave. What other choice do I have? That's what they expect, my family.

The fact there is still no sign of Shae is more of a worry. When I try to ask Petra, my bodyguard gives me the strangest look – a mix of pity and endurance – before saying he's overseeing security arrangements with the council.

But she doesn't seem comfortable giving that answer.

'What's wrong?' I ask, in earnest, refusing to be put off.

Petra scowls and glances from side to side before leaning in a little closer. So no one else can hear.

'He's monitoring the airwaves, trying to work out what the disruption is. He tried to tell the Anthaese that the wedding is the most likely time for a Gravian attack, but they won't hear of it. I've never seen him so angry.'

I have, but I don't say it.

'What does he want them to do?'

'Postpone it. Call in reinforcements from the Empire. Anything but let it go ahead today.'

Deep in my core, a dark vortex opens, sucking all the remaining life and happiness out of me. He's trying to stop the wedding. Of course he is. After last night... even though I chose Con. Even though I have no choice and he knows that.

'And they won't listen?'

That must be the most humiliating thing of all for him. Why make him part of the war council, if not for his experience and expertise? To refuse to listen to him now is an insult. Is Con doing it deliberately? He wouldn't be that petty, would he? Am I going to be forever torn in two between them?

Something else I don't dare to ask. Not out loud. But I wish he was there. Even knowing what I know. Even with the full realisation of what happened last night. What could have happened... what almost happened...

Am I doing the right thing? Is there any way to do anything else now?

'There.' Elara examines me from head to foot exactly the way she might do a work of art. 'Don't bite your lower lip, your Highness. And smile. It's your wedding day. A bride should be radiant. A royal bride most of all.'

Hardly, I think. It's a bitter realisation. A royal bride is more likely than not sold off for the sake of her people – a glorious bartering chip, or a clever chess move. A royal bride has nothing to be happy about. But radiant also means dazzling – something to distract attention from what is really going on – and that I can do. That's the reason I'm here.

'When do we leave?' My voice sounds confident, assured, a lie.

'A few minutes. There's a procession through the city in a horse-drawn carriage and then we move on to the Rondet – cross country this time rather than flying. It's slower but it has more grandeur. Are you ready?'

I nod without speaking and Elara studies my face for a long moment.

'I wasn't sure what to make of you, how you would manage here, what you would make of our customs and our ways. But I'm glad you came, Belengaria. Glad for Con too. He needs someone like you.'

That's the last thing I expect from Elara. 'Like me?'

Elara smiles ruefully. 'He's a dreamer. It's not my place to say, but—'

'But you will anyway?'

A brief laugh breaks from the other woman's lips and I blush. 'He needs someone to care for him. Just him. Not the crown or Anthaeus. But you understand that. I heard what you said at the Rondet.'

Yes. I understood that. Everything fell on Con's shoulders. Or he brought it there. Someone needs to share that burden. 'I'll try.'

'We don't always get what we wish for,' Elara goes on. 'But sometimes the responsibility is worth more than wishes. Sometimes we need the things we are given.' She steps back and smiles up at me. I never expected to like her, not really, not the way I do. I rely on her more than anyone else on Anthaeus. More than that. I think she's my friend.

I mount the carriage which stands waiting for me outside while Jessam takes his place behind me. Petra and Thom stood to one side. The horse are real this time, and beautiful animals, white as snow with long flowing manes and tails. Perhaps the journey is too far for the mechanical ones.

'We'll be going ahead to the Rondet,' Petra says. 'Jessam and the Anthaese security team have you now. It'll be okay, Bel. Just remember to breathe.'

'I thought Zander would be here. To represent me?'

A flicker of concern crosses Petra's face but she tries to hide it with a smile. I'm not fooled. Something is up with my guards. 'You've spent too much time with the Anthaese. You'll have to represent yourself, like a good Vairian warrior. But I'll find out when he's arriving, if you want. They could have been delayed along the way, you know? I'll ask Shae.'

Of course she will. And Shae will have an answer. I hope.

'I have something for you.' Petra looks a little uncertain suddenly. 'From us. From all of us.'

She hands me a gift wrapped in silk. When I open it I discover an elaborate Vairian knife belt. It looks like an intricate knot of silver and gemstones but is in fact made of nine wickedly sharp knives, each one of which can be removed and used. A weapon store I can wear.

Unaccountably, tears sting my eyes. I hurry to put it on but find my hands shaking too much.

'Here.' Petra sounds both amused and impatient. She leans forward to help. The knives hug my waist and hips as if the belt had been made for me. Which of course, it probably has been. My guards had picked the design out for me, had it made for me, and bought it for me. It is the perfect gift. I suspect they must have brought it all the way here from home because I can't imagine they could get this made here. Anything else, perhaps, but not a Vairian knife belt. Not like this. It makes me feel safe. It's a reminder of home, of our craftsmanship, our strength. 'There now. That's more like a Vairian Queen.'

'I don't know if I can do this, Petra. I don't know—'

'Shhh, you're going into battle, Bel. A different kind of battle no doubt but still… a battle. You never know. You just hope, stay sharp and try to do your duty. You just do what you can. You'll manage and we'll be here with you. Be a soldier now.'

'Good luck, Princess.' Thom's big, boyish eyes are full of care. 'It'll be all right.'

It'd help if they sounded a little less like they were trying to convince themselves as well as me.

The people of Limasyll cheer from the terraces of the palace and the upper windows and roofs of the city buildings. They throw flowers, the petals like rain. Music plays everywhere and I wave until I think I'll lose all feeling in my arm, but I don't stop doing it. I can't. Travelling by carriage is going to take hours but I remember what Con said when I first arrived about how much his people love to see him. Us, I suppose. Me.

I hear people shouting my name and there's joy in the sound. I can't believe it. They are actually cheering me, celebrating my wedding. Perhaps any royal wedding would engender the same thing. But this isn't what I had expected. Joy, delight, pleasure... swirling around me, making my heart beat even faster. For a moment I actually start to believe that Thom is correct, that it is indeed going to be all right.

Just for a moment.

A silent concussion bursts in the air overhead. We freeze, everyone, a still moment, frozen in shock, looking for the source. And in an instant, everything changes. The earth bucks and roars, rumbling violently. A blast of scalding air rips through the upper levels of the city, incinerating banners and streamers, and the people leaning from the highest places for a vantage point. They're like meteorites, blazing as they fall. Screams take the place of music, cries of agony and panic instead of cheers. The horses break free of the carriage, tearing madly away through the stampeding crowd. Under my feet, the carriage jerks and then plummets to one side. Jessam throws himself forward to protect me, stopping my fall and shielding me.

'We're under attack,' someone is screaming, panic twisting their voice. I don't know who. No one I know. Chaos breaks loose everywhere.

'Retreat,' Jessam tells me. His grip is firm as he helps me to my feet. We flatten ourselves against the wreckage of the carriage and he barks out orders to the security teams nearest to us, shouting into his coms.

My whole body vibrates, both panicked and frustrated. They've done it, the Gravians. Just as Ambassador Choltus threatened. Just as Shae feared. The wedding won't take place. Not now. How could it? We'll be lucky to survive the day.

Where is Con? Where is Shae? Has my brother even made it to Anthaese space or did he find a Gravian fleet waiting for him? The ship movements Con had spoken of, interstellar disruption... I should have thought! A classic prelude to an attack. How far does this go?

I push all those new fears aside. We have to get back to the palace – that is the first priority. Regroup and get some intel once our position is secure. But can Limasyll be made secure? It hadn't been built for defence. It was beautiful. Now it's burning.

'Palace under attack,' the voice crackles in Jessam's radio. I know it at once, even scrambled by static. It's Shae. I snatch the com from Jessam's hand.

'Shae, where's the Anthaem?'

I can't make out the answer, aside from my own name, which is little more than a bark. There's swearing involved. I can hear that. It finishes with an order that I get under cover.

'I'm on my way there!' I tell him and then shove the com at Jessam before Shae can argue. Let them try to stop me. I might not know how to be a princess but a soldier – now that is something I understand. I know Gravian tactics all too well and I don't imagine that a change of location will change their thinking. It isn't in their nature. 'Someone get me a weapon. They'll land ground troops and flyers as soon as they can. We need to take our key positions and hold them before they come. We need to secure the Anthaem. Who's with me?'

They sound off – Vairian and Anthaese – more of them than I would have thought possible. Maybe they just need someone – anyone – to lead the way, someone they can follow. Knowing that if I hesitate now I'll lose them, I lead the way through the embattled city in my ridiculous silver wedding dress, with a Vairian knife belt around my waist and a borrowed plasma gun in my hands.

*

The entrance to the palace isn't far. The ground shakes and trembles as if giants are stamping their feet just beyond the next junction. I can guess what it means. I look to Jessam, and see the same realisation in his eyes, as he directs the security guards with us to fan out, and usher as many of the panicking Anthaese civilians to safety. There is no safety. The ground troops are landing. Pretty soon the whole area will be swarming with Grunts and Mechas. This isn't a small incursion. The Gravians know there is next to no resistance to be had here. It's a full scale invasion. They'd learned their lesson with the capture of Kelta. The Anthaese aren't widespread across their world. They live in the few cities or in the wild, in isolated homesteads, alone and no threat to anyone. All it will take is capturing a few key places and—

'Communications are breaking up,' Jessam yells, as an explosion rents the air overhead. 'EMP or jamming.'

'We need to find somewhere defensible. Hold them off and get these people to safety.' And I need to find Shae. And Con. I desperately need to find them both. I can't explain it, can't bear to think of either of them in danger, or hurt, or worse.

Safety, that's another problem. Where is safe? Where are our defence forces? Where are our allies?

Does the Empire know? There are patrols in this quadrant and they must have reported something. Or have the Gravians wiped them out too? Too many questions. There isn't time for this, for any of it. I can't panic.

'Princess?' Jessam nods to the left and I see them, a group of flyers sweeping in – Gravian, grey bricks in the sky, held aloft by sheer power and malevolence. 'Time's up.'

'Get the people to the palace!' I fire without pause, standing up and letting the plasma gun bark as it discharges, focusing on the target, on the vulnerable intake valves below the engines. The next thing I know Jessam is with me, standing slightly ahead of me, firing as well. One flyer stutters and leaps in the air. Then it explodes. The blast sends us rolling backwards. I lie there stunned as another flyer swoops over us and the ground erupts with weapons fire. Jessam throws himself over me and pulls me to safety, hard against the wall of the palace.

The civilians with us are already through the gates. That's when I see him, standing there, yelling at me.

He's always yelling.

Shae.

I can't hear what he's saying. The noise of weapons and explosions are bad enough and my head rings with a possible concussion. But it's Shae, alive, in command, armed to the teeth.

Jessam pulls me forward and I don't resist. A moment later I have my legs under control again and I sprint. I can hear Shae now, shouting something about evacuation. I see transports, the civilians piling into them. Just a few unarmed Anthaese transports. Not enough of them.

'Bel!' Shae yells. 'Get in the lead transport. Get in it now.'

'Where's Con?'

'He's still inside. But you have to go. Now!'

'We can't leave him here. If they capture the Anthaem—' He's going to argue. I know it. Shae thinks only of protecting me, not of the Anthaese. Not really.

He grabs my arm, shakes me roughly as if trying to force some sense into me. I pull away angrily. 'Get in the transport.'

'Not without Con.'

'They've blocked the space-lanes. They've cut this world off from outside help and they're targeting all the major centres. You need to get to safety now, while there's time. Out into the wilds where they won't look. Then we'll sort out an escape route, back to Vairian.'

'And what will happen if they take Con? Come on, Shae, you know how the Anthaese feel about him. His people will do anything to save him, even hand over their entire world to Gravian occupation. We've got to get him out too. He's our ally.'

'There's been no marriage, so no alliance. Bel, please!'

I can't believe he's saying this. Him, of all people.

'The marriage is a symbol. Of course there's an alliance. I wouldn't be here otherwise.'

Besides if I leave and somehow manage to make my way back home, how determined would my family be then? They'd still want to help, but would they? If the stakes weren't so personal? Which is only half a problem anyway, because if I do make it to safety now, I can't get off the planet, let alone out of Anthaese space, if what Shae says is true. I could be flying straight into a trap and a new role as a hostage myself. Or worse.

I glare at Shae. There isn't time. Not for us. Not for any of this. 'I can't go without him.'

He snarls and curses, not exactly coherent.

'Con won't leave,' says Shae at last.

'He won't *what*?'

But it makes sense. Of course he won't leave. Why am I not surprised? He'd gone to fix the sabotaged engine rather than fleeing a dying spacecraft. He'd never leave his people at a time like this. Not without encouragement, anyway.

'Right,' I mutter. 'Then we'll have to *make* him.'

'And you'll go with him,' Shae tells me. 'No arguments, Bel. If I get you to him and find a way out, you'll leave too. This isn't your fight.'

It isn't his either. I nod, too stunned to argue. Because it really isn't a fight for either of us any more. It's a rout. Will there even be a wedding now? Peace has failed. Anthaeus will be occupied by the Gravians and a long drawn out war is the best we can hope for. Unless Con is taken and then the Anthaese will give up any semblance of resistance. Fighting isn't in them.

'I'll get him to safety, if that's what you mean. But we have to fight the Gravians. It's why we're here. It's what we were made for.'

He doesn't answer that, but ushers me forwards. 'This way.'

Chapter Fifteen

I run along behind Shae, aware that the men laying down covering fire are falling back to the transports as well. They take to the air. Three speed off into the skies – to safety, I hope – but the fourth has barely lurched over the height of the gates when it explodes in a fireball, taking everyone on board with it. Shards of smoking metal rain down on the flowered gardens, setting them alight.

Shae flinches, but doesn't react beyond that. There isn't time. Those words keep repeating through my head. *There isn't time.* Another massive explosion takes out the gates, but blocks them with rubble.

'We don't stand a chance here,' he shouts over the noise. 'In the forests maybe, out by the Rondet. Or the mountains, up around Montserratt. Anywhere but here.'

'We'll get there,' I tell him. 'And the Vairian fleet will breach the blockade with all the power of the Empire behind it. Maybe we just need to hold out until then. You'll see, Zander is probably already engaged and summoning help.' *And if wishes were horses, beggars would ride.* Nerysse used to say that.

Nerysse died for me. How many others will die today?

Where are my other bodyguards? Where are Elara and the maids? Are they okay? I can't think that. I have to keep going.

Shae is right ahead of me. 'Any response from the fleet will take time, which we don't have. If they can force a surrender beforehand, what can the Empress do? It could be all over before the Empire has a chance to respond. And Anthaeus isn't even part of the Empire. You're the only reason they might still try to get here. The Gravians will have this over in hours, Bel.'

And the key piece to that Gravian endgame is Con. I look up to the tower where he has his study. I've never been there but I'm sure that is where he'll be. I have to get him out of there before he's captured or killed. Otherwise his whole world is lost. Gravians are dropping Grunts and Mechas into the courtyards, each terrace below us already swarming with them. As we reach the tower, Shae, Jessam and the others form up with the royal guard who have so far managed to keep back the tide. Hundreds of them, holding the tower, keeping Con safe inside. Or trapped.

'Go!' Shae shouts. 'Go now. We'll hold the stairs.'

I have to find Con. That's my one mission. Without him everything will fall apart. And if they take him captive...

His people will do anything to free him.

He didn't think they'd actually attack. He'd never believed Choltus' threats.

I run up the stairs, my legs aching, my head spinning. The gown hampers my movements, but I can't stop for anything. Not now. The plasma gun is flat and though I cling to it I know it's useless. Maybe it could be a threat, but nothing more, unless I use it as a club. At least I have the belt of knives, if it comes to a close quartered fight.

At the top I come to a locked door. Con's study. I've never been allowed near it, but I studied the palace enough to know where it is. It's his refuge. I hammer my fist on the door.

'Con? Con, let me in. We're under attack. Con!'

A brass box on the wall by my head lets out a high pitched shriek of static and then I hear his voice, tinny and distant. It's a tablet, a small one, buried in the wall.

'Bel? What are you still doing here?'

'We're under attack!'

The static crackles again. 'You have to press the screen or I can't hear you.'

Damn his stupid tinkering. Why can't he just open the door? What's he doing in there anyway? I slam my hand against the box, hitting it and the screen all at once. I'm lucky it doesn't break.

'We're under attack. Limasyll is falling. Let me in.'

The door whirs and groans, gears and levers clicking away inside it. Slowly it creaks open.

A huge room, ceilinged in a dome of multi-coloured glass similar to the Rondet, opens out before me. And Con's various contraptions fill it. They hang from the ceiling, lie scattered in pieces on workbenches either in a state of construction or recycling. They're jumbled on the shelves lining the walls with his books and charts.

Con stands in the centre, hair dishevelled, his eyes startled as if from sleep. He's holding a coms unit and I think I hear Jondar's voice coming from it. Desperate with panic. But Con isn't paying any attention to it now. The apron he wears over his clothes hadn't protected his face or sleeves from smears of oil and soot.

My husband-to-be looks like a blacksmith, albeit the richest blacksmith in the world.

Weren't we meant to be getting married about now?

'What are you—?' I begin, but when I see his project my voice jams up in my throat.

A flying machine. It's based on the memories of my Wasp and the dragonflies of Vairian, all the things I showed the Rondet, and which they in turn had shared with him. Every detail is perfect, every part of it unique and flawless. Transparent panels gleam in the wings – the solar cells he'd been going on about two days ago when we sat in the garden and all I could think about was assassins and autopsies – light enough but so very powerful. Its frame isn't wood but some kind of clear plastic. The canvas isn't canvas but silk.

'Con,' I breathe his name like a prayer. 'What have you done?'

He waves his hands at it, flustered. 'It's not finished. I thought… a wedding gift. But I got distracted by everything, and I ran out of time so it isn't completely finished.' His emerald eyes flicker over my face and quickly dart away. 'When you thought of flying your Wasp, it brought you such pleasure and when you showed us the beauty of the insects, I thought—'

I stare at it, hardly daring to believe it. Shouts from below bring me crashing back to my senses.

My voice comes out harsher than I'd thought it would. 'You have to leave it. We have to go. The Citadel is taken. Limasyll has fallen. They're coming.' His expression crumbles, devastated at my callous words. Well too bad. I can hate myself later for it, but it's the truth and he has to hear it.

Thunder on the stairs heralds Shae and his troops. They flood the doorway, but I can't help but see there are fewer than before. Barely enough to hold the way. I catch a glimpse of my captain's face and my heart freezes. It is bad. I know from just one look that it is bad. But then, I hadn't expected a miracle. I know better.

'We're cut off,' he reports, his words succinct and to the point. 'We can't hold them.'

'No. You have to get the Anthaem out!'

Con can't be taken. Even now he's talking into one of the wrist coms, receiving reports and rattling off instructions. His people need him. Now more than ever before.

'There's no way, your Highness.' Shae bites out the title like a curse.

'Yes, there is,' Con interrupts. 'But Bel's taking it, not me.' He stands by his flying machine, holding a pair of goggles.

'You said it wasn't finished.'

Con smiles his self-deprecating smile. 'Nothing I work on is ever finished. Not to me. But it's as good as. This would be its test flight, if you're willing. But the aerodynamics and engineering are sound. You only have to get to the south wing. Jondar is holding open a way through there.'

That's what he's been on the coms about? Securing *my* escape? I push the goggles at him. Jondar would never have agreed to rescuing me over Con. I know at once that this was not the plan. 'You have to take it.'

'I can't fly. Flying is more than understanding the mechanics.' I know that. Of course I know that. But he still needs to get out of here. He brushes his fingertips lightly against the curve of my cheekbone. It's the most tender gesture I have ever known and I don't deserve it. I can't possibly leave him here. Not like this. It has to be him. His world needs him. 'It takes heart, Bel, instinct and belief. You have that. Not me.'

'And how am I meant to fly in this ridiculous gown?'

'There are overalls in that cupboard.'

Ancestors! Does he have an answer for everything? 'I'm not leaving you.' I glance back at Shae. 'Either of you!'

'Yes, you are, Highness,' Shae replies. 'Both of you are, in fact. You can get him to safety. It looks strong enough to hold you both. And it's only a short flight, as his Majesty pointed out.' He stares at Con meaningfully.

'As if you'd know,' I snap, realising at the same moment that he does. He knows flying machines almost as well as I do. He's spent most of his life around them, thanks to me. This can't be happening. Panic makes me reckless. 'I'm staying with you, Shae. I won't go. I won't leave you to die.'

There's a struggle on his face, just for an instant. He closes it down in the next second. Dangerous words, I realise, but true, all the same. What does it matter now, anyway? Acid tears fill my eyes – anger, despair and rage fuelling them. Rage at this hopeless situation. Rage at this political game which has stolen the man I love from me before I could ever make him mine, while still keeping him at my side.

He says nothing. He isn't giving me a choice. Not now.

'I can't,' I whisper.

Shae takes my hand, squeezing it. 'You must. You have to live, Bel. It's the only reason I'm here. Understand?' The agony in his blue eyes tells me all I need to know. I can't argue with him any more. He stares at me, willing me to do as he says just this once. And I have to. I know that. Then his gaze focuses behind me on Con, standing behind me, watching everything. He's always watching everything. I'm a fool. 'Both of you. These people need you both if they are to survive, if they are to be willing to fight for their freedom.' He regards Con gravely. 'And your people *must* learn how to fight. Bel can teach them that. Besides which, the Vairians will raise heaven and hell to help you if she's with you. You know this.'

Gun fire comes from the stairs, followed by the blast of grenades. The floor shakes, groans.

'Bel should go,' Con still protests. 'A lighter load, an experienced pilot—'

'You both go,' Shae insists. 'You only have to make it to the south wing, remember?'

With a snarl of frustration, I grab the goggles and stride to the cupboard to pull out a set of overalls. I don't pause for modesty, stepping out of the stupid gown to leave myself in just chemise, drawers and corset. I try to breathe and then growl to myself, struggling out of the corset as well. As I pull on the overalls and strap the knife belt back around my waist, I hear Shae questioning Con.

'You have explosive materials here? Something we can use to booby-trap the door?'

'It's already done,' the Anthaem says. 'Did you think I was just sitting up here waiting?'

I push their voices from my mind. It can't be dwelt on, not now, not if I'm to continue to function.

Shae will die here today, to ensure that I escape with Con. Shae will sacrifice himself for me and for my husband-to-be. Because that's his job. That's what he's here to do and always has been. He was never mine. He never loved me as just me. And yet… he has. He has loved me all along, that's what he was trying to say, and now it's too late. I'm the only reason he's here. I dash away more treacherous tears and pull on the goggles to hide them, knotting my hair at the nape of my neck.

I advance on Con. I can't make my voice kind. It comes out harsh and bitter.

'Are you ready? Show me the controls and climb aboard.' Con recoils, swallows hard and then nods. Reluctant. Shocked, maybe. It doesn't matter. I have to get him out. That's my mission. Shae has made that clear and I owe it to him.

It only takes moments. Con's instructions are precise, rapid but clear. He would make a good teacher, I think absently, aware all the time of the approaching gunfire. And beyond it, the sounds of men and women dying.

I push that away too. Because I have to.

Con climbs in first, lying along the length of the Dragonfly body. I slip in beneath him, pressing against his chest and I take the controls.

Vision is perfect. The controls layout is instinctive and they respond readily. There's only one problem.

'Where's our exit?'

Con calls past me. 'Shae, there's a control to open the dome over—'

The violent staccato of gunfire fills the air. Both of us flinch and the dome collapses, millions of shards scattering about us, tinkling over the workroom like a fall of deadly snow.

Shae lowers his gun. 'Go.'

'A waste,' I mutter darkly. 'Idiot.'

'It's only glass.' Con's voice shakes. But it wasn't. I know that. It had been beautiful, the dome, an echo of all I had seen at the Rondet. So beautiful. Probably ancient too. The craftsmanship alone made it priceless. Even I can concede that. But if I do so at this moment, I might break just like the glass.

'I meant the bullets.' I suspect Con knows I'm lying. 'Hold on.'

I can't look at Shae as I start the Dragonfly up. It pulses around me, the engine a soft hum against my chest, another heart pressed against mine. With a gentle squeeze I ignite the lifts and the Dragonfly leaps into the air.

I glance down, even though I shouldn't. Below me, I can see Shae retreating, see figures in black swarming into the room. Shae looks up, just for a moment as we clear the shattered dome and he smiles. I'm sure he smiles. No exactly joyful, but satisfied, and his blue eyes are locked on mine. I don't know if he can see me, but it doesn't really matter. He does this for me. He raises one hand, presses it to his heart and then closes it into a fist. A salute.

A trigger.

The upper floor explodes. The blast shakes the Dragonfly, buffeting it in a hurricane of heat and fire. An inferno lifts us even further, throwing us into the sky.

'Steady,' Con whispers. His hand closes on my shoulder, a single press of comfort, of concern.

'I've got it,' I reply, through a tight throat, and bring the controls up so I can bank right. 'She's okay.' The ship responds beautifully, dancing on the tumultuous air, finding a current and taking to it. Gliding, free.

It's a beautiful thing, the ship Con created for me. A wondrous thing. Everything I could wish for in a flyer.

Tears roll down my cheeks. I blink them away furiously, but they won't be stopped. Damn it, there's no time for this.

But Shae... my chest aches as I try to keep the sobs inside me... Shae...

Con wraps his arms around my body, managing to do it without hampering me at all. He buries his face in my hair and sighs. His breath is warm, shaking, but a comfort. A tiny, sliver of comfort.

'I'm sorry, Bel. I'm so sorry.'

It's all either of us say for the rest of the short flight.

The Dragonfly soars over the flames of Limasyll, over the scattered refugees and the black clad Gravian troops, over the flaming gardens and the terraces awash with blood and the inferno which had been the royal library below Con's workroom. All those books. All those precious books.

Limasyll falls. I never dreamed I would mourn the place so. The airships are in flames, plummeting from the sky and everything is in ruins. Everything.

And Shae is gone.

The south wing, with its gate still secure, comes up more quickly than I imagined. We pass over the thickest press of battle and suddenly the Dragonfly bucks, twisting off course. Pain slices into my thigh, but I grasp the controls even tighter, wrestling them back under control.

'What is it?' Con holds me against him.

'Nothing,' I lie. 'It's nothing.' I have to bite down on the wave of agony, to hide it from him. There's no time, no hope left. We're almost there. I have to make it. 'I'm going to land there, by the gate. Okay?'

How I bring the Dragonfly down so smoothly beyond the south wing of the palace I can't say. A testament to his design, in all likelihood. Black spots dance across my vision. Even as we touch down, his remaining honour guard speeds towards us, and Jondar with a group of the nobility in hot pursuit.

Safe. Something inside me wilts. We're safe.

I slip out of the flying machine, because he can't get out if I don't and they need to see him safe. As I try to stand on my burning leg I go down with a soundless cry.

'Bel!' Con's voice sounds thin, as if I'm listening to him through his brass box again. But the static is inside my head this time. Pain slices into my thigh as I try to move again, and I'm burning just as Limasyll is burning.

Strong arms gather me up, holding me. The body I rest against smells of Con, but it can't be. He would never tremble this way.

'Bel, answer me. Someone get a medic. The princess is injured. Get me a damned medic. Now!'

I smile as I pass out, thinking how much like Shae he sounds.

And then I remember. Shae will never bark another order at anyone. Coupled with the agony spreading from my wound, the thought is too painful by far. I give myself up to the shadow at the end of the darkness.

Chapter Sixteen

I awake to a pale billowing ceiling that makes my stomach twist and lurch from just a glimpse. I squeeze my eyelids together until lines and dots dance before me, and I take a deep breath before opening them again. A tent, I realise as my vision adjusts. I lie on a low cot in a tent, with gauze curtains screening my corner off from the rest. I'm dressed in the ragged remains of my flight suit, although the material covering my leg has been cut away. There are bandages all down my thigh and winding around my stomach too. White and tight, layers and layers of bandages. But I'm still alive. It hurts so much I have to be still alive.

Twisting around I see the knife belt folded carefully on the chair beside me. Nothing else of note.

I try to sit up, to reach it, but my head swims again as pain engulfs me. It lances through me, originating from my leg, but it hurts everywhere, slicing through my nerves with a blade of ice. And then I remember – taking to the air with Con, looking down in time to see the fireball engulf the tower. And knowing… just knowing…

Shae's gone. So are Jessam and Dan, so many good soldiers, both Vairian and Anthaese. They're gone. The ancestors only know where Petra and Thom are, what happened to them. And Elara, with her dressmakers and designers, all the maids that had attended me. I watched the city burn beneath me and flew away. I felt the heat lick over my body.

And Shae is gone.

Sinking onto the bed, I stare at the roof, willing my heart to crack with the agony of that thought, willing myself to give up and die so I can follow him wherever he has gone. In the summer fields with our ancestors, we'll meet again as warriors, as heroes.

Shae is gone.

I can't even cry.

It isn't long before someone comes in – a weary-faced medic who probably never dealt with anything more serious than a fracture before today, or some disease of peacetime and indolence. A girl really. She looks as if she hasn't slept in days and for a moment she seems too shocked to realise what she is seeing.

'You're awake.' She blurts out the words and then stops. 'I need to… I'll just… how do you feel?'

I give her a level stare. 'It hurts. Everywhere.'

'Of course it does. How's your vision? Any headaches?'

'I'm Princess Belengaria of Vairian, Duchess of Elveden, Countess of Duneen. I was in a flyer that crashed and I need to know what happened to my passenger and what news there is.' I don't mention who my passenger was. One small protection, I hope, just in case.

The medic smiles, completely unfazed by her patient's belligerent tone.

'I'll fetch someone to answer all your questions, Princess, as soon as I'm sure you're up to it.'

'Of course I'm up to it.' My stomach heaves and suddenly it seems there are three identical medics gazing down on me, each face wearing the same stern look of disbelief. I'm cold, as if all the heat has been sucked out of me.

The medic has the measure of me, that's the problem. I can see it in her eyes, in the way she coolly folds her arms and waits. Cooperate with her, and she'll get me whatever I want. Otherwise we'll wait until I feel more like doing as I'm told. She's Anthaese. Maybe there's some of the stubbornness I saw in Con in all of them after all, so that's a hope. I'll have to cooperate.

'I need to check your wounds first.'

'How long ago?'

'Three days. You were unconscious for most of it, sedated for the rest. But you were lucky. There weren't many who made it out of Limasyll.'

I suck in a jagged breath. A terrible cold grief settles a wet blanket over me, smothering my aching heart and mind. Of course, not many made it out of Limasyll. I saw how much firepower the Gravians directed there. I saw it burn, felt it.

And Shae is gone.

Once the medic, Dr Halie, is satisfied with me, and I take some medication from the pitifully small store they have, I'm left on my own again. But only for a moment.

There's a flurry of activity outside. Then Petra and Thom burst in.

They too are bandaged. Thom limps badly, though he tries to hide it, and Petra has bruises all down one side of her face and neck and holds her arm awkwardly. But they're alive. Dear ancestors, they're alive.

The three of us hold each other, reassuring ourselves that this is real, that we are actually all three of us here and alive. I cling to them until the pain of moving threatens to make me black out again and I disentangle myself. Petra and Thom seem to understand, at least, and straighten up, standing to attention as best they can until I tell them to sit down and stop being stupid. At the same time I struggle upright, ignoring the roiling sickness that fills my stomach as I try.

'What news?' I ask at length. 'Did anyone else—?'

Petra shakes her head before I can finish. 'The city is in ruins. Most of the population centres are. We haven't heard anything from the southern continent. The palace – well, what's left of it, seems to be where they've set up their HQ. They've prison camps springing up, labour camps, that kind of shit. There may be some resistance, but it's scattered, disconnected. They'll wipe it out in their own time. That bloody ambassador of theirs keeps issuing demands and proclamations. In the name of the Anthaem, no less.'

'Con?' I try to push myself up from the bed. But I flew out with Con. That had been the whole reason for Shae's sacrifice. *How did they capture Con?*

Petra sits down beside me, perching on the edge of the cot. She reaches out and wraps me in her arms. Holds me close. She strokes my hair.

'It's okay. Con is here. He's safe, my princess. The Gravians have set up some sort of puppet government with that prince of theirs.'

'Kendal.' Thom's voice seethes with loathing. 'Claims Con is dead and he's the heir apparent, but he isn't fooling anyone. Without a body, no one is buying it. They're wonderfully stubborn, these Anthaese.' His laugh is short. 'Plus, Con's here. Preparing his own broadcast, which involves building a system to do it first. Not that it bothers him. It'll just take time. They're bluffing. Jondar's furious. You should hear him. I never thought he knew how to swear like that.'

'Con can't broadcast. What if they get our position? Where are we anyway?'

'Safe for now,' Petra replies. 'And that's exactly what Prince Jondar said about the whole idea too.'

Thom grins at me. 'Anyway, your fiancé has it covered. He says he has a plan. He's full of them these days.' He starts telling me more, detailing locations and numbers, supplies, weaponry, but I can't follow him. All his words jumble together…

I'm not sure when I fell asleep, or how long I was unconscious. My dreams are brutal, confused, terrifying. The world burns and Shae is burning. I burn with him. I wish the darkness would swallow me once and for all.

Something cool soothes my fevered brow. A voice whispers to me, calling me, comforting me when the nightmare is ready to swallow me up. I cry out and strong arms hold me. It feels like Shae. I wish it was Shae. But I can't bring myself to say his name, because I know Shae is gone. It's all I can think of. I just want to follow him.

I wake later, cold and shivering, despite the blankets tucked in around me, tight as a shroud. It takes me a moment to struggle free and take in my surroundings again. Still the tent, but it's dark outside now. A single lamp flickers on the cabinet.

Con sits beside me, his shoulders bent, his eyes closed. I watch him with hooded eyes. He looks like a man lost in prayer.

It's only when I push myself up on my elbows, still unable to do so without giving a gasp of pain, that he stirs.

'You should be resting, Princess. Lie down. Don't move.'

'I think I've rested too long. What news do you have?'

'Whatever news, it's all bad. Limasyll has fallen. My people are enslaved and we are cut off from the rest of the galaxy, from everything.'

'Cut off?'

'They've some sort of jamming device. No word has got in or out to my knowledge since before the attack. That must be why we never heard from your brother. I'm sorry, Bel. I'll find a way to crack it but until then you're stuck here with the rest of us in an occupied world.' He's so sure he'll break through whatever is jamming the signals and so am I. He can do anything when it comes to tech. But there's a bleakness behind his words. Ancestors, Con is so lost. His life has fallen apart. His beloved world has been stolen from him.

'Occupied, perhaps.' I reach out and squeeze his tense grip. 'But not conquered.' Although that won't be long from the bleak picture Thom and Petra had painted. But I can't say that to Con.

Con wraps his free hand around my fingers, grateful for the contact. 'This isn't your war. You were here to marry me as part of a treaty, a mutual defence pact, which hardly seems to have much of a point now.'

I shake my head, bemused at his defeatism. Is he saying he doesn't want me here any more? 'That doesn't mean we give up, Con. We never stop fighting until we've driven them out. The Vairian fleet will bring the Imperial vanguard after it, and you and I will lead the attack from here. We need to contact the other survivors, organise resistance and fight back.'

Con breathes out, a long, low sound of relief. 'My thanks. I don't deserve so much, especially not when you've suffered such loss.'

My loss? There's only one thing he can mean.

Shae. The thought of him is a barb inside me, sharp and bright and terrible. I flinch. All the blood drains out of me again. Shae is dead. And Jessam, and Dan... Elara and my maids... But the only one I can think of is Shae.

Shae is dead. I wish I was too.

From somewhere tight and painful, I find my voice. 'My bodyguards did their duty and saved us both. They are heroes...' I choke on the word, struggle and force myself on. 'They were heroes of Vairian and Anthaeus.'

'There were a lot of heroes that day.'

A lot of people dead, he means.

The walls between us go up again. How can I open up my grief to him when it shames him as well as me? How can I speak of loss compared to everything he has lost? I lost Shae, but he lost everyone.

The silence drags out until he tries again.

'Bel… Shae wouldn't—'

'No, please.' I have to stop him. I can't stand it any more. I can't bear it. 'Don't. Don't talk about him. Or say his name. Just… please…'

And to my horror, my body seems to just fold in on itself. Great racking sobs I'd sworn not to release wrench their way up through me. I wrap my arms around my knees, even though the agony in my leg screams through me. But the pain is real, and though it doesn't diminish my grief, it works in a dreadful tandem with it. I've lost him, and the pain reminds me I am still alive. And maybe eventually the pain will grow so great that it will block out the agony of having lost him. So pain can be my friend and I can drown in it and forget.

When I'm aware again, Con is holding me. I've buried my face in his chest. He strokes my shoulders, my neck, and I hear him whisper that I must let it out, that he's here, until I finally descend into the depths of unconsciousness. But my last thought is relief – that it had been him, that I hadn't broken in front of a stranger, or worse, in front of Petra or Thom, who would finally see how weak I truly am.

*

The fever returns and I pray for it to take me, to end me. I wake with ants crawling under my skin, my vision swimming. Someone keeps bringing a foul sort of herb soup and making me drink it. I spit it out or weep, or purse my lips tight, but in the end, I drink. It tastes of stinging nettles. It's dark and then light again and Dr Halie is never far away. I have terrible dreams, dark and twisted. I see Shae die over and over again. Elara screams for help but I can't reach her. Limasyll burns.

When I finally wake with a clear head, and the agony of my wounds are nothing but a dull ache, Jondar is there, watching over me, his dark eyes distant and filled with worries. Thom stands at the door with his back to us, although I know he is listening to every word. Of course he is. Listening, monitoring, ever vigilant.

My first thought is to remember that Shae is dead. I take a breath and lock that grief away once again.

'Where's Con?' I ask.

'Not far. Working.'

'How long have I been…'

'Nine days. Do you feel up to getting out of bed? Just for a little while?'

Since when had Jondar been so solicitous? I give him a wary look and he manages a smile.

'You brought our Anthaem safe out of the fire, Belengaria,' he says in overly formal tones. 'We owe you a great debt.'

Belengaria. Not Princess, not your Highness. Now that there is no wedding I'm just me again. Or is he trying to be kind? I can never tell with him.

He helps me to my feet and I'm mortified by how much I need to lean on him. But at least it's Jondar – stiff and formal, never too amiable, always judging me – because someone else would see me as I really am. Jondar, somehow, already knows. He always knew.

Even if he is suddenly looking at me in quite a different way. The reserve is still there, the withdrawal, and the slight hint of disdain, and yet something else is there too. I wish I knew what it was.

'Come on. Just a short walk.'

It takes a moment to find a pair of shoes and he doesn't say a word as he helps me wrap a robe around the plain tunic and trousers I slept in. I wonder who they belong to… or belonged to. I wonder how they got here. Or how I did for that matter.

The camp is scattered through the trees, and not so makeshift as I'd feared. There are about thirty of the low, billowing tents in all kinds of muted colours. From overhead, they must visually form part of the forest floor and canopy. I breathe a little sigh of relief.

'Not so innocent after all, are we?' Jondar grins, like he's reading my mind. 'We have ways of fighting.'

'To be fair, this isn't fighting. It's hiding.'

He laughs, a brief, cut off sound. 'Yes. For now. But Petra says we have to survive before we can fight. So we did this.'

He has a point. But then again, I'm surprised he's quoting Petra – I wonder if she is bossing them all about now. 'Where is she?'

'Rallying the troops. Or at least stopping the desertions. And dealing with refugees. She's a remarkable woman. People look to her for protection.'

Well of course they do. I can't think of anyone else I'd rather follow in times of danger. Petra doesn't hesitate. Duty is everything to her. And right now, clearly, she sees a duty to the Anthaese, even if, technically, we no longer have one. There was no wedding. The planet is in Gravian hands. Our mission, such as it was, is a failure. I don't know where that puts us now.

I deliberately push those thoughts out of my mind. Jondar is the last person I want to catch wind of them. What would he do, if there was suddenly a way to get rid of me?

'How many refugees?'

'Almost a hundred here. More on the way. A huge number took to the caves in Montserratt. We've no way of knowing how many yet. But we're working on it. Trying to make contact with the other settlements, refugees, and those who scattered into the wilds. Petra is sending out runners, but there aren't many and they have to be careful. One mis-step and we're all exposed.'

He sits me down in a patch of sunlight and Thom circles us, not too close, but close enough.

Everywhere else around me there is activity. Not fevered, but determined, as if by throwing themselves into all their various tasks – weapons training, food gathering, construction – the inhabitants can forget for a while what is happening, what they've seen. *Work focuses the mind,* my father always said and I can see it now. That's how he'd survived the loss of my mother, and being thrust into his present role.

I have to do the same.

I force myself to my feet again, but before I can say a word, my head swims in syrup. Thom turns, his face filling with concern and moves towards me, but Jondar catches my arm instead, steadying me. Thom stops, nods, his eye contact with Jondar lingering meaningfully.

Oh yes, he's watching. Thom's furious that I was hurt. He blames himself. He's going to police my recovery and everyone else needs to fall in line. Wonderful. And I thought Petra would be the problem.

'Easy now,' Jondar says. 'Sit.'

I can't. Not with everyone else working. 'I should be doing something.'

'You are,' he replies, not unkindly. 'You're recuperating. Take your time.'

'But there isn't time, is there? What else is happening out there? Where's Elara?'

A pained look sharpens his gaze. Mentioning her name was probably not the best move. 'We don't know. There are so many…' His voice trails off but I know what he was going to say. Missing. There are so many missing.

And Elara is among them. I'd guessed as much when she hadn't been there when I woke up. My throat tightens, hard and painful and I have to swallow reflectively. More things to repress, more things to deal with later. My mother, Nerysse, Elara… everyone I care for is taken from me. Everyone.

I won't think of Shae. I just won't.

'Of course.' I force my voice to be steady and calm. 'Why act when we can sit around waiting to be captured?'

'Why rush in and die when we can gather information that might save us? We're a peace-loving people, your Highness. That doesn't mean we're stupid.' He looks fierce. Maybe there is hope.

It's the first time I've felt the urge to smile since… well, I can't remember when. 'Okay. Not stupid. I'll remember that.'

Jondar smiles too and the relief makes him look human at last. 'Good.'

*

For the next ten days, I rest and work on my physical strength, making myself endure the exercises that will help me recover, doing whatever Dr Halie tells me.

Try as I might not to dwell on the dead and missing, I can't help it. Elara was my friend, whether I realised it or not, and no one has heard anything of her since the fall of Limasyll. And as for my guards… well, I saw the tower go up.

I should have been with them. I should have stayed. I know logically there was no one else to pilot the Dragonfly out, but still. I'm Vairian.

I don't have a place here. I wish I'd stayed with him. There must have been something I could have done.

He should be here, protecting these people. Then they might stand a chance. I should have stayed behind.

I wait for news. Any news. Word of Zander, word of what's happening in Limasyll, of the labour camps and the prisoners. But nothing seems to be happening. Nothing at all.

Kendal releases statements, broadcast on all frequencies, promising peace if we cooperate, assuring the people of Anthaeus that the Gravians will not harm them. Some of the people here have tablets that still work. Word of mouth does the rest of the work. His lies are fooling no one, or at least I hope that's true. But some of the Anthaese must be working with the invaders willingly or unwillingly. And there are more Gravians landing all the time.

Con might as well be a ghost too. I can feel his presence in the camp. Everyone talks about him. I can tell where he's been, and when I have just missed him. Sometimes I wake with the feeling that he has been there, as if the scent of him still lingers beside my bed. I wonder if he's trying to give me space. Or avoid me.

And yet the one ghost I'm certain lingers beside me, all the time, is Shae. I'm so used to having him nearby. He could have been with me just a moment earlier and each time I wake I have to remind myself all over again that he's dead. Sometimes, I'm certain, he speaks to me in my dreams, tells me to be strong, especially when all I want to do is give up.

All those days flow together since the fall of Limasyll and I go a little further each day, though never on my own. I watch Thom and Petra in their morning training routines, the salutations to the ancestors, the various forms, fluid and graceful, faster by turns. I don't have the strength to join them, but at least I can watch them and dream of home.

I can almost sense Shae, like a phantom alongside them, a shadow on both their faces. And on mine as well. After the first few days some of the refugees watching along with me join in. And then some more. By the time I regain enough strength to partake, there are over twenty of us, our bodies in unison, our minds focused. Dancing the dance of warriors. And the ghosts of the lost dance with us.

Con remains elusive.

When I finally ask Jondar where he is, he gives that infuriating smile again. Delighted to know something I don't, no doubt, back in his place of power, guardian of the Anthaem.

'Come and see,' he says. 'We've got a surprise for you.'

I'm too taken aback by the invitation to argue.

It's early morning, more than three weeks after the fall of Limasyll. I've lost track of the days and I'm too embarrassed to ask. Besides, who has the time to humour me? Everyone has a task to do, and the camp is quiet. Jondar leads me through the trees to a clearing. Machines are scattered around the edges, in various states of repair, or disassembly. But in the middle... ancestors, in the middle...

It's the Dragonfly. Somehow they managed to salvage it and put it back together. I draw in a breath and can't quite manage to let go of it.

'How?' I ask.

'Con had time on his hands.' Jondar wears a wry grin. 'Well... not really, but it's better if he's occupied. He's happier busy, so he worked on it when he could. In between everything else – securing our defences here, hacking the Gravian security grid, building a communicator and comforting his people. You know.'

'About half an hour then?'

How strange I can joke with him now. It shouldn't be possible, and yet here we are.

Jondar smiles with an easiness that seems to surprise him as well. 'He wanted to fix it for you.'

I'm not fooled. He'd wanted to fix me, probably, but had to leave that to Dr Halie, so he'd turned his attention to the Dragonfly instead. Is that why he hadn't come to see me again? No, that isn't fair. His time is better occupied than sitting watching me. And this is the result. It's so beautiful my eyes threaten tears. I push them back with ruthless efficiency.

'One isn't going to help a lot, although I could fly reconnaissance I guess, and—'

'He's making more. We have pilots and some working airships. They got the airfields but not all the ships. Some of them made it aloft and got away. The trees offer cover for hiding them.'

But trees are not so great for take-off and landing, unless the flyers can manoeuvre the same way as the Dragonfly and—

'Oh,' I exclaim, oddly delighted with the revelation at which I've suddenly arrived. 'He's going to reverse-engineer the older flyers, adapt them.'

'Precisely. Or use them for parts to build more of these where he can.'

It's a clever plan – from what I know of Con, I'd expect no less – but they'll still be too few. And it will take too long. But still, he's a genius. He's their best hope.

'Where is he?'

Jondar nods through the trees and I see something hidden there. A structure, broken and twisted. I frown and start towards it before I realise it's the shattered dome of the Rondet. Coloured glass, blackened and melted together, is strewn around the grass and the great crystal is gone. I hadn't realised we were so close. It must have been bombed, like everywhere else. Destroyed, looted and then abandoned. I think of the Gravians ransacking that beautiful, sacred space and my heart goes cold.

'He's communing.'

Somewhere I find the will to breathe again. They're safe then, and Con is with them. Underground, he's sharing his plans with the Maesters and Maestras. I only hope they're helping him rather than just marvelling at his cleverness. The hive mind probably delight in all his new inventions, these novel ideas and wonders he conjures up for them. That's what they love the most.

But are they helping?

So how will they feel when their land is taken apart and left a husk? Rhenna said they felt everything on Anthaeus, saw everything. What do they make of events now?

'Ancestors,' I breathe the word as another realisation sweeps over me.

'Highness?' Jondar holds me carefully, watching me for another sign of fever.

'I need to see him now.'

'But he's… it's forbidden.'

'Oh never mind.' I pull free of him and make for the Rondet. Jondar follows nervously, even when I carry on past the hole where crystal had been, down into the little gully and up to the secret entrance. Not so secret, since he clearly knows about it as well. It never crosses my mind that the Rondet might refuse me access. I'm inside before Jondar can stop me or even question what I'm doing. Jondar stops at the doorway, his face strained with conflict.

'Bel, please. It's forbidden.'

Bel? Since when has he called me Bel? Even Belengaria had sounded strange from his mouth. I raise an eyebrow. 'Stay there then.'

'With respect, Princess…'

And suddenly there it is. *Princess*. Yes, I am a princess. Maybe not of here any more, but I'm still a princess of Vairian. They need to remember that.

'No.' I leave no doubt in my voice. I have every right to be here. I earned the place at Con's side as far as they were concerned. They had welcomed me, hadn't they? Spoken to me. Picked through my memories. But then Jondar probably doesn't know that. He ought to though. The marriage wouldn't have gone ahead without their agreement. But then… the marriage hasn't happened. The Gravians saw to that. 'Wait here.'

He tries to follow, but can't seem to make himself do it. He wants to argue, that his place is by Con's side, that he would do anything to be there, but he can't.

And I remember what he had said about Elara. How she hated him because he didn't marry her, because he didn't love her. Of course he didn't. He can't love two people. Not like that.

It's like I mentally trip over my own feet in a moment of blinding clarity.

He loves Con. He's always loved Con. In the same way that I loved Shae. I have to hold myself still to let another wave of agony wash over me at that thought. Jondar loves Con and Con is still alive. Con is still here, part of his life, every day, and Jondar is torn between his duty and his love, *every single day*.

'You…' I don't finish it. I don't know how to. On Vairian partnerships are just that and opinions about them flexible. People live together, fight together, love. So much loss means that love is cherished, whatever form it takes. Outdated moralities don't have a place on my world and for that I'm grateful. But here, on Anthaeus, where court and culture and society rule, where tradition dictates clothes, marriages and position, where an individual's standing in that hierarchy is everything... I don't know. I just don't know. What to say, or how others would react if they heard. How he would react if I said those words, laid his secret bare?

I look at him too long, with too much knowledge in my eyes.

When he brought me here, did he think I'd replace him? And now... now that everything lies in ruins, that I don't even know if I have a place here, *now* what does he think?

Jondar flushes and hangs his head. He isn't wearing court finery any more because no one here is, though the shirt and waistcoat implies he's still making every effort he can. He's still aware of position and protocol because they're part of him, grafted onto his bones.

'Yes, Highness. I'll be right here.' He steps outside and seals the door. Running away from me. From what I've guessed.

I swallow hard. There isn't time for this. What would Con make of it though? My stomach quivers with nerves. Should I tell him? But how is it my place to do that?

And honestly, what does it matter now? It isn't my choice to make.

Chapter Seventeen

I square my shoulders and continue down the passage. It's tougher than I thought on my own, with my legs aching and my body still out of condition in spite of my morning training sessions. It isn't enough. I'll have to work harder, though I push that away for now. *Focus on one thing at a time. No matter what.*

'Con?'

My voice echoes back, empty and too loud.

Con is asleep, or at least he looks asleep. His face is so still and calm. Peaceful. He looks younger than I've seen him look since I arrived and I envy him that peace. He sits on the floor, his legs stretched out in front of him and his head tilted back, leaning against the crystal panel of Aeron's chamber. He's dressed as simply as I am. A moment of fondness sweeps through me. Without all the pomp to make him the Anthaem, the engineer has reverted to his true form.

'Con?' I whisper, and crouch down before him. The urge to touch him flares strongly in my mind, to curl in against him and feel my body warm against his. To open to him and let him in – body, mind and soul.

But my heart is stone, my body broken, my mind too sick with grief. If I even touched him, I'd hurt him.

'Con,' I say again, a little louder.

'*He's far off, young Queen,*' Rhenna's voice informs me. '*Would you join him?*'

'I need to talk to him, not commune. Or entertain you.'

Rhenna laughs. '*He's exhausted. We offer him rest and renewal. He needs it.*' There's a definite touch of reprove in her voice.

I school my tone. Rhenna is the kindest of them. I don't want to annoy her. But this is important. 'I realise that, but Rhenna... Oh ancestors, Rhenna, you can help us, can't you? All of you. Please?'

'*We aren't supposed to get involved in your disputes,*' Aeron interrupts.

'But it affects you too. You live here. It's your land they'll strip-mine. I'm not asking you to *do* anything. Just help us to see, to look afar, to know their plans and movements. You do that anyway to amuse yourselves. Put it to use.'

Con laughs. I hear him in my mind, linked as he is to the Rondet. The sound is startling, warm and rich, fond. So intimate.

'*Didn't I tell you she's a strategist?*'

It's Con's voice, faint and weak, exhausted and so far away. But right inside my head just like Rhenna and Aeron.

I can't allow them to see what's in my mind. There are too many thoughts in my head, things that will hurt him, things that will hurt us both, and others.

I dig a hole deep in the back of my mind and bury my thoughts about Shae and Jondar in it, sealing them away. I have my own secrets, ones that can't be shared. Not now. Not ever. And as for Jondar... It isn't my secret to share in the first place. I hide it all before he gets too close and pray I am doing the right thing.

'*What do you think Con is already doing?*' asks Rhenna. '*Gathering information. Come. Two pair of eyes will see all the better.*'

'All right…' I begin but before I can say another word, I feel myself falling. My body slumps to the ground beside Con but I don't.

I am flying.

*

I soar, high over the mountains which hide the Rondet in their deep valleys. The trees cram into the spaces between the heights, obscuring everything – the dome, and further off the tents, even the landing strip. The location is perfect. You can't see it from the air.

Wind lifts my hair around my face, strands spreading out like ink in water. I am weightless, ecstatic. It's just me, in the air, flying and for a moment the wonder is almost too great. I have to get a hold of myself, concentrate. Focus. Just like flying my Wasp. I catch an air current, wheel around and swoop low over the canopy, flying like a bird of prey, letting instinct guide me. I see everything, feel the air. Still no sign to betray those below. The camp is better hidden than I could hope.

'*First thing I did,*' comes Con's voice from far away, and yet as clear as if he is right beside me. Which he is, really. He sounds different from the members of the Rondet. Less alien. And yet, less human as well. '*I set up shielding arrays. They'll last unless something big passes through them, but they work well. Solar cells keep them powered, but we can't extend much further, not without extra parts. We need to find somewhere more secure. If we grow any greater in number… It's good to see you up and about, Bel.*'

Con did it. Of course he did. For a moment I'd thought the ancient Anthaese had somehow commanded the trees. But no, just Con. Not that there's anything 'just' about him.

The wind whistles by me. He can't see me, can he? Up and about… up here. I'm lying unconscious beside him in the inner chamber of the

Rondet, but what's the point of saying it now. Here in the hive mind, he knows, or at least senses my thoughts.

'*Where are you, Con?*'

'*Here. Come, join me.*' He doesn't show me, exactly. I just know.

The sky of Anthaeus speeds by around me, blurring, twisting as I'm drawn to his side. Limasyll spreads out below me, or rather its ruins. The city is devastated, the palace not much better. There's a gaping, blackened hole where the tower had been. It makes me quail and I shy away, ready to flee, but a hand closes around mine, stops me.

His hand, warm and gentle. Strong. Real, even in this dream state.

'*I know it's hard,*' Con says. '*But it's necessary.*'

He squeezes my fingers, a by now familiar gesture from him which I return gratefully. Hard for me but how much more so for him?

He'd lost Matilde, and then everything linked to her. Just as I lost Shae.

The pain is a spear running me through. A sob of pure agony bursts out. Here there is no body to smother it with, nowhere to push it down deep inside me. It rips through the air around me, through the hive mind, and the others join in. Con loudest of all.

'*I'm sorry,*' I try to say. '*I'm so sorry.*'

'*Do not be sorry.*' Aeron recovers first. '*You cannot hold in such emotions, little queen. It is folly to try.*'

'*I'm not a queen. I don't know what I am any more. I mean, everything's changed now. The whole thing was a political alliance to prevent this and it failed.*'

Con stares at me, his mouth open but when my eyes meet his, he turns away, hiding the pain reflected there. I close my eyes, cursing myself, forcing my pain back under control, and when I look again he's counting troops, noting their movements, determining their plans. As if nothing had happened. As if I have not spilled out all the grief and pain I've been hoarding in an instant.

'*There's a convoy going east,*' he says. '*Can you see it?*'

I draw in a breath, even though there is no need here. Reflexive, instinctual, so strange. Better to focus on what we can do, the things that will help. Better to focus on anything but losing Shae. One of the Rondet reels off co-ordinates and then we are there, the land below rushing by in the same sickening flash.

The line of the convoy runs through the valley like a black snake.

'*Prisoners.*' Rhenna bleeds her disgust into mine. '*Treated no better than slaves.*'

I can't suppress a shudder, or at least the mental ghost of one. '*To the Gravians, they aren't any better than slaves. Worse, they're animals, to be worked or slaughtered. You don't know them, Con. They don't have a high opinion of captives. We have to help them.*'

'*There isn't the manpower,*' Con whispers, pausing in his surveillance.

'*Precisely. Where do you expect to get it with your people being killed or shipped to their work camps? Not to mention our lack of supplies. Look, they're heading to those hills over there. Through that valley.*'

'*Escon Falls,*' he says simply. I can almost feel his mind at work, the need to do something, the knowledge of what needs to be done, the inability to figure out how. I can help with that. I'm sure I can if I can just think for a minute. '*We've had some success with the deeper mines there and there's evidence of large crystal deposits, but the ground is treacherous, too dangerous to dig deep.*'

'*That won't matter to the Gravians, not when they're sending Mechas and prisoners down there. This is their regular route, isn't it? They aren't known for changing their methods once something works efficiently.*'

Con hesitates, looks at me, his eyes the green of the leaves beneath him, his hair like the sun. We're back in the chamber and I can still hear him in my mind. '*I… yes, I think so. There aren't many roads through to the mountains.*'

'*Then I may have an idea.*'

*

Oh, how we argue. And we really do argue. It's been coming all along. Since the first day I arrived on Anthaeus, a little over a month ago. It seems longer, so much longer. Since I tried to tell him about Choltus and he didn't listen. Round after round of arguments. All through the evening and again the next morning, all through the preparations and planning, we argue. It's the most animated I've ever seen Con. He calls me insane, and reckless, insists that my injuries have robbed me of my senses.

He falls short of calling me suicidal, probably because he fears that I am. Perhaps that's true.

But I don't care. They can't deny that the idea will work, that I'm right. No, the argument centres around who should go and it doesn't include me. As one of the only three Vairian warriors left to them, I'm pretty quick to disabuse the sorry remains of his Martial Council of the notion that the princess should stay behind in safety. Con keeps stubbornly refusing to concede it for days, but I wear him down in the end.

I've won arguments against Zander. When you look at it that way, Con didn't stand a chance.

Getting past Thom and Petra is another matter.

'They need me,' I insist. 'They need all three of us. You know that.'

'With respect, Highness—' Petra begins. That's her go-to phrase when she's about to be stubborn. Respect? She doesn't mean it at all.

'Oh stop it, both of you,' I cut her off. 'We don't have time for nonsense. We all know what we are here, so knock off the titles and the second guessing. I'm not letting them be enslaved and massacred, so unless you're planning to tie me up...' They exchange an all-too-conspiratorial glance. It's only half in jest. Or at least it had better be. If they thought they could get away with it, they would. 'Stop it. Thom, Petra, they need us. They'll hide here and slowly be picked off, a few at a time. And eventually the shielding will fail and the Gravians will find the Rondet too which will mean we're all wiped out or captured. Con's plans are no use if no one will carry them out. We need to give them heart, or I tell you this, the Gravians will have won. I won't see them driven off Vairian, and out of the Empire, to embed themselves like parasites in an even richer world like this, a vulnerable world, where they can garner wealth and build their strength to attack Vairian again. I can't do it. I won't.'

Before leaving camp, Thom removes any shred of uniform our little unit still clings to, putting them instead into scavenged browns and greens, smearing their faces with mud and glaring at them every second.

'When did he get to be such a sergeant-at-arms?' I ask Petra as we watch him stalk along their line.

'He learned from the best,' Petra replies, sorrow dragging behind her words.

I recall Shae doing the same sort of final inspection on his troops and swallow hard. On the far side of the camp, Con looks up, concern flickering over his features. Has he felt my heartache? Impossible, surely, but I don't know how the hive mind works, or what the after-effects of sinking so deeply into it could be. I try to think of something – anything – else to say to Petra, but grief smothers my thoughts.

As we make ready to depart, Con comes over.

'I modified these for you.' He offers me a pair of ornate brass field glasses. 'Only ones we have, I'm afraid, but they work.'

I lift them to my eyes. The magnification is incredible. I can make out details of the bark and leaves on the far side of the clearing. They focus and a readout reels up on the tiny inbuilt screen – distance, wind speed, temperature, a dozen other pieces of information. All of it useful, vital. He thinks of everything.

I lower the glasses and stare at him, trying to think of something to say. But the words don't come out.

'And this,' he goes on without pause. It's my coms bracelet, although he has simplified it. Less decorative now, more practical, so much better. I love it. 'The range is greatly improved, and I've installed a tracker – in all the coms, actually. Just in case.'

In case it all goes wrong, he means. In case we're all captured or killed. To find us. Or bring back our bodies.

'Thank you,' I say quietly. And I have never meant it more.

He hesitates, as if he wants to say more, or stop me. Well, naturally. I know he wants to stop me. He's so intent on me that for a moment I wonder if he'll try to kiss me goodbye.

The last kiss, my only kiss, was with Shae. I flinch back without meaning to.

But Con doesn't move. Sunlight gleams off his golden hair, and glints in those strange, tell-tale marks in his skin. His eyes glow, green and alien, just for a moment.

'I should let you go,' he mutters at last, just loud enough for me to hear. The words stop me. Let me go on the mission? Or does he mean more? I frown and he looks away. 'Or at least… I should be going instead of you.'

'Out of the question,' Jondar interrupts. So he's been listening after all and Con is not as stealthy as he thinks. No surprise there.

Poor Con. 'The risk is too great. If you were captured we would lose everything. Our people would insist on paying any price for your return. You know that.'

I had been about to say the same thing. I glance sharply at the prince, who catches my look aggressively, but softens when I nod.

'We'll be back in no time,' I tell Con.

'And I'll be waiting, watching.'

A smile tugs at the corners of my mouth again as I think of Con and the Rondet watching over me from above in the hive mind's dreaming, my guardian spirits, like in the old tales he loves so much.

'I'm counting on it.' I hold his hand to my chest and bow my head. 'Stay safe, my Anthaem.'

The others bow, and the silence which falls over the area is complete. I look up to see Con's eyes glittering with unsheddable tears and realise that apart from him and the troop going with me, the Anthaese are all holding their hands to their hearts. For us.

I take my leave, the others falling in silently behind me.

*

We take up position as soon as we arrive, with twelve members of the Anthaese royal guard and artillery scattered among the trees and boulders littering the hillside, overlooking the narrow road below. It smells like home, the scent of forests and earth.

It's as if I never left Vairian, as if the whole nightmare which began with the destruction of Higher Cape never happened. It's only when I feel the need to say as much to Shae that I remember again, and each time that happens grief pushes my rage higher and higher.

But it isn't a wild and fruitless rage. Not this. It's an arrow, aimed with purpose and directed straight at my enemy. I crouch behind cover on the hillside over the road which cuts a fresh scar through Anthaese forest. My troops are so still that even the birds have started to sing again.

It takes forever. It takes no time at all. My father always said that about ambushes.

Petra signals, a silent gesture from the far side of the track – *target in view*. I wait, counting silently to measure the moments.

Petra signals again – *target in range*.

Come on then, I think, willing my men and women to stay calm. One moment of over-anticipation could ruin this. Could ruin everything. I lift the glasses, scan the trail below them. Wait.

Someone shifts behind me, the undergrowth giving a rustle, and I wince, suppressing the urge to make it worse by cursing. But they're immediately silent again. Everything falls still. We wait.

The convoy heaves into view, the Anthaese prisoners dragging behind it, some caged, some tethered. There are Mechas, but only a few. The Gravian guards aren't exactly doing their job, riding on the wagons, weapons down. Clearly they believe no one will dare to attack them. No one has dared since they invaded, so why would that change now? Their arrogance is galling, an insult.

A snarl wrenches its way up inside me. I give the signal, my hand punching the air.

All around me the Anthaese guard rise up as one. They plummet down the slope, or burst up from the undergrowth, silent and terrible. Kick anything long and hard enough and it will bite back. The meekest among us still have teeth.

I fire directly on the Mechas, taking to task the strongest threat first. More machine than human now, creatures of destruction – they will kill without compunction so I return the favour without a qualm.

'*Remember*,' Shae told me long ago. '*They aren't what they were. Their lives are over and constant agony is all that awaits them. You're doing them a favour, putting them out of their misery.*'

The first goes down in a shower of sparks. I can't see a face – it's all machine. Just as well. The second begins firing, hitting the tree behind me before Thom blows it apart.

The Gravians turn their weapons on their attackers too late. Amid the chaos those prisoners who are still shackled to the wagons break free, setting others loose. Many panic and run for the trees, desperate and terrified. I don't blame them. But the rest stay, turning chains into weapons, or seizing firearms from the fallen Gravians. Even without training or skill, they can shoot plasma rifles. Not accurately, but that doesn't stop them. So long as they don't hit one of their own.

Everything is over almost as soon as it begins. We pick our way through the Gravians, dispatching the survivors with alacrity. Not a pleasant task, but what choice do we have? Prisoners are no use. Survivors will tell tales. Better that this convoy just vanish. As if the forests of Anthaeus have swallowed it up.

Not the honourable thing to do perhaps, but no one disputes my orders. There's a certain revenge to it as well. I'm not proud of that. We do what has to be done.

Chapter Eighteen

Con gets up from his chair slowly, towering over me. 'Again? But you can't do the same thing? Won't they be prepared?'

I looked up at him, weary of this. It's been a week. The latest announcements from Kendal and the Gravian command are denunciations and threats. I couldn't have hoped for better. He's advertising our resistance to other survivors for us. We need to do something else. Something fast. 'Not the very same thing then. But to the same ends. There's that work camp they were heading to, for example. And countless others like it. They have mining operations. Do you really want them having an endless supply of crystals to power their weapons? Do you want them to find something the size of the Rondet crystal? Because the things they could power with that don't bear thinking about. How are we for explosives? Mines need explosives, and that's where we can get some, from their supplies, and then we can turn the tide. What weapons do we have?'

'You added to the weapons store with your first raid,' Jondar says. 'I'll give you that, but not to the people able to wield them.'

Thom, who stands by the door the whole time, as silent as a statue, clears his throat. 'We added the people,' he says in his calm, quiet voice. 'Now they just need training. I can arrange that for you. With your leave?'

Con stops, looking from one to the other. Then he nods.

And like that, we have another mission in the works.

*

We throw ourselves into training, organisation and good old-fashioned sneaking around. There are more proclamations from the Gravians, and visions of Kendal's strained and pale face everywhere, warnings of dire retribution for the vanishing convoys, supplies and liberated prisoners, for the acts of sabotage and for the deaths of their people. I have only led a few such missions so far which tells me one key thing – we are not alone. It sends a wild exhilaration through me. Elsewhere other groups are taking on the invaders as well. They have to be. Anthaese? Or Vairian infiltration units? Perhaps a mixture of both. I don't know and can't afford to try to make contact with them, tempting though the prospect is. If we link up, when one falls we would all fall. The risk is too great. I can only do what is possible here and now, isolated in our one small area. So I throw myself into the moments of action and survive everything else. Along with Thom and Petra, I oversee weapons training with the remains of the Anthaese guard, as well as those refugees and freed prisoners fit for it.

Thom doesn't bark orders the way Shae would have. Not as he had the first day. He doesn't need to. Everyone here is filled with a focused determination. It isn't just hatred, but stronger than that. We have turned away three times as many who would have joined this group. There are roles for everyone. Many of those train with Petra and a group of gamekeepers and hunters familiar with the forests around us. They aren't just gathering food, but learning to hunt, to lay traps, to face danger with their wits and a blade. Soldiers come in all shapes and sizes. It's another form of warfare.

But this group, I think as I watch them train, *are special.* They always will be. Thom throws everything into their training, and they dig deep inside themselves so as to return it.

They run through target practice, static and in motion. There's hand to hand combat and long range marksmanship. I'm impressed with the speed at which they learn the new skills. Thom has picked them with the utmost care and it doesn't take a genius to see why he's selected those he has.

Each of them has lost someone. No surprise there. But instead of falling apart, they have a stillness about them, an expectation, a hunger. The weapon is all that matters. They are becoming weapons. He's forging a warrior elite.

I join in myself, for a while, but the way they watch me and step away from me rather than engage soon grates. They aren't just an elite. He's selected them for something else, and I realise suddenly, standing in their midst, what that is. They all look to me, with a devotion that outshines even the way they look to Con. A different kind of respect and admiration. Fierce and terrible. As if they would do anything for me. They were to be mine then, a Queen's Guard.

I retreat and watch them again. The weapons training makes me think of Shae and the need to crawl under a pile of blankets and never come out again, the need I fight daily, rears its head again. What would he say, if he saw them? That I deserve it? But I don't. Not of the Anthaese. I'm such a fraud. I'm not their queen and I might never be. With the fall of Anthaeus, I don't know what the Empire has decreed. If they have abandoned this world to the Gravians, or if I still have a role to play. Other than that of a soldier, that is. I don't know what I am any more. I'm a lost soul, denied entry to the halls of my ancestors. That makes me think of Shae again and I offer up a prayer for him, that he's at peace. That makes the pain sharpen all over again.

The only time the veil of grief lifts is on a raid, waiting in the trees, ready to fight. When I have a purpose of my own.

Con joins me in my observation, quiet and watchful as ever. He doesn't say a word, although he looks as if he wants to. I wish I could share my thoughts, but I don't know where to begin.

'How are your machines?' I ask, more to have something to say than anything else.

Con smiles, a distant, troubled expression. Not good then. 'In need of the appropriate parts, like a signal booster. How are your recruits?'

'They try.' I don't share my suspicions. 'But they are getting better.'

'These other groups...'

I know what he's thinking, the same temptation that I would have given into in a heartbeat if I could. 'We can't contact them. It would put you at risk.'

'Oh, *me*. It's all about *me*.' Bitterness twists his voice.

I need to be patient with him, gentle. I'm terrible at that.

'Yes, Con. I'm afraid it is. What if you were captured? And them too. What if we led the Gravians to them, or did something to make them give themselves away?'

He reaches out, as if to touch my hand, but stops. I swallow and force my skittish heart to be calm. I want very much to reach out to him as well, to offer him some comfort. Because though he hides it beneath a strong and determined exterior, though he holds himself together for everyone else, he needs comfort and support too. He blames himself for everything that is happening. Tortures himself.

'Look!' he says suddenly and points skywards. From where we sit, through a gap in the canopy, we can see vapour trails crossing the sky, white ghostly lines against the blue. They twist in on each other, an elaborate pattern becoming more complex by the second.

'It's a dogfight.' I stand up so quickly my head swims, but I can't sit down again. My heart thunders against the inside of my ribcage, my breath jamming up inside me. 'Five... no, six of them. Those are Vairian ships, those three. They're Falcons. Two of them are. The other... I'm not sure. But they're Vairian!'

All over the clearing, people stop what they're doing, all over the encampment. They come out of the tents and shelters, standing with their faces tilted to the sky. Some, like Petra and Thom, know what's happening, can trace the manoeuvres, the lines of that deadly dance. It's bewitching, terrible. It could end in flames at any second, but I can't tear my gaze away.

They're fighting up there. They're fighting, trying to get through the blockade. My heart forces its way up my throat but I can't stop watching. Con's hand closes on mine, holding me tightly.

The explosion is so distant, a puff of smoke and the flare of a match.

A ship spirals down.

'Who is it?' Con asks. 'One of us or one of them?'

'One of them!' I gasp out the words. 'Ancestors bless us, it's one of them.'

I follow its fall. The flyer vanishes into the mountains to the north and a plume of smoke replaces it.

A cheer goes up. People hug each other and grin, laugh out loud. It's a moment of pure joy. And we need this. We need it so much.

But the dogfight isn't over yet. The next explosion wipes a Vairian ship from the sky and the joy shatters. I choke back a cry, smothering it as debris plummets towards the mountains. No way anyone is getting out of that one. It isn't possible. I don't want to think about it. Can't let myself give in to that. Someone is in it. One of my people, one of my own.

And all around the encampment, *my* people are watching. My new people, those who really need me now.

Two ships break off, a Vairian and a Gravian. I know the tactic. He's leading one away, breaking up the threat. I hope. The roar of a sonic boom shakes the air, sends leaves swirling down over us. Everyone instinctively ducks.

Birds scatter from the trees and the noise explodes in my chest. I can't tear my gaze from the sky. I'm frozen, watching helpless as it unfolds before me.

They speed down, roaring over the treetops, shaking the world around us. I stretch up on my toes, trying to see. I need higher ground. I need to see.

'Do it,' I whisper, to myself, but also to that pilot, whoever it is. 'Do it.'

The Vairian ship flips. High in the sky overhead, it heads higher and then loops back on itself. It's a risky move, dangerous, but he's good. So good. It's like watching a master swordsman. The Gravian can't adjust and speeds by, straight into the Vairian ship's targeting range. Everything seems to slow down, to pause. I stare into the sky, aching with the need to do something, to help in some way, but there's nothing I can do. Nothing any of us can do. I hear someone gasp, someone else start to pray. And then I see it – the Vairian fires. Streaks of white shoot from the front of the ship, straight at the Gravian.

The shots are good. I know it before they strike home, directly on the Gravian engine coil. It bucks in the sky, shudders, and for a second there's nothing. Nothing at all. The whole thing goes up in a fireball, the ship igniting and shattering into pieces.

'Yes!' I scream the word, but too soon. The Vairian flyer – a Falcon, I can see it now clearly, it's a Falcon with Imperial markings, a Vairian ship in service to the Imperial fleet – jerks awkwardly, shrapnel striking it. A Falcon is short range, not designed for a space flight. Which means that there has to be another ship. A bigger ship. One to get it here, to drop it into the atmosphere.

The Falcon's engine splutters, fails and the ship jolts back in the air.

'No,' I say and Con pulls me closer, hoping to protect me from what will happen next, what is inevitable.

The Falcon goes down, spinning out of control. The impact shakes the earth and the air alike. I feel the breath sucked out of my lungs and I pull free.

'We have to help!' I yell, sprinting for the Dragonfly before anyone can stop me. Con runs after me, calling to me to wait, but all I can think is that the pilot might still be alive. He might have survived. Someone from Vairian in one of our ships. Someone I might know. He could have information, might be able to tell us if help is coming. Ancestors defend us, help has to be coming.

It might even be Zander.

It can't be. I know that, logically. They'd never let him out in a dogfight. Not when he's the Crown Prince.

But it could be.

He's stubborn, my brother. Like me.

I vault into the cockpit of the Dragonfly. Con's hands close on the edge before I can close the hatch. 'You can't. Please, Bel. *Think*. You can't just go.'

'I have to. Who else is there? I'm not fighting, I swear. I have to help them.'

'No one could survive that.'

'Yes. They could. Someone in a Falcon could. I promise. I know this. Please Con, I'll stay low, out of trouble. Get the others, and tell them to follow me. Please.'

He steps away, releasing me. Amazed, I can only stare for a moment and then my instincts kick in. I slam the controls forward, ignoring the shouts of Thom and Petra, and take to the air, trusting that they'll follow. They know their way around a cockpit and the other ships they saved are mostly operational now. Or they'll come on foot through the trees. It'll just take longer, but I know. They'll follow me. Because they have to, or I'll have to do this alone.

Chapter Nineteen

The Dragonfly darts between the trees, responding to my every touch, almost before I move the controls. Con had worked on it more than I'd known. Normally I'd revel in her, in the speed and the way she moves, but there isn't time. I push her to give me all she has. And she does. All she has and more.

The crash zone is a scar in the hillside, away from the forest. Thick smoke comes from the downed craft but I can still tell that I have the right one. A Vairian Falcon is unmistakable to me. I would know it anywhere. The only ship I know better is a Wasp. I hook over the debris, letting my Dragonfly glide low. The central section is intact, though the wings and tail are shredded. There's hope.

I set down safely away from the crash site and sprint across the space between. Open ground is dangerous, and I know I can't afford to be caught out here. Or even seen. But I can't just leave the pilot there.

I scrabble with the hatch and finally manage to open it. The whine of a gun charging makes me duck.

'Don't fire. I'm a friend. Hold your fire!'

The whine fades and I stand up again, pushing the hatch open cautiously. The pilot lies in her seat, her mask hanging down, the helmet pushed back. Her whole chest is a bloody mess, but she still holds the gun in an unshaking hand.

'Who are you?' I say, but I see the recognition in the pilot's eyes.

'Princess?' She struggles to rise but fails, coughing up blood.

'No. I mean yes, but don't try to move. Help's coming. Stay there. Help's on the way.'

Help had better be on the way because she isn't going anywhere. She's dying in front of my eyes.

'Help,' she says and tries to smile. 'We came to help you.' Her eyes search my face. 'Your brother... your brother brought us... Prince Lysander...'

'He's okay? He's alive?'

'Yes, Highness. Fighting... every battle, trying to break the blockade above the outer atmosphere.'

Zander...

I wrap my hand around the pilot's hand, squeezing it, but she doesn't seem to feel anything. She doesn't react. 'What's your name?'

Where are the others? Maybe they haven't followed. Maybe I've lost them. I curse mentally.

The pilot's voice is the faintest whisper. 'Devra. Devra Colvil of Masonis.'

'I remember Masonis. There are pine forests and a lake.'

'I lived... Princess...'

Her breath rattles in her throat.

'Devra? Devra, please.' I reach across her, trying to feel for a pulse and knowing already that it is too late. Far too late.

The radio unit crackles, and a voice breaks through.

'Report, 371-alpha. Check in.'

I freeze, staring at it, as if to deny the voice that's coming from it. From beyond the blockade, from a command ship – it has to be. A Vairian command ship.

Muttering under my breath, prayers and curses and anything else that came to mind, I pull the helmet gently off Devra's head and shove it on my own.

It had better be a secure transmission. Or I'm dead.

'Control? This is Belengaria. Come in.' *Please, please, please…*

'My Lady?' The voice is startled, horrified. There's a scramble of activity at the other end, frantic mutterings and then a voice. A wonderful, dreamed-for voice.

'Bel?'

Zander. I let out a whoop of delight.

The engine bursts into sparks and billows out black smoke. A hiss fills my ears. 'No!'

Zander's voice dissolves into static.

But I could bring it back with me, couldn't I? Con will be able to fix it. I just need to get it out without damaging it. I lean it, trying to work my fingers around the edges of the unit.

'*Bel, look out! Behind you!*'

Con's voice bursts into my mind, as clear as if we are sitting together, as if we are in the hive mind and linked together. For a moment I'm too shocked to respond, and then the words filter through.

Behind you!

Something glances off the helmet, heat searing against my cheek. Plasma fire. If I hadn't been wearing the helmet it would have taken my head off.

I snatch the plasma gun from Devra's unresisting hand and throw myself to one side, as weapon fire bursts against the side of the ship, tearing through the hull. The material rips like paper, the stench of plasma filling the air. I hit the ground and roll, bringing my own weapon up.

A Gravian pilot lurches over the rim of the crash site, his weapon trained on me. He's lost his helmet and his face is a ghastly chalk, his hair almost shaved to the scalp. No Mecha implants that I could see. No enhancements at all. That doesn't mean he isn't dangerous. I fire, hitting his shoulder, but that doesn't stop him. It doesn't even slow him down.

Think, Bel. Think!

Where are the others? Why did I go off on my own?

The swirling hypersensitivity of the hive mind settles on me, and I see the world as I had before, soaring above it with Con.

Everything sharpens into pained focus. The Gravian comes towards me, snarling, his teeth bare and his mouth so very red around them.

I fire again, twice in quick succession, full in the stomach, again in the knees, because I'm too shocked that I hit him to aim properly. He jerks and goes down. Blood splatters my face and I realise he's only a few feet away. Right on top of me.

My heart thunders against my ribs, threatening to tear itself out. The world blurs and I'm wrung out, empty.

'Bel!' It's Petra, calling to me. But I can't find the strength to answer, or the voice. 'Bel, are you hurt? Bel, answer me!'

They pull me out of the wreckage, dragging me with hands that are violent with their terror, the fear that they have lost me.

'Ancestors,' Thom says, amid a thousand muttered curses. 'Thank the ancestors. We thought... we thought...'

I struggle free of them and lurch to the cockpit of the downed Falcon. Someone has removed Devra's body, but there's blood everywhere. Still, I force my way inside, reaching into the panel and tugging out the unit I want. I'm too late. The radio is dead.

*

As soon as I'm back at the camp, I make for the Rondet, sure that had to be where Con has hidden himself away. But he isn't there. The door won't even open.

'Where is he?' No one answers. I feel numb, lost, and empty. Devra's dead and I almost died. I should have died. And yet here I am, and somewhere out there people are dying trying to get through the blockade, trying to bring help. I spoke to the Vairian flagship, I'd heard Zander's voice. And here I am, hiding in the woods, farting around with guerrilla raids and picking off convoys. It can't go on.

'Where is Con?' I shout, frustrated beyond belief.

No one moves. At length, Jondar nods to the shelter which Con had commandeered as his workroom. I push open the door, and step inside.

Something fills the middle of the one room. A construction that can only have come from Con's unique mind.

It doesn't look like a communications system. That's what I'd been told he was building when I was ill. But this… I'm not entirely sure what it looks like – cobbled together, a cannibal machine made up of bits and pieces, cranks and gears, valves and crystals, and threaded throughout with a rainbow of coloured wires.

I reach out, fascinated, my anger and despair suddenly melting away.

'Don't touch it!' Con's voice snaps out from somewhere underneath. How he saw me I don't know. He just seems to sense the threat to his creation from my bumbling fingers.

'All right,' I assure him. 'Just looking.'

'You don't have eyes in your hands,' he replies, anger making his tone bitter.

'What does it do? Does it work?'

He mutters something that I can't quite make out. From the tone it's probably better that way. Not very regal.

I just survived a firefight with a Gravian. I'm not putting up with this from a disgruntled engineer. I'm feeling positively reckless. 'That well?'

'I'm working on it.'

The frustration in his tone makes me pause and regret my taunting. An uncomfortable silence stretches out. He warned me at the crashed ship. He helped me. I'd heard his voice, and he'd helped me in some way, helped me to be faster than the Gravian. I don't know how and it doesn't seem possible. Had he been with the Rondet? Had they reached out to me somehow? But it had been his voice I heard. Unmistakably. I'd be dead without him.

And yet now… now… I don't know what to say. Neither, it seems, does he. I left him. I flew away to an uncertain fate and almost got myself killed. And if he did warn me, then he knew the danger I was in.

So he does what he always does. He talks about something else entirely. His work, this invention, whatever it is.

'The harmonics are wrong. I was hoping some of the local crystals would compensate but I need… so many things. This room is all wrong. I don't have the parts.'

'Tell me what you need. I said I'll get it for you.'

'Haven't we been through this?'

'No, we haven't.' At least not out loud. Over these past two months I have learned that Con sometimes means to tell me things, but forgets, thinking that he has already done so. Or writes it down so he doesn't have to remember. And then loses the note in the scramble to get the work done.

'I made a list and put it somewhere. Over there.' His hand appears and waves towards a jumble of papers and equipment beneath which might conceivably be a desk. Perhaps. 'Part of a list anyway.' He sounds so distracted I almost smile. But that would just irritate him more. Not that he'd be able to see from under there, but somehow, he'd know. He'd figure it out. I'm sure of it. 'A signal booster for one, but we aren't going to find one of those lying around.'

'Depends on what we knock over first, I suppose. Or we might find one just lying around.'

Con pauses in his work, the sound of clanks and tinkering halting. 'I don't like that tone. It's a foolhardy tone.'

'Yes, your Majesty.' My voice is all sweetness. So, he gets edgy when I tease him. I'll have to remember that. I need to do it more, if only for this reaction. Being in danger makes the thrill of being back here with him even more exhilarating. Plus, I know what I have in my hands. I'm anticipating the reaction. I can't wait. 'Are you going to come out and see what I've brought you then?'

He pushes himself out. There's oil in his hair again, staining the gold with its darkness. His eyes have dark circles around them and he looks painfully drawn. I know he's been under strain, but he looks terrible. I wonder when he last ate. The momentary thrill of teasing him fades away.

His eyes latch on to the Vairian radio unit in my hands, the one that comes with a signal booster built in. Their colour ignites, bright green and terrible to behold, the eyes of an obsessive or an addict.

'You got one?'

'I hope it's the right thing. And I may have broken it getting it out.' Not to mention the blood on it. Even I know sticky liquids and finely balanced machinery aren't a good mix. But I don't want to say that to Con. Not the sort of joke to make right now. Thom or Petra might get it, but not the Anthaem. He doesn't have their black humour. He isn't a fighter, except when it counts most. Except when I had needed him, when I could have been dead without his warning. How did he do it? He saved me. My engineer. Besides which, Devra died in that ship. The amusement dies with that thought. But still, I need to know how he warned me. 'Con, when I was back there…'

He waves my words away as he takes the booster, and examined it, turning it over gingerly with his hands. It's the most important thing in the world right now.

'I can fix this.'

I smile, heartened by his obvious delight. Explanations of how and why can wait. I'm just relieved. One good thing has come from this debacle. One good thing.

He sets it down with the greatest of care and turns to me again, trapping me with his solemn gaze.

'What is it?' I ask.

'Bel, I thought… I thought…' But words fail him. Frustration makes him wince and I wonder what on earth is the matter now? Isn't he happy with the radio?

Con grabs my arms, pulls me into his embrace and kisses me.

It's no courtly kiss, no peck on the cheek or the hand. His arms wrap around me and his lips meet mine. I stiffen with shock and an unexpected vibration of desire shakes its way through my body.

I freeze, feeling his warmth, his touch, smelling the oil and sweat with the scent of him beneath it. Beguiling, bewitching. He doesn't have to do this. He doesn't have to marry me any more. Why is he kissing me? But I can't think about that right now. I can't think about anything but this kiss. My breath is caught in my throat. My heart beats so hard I can hear it and I stare at his half-lidded eyes, the sliver of green so bright. He moves his jaw as he kisses me in a way that makes warmth spread through me, coiling in my abdomen. My eyes slide shut in surrender. And my heartbeat has become everything.

My heartbeat and his. I can feel it too, echoing through his body and into mine.

Since Shae, nothing and no one has moved me. In an instant all my walls crumble.

The kiss breaks and he pulls away, as though suddenly aware of what he has done, that I'm not responding. Con studies me and his face falls solemn again. Disappointment, followed by a large dose of shock at what he just did. 'I shouldn't have... I didn't mean... I'm sorry, Bel.'

But he isn't sorry. Not really. Not for what he just did. I can see that in the new glow infecting the depths of his eyes. No. Con isn't sorry at all.

'Liar,' I whisper back and lean in to kiss him myself. I'm not sure who, between the two of us, is more surprised as my lips brush his, as my arms wrap around his neck. He makes a noise of submission this time, deep in his throat and I melt at the sound. Something fierce and primal in the base of my brain whispers. *Mine.*

And I mean it, I realise. I really mean it. I'm not here with him because I have a duty, or because I have a job to do. I'm not here because my father and the Empress sent me. I can't leave him. Not now.

'I thought this time I was really going to lose you,' he whispers against me, like a confession.

I shake my head, nuzzling into his skin. He smells like oil and plasma, and underneath that, like Con. Or maybe that's all part of his scent, that heady mixture which shouldn't be quite this intoxicating. 'I heard you. You warned me.'

'I tried to. I was in the Rondet, communing with them, trying to see...'

'But you *did*. You saved me. You helped me. I should have waited. I know that. But Devra... the pilot would have died alone, if I hadn't.

Con, she would have…' And abruptly, my tears come too, tears and sobs and all the emptiness I had tried to hide.

'Don't,' he says. 'Don't. Please. It wasn't your fault.'

He whispers my name and holds me until I find myself again, find the strength I need. I struggled back into the shell of control, of self-containment that will let me speak again. I wipe my face but don't pull away from him. I can't.

'You need to fix the communications device. Zander's out there. I heard him. I made contact and that means that booster is powerful enough. We can coordinate this. And we've got to. It's got to stop. We have to get them off Anthaeus.'

Chapter Twenty

Con doesn't sleep, that's the problem. Even when he does go to bed, he'll be up again soon afterwards with an idea to try, a plan to jot down, or a design to amend. His inventions might be giving his people what they need to survive and fight, but they're slowly killing him. I can see it. But there's nothing I can do about it. Nothing except try to keep an eye on him, try to keep him from being his own worst enemy.

The way Shae looked after me, I suppose. Duty, of course, but more than duty. Whenever I think of him something inside me twists. I can't help it. He should be here, not me. Or at least he should be here with me. And then, whenever I think that, I think of Con and the guilt of it all nearly smothers me. I can't help myself. I thought it was difficult when Shae was alive. Now, every thought of Con is tinged with a memory of Shae. Even the kiss. I'm a terrible human being.

In a camp this size, there are few secrets. Not with everyone heaped on top of each other. Con sleeps, in theory at least, no more than five feet away from me most nights. I'm keenly aware of it, the sound of him, the scent of him, everywhere I go. It's like my body is tuned to his, reacting to his presence. I watch him as carefully as Jondar, guarding him in the same way Thom and Petra guard me. Although with Con, the greatest threat looks to be himself. I try to, and sometimes I can, draw him away from slaving at the communications system, or the

Dragonflies, of whatever else has captured his attention, just for a little while. When he's exhausted, I make him rest, or go with him to the Rondet which rests his body if not his mind. I sit at the Council with him, make sure he eats, and try so hard to keep him whole.

I want to explore the kiss more, but I'm not sure how to approach it. Not now. It isn't as if I can flirt. It isn't in my nature to begin with, and the camp is not the place to do it. We're fighting a war, after all. But it wasn't the polite kiss of the Anthaem. That passion was all Con, and it stunned me. There's no political need for it. No reason behind it other than… that he might actually care. Something about that frightens me. It's almost too much to bear, with everything we've lost, everything we stand to lose. The thought of losing him… I can't. Duty and love are bad bedfellows, I know that better than anyone. So I just try to be there for him, with him, and try to make sure – in my own way – that he's protected.

Our mission almost goes horribly wrong a few days later, when we're pinned down by multiple snipers behind a rock outcrop. It's only when I feel the touch of Rhenna's mind on mine that I can see the positions of the enemy combatants in my mind. No sense of Con, this time. But I count to three, breathe out and come up in a rush, three shots taking out three snipers and I'm down again, staring at Jondar and Thom's startled faces. Behind them, one of the Anthaese starts saying a prayer of thanks. He's looking at me the way they look at Con, the way they looked at Matilde. So be it, I decide. Let them believe whatever they want.

I need to get back to Con. That's all that matters.

In the meantime, my recklessness is catching. Jondar is showing off, I suspect in my ungracious moments, now that Con and I spend more time together. Or perhaps he just doesn't care if he dies any more. I try to tell Con that much, one evening as we sit with the Rondet. But he just smiles.

'You would recognise that in another, I suppose.' He links his fingers with mine as he speaks and his touch feels like coming home. Something I couldn't bear to lose now. I'm not so reckless all of a sudden.

'Just doing what needs to be done, Anthaem.'

A smile tugs at his lips, more resigned than happy. 'It's getting more dangerous. The last raid… you barely got out in time.'

'I know. They're starting to anticipate us. Or at least prepare more thoroughly.'

'Anticipating…' he says. 'But at least we have this.'

'*Glad to hear we are but an advantage.*' Rhenna has a teasing tone in her voice.

'He should be resting, not here communing.' I'm not in the mood for Rhenna's games.

'*So tetchy,*' is her only reply.

'Almost got shot today.' If Rhenna is going to accuse me of tetchiness, I might as well own it. 'Again.'

'*We saved you.*' Aeron doesn't sound in the humour for games either. '*Again.*' Petulance, maybe, but not games. Their guidance is invaluable. Their moods, less so.

'Besides,' Con interrupts, the eternal peacemaker. 'Being here is restful. Close your eyes, Bel.' He draws me against him, kisses the top of my head, his arms wrapping around me. I want to lift my face to his, to kiss him, to do so much more than kiss. We would have been married by now, if things had been different. We might never be now. And yet… I don't want to think about that. The fear of loss – the way I lose everyone I care about – is too great. But Con has other matters on his mind. I can't bother him with my doubts and fears. In spite of everything I close my eyes as he asks. There's very little I can deny him. It happened so suddenly, but it also feels like it was happening from the first moment we met. What would Shae say to me? Would he be angry? Jealous?

I can't think about that. It's not that I push thoughts of him away. It's more like I wrap them up carefully, like an heirloom, and store them for another time.

'Can you show me my brother?' I ask. But all I see are stars. So many stars. Zander is still too far away. But at least I know that he's there. He's definitely there.

*

Jondar remains a problem. He stalks around the camp, his sword at his side, his eyes finding fault with everything. I don't know what to say to him, or even if I should try. He insists on accompanying me on every raid. He's not a soldier. True, I've seen him joining in the training sessions and his skill with that sword is undeniable, but he's a courtier at heart and always will be. He wasn't made for war. However, like Thom and Petra, Jondar seems to have appointed himself my bodyguard. Maybe he's just determined to bring me back alive to Con, no matter what. Maybe he blames himself for landing me here where a princess is no longer needed. But soldiers are. I'm not sure he's able to see me that way. I'm always going to be a dishevelled girl in a muddy flight suit who burst in on his meeting with my father.

The raids themselves are increasingly difficult. For every plan we lay, it seems that the Gravians have already anticipated it. The supply lines start to dry up, and easy raids are now pitched battles. I throw myself into planning and when word filters through that a transfer of food and prisoners is taking place on an old route, one of the first we ever attacked in the days of our greatest successes, I want to fall on them headlong. We know everything about that route, every hiding place, every bolt-hole. But I pause, studying the details.

'What is it?' Con asks, as I pour over the maps of the forest. He puts down a bowl of fragrant stew with black bread on the side and pushes it towards me, right across the section I was studying. I frown at him, but he just wears the same patient face I use on him at moments like this, so I take it and eat while I explain.

'Something strange, maybe. Or something good. I'm not sure.'

'Then we don't go.'

I glare at him for a long moment. I know what's on his mind, perhaps better than he does. 'Well, *you* don't. That's for sure.'

Con shrugs, frustrated and annoyed. 'As if they'd let me.'

My smile creeps across my lips. 'No. We're lucky they let me.'

'Ah.' He returns the smile, with a little cynical twist. 'If Jondar thought he could stop you, he would. Besides which, I doubt they'd have the first clue without you.'

'Not true. Your hunters, your guards—'

'*Your* guards. Petra and Thom are an inspiration. So many try to emulate them. But the people follow you, Bel. Do you still doubt that?'

I shake my head. 'Only because of you.' But my face heats all the same. Why would they follow me? I'm not Anthaese. I never will be, as everyone was so fond of reminding me before the invasion. I don't know how to fit in, how to be anything other than I am. Eventually, somehow, we'll drive the Gravians off and then what? What good is an alliance now for either of our worlds or the Empire? And if I'm of no use to them here, will they whisk me off to be a pawn somewhere else?

What would Shae say? I close my eyes and I can picture him, frowning as usual. He'd tell me to stop moping and get on with things. To do my duty. Like a Vairian.

Con reaches out and brushes a stray lock of hair back from my face, tucking it behind my ear. 'You're a wonder, my princess. Funny how the person who takes the most convincing is you.'

I shake my head in disbelief, which he seems to find even more amusing. But really. I'm here in cast-off clothing, bits and pieces of fatigues and body armour instead of the elegant gowns of the court. My hair is a knot at the back of my head rather than the sleek and beautiful hairstyles I once wore. I'm sure I've probably got mud on my face again.

He leans in closer, and I gaze into his green eyes, see myself reflected there. I part my lips on a breath and feel that same flush that colours my face spread all over my body. My eyes close as Con kisses me, his lips gentle but demanding, intoxicating. I just want this, that's all. Being a princess, a queen or even a warrior, doesn't seem to matter any more. I just need him.

A subtle cough interrupts us and we spring apart, trying to disguise what has just been happening, while I curse inwardly. Both at the interruption and our reaction. We've never been easy together, not with so many eyes on us. And we were never going to get the luxury of the time we need. Or so it seems. We need to get used to that.

'Your Majesty,' says Jondar, apparently looking at anything other than the two of us. 'Your Highness, we're ready.'

'You're coming with me?' I already know the answer to that.

'Yes,' says Con, before Jondar can answer. Suddenly I realise why Jondar is always there. Con looks guilty. My frown takes just a moment to work and he rushes to explain. 'I've asked him to. I want you kept safe. No arguments.'

And there aren't. Not out loud. So that's what's been happening. In my mind, I rail against him, and against Jondar's presence, but he is the Anthaem. So there's nothing I can do about it.

Con too can be devious, and I never for a moment guessed it.

*

We wait in the shadows of the massive oaks, crouching in undergrowth. I've said it before, ambushes are the worst. But what else can I do? We don't have the tactical advantages needed for an outright battle. Not yet.

The attack comes in an instant, sudden and swift, the moment the supply caravan hoves into view. There are prisoners, more than before and many of them have clearly been in captivity from the first. They are starved, worked to the bone and desperate. At the first sign of attack, where others might have panicked or fled, or even fought to be free, they only stand where they are, or sink to the ground, helpless. Like they can't believe what's happening, like they have nothing left inside them.

I take on the nearest Gravian troops, three Mechas and their pale masters who fight back with a vicious effectiveness. We haven't encountered troops like this before. Fresh in and dangerous. They have things to prove. The Mechas under their command fling themselves at the Anthaese, firing shot after shot. More armaments have been built into them, more targeting equipment. The guards on either side of me go down in a hail of bullets and I throw myself aside. Getting into the cover of a boulder by scrabbling along the ground, I try to centre myself. The earth shakes and they are coming. I know they're coming.

Terror tastes metallic in the back of my throat. I reload, and brace myself as the first one tears towards me. Where are the others? Where's

Thom? It doesn't matter, can't matter now. I only have myself or I'm dead. Weapons fire sears the air over my head, smacks into the nearest tree and leaves it smoking and creaking. *Wait*, I tell myself. *You have to wait.*

I burst from my cover, firing at the Mecha until it collapses. Another rears up behind it and I fire again. To no effect. It has a personal shield. No one gives a Mecha a personal shield. Why would they? They're disposable. This is different. Dangerous. This feels wrong. How many of them have shields?

This is a trap.

It bears down on me. I catch glimpses of the man it had once been behind the implants. He'd been so young, I think with a kind of abstract fascination that means my mind has already accepted I can do nothing now.

The sword comes out of nowhere. It bursts through the Mecha's chest, cutting through internal organs and circuitry with brutal efficiency. The thing falls, a heap of metal and flesh and Jondar stands there instead. He doesn't hesitate, just grabs my arm.

'Quickly, we have to regroup.'

I don't have time to argue or question but stumble along with him. Thom yells as we come into view and immediately I'm surrounded again. Safe. And I watch as Jondar throws himself into the fight once more, wielding those ridiculous swords I'd thought of as an affectation with startling skill against the shielded Mechas.

The shields have a weakness after all. Anthaese steel. I take a deep, calming breath. I've focused on blasters and plasma rifles. Modern weapons, not ancient ones.

How many swords can we get hold of? I'll get Thom on to it as soon as possible.

The battle, such as it is, doesn't take that long. I watch, out of the combat area now, as we finish it. Driven back, the Gravians fight hard, but not as hard as the Anthaese, who need to help their own.

I find Jondar, sitting down, his long legs splayed out in front of him, catching his breath perhaps, or lost in thought.

'Thank you,' I say. He looks up at me, startled. 'You saved me.'

'I… of course I did. It's my duty, Princess.'

Of course it is. Why would I have thought otherwise? I sigh. 'Because he asked you to. You've nothing to prove to me, Jondar.'

His face falls, the expression freezes. 'Because he loves you.'

And not him. Oh ancestors, I didn't mean that. I can see the agony on his features. I say it, even though I shouldn't. 'And you love him.'

The world seems to jolt to a stop. Then, Jondar pushes himself to his feet. 'I saved you because you were in danger, Bel. Because we need you.' And with that, he stalks off. I hesitate to follow him. I should just keep my mouth shut. I'm an idiot.

The prisoners stumble free, though I suspect they barely notice. The trauma is evident on every face. Shock, horror too great to fathom. Where were they being taken? If they were so useless now that they were just being disposed of, then why not just slaughter them wherever they'd been held? I don't want to think about it. I pick my way along the caravan as my warriors sort through the useful equipment and supplies, and I try to help those we've rescued.

And then one voice rings out over all the rest. 'Princess? Princess Belengaria? Please!'

My feet are rooted to the spot, unable to move, unable to believe what I'm hearing.

Elara? It can't be. Elara's dead. Elara *has* to be dead, because otherwise—

'Princess, please!'

I tear towards the voice, racing back along the caravan, throwing back covers and searching the hollow faces I find there. I stumble, and grab the bars to hold myself up, scrambling to my feet again.

'Elara? Where are you? *Elara?*'

It's her. It has to be her. I know her voice. I can't believe we gave up and just believed her dead. All this time.

I find her in one of the cages, ragged and beaten, her face almost unrecognisable. Soldiers force the door open and Elara scrambles towards me. I seize her in fierce arms and Elara sobs out her relief. Tearless, desperate sobs, sounds which wrench their way out of her like an act of violence.

'I didn't tell them anything, Highness. I didn't tell them anything. They had a machine, a terrible machine. But I didn't tell them anything.'

It's a miracle. We'd lost her and now here she is, back, like an emissary of all the ghosts of those we've lost. One life saved. One person home. I hold her close and tears stream down my face.

'I'm sorry,' is all I can say to her. 'I'm sorry.'

Jondar sprints from the far end of the caravan where he had been overseeing the unloading of the meagre medical supplies found there. He comes to an abrupt halt, his face white as marble, his hands twitching as if looking for something to do but finding nothing.

'Elara?' he whispers.

She cries out and shies away from him, hiding behind me and sobbing.

'It's okay,' I tell her. 'It's just Jondar. Elara, please. You're safe now. We have you.'

But Elara just babbles, and won't calm down until Thom escorts Jondar away.

'We'll go home.' I speak calmly to her but she just sits there in her rags and shudders. 'It will be fine, Elara, you'll see.'

But Elara won't, or can't, answer.

Chapter Twenty-One

Back at our camp, Jondar stands by the door to Con's command tent, his arms folded, his rage simmering. He won't leave, won't sit down, just stands there vibrating with anger. And Elara won't see him.

'How long did they have her?'

I sit on the travel chest, elbows on my knees, my head in my hands. 'Long enough. More than long enough.'

Con hasn't stopped pacing. 'What has she said?'

'Nothing. Just that she didn't say anything. So they interrogated her. At length. And worse. She's a beautiful woman. You can guess what else they've done.'

Colour drains from Con's face.

'Will she—' Jondar stops, clears his throat. 'Will she recover?'

'Who knows? I left her with Dr Halie. It depends on so many things. She isn't the only one, Jondar.' *She can't cope with any man near her. She only seems to truly feel safe near me.*

'I'm painfully aware of that, Highness.' He spits out the words.

'Jondar,' Con snaps, his patience shattered. 'We're *all* aware. This is hardly a shock. That it's Elara… of course… But there *are* so many others. We have learned what cruelties the Gravians are capable of. They revel in them. If they wanted information from her, I'm stunned they didn't get it, which says more about her than I could have imagined.

We're livestock to them, understand? Slaves and cattle. We need to be aware of what we're up against. What they'll do to us and to our land. They have to be stopped.'

'By any means necessary,' I add. 'But you have to be prepared to pay a price. We got lucky today, and lucky if it's true, that she didn't tell them anything of use. It won't always be that way.'

'We are prepared.'

'Not really. Not yet. But you will be. When those we rescued today start telling their stories. When people see Elara. When we go to rescue more tomorrow.'

*

While our raids continue, the Gravians are still better prepared. With the Dragonflies Con has adapted, we can fly further afield, but that just seems to make matters worse. Convoys take different routes at the last minute, or are more heavily guarded than before, usually more than we can deal with. Word of the last raid spreads quickly, and everyone is talking about it now. Thom can't praise Jondar highly enough. Next thing I know, they're always together. Jondar joins in training the recruits and glows with purpose. Swords are the new weapon of choice, alongside plasma guns and any number of knives. Especially now that we know the steel works against the shields. And Jondar knows how to handle a sword better than anyone I've ever known. Except Shae. Because I still firmly believe there is... was... nothing Shae couldn't do.

I have to push thoughts of Shae to the back of my mind. Whenever they reappear everything becomes jumbled and confused. I don't know what to think so I prefer not to think about it at all. Guilt isn't a good sensation. It's bewildering at a time when I need to focus. I should just stop, stop feeling things for Con, stop worrying about him. Stop thinking about him.

If anything Jondar seems more reticent with me than ever. Even though he saved my life, I'm not under any illusions. It doesn't make us any closer. It couldn't.

I know his secret, his desires and have no problem with that. But the object of his affections is another matter. Con.

I glance at them now, deep in conversation over a sprawl of maps. They laugh together, argue and debate. They are friends. How would Con react to the revelation, if he ever found out?

I want to think he'd be okay. He doesn't have it in him to be a bigot. But to be the object, to be the one Jondar loves...

He can't find out. If wouldn't be fair to any of us. And that's what Jondar fears, that Con would discover the secret. I should never have said it out loud. It's too big of a burden for any of us.

It's none of my business. I don't want it to be something I have to deal with. Shae would know what to do, wouldn't he? Sometimes, in spite of all I share with Con, I miss him so much it's painful, actually painful. My mind goes back to that moment in the garden, while the ball glittered on beyond the doors. When he kissed me. It wasn't like Con's kiss. I don't know how to compare them. And I probably shouldn't.

The two of them are night and day. I love them both.

Loved them both. Loved Shae.

Jondar isn't the problem. Shae is the ghost that lingers on, standing between Con and myself.

*

I return to a subdued camp with little to show for the last week, and the start of a headache pounding at the back of my head. Dinner is a dish of eggs and smoked meat, with small black mushrooms and dry bread which is fast running out. Hardly the luxurious banquets of the Anthaese court. The memory of them seems like a wild fantasy now. We need more supplies and I have nothing to show for the day. Not today. All the same no one seems ready to complain. Not even Elara, but then Elara never complains about anything these days. She sits in silence most of the time, and gazes wide-eyed at anyone who approaches. She's been here a week and only engages with one person. Me.

'I don't like it,' Jondar says as she settles herself across from me to eat. 'She's changed.'

It probably doesn't help that people like him talk about her like she isn't there. But at least he's talking to me. And about a safe subject.

'Of course she's changed.'

'Leave it, Jon.' With a brief nod, Con accepts a cup of the bitter wine from one of his company and joins us. 'Don't. She's right there.'

'It's not as if she's even listening.'

I look up, directly into Elara's wide, vacant eyes across from me. She is listening. No doubt about that. She just isn't reacting.

She's always listening.

A chill creeps through my body and my appetite evaporates. No one takes care with what they say around Elara, especially not now. She's in the heart of the camp, trusted by everyone, able to go anywhere. By my side all the time.

Because I trust her.

They had a machine, she had said. *But I didn't tell them anything.* What if they hadn't wanted her to tell them anything? What sort of machine?

'Are you all right, Princess?' asks Thom.

No, cold dread is smothering me. 'Yes, I'm... Con, I need a word. Please? In private?'

Private means the Rondet chamber. Even with the Rondet listening in, it's the most private place the two of us have.

He must have caught my alarm. 'Of course. Excuse us, everyone.'

I link my arm with his, wondering if they're gossiping behind us, a little mortified by the thought. They all know. They all know better than I do what's between us now.

It's too difficult to sort through my feelings. And now... now, if I'm right...

I glance over my shoulder. Elara is following us. Not directly perhaps, but in a random, meaningless way, which isn't actually random or meaningless at all.

I stop at the tunnel entrance. 'You go on.'

'What is it?'

'Trust me. I think... I need to talk to Elara.'

'Elara?'

I don't want to alarm him. What if I'm wrong? All the same, I need to get rid of Elara, whether I'm right or not. 'Please, Con. Just give me a minute.'

He nods his acquiescence and vanishes inside. I know him too well though. He'll head straight down the tunnel and wake the Rondet, link his mind with theirs to watch over me. Or at least I hope so.

Elara stops when she sees me, a slight flush reddening her cheeks.

'Watching us, were you?' I ask, unable to keep my voice even. I shake too much, ball my hands into fists so hard that my nails dig into the palms. I have to stay calm. Because this – if it is what I fear – could be dangerous.

I mean, really dangerous.

'I have to watch,' Elara replies. 'It's all I was to do. Just watch and... and report. Just let them know. I'm so sorry, Bel. So... so sorry. They had a machine.' Her voice shakes, and she sobs. But there are no tears. She hasn't cried since we rescued her. When she'd been accused of the assassination attempt on the Adeline, there had been so many tears. When she'd been injured by the assassin when I became the Bloody Bride... But not now. Not any more. And I know why.

Mechas can't cry.

The assassin who had come with the dressmakers hadn't looked like a Mecha either. I remember the circuitry and gears, the wiring inside that the autopsy revealed. Never a clue from the outside. Except for scars. They must have cut her apart and put her back together again. She'd been covered with scars, a fine tracery of tiny white scars all over her skin. Bruising would have hidden that. The beating Elara had taken, the physical punishment, the abuse... it was to disguise what they'd done. So many scars. Everywhere.

Elara steps closer, each movement fluid and measured, a hunter stalking prey. Not a fragile, broken thing now. A dangerous thing.

A really dangerous thing.

'They changed me. And then they sent me to you. They knew you'd take me in, keep me close. Even broken and damaged. The ambassador knows you, Bel. He knows everything.'

'Who is he, Elara?'

'Choltus? He's one of the High Command, one of the rulers of Gravia. He answers to no one, Bel.'

I don't need to ask why she's telling me that. It doesn't matter any more. She's going to kill me.

I swallow to fight back the scream inside me. It isn't fair. Not Elara. I saved her. I'd got her back.

'Can't you stop? Or send them false data. Can't you do something?'

Elara shakes her head. 'I have my programming. I'm so sorry.' She stops in her tracks, her body seizing up. Her voice changes subtly, emotion leeching from it as she says two words. 'Counting down.'

'Elara, think. Please. This isn't you.'

Elara shudders, and an expression of shock spreads over her face.

'No,' her voice is her own again and full of horror. 'But that doesn't change it. I want to think I died back there. That this isn't me. But I remember being me. I didn't die, Bel. I was alive until... until... Please... please...' She tries to take a step back but can't. She just jerks and then gives up, wrapping her arms around her chest. She shivers from head to toe and panic fills her voice. 'Please get away, Bel. Get to shelter. Now.'

'You can stop this, Elara! Please try.'

I hear frantic footsteps behind me, Con running up the tunnel, screaming my name. He knows. He's seen. He wants to stop it. But he can't. He won't make it in time and I won't get away in time. It doesn't matter.

Elara drops to her knees, her face creased up, her body a ball of pain. 'None of us can. I liked you from the first. I grew to love and respect you. I would have done anything for you. And so would he. But it's too late now. I knew you too well. That's why they chose me. I'm not alone. I'm so sorry. Run! You've got to run.'

'Bel!' Con grabs me, flinging me into the tunnel behind him. He moved faster than I thought he could but now he's here too. Now he's in the open.

'Transmitting location,' Elara says in that other crisp, inhuman voice. 'Detonating.'

Con slams the door to the Rondet just as the explosion rips through the hillside. I throw my arms over my head and the tunnel collapses around me.

Chapter Twenty-Two

I can't move. I can barely draw breath. In the darkness, the weight of stones and soil crush down on me. I can hear nothing but the whining in my ears. And I can't feel my legs. That can't be good, can it?

I fight my way through panic, try to think. There has to be a way out, some escape. I can't die like this. Where's Con?

I try to stretch, but there's no give anywhere, and I'm held firm, a pocket of air keeping me alive. For now. The air won't last.

Con has to be in here too. Somewhere. I can't see anything, or hear him. It's not a good sign. In fact it's bad in the extreme. Why can't I hear him?

'Con?' My voice comes out in a harsh croak. 'Con? Can you hear me?'

Nothing. Nothing at all. Even if he can answer, I can't hear, not with the ringing in my ears.

But he has reached my mind before, while in communion with the Rondet. And they aren't that far away. If they're still alive. Their crystal chambers would have protected them, wouldn't they?

'Rhenna? Please, Rhenna, hear me...'

Darkness wells up around me like tar and I sink into it, unable to resist, too weak, too hurt.

'*Hush, little queen. We are here. Do not move. You are hurt.*'

But how can I lie there when...

Where's Con? Is he okay?

I can't even form the words, just think them, but by some miracle she hears and replies.

'*He lives. He breathes.*'

Show me. Please.

He's trapped in rubble by the door and he's hurt. There's blood all down the side of his face, and his right arm is twisted at an unnatural angle. That's all I can see of him. He stirs, as my consciousness brushes against him, trying to wake. For me.

'*Bel?*' Is it his voice or his mind? Am I hearing him in my head or with my ears?

Another noise filters through my mind now, a sound I am hearing through him rather than one I can discern for myself. The soft woomph of transport engines, low and rhythmic, making the air vibrate.

'*Who is it?*' They don't sound Anthaese. Or Vairian.

'*Bel, be quiet,*' Con hisses. '*Don't make a sound. Just... just...*'

The field of vision changes, sweeping up across a devastated camp, and a shattered forest canopy, through acrid smoke to the dark shadows descending from the sky.

Gravian transports.

'*No!*'

'*Bel, you have to be quiet. They won't see you. They won't...*'

'*But they can't miss you. Con...*'

I struggle, aware again of the tunnel's rubble pressing down on me, the ache of my body, the ongoing whine in my ears. The air is growing stale and as I try to force my way out of it, the rocks are shifting, grinding down on me, crushing me.

'*Bel. Stay still. Stay quiet!*'

'Con!' I scream his name out loud and a backlash of mental energy slams against me. The Rondet's minds close around me, smothering my efforts to fight him, to stay with him and… I don't know what to do. They're on his side in this. Even though I know he'll be captured, even though I cling to his consciousness.

I try to shout again, as the Gravians drag him from the rubble. He can't fight them. I can feel his pain, his helplessness. They aren't gentle and I try to tear myself free to reach him.

'*Bel, no.*'

'*I won't lose you! I won't lose you too!*'

The whine of a plasma weapon charging is a familiar, terrible sound. I know it too well to mistake it. Con drops to his knees as they release him, hitting the ground hard. I feel the spike of agony run through him like it's my own. The weapon nudges the back of his head, runs down the length of his neck.

Bel, he thinks, a warning, a prayer.

Stabbing pain, and blackness. Nothing.

It feels as if something vital has been ripped out of me, leaving a tattered connection that stretches to breaking point. And then that is gone as well. Ripped away.

My mind screams but my lungs can't draw breath to voice it. I just sob but can't quite form his name, or a sound above a breath. Rhenna encircles me in a cocoon of shadows and silence, holding my mind in a cradle and singing softly to me until the darkness swallows me again.

Con… Con is gone.

*

The sound of rubble moving wakes me from a nightmare of being buried alive, which is less my imagination and more my fevered memory. Not to mention my reality.

'Here!' a voice cries out. 'Quickly, down here!' A human voice, with an Anthaese accent.

The movement increases, frantic and desperate. And then there is light. The carved panels roll away, and the fresh air hits me. I gasp in a breath, a bright and perfect breath spearing right through me. I try to push myself up and pain makes me cough. My vision turns white and I cry out, my voice twisted and hoarse. Not just pain, grief too.

'Stay down.'

I tip my head so I can see the source of the rough voice. Jondar crouches down to my left. Blood and dirt smears his face and beneath that he looks terribly pale.

'Con?' I whisper, terrified of the answer I might hear, and yet desperate to know, hoping against hope for a miracle.

Jondar shakes his head and my world crashes down around me. Ice washes over me, crystallising around my heart. First Shae, now Con? It isn't fair. It can't be true. To have lost him now, when I've only just realised how much I need him—

'Was it—?' My voice breaks and tears stab at my eyes again. I force them away ruthlessly, choke on the sob threatening my last shreds of dignity, and try again. 'Was it quick?'

Jondar ceases his work on the debris pinning me down and gazes at my stricken face. Studying me. He will be the Anthaem now, I suppose. Their ruler. But ruler of what? Rubble, disaster, ruin…

I almost miss his reply. My reeling mind takes a moment to realise he is speaking. He strokes the side of my face, a strangely comforting gesture from a man who loathes me. 'He isn't dead, Bel. They didn't kill him. They captured him. Took him in the chaos after the explosion. Sedative dart I think. They airlifted him out.'

I close my eyes, elation robbing my breath. Still alive. For now anyway. No, they won't kill him for a while yet. While they have him, they have this world. While they hold Con, his people will do anything to ensure his safety. And the Empire will be powerless.

Tears trickle down my cheeks and Jondar brushes them away with a touch almost as tender as Con's.

'They used Elara. Made her a Mecha and sent her here.'

'I should have seen it. I've known her all my life.' Jondar closes his eyes, his forehead tightening with stress and grief. 'I knew there was something wrong. I *knew* it. I thought…'

'I know. But she's dead.'

'She's been dead since they first altered her.'

'She tried to warn me. Even as they controlled her. She tried to…' The weight shifts on me and I gasp. I grit my teeth and force myself to continue. 'Another life. The last one.' I open my eyes again, fierce determination taking the place of bleak despair. It's not going to be the last death on my conscience. I know that. Life after life, everyone I care for, everyone who cares for me… My mother, Nerysse, Shae, Dan, Jessam, Elara… everyone. 'We have to get Con. Have you regrouped? I need a casualty report and I need to know what we still have, what we can use.' I push uselessly at the remaining rubble pressing against my chest. 'Get me out of here.'

A strange smile tugs at his dour face, just for a moment. I stare up at him, fired with the need to help Con, to rescue him, but then doubt fills me. If Jondar leaves me here would anyone else find me? Who else knows the entrance to the Rondet chamber is here? Not many. If he said he'd searched the remains and found nothing, would anyone else bother to check? I'd be out of his way then. Nothing between him and Con, just as it used to be.

He must have seen it in my eyes, or thought it himself. The smile changes, gentler, that amusement that had so irritated me before. I find it a comfort now.

'Yes, Majesty,' he says and bows his head. 'They mustn't have heard me shouting.' He pulls the communicator from his belt – another of Con's contraptions now put to perfect use. 'I've found the princess. The tracker the Anthaem gave her is still working. She's unharmed but trapped. Need a bit of help down here.'

Con's tracker, the one in the bracelet. I'd forgotten about that. He's still rescuing people, his brilliant mind still helping us all, finding those who are lost. Like me. I reach out for Jondar, holding his hand, and try to stay calm rather than wriggle and make matters even worse.

In moments, relieved and eager troops surround me, lifting the rubble aside until I'm free. I struggle to my feet, aware that Jondar never moves more than two feet from my side, ever there, ever ready to catch me should I stumble. Just as he always was for Con.

I prepare myself for the reports, knowing that they'll be bad, that casualties will be high. Our hiding place has been betrayed. If we are to help Con, I need every bit of information, need to evaluate every option. I don't dare think about not getting him back.

Because if we don't, if we can't—

I must have swayed on my feet. Certainly, my shoulders tremble.

Jondar's hand closes my elbow, an inconspicuous reassurance. He leans in, just for a moment, his voice unexpectedly warm and soft against my ear. 'We *will* get him back, Bel. Even if we have to die to do so.'

That clothes me in steel. I'm unable to voice gratitude right now, but I hope he feels it anyway. He reminds me suddenly of my brother Art at our father's side. My three brothers are so different. Zander is all passion and energy. He'd throw himself right in to the fray and everyone would follow. Because everyone always follows Zander. Luc would be there with him, leading his Wing like something from legend, his knowledge of tactics second to none. Art would plan every detail, winnow out just the perfect bit of information. Together they're indomitable.

My brothers always knows what to do. If only I could contact Zander. I've spent my life in his shadow. So I know him, I know how he thinks. I know all of them. I know where they came from because I come from the same place – mother and father, and all they taught us all through the years… And then I have it. I just have to imagine I am one of them and the answers start to come right away.

'I need a command centre,' I tell Jondar. 'And I need to know everything we have, everything we need. Now. Was the communications machine damaged? Did Con finish it?'

But I know from the expressions all around me that every bit of news is bad.

*

Con's machine is devastated. There's no other word for it. Pieces are strewn all over the little tent in which he worked. I stand in the broken doorway, staring at it, a black pit opening up in my stomach. It's gone. All of it. In pieces. Not broken perhaps, but shaken to bits by the blast.

Jondar curses softly. 'Is there anything left of it?'

I feel even more lost than I did trapped under the rubble. 'I don't know. This was his creation. I don't know how it works.'

'What are we going to do?'

'They have our location. We need to move immediately.'

'Send out runners to the other camps. Warn them.'

'We need a working communications network, your Highness.'

'Yes, we do.' I bite my lower lip. A bad habit. Elara and Nerysse would have given me hell for it. It's a sign of weakness. And I can't show weakness now. 'Pack it up. All of it. We'll take it with us.'

'But where? The mountains?'

'Can you get me a rope?'

He looks startled. 'A rope?'

I don't have time to explain. What worries me are the voices I can't hear, not any more. The Rondet are silent. Completely silent. And I need to know they're okay. I can't lose them too. I should have thought of them sooner.

I pick my way through the camp. With the Gravians gone, a few of the Anthaese have returned, trying to salvage what they can. They watch me as I pass but say nothing. Not a good sign. Not at all.

A familiar figure falls into step beside me.

'Princess?' Thom won't leave me, naturally. I wonder where Petra is, but know she won't be far. I hope. Ancestors, what if she...?

I cut that thought off. 'Where's Petra?'

He sees my panic. 'Securing the perimeter.'

I breathe a sigh of relief and a smile twitches on Thom's lips. He knows what I thought, that fear. He'd probably felt it himself for both of us.

But his question surprises me. It's only two words but they have so many meanings. 'Jondar's okay?'

Jondar? I study him carefully. So that's it? Well, why not? Although I wouldn't have said he's Thom's type. But then again, what do I know? I don't even know my own type.

'Yes. I sent him for something. He'll be here shortly. I need to get into the Rondet chamber. It's down here but the tunnel is blocked. Can you help?'

Shards of glass and crystal still twinkle in the grass and there's a gaping hole leading down.

Jondar jogs up to me with the rope, a long length of it coiled around his arm. 'Princess.'

Princess this, Highness that. It's really getting on my nerves. I don't have time for it. Why, in the midst of war, in the centre of this maelstrom of chaos, are they still clinging on to these wretched titles?

'Oh, stop it both of you. Bel is shorter. Just use it.'

I circle the hole. Are they still down there? Are they still alive? There's only one way to find out and I don't like the thought of dropping into that dark pit. But what else can I do? The tunnel had come down on top of me. Clearing the rubble would take too long.

So down it is.

I glance at the two men, know there's no way they are letting me go without them. There's no point in even arguing. So I don't bother. I'll skip a step.

'Bel?' Jondar asks, waiting for my orders. And, I suspect, dreading them. Maybe he's afraid of heights. Maybe it's the dark.

'Secure the rope. We're going down.'

*

We climb in silence, me first, shimmying down the rope in the darkness until I feel the ground beneath my feet. My aching body protests, but I ignore it. There's no serious damage and I don't have time for cuts and bruises. The chamber is dark, the crystals still and silent. Thom joins me, followed by a reluctant Jondar. This is a sacred place, so sacred he couldn't enter once. And now it has been desecrated.

If it is the dark he fears, this is very much the wrong place for him.

The light overhead is pale and distant, leaving us in shadows.

'We shouldn't be down here,' Jondar mutters.

'Oh stop it. You're Matilde's brother. You have as much right as me. More probably. You're Anthaese.'

'Which makes *me* feel so welcome,' Thom adds in an undertone.

Thank the ancestors for Thom and his sense of humour.

I smile and leave them where they stand. I approach the nearest wall, my fingers touching the rough stone and then the smooth panel.

'Rhenna?' It's too quiet. I draw in a breath which trembles far too much for comfort. 'Rhenna, are you there? Aeron? Please. Answer me.'

'*We are here still, Princess. Just.*' It's Aeron, his sombre voice surprisingly frail.

'Are you hurt?'

'*Not hurt. Not really. But our land... our land is screaming. Our Anthaem...*'

'Con? Where is he? Can you show me?'

Aeron hesitates, reluctant to answer. Or wondering what to say perhaps. But he answers eventually. But not the answer I want. '*No.*'

'No, you can't or no, you won't?'

The response is petulant in the extreme. 'We will not.'

'I'm not a child, Aeron.'

'*Yes, you are. To us. Rhenna, Favre and I concur. Our sister watches him.*'

Great, they're still trying to protect us, cosset us.

'Is he still alive?'

'*Yes, Bel. He is. And his pain is... terrible.*'

'What did they say, Bel?' Jondar interrupts. 'What did they say about Con?' He takes an urgent step forward, but Thom closes a hand on his shoulder, stopping him. So he knows about them too. I wonder if Matilde told him. Or Con.

I look at the concern in his face and see perhaps what Aeron sees in mine, or in my mind at least. And I understand. I don't want Jondar to know how Con suffers either. I'm not sure he could take it. Perhaps we're more alike than I thought. 'They don't know. He's alive, but they can't... He's alive.'

It's enough, isn't it? It has to be. Pain, such pain as an ancient, alien creature would consider terrible... I don't want to think about that myself, let alone share the burden further.

'There must be more they can tell us.'

'Not now. That's not why we're here. I need somewhere we can be safe, somewhere the Gravians can't find us. And I need to find out how to fix the coms. Or some way to contact Zander.'

'*Bel?*' It's Rhenna, and I've never been so happy to hear her voice. Apparently it's mutual. '*It is good to hear you. We thought... we feared...*'

I press my forehead against the glass, reaching for her. 'I know. Me too. But I need your help now. Do you understand?'

Closing my eyes, I pour all my needs out, all my fears, all my concerns, the grief over what had happened to Elara, over Con's capture. I need to find somewhere to hide his people, somewhere safe for those who trust me. Those who think I can keep them safe. All those I've failed.

And the image sweeps over me as I fall into communion with them, as if I'm stepping into fresh air. I see the caves, feel them close around me, deep within the earth beneath us. Caves that run like a rabbit warren, a labyrinth.

Where we can hide. So many of us could hide in there. Con had mentioned caves, that he thought the ancient Anthaese lived underground. Under the palace, under the Rondet. Somehow connecting the two.

Tunnels, that's what he meant. I follow them, my mind flowing through them like floodwater. Tunnels which come up everywhere. Tunnels which could be defended, given the right tactics, which could be used to move silently and unseen.

'Why didn't you show Con this before?'

Another hesitation. Rhenna doesn't answer this time. Aeron's voice sounds angry, bitter. '*This is our place. Not yours. It is sacred ground. You didn't need it before now.*'

'But we did. We could have used this.'

'*Used it. But you didn't need it.*'

He's stubborn, so horribly stubborn. Just like Con but without the innocence and kindness. And he's annoyingly literal. I push my frustration aside, but I can tell by the way his mind feels that he's aware of it. Well, good. 'How do we get there?'

The route flares in my mind like fireflies in the night.

But it isn't enough to hide.

'I need more. I need your help. We have to fight back. Aeron, Rhenna, please.'

'*What do you ask of us, little queen?*' Rhenna sounds bemused.

'You. I've seen you. Wake up. Help us.'

'*That is out of the question!*' A new voice roars through me, leaving me shaken.

Favre. It has to be him. This is the first time he's ever spoken to me, which tells me how shaken they all are. The third and fourth voices have never deigned to speak to me before. But everything is different now.

'Help me. Con and I did everything you asked, shared with you all we felt. Please, help me. I have to find Con, I have to reach Zander, I have to stop this invasion before it's too late and your land is left a husk stranded at the end of the galaxy. Is that what you want? The death of Anthaeus?'

He snarls. I feel that too, an alien mind snarling inside me. The shock of it drives me back, almost makes me disconnect, but it lowers to a rumble, a warning. I manage to breathe and reach out to include him. And it feels right, as if like Rhenna and Aeron, he has always belonged there. The Rondet are part of me now, and I'm part of them.

'Where's Con?' I whisper and reach out for him across the blackness.

Rhenna's mind rises in a shield. *'No, my love. No. He begs you to stay away.'* Her voice is a sob, and I know it's an echo of Con's voice leaking through. *My love...* did he really say *my love*?

'What are they doing to him?'

But Rhenna doesn't reply. The silence is painful in itself.

'Help me!'

'There is something,' Aeron says. *'One thing, we can do. We watched Con build his machine. Kept him company, helped him, listened to him talking it through, discerning how it might work. He left his designs. He thought he could do it alone, but he couldn't. No one could.'*

And two other minds join me, two human minds as scared and bewildered as I am, more so because this is new to them. I reach for them, praying one is Con, but find Jondar and Thom instead.

'Bel? What's happening? What is this?' Panic surges through Jondar, full-on terror, but Thom steadies him, reaching out to him and keeping him there. A soldier, a guardian, always reliable, my Thom.

'Hush,' I say as they struggle. 'Don't. You're needed.'

'These two.' Aeron's voice is soft as silk, gentle with them. *'They can do it. They complement each other, will work well together.'*

'And your help. The caves, Aeron...' I try again.

'*They are sacred,*' says Favre as if that is the end of it. He doesn't know me. But before I can argue, Aeron continues for me.

'*Favre, we have no choice. She is right.*'

They release me and I stumble in the darkness, as images of locations and maps pour into my mind. Thom and Jondar stand still as statues, their hands pressed to the wall on the crystals which hold the other members of the Rondet. In communion as I had been. Not the deep sharing, or the intimate connection Con and I had shared with them, maybe. Jondar's shoulders tremble and Thom's eyes move behind his eyelids. He breathes out slowly and then snatches his hand away, a hiss escaping his lips.

'What was that?'

I smile at my bodyguard. 'They don't take no as an answer.'

'They were in my mind. And still are. And the machine... I could see Con building it. Everything, how it fits together, how the pieces interlock and work. He's brilliant, isn't he? I mean I knew that, but to see it... Bel...' He pinches the bridge of his nose as if fighting off a headache. 'But I'll never remember it all. Bel, I'm just a soldier. It's all I know. This is...'

Jondar's hand moves down the panel more gently, almost reluctantly. His long fingers caress the smooth surface. 'It's a blessing,' he whispers. 'I never thought...'

'What did they say?' I ask. He's been in there longer, just a moment longer.

'They told me...' He glances at Thom and I'm sure he blushes. I can't tell for certain, not in the chamber with this light. But I'm still sure. 'They... um... told me to build the machine of course.'

'But how?' Thom asks. 'The things I saw are already fading. And Con was a gifted engineer. We're just... just us.'

It's my turn to be inspired, and not by the Rondet. I think of Con, of the time he spent down here. It was his place, his retreat. He left designs, Aeron had said. Of course he did. And where else would he leave them?

It takes me only moments searching before I find the small chest by the wall, beneath Aeron's chamber. I pounce on it, sweeping off dust and stones and throwing it open to find the pages. His writing, his drawings, his thoughts, laid out for them to follow. Notebook after notebook, everything he had done carefully drawn and documented, all his ideas sketched out and elaborated, layer on layer of writing. I gather them all in my arms and a sob breaks out of me. Relief, love and grief overwhelm me. Con has left us what we need. Of course he has. I can sense his mind in these precious pages, almost catch his scent on them. I hold them against my body as I would have held him and I weep.

Chapter Twenty-Three

The caves lead down, as promised, into a rabbit warren of tunnels, into a city built beneath the ground, lit from above with crystals like the one which had shattered above the Rondet, huge and powerful. Others stud the walls, running in veins through the rock. Crystals which could power the entire Empire and more. It was all there, under our feet, all the time. Wide plazas with fresh running water and pools which reflect quartz and mica like stars. Great domed meeting halls, which rang with laughter and song long ago and now do so once again as the people of Anthaeus flood down here. To safety. There are wall carvings of elegant creatures, winged and alabaster smooth. They fly in skies made of polished lapis tiles. The Anthaese, the native Anthaese, I'm sure of it. I study their insectile faces and tried to persuade the Rondet to tell me more, but they remain obstinately silent. I wonder if they don't want to be reminded of what their civilisation had once achieved. And lost.

Because they are gone. All except the Rondet, the four of them sleeping in crystal, wandering with only their minds and help from the minds of others. What had happened to them? Where had all the others gone? There must have been thousands of them in this city alone.

I wander the halls with Petra, checking on the newcomers, testing for Mechas among them. Children play in the great courtyards and wave at me as I pass, calling out my name. The evacuation has been quick, given the circumstances. Runners sent from place to place made contact with more survivors than I'd expected, to be honest. Getting them back here in secret was another matter. But the underground city has entrances in several places. And there's more beneath us. We'll have to map it somehow and that will take time. But for now we're safe.

It's all I can do not to weep for them, especially when they don't seem so desperate down here. They can't stay underground forever. These halls weren't made for them, and humans need the sun and the open air. While we have fresh water and can forage for food, this is a temporary solution.

We arrange scouting parties, some going on raids, others on hunting trips, bringing back game from the forest, mushrooms, nuts and berries, roots and such goods as we need that can be pilfered, especially medicine. And information. That's the most important thing of all. I think back to my lessons with Nerysse. Anaran would be so proud.

The Gravians, realising that the Anthaese are vanishing from the land above, have stepped up their patrols, searching everywhere by air and by foot. But the entrances have a way of shielding themselves, much as the one to the Rondet had. It's like the world itself is looking after us.

And there is no word of Con. Not a breath of a word.

No announcement, no threats, no demands. Nothing from Kendal, nothing from Choltus. Nothing.

That makes me more nervous than ever.

Thom and Jondar supervise moving the remains of the communications machine down below. They pick a chamber seemingly at random, in unspoken agreement. The rock that forms it is thickly encrusted with crystals. They hum when I touch them. I remember Con talking about the ones in the Rondet chamber.

And as for the crystals here, they're more like a network, or veins…

'Don't,' says Jondar, in a tone very like Aeron's. 'Please, leave them be. For now. I think, I—'

'Yes,' Thom cuts in. He smiles. I like that expression on his face, that of a child delighting in a mystery solved. It suits him. 'Yes, I see it too. Let's get to it.'

It's fascinating to watch them work. They rarely speak, and when they do it's usually to finish one another's sentences. They move together, a subtle dance, each one filling the space complimentary to the other. They spread the designs over a table and lean in close together, studying them, their minds in unison, focused on their task. Whatever the Rondet has awoken in them, it leaves them tireless, dedicated and absorbed in their work. In each other. I've never seen either of them so complete.

The machine grows in an organic structure. Con's machine and yet something more as well. Jondar and Thom are leaving their own stamp on it as well. It's beautiful.

When they rest or eat, they talk quietly, intimately, and I feel the need to step away from them. It doesn't seem fair to intrude.

'I've never seen him so… comfortable with anyone,' says Petra one day.

'Jondar?'

'No, Thom. But now that you mention it, yeah… him too.'

They are happy, that's it. More than that. Content. It's the way I'd felt with Con.

The thought makes my heart twist inside me. I never felt that way with Shae. That had been need, a fire, but no peace, no sense of belonging.

And I have lost him. Lost them both.

I can do nothing for Shae, not now, I remind myself time and again. But Con... I have to do something for Con.

I watch and wait. Days grind by, sluggish and marked by increasing desperation. I range further and further in the caves, with Petra and a number of the other guards my constant shadows. They aren't going to let me give them the slip again. It's fair enough, given what happened. I accept that now.

But there are still the Dragonflies. A flight of them still operates and can be kept in the air. Without Con, I'm not sure how long that will be the case, but I drill the pilots daily in maintenance, in safety, in proper manoeuvres. They can even fly in the great caverns, but my trips above ground are few and far between.

They almost lost me once, I'm daily reminded in turn. It's not going to happen again. Just like Zander, on his free-wings. And look where that had got him. Command of a whole damned armada and not a moment in the air. Flying to our rescue but trapped out of reach by the blockade.

They are good, my pilots. Skilled and smart, everything I could hope for in a Wing.

I always wanted to command a Wing. I ought to have been more careful what I'd wished for. Sometimes I wonder who's in command of whom.

Making my way to the Rondet is something I can still do. There's precious little space to cover above ground under the trees and it's bliss to feel sunlight on my face. I stand straighter, and taste the wind, expecting freshness and relief, but today there's something on it – an acrid tang which make my senses recoil.

'What is that?'

'They've been blasting the mountains at Monserratt,' Petra says. 'You can smell the dust and explosives. There were still people in those caves.'

'We should send out runners, try to get them out.'

'The Gravians are looking for us,' one of the younger guards continues. He grits his teeth. I know what he's thinking. Sending runners to help those still at Monserratt might give our location away. I hope we've trained them better than that.

'Well, they won't find us there.' I try to sound lighter in mood than I feel. Con and I talked about this eventuality, that they'd come after us. They must have known Montserratt was a base for some time. It's only a matter of time before they start blasting elsewhere. Sooner or later something will give us away.

I push aside thought of the tunnels collapsing like the tunnel to the Rondet, that beautiful underground fortress falling in on us, condemning us as it saves us now.

We can't go to the Rondet every day. Sometimes several days pass between my visits. It's too dangerous. I risk capture. Everyone tells me so. It makes Rhenna edgy and Aeron grumpy. They want to share with me, to know what I know, to see their world as I see it. Perhaps they really do want to help in their way. They weep for the refugees, rail against the invader. But still, they don't do anything, which makes me all the more frustrated with them. They're like spoilt children sometimes. So self-obsessed, and egotistical... but I need them still. And it isn't just that. I sometimes wonder if any of this is real to them, as if they think we are just dreams, there to amuse them. It's a chilling thought. I'm on the verge of asking them to dream better dreams, or to wake from this nightmare, but I haven't managed to get up the courage yet.

Favre says nothing more. Funny, I always thought Aeron was the leader of the group. But now I'm sure it's Favre, or the other silent party, the fourth one who never speaks at all. I don't even know her name.

Just that it is indeed a female mind. One which does not deign to talk to me at all but instead – I hope Aeron is right – watches over Con.

Climbing down the rope, I try not to think about what might be happening to Con. Thoughts of what it might be haunts me. I wake from nightmares where I crawl through rubble to try to reach him. Only to feel him push me away. It hurts every time.

'*Little queen, how long has it been?*' Rhenna asks, sleep muffling her mind. They always call me that, I realise. Even though I'm not and probably never will be a queen. Not if we don't get Con back. Perhaps not even then.

'Three days,' I reply, settling myself down on the floor as far away as possible from the place I had once sat curled in against Con. I stare at the spot, an accusation. 'I couldn't get away. They're getting bolder. Blasting the caves at Montserratt to drive us out.'

'*But explosives will not touch you in the city beneath,*' says Aeron. '*We have watched. We will continue to watch. This is our task.*'

'You could do more than watch.'

He sighs at my belligerent tone, used to it, sick of it. As sick as I am to still use it and be ignored. '*It is not yet time. Shall we begin? Troop positions, convoys, the movements of their ships in the air and—*'

'And Con?'

'*No, child. He does not wish it.*'

'I wish it. Please, Aeron. I need to know. I need to see that he's still alive.'

'*Impossible. We have a task. You have a role. Enough argument.*'

It's always the same. 'All right. Let us begin.' I close my eyes and sink into the hive mind. It's becoming easier, every time I go a little deeper, sooner, with less of a struggle. Is it that they accept me, or I accept them? Con would have an explanation. But I can't think of Con. Not now. It just hurts. It hurts far too much.

We soar over the land, as high as we can go. The world is a toy map with moving parts, one which is more devastated every day. The forests are scythed and pulped, the water runs black from the ore extraction process, the mountains are crumbling.

I recall the green and verdant land I had first seen and I want to weep. At least Con can't see it. At least he's spared this.

'*I know.*' Rhenna's voice trembles.

'*Enough,*' Aeron informs us. Maybe he doesn't feel emotions, not like we do. But I know Rhenna does. No, his alien nature doesn't explain it. Maybe he's just a bastard, cold through and through. '*We have work to do.*'

Work, that is how he thinks of it. Perhaps it's better that way. Think of it as work and it becomes something we can manage, something we can overcome. It's a good approach, one of which my father would approve. I'm starting to understand why Con buries himself in his work too.

Deal in the practical, not in emotion. Emotion will betray you, get you killed. My emotions are all over the place. I have to think instead.

Think. That's easy to say when my mind is awhirl. I push my emotions down inside me and breathe in the martyred air of Anthaeus. And I focus, my attention needle sharp. I note the troop movements, search for the weaknesses, and store each one away for my report. Rhenna points out chinks in their armour, the way they leave gaps in the perimeter patrols around the Citadel at Limasyll.

Poor broken Limasyll.

The capital is transformed. They burned the gardens. The opal sheen of the walls is soot-blackened and streaked with blood where they've lined up victims for execution.

Con is in there somewhere. Trapped inside. At their mercy. He has to be. Where else would they keep him? It's almost like I can sense him there, as if my mind calls out to him and finds an answer, whether he wants it or not.

My fiancé. My husband to be. Or rather my husband who would have been. In another life. My heart wrenches as if someone has torn it in two. I want to see him, to know he's not dead, to be certain…

'*Go then*,' whispers the fourth voice, unexpected, uncalled for. I'm so startled I drop through the air, flailing as if I had wings which I have suddenly lost. I catch myself again so I'm hanging there, helpless. Did she really just say that? '*He needs you as you need him.*'

I don't hesitate again. It's my only chance, because Aeron and Rhenna will drag me back in a second to protect me. And Favre will be furious that I have disobeyed. But it doesn't matter. Not now. Con is in there. I dive down towards the walls of Limasyll, through them and down into the foundations beneath.

Darkness grabs me and slams me onto cold, hard ground. The stink of blood and filth assails me, and pain follows, raw and terrible. It rips through me, barbs beneath my skin. Electricity courses over my body, digs nails in behind my eyes. My mouth opens, further than I could have imagined possible and the scream is wrenched from me.

The image that comes to me is blurred and twisted. A figure, a woman with many arms, her skin a deathly white and her eyes black and endless. The death goddess of the Gravians. She looms over me, grinning and terrible.

And I know I see what Con sees, through horrific agony, through the torture he endures. For me. They are using him for their rites, dragging every inch of torment from him in honour of that goddess. I've heard tell of such things but never really believed them. Religion like that is an anathema to my people. We honour our ancestors, our families, those who went before us, not monsters from supernatural realms who demand blood and agony. But their religion is everything to the Gravians. It's an integral part of their culture.

I know it's him. This is what he's feeling, enduring. This is Con, as if he is wrapped around me like a shroud. Or perhaps I'm a ghost under his skin. I know his mind, his spirit. It called to me and drew me in. Because his mind isn't quite connected to his body any more, because he's slipping away into that chasm of pain and despair.

'*I'm here,*' I whisper, reaching for him. Trying to comfort him, to bear some of his pain. '*I'm here, my love.*'

'*No.*' Even his mental voice is ragged, almost broken. '*No, Bel. Please.*' Con pushes me back, weak but determined. '*You cannot be here. You cannot feel this. You must go. Tell me nothing. Just go.*'

But still I reach out, try to cradle him as Rhenna had cradled me. He fights me, trying to force me away from him. But I hang on to him.

'*I am coming for you. I will be here. Don't give up.*'

'*Aeron! Favre!*' he screams out loud. His voice bounces off cold stone and echoes back at his torturers like the ravings of a madman. They laugh, the Gravians tormenting him, I hear them laugh. One of them leans in close, examining Con's face. I know those eyes. I know him. Choltus. He bares all his teeth in a rictus grin and I recoil at the mockery I see there. '*Make her go. Please! Make her go!*'

The Rondet comes for me. I can't stop them, no more than I can stop Con. I can't fight the wave of pain and fear engulfing me. It's a hurricane and I'm just a moth caught in it. They dive into the swirling vortex of agony that is Con's existence and pull me clear. But not before they feel it too, endure all that he endures. If only for a moment.

They scream, as I scream, as Con screams, and they drag me clear on his anguished command. Drag me away from him as if they are tearing us apart. Their inhuman voices rise in terrible harmony, ringing together like chimes in the night.

I shudder awake to the sound of someone sobbing. A broken and desperate sound that doesn't seem to come from any one source but ripples through the rocks around me.

I'm part of it, this sound that comes from five souls, and is still only a faint echo of Con's torture.

'*Go now*,' says the fourth voice. She sounds distressed, but not as bad as the others. She had been caring for Con all along. Enduring it too, I realise, trying to shoulder the burden and support him. She knows what she's doing. She needed the others to see. And I was the tool to do that. She used me. And yet I would have done exactly the same thing. '*Go. Leave us.*'

I want to beg them to help him again, to help me to get to him, to do something, but I know they won't thank me. Not now. If anything they might never speak to me again.

But the fourth voice… she knew what she was doing, didn't she? I could only hope.

Tell me nothing, he said. Because he didn't trust himself not to talk, not to tell them everything he knows. My Con is broken. He is in a world of constant agony.

When had the Rondet last felt such pain? And it's worse, so much worse, when the source is someone they love so dearly as Con.

Chapter Twenty-Four

'Bel.' Someone shakes me awake with a roughness I have long forgotten. Being a princess has made me soft. Being away from my brothers has made me complacent. My dreams are of a better time which is good. I couldn't bear to dwell in the nightmare world where I left Con. And I hate myself for it. 'Bel, come on.'

It's early evening, or morning. I don't know which. The light is dim outside. Then I remember, that I'm far underground and that the light is always like this, except on the brightest of days. How long have I slept? I remember stumbling out of the Rondet chamber last night and back here, an automaton. When Petra quizzed me, I hadn't answered. When my bodyguard persisted, I just reeled off the troops and defence information I needed to pass on and ignored the rest. Ignored everything. Tried to blot out the agony. The disaster. I collapsed into the cot bed and slept.

All that Con is enduring, I felt it too. Only he is still in anguish and he sent me away. And the Rondet had felt it. They know now what he is suffering to protect... *them*. Oh it's suddenly so painfully obvious that it almost hurts more than the echoes of his torture. He's protecting them, keeping them secret. He's going through all that so that the Gravians won't find out about the Rondet and their cave. Because who knows what they'll do? The gems in that cave have to be worth a fortune, and an undiscovered race… a vulnerable, hibernating race… The last of them… if the crystals are valuable, the Rondet are beyond value.

'Bel, please, my princess. You have to come.'

It's Petra, my guard, my friend, drawing me back to the present. I drag myself out of the pit of depression which I wish would just swallow me up, and I blink at her.

'What is it?'

'Jondar and Thom, they've got something. They want you.'

I scramble up, brain bleary from sleep and exhaustion. 'Is it working? Do they have a contact?'

'Not yet.'

I don't want to waste any more time in discussion. I pull on a robe, a thick red velvet that someone has brought down here for me. It's blissfully warm, especially as the air around me is deathly cold. But then I think of Con again, and the awful persistent cold surrounding him in the dungeons beneath Limasyll and my heart falters a little. Guilt, that insidious worm, burrows deeper into my heart and leaves me sickened.

Jondar and Thom talk, locked deep in conversation. More words flow between them than I've heard them say in days. The machine fills the cave, intricate and beautiful, just as Con's had been. It gleams in the half light, more art than mechanics. No, that's wrong. All of Con's creations are works of art, as well as works of perfect mechanics. The two go hand in hand when he makes things.

And this, though other hands had built it, is no exception.

I notice changes though. That bit there looks more like something the native Anthaese might have left behind – Aeron's work perhaps. Airy wiring at the top reminds me of nothing so much as Jondar – I can't say why – making things beautiful with regimented order. And beneath it, balancing the whole affair, adding weight and contrast, perfect support – that's pure Vairian work.

Thom beams at me when he sees me. He grabs Jondar's hand and pulls him forward. If Jondar looks shocked at the intimacy in front of others, Thom doesn't seem to care. Why would he? Thom has never had a problem. He loves where he loves. He's lucky. But I can't help but be glad for him.

'You should have seen him doing this. It was brilliant. He just *knew*.'

Jondar turns red. 'I wasn't alone. Besides, we don't know that it works. Just that it *should*.'

'Of course it will. That's why we thought you should be here.'

'You haven't tested it yet?' I ask.

'Not yet, your Highness.' Jondar probably wanted more time to test it before bringing me here. I can read him much more easily now. Understand him too. He doesn't like just throwing himself into things. It's chaotic, disorderly, improper. Poor Jondar. He hasn't a hope.

'So do it.' Thom shoulders Jondar gently and grins even more widely. He's irrepressible. Another thing Jondar doesn't have a chance against. 'Go on.'

'It isn't my place. Bel?'

That makes me smile too. He's finally using my name. In front of other people and not just when someone is actually trying to kill us. That's a start. It almost feels like friendship.

'You fixed it. Turn it on.'

Jondar frowns. Lack of propriety again, my eternal flaw when it comes to court. But somehow that doesn't matter any more. He gives up and crosses to the control panel. Most of the lights are already aglow, and as he lifts the switches, they grow brighter. Something hums, a deep reverberation that starts in my stomach and ripples through my body.

It feels as if it's part of me. And the part of the rocks around me, part of the crystals. But the vibrations feel wrong, almost out of tune.

'What's is it?' asks Thom, his voice suddenly concerned. 'Jon?'

'I don't know. It's just—'

'—signal strength, yes, I see it. But there isn't a—'

'—booster. Yes, there is. The crystals. Bel did it before, remember?'

They both look at me that same moment, in perfect synchronisation, so perfectly in tune it makes me take a step away from them. 'Stop doing that,' I tell them. 'What did I do?'

'You tapped the crystals, when we first came here.' Jondar's enthusiasm spills out between his words. 'Do it again.'

'What? This?' I flick the nearest crystals embedded in the walls and light flares all around them. Thom gives a whoop of delight, the kind I've heard him give on chute jumps back home or heading into battle.

Of course, Con called them a network, veins of crystal threading through the rock of Anthaeus itself.

'That's it. Do it again. They're amplifying the signal. Do it again. Go on!'

So I do. And bemused, Petra joins in, tapping at the glowing rocks beside me. We're like children, tapping and giggling, making the stones shine with energy. With power.

And then I hear it.

'Come in… receiving you… Control… massive interference… code 371 alpha… Come in…'

'Code 371-alpha!' I gasp, locking eyes with Thom. 'That's them. That's Devra's code. Ancestors, that's them. Where's the mic, Thom? How do I talk to them?'

'There's no mic. It's a field. Just talk. Do it.'

'Come in, this is… I don't have a code name. But it's me, Control. It's Bel.'

The connection crackles and screams with static and then I hear it. Zander's voice. It's my brother's voice.

'Is this a secure line? Are you unhurt? Are you safe?'

'Yes. I mean, I think so.' I look to Jondar, who shrugs. Secure? I don't even know how it works. 'As secure as it can be. We're safe, Zander, but they have Con. We have to get him out. And soon. They're torturing him. To make him hand over his crown, or sign a treaty or… I don't know. Just for fun maybe. Zander?'

'Where's Shae? Let me talk to him.'

I choke, my voice lodged in my throat for a moment. *He doesn't know.* Of course he doesn't. How could he? I haven't had to say it out loud because everyone knows. Everyone else knows. And I don't want to say it, not out loud. Because that makes it true.

But I have no choice. 'He's dead.'

Silence follows the words. Shae had been his friend too. Always. 'When? How?'

'At the fall of Limasyll, two and a half months ago. He died to get us out. Con and me. And now they have Con and I need to rescue him. I have to. Are you listening to me?'

A silent Zander is never a good sign. I wait, tapping on the crystal more out of frustration than the need to boost the signal any further.

'Transmit your position. We're coming to pick you up, and get you home as soon as possible.'

I suck in a shocked breath and my eyes lock on Jondar's. Zander thinks he's just spiriting me away? No. Not a chance. Something hard passes through the Anthaese prince's eyes, resignation… and agreement. He nods, he actually nods. *Oh sure, get the little woman out of the way.*

'No.' I make sure no one can doubt that I mean it. 'No way in all the worlds, brother.'

'Bel, listen to reason. As a hostage—'

'And you listen to me. They don't need another hostage when they have Con. I can't leave here.'

'They're blockading the planet but we can punch our way through for a limited strike.'

'I can't leave them. More than that, I *won't*. Now are you going to help me or not?'

Zander growls something obscene. 'Thom? Are you there?'

Thom stares at Jondar, and something unspoken passes between them again. A struggle, no doubt about that from his expression, but he doesn't speak, though every inch of him wants to. He closes his eyes, and doesn't answer. Jondar looks at him in adoration.

'Corporal Kel!' Zander barks and Petra jerks to attention. Training runs deep. She can't avoid it. And she served with Zander. He's been her commanding officer. It's drilled into every fibre of her being.

'Yes, your Highness?'

'Give me your coordinates and prepare my sister for airlift.'

I stiffen, staring at my bodyguard in horror. She wouldn't. She couldn't! But I've never known Petra to disobey a direct order. It isn't in her nature. She's a Vairian soldier through and through. Always has been and always will be.

Petra shifts on the balls of her feet, and then bows her head. She picks her words so carefully. 'With all due respect, your Highness, I can't do that. My fealty is to Princess Belengaria and the Anthaem Conleith.'

Zander's language degenerates into the type of things a crowned prince and heir apparent shouldn't know. But the commander of a fleet of warships might have picked up a few of them. A soldier definitely would. I wait, my heart pounding until he runs out of steam.

Then I speak, as gently as I can. I know he's angry. I'm probably going to make him angrier. But what else are little sisters for?

'I have a plan, Zander. I'm going to need your help.'

*

As we make our way through the tunnels, Petra is her silent self, but there's something different to this silence. Stoic, naturally, but also sullen, and most unlike her. I march ahead, unwilling to have yet another argument about how I should, at the very least, be upwards of two hundred miles above the surface of the warzone. The discussion isn't going to go anywhere. I'm not leaving. They really need to all get their heads around that so we can just move on.

'Did you think I'd back anyone over you?' Petra asks abruptly. 'Did you think I'd bundle you up and send you home?'

It's more awkward than I can bear. I try to think of anything to say. Anything at all.

'He's your commander, isn't he?'

Petra folds her arms. 'He was. But that was a long time ago. And anyway, what does that make you?'

'I... I don't... what?'

Petra shakes her head and smiles. 'Let's not ask you to give any speeches, shall we? Honestly, Bel, why do you think I'm here? For you. It's what I do. I look after you. Just as Shae did. It's what he would have wanted.'

'Shae...'

'I don't imagine he'd think that Zander was right to just swoop in and demand your return, no matter what the circumstances. He'd want you safe, but if he saw you here, he'd understand.'

Would he? I hope so.

'I thought I loved him, Petra.' It's a terrible admission. I see her gaze soften.

'I know. But I've seen you with Con. *That's* love, Bel.' When I start to protest, Petra waves me to silence. 'Don't. All this… you're doing it for him. *That* I understand.'

'Then you know why I have to get him back. Otherwise, everything, especially Shae's death, will have been pointless.'

'We can't have that. We are both warriors, my princess. It's what we're trained for. Vairians by blood.'

I grin. 'And by stubbornness.'

'That most of all.' Petra holds out her hands. 'I have kept you safe. I'll continue to do so. I swear this, my princess. And if the ancestors are willing, my Queen of Anthaeus.'

'I'm not the queen. Not without Con. And I don't… don't know…'

The panic and loss roils up inside me again. I'm intimately familiar with it now but that doesn't make it any easier to bear.

'I do,' she tells me. 'Believe me. And them. Ask the Anthaese if they'll follow you. Then you'll see.'

I link fingers with her, and my eyes sting with unshed tears of gratitude and relief. I've never actually had a friend. Not a friend like her. Sheltered upbringing, family ties and all that. To find out that I do is a revelation. Petra is more or less my own age but she seems older because I know I can always rely on her. Always.

She pulls me into a brief but heartfelt hug then clasps my shoulders as if grounding me, making me centre myself and driving her strength in to me.

'But first, Bel, we need to rescue your Anthaem. Shall we?'

'Who else will do it?'

Petra shrugs and her grin turns positively wicked. 'You can't leave a job like that to our men. Can you imagine?'

*

The light in the Rondet chamber is pale and cold. Nervously, I reach for the hive mind. They don't want me here, that much is certain. The resistance is stronger than I've ever felt it before. Those eager, hungry minds are closed to me, determined to keep me away.

'Oh, come on,' I groan. 'Rhenna, please. Talk to me.'

There's nothing. If anything the barrier between us hardens, crystalline and impenetrable.

'I need to help Con. I need your help to do it. I know what you are, what you were. Wake up.'

No answer. Nothing.

I punch one of the panels, which achieves nothing but pain. I've no choice but to stand there, nursing my arm and glaring.

'And I'm not going anywhere. I'll break you out of there if I have to. I can come back with enough explosives to resurrect you *and* blow you to pieces.'

'*You are quite the most infuriating female we've ever allowed in here,*' Aeron says.

'Oh, not entirely, I'm sure. Isn't that right, *Matilde?*'

There's a smothering silence. I hold my breath, waiting. Stubbornness, Petra had called it. It's a Vairian virtue. One I hold higher than duty or honour, because it is only through stubbornness that either of them can be achieved.

'*Have you known for long?*' the fourth voice asks at last. She's almost timid. The last thing I would have expected.

I press my hand on the crystal of the last panel in the chamber. I can see the creature inside, that it stills sleeps, that it isn't human in any way. It might even be made of stone. But that doesn't matter. I know who is inside. Somehow.

'Not until you allowed me go to him. Because he needed me, even if he couldn't see it. Thank you.'

'And does he know who I am?'

'I didn't tell him, Anthaem. But how is it even possible?'

It is a sigh in the depths of my brain. *'I knew I was dying. My own body, betraying me... I wouldn't be able to help Con, or protect him. His mind, Belengaria — such an impeccable mind. He was bright and fiery with ideas and inventions. I couldn't let that be lost. I couldn't see him ground down. So I reached out to the hive mind.'* I can feel them all now, bound intricately together, woven in a pattern so beautiful I can't bear not to reach out myself, to touch it. But one thread is missing. One, as Matilde said, brighter than all the others. Con. *'I knew them so well, you see. We fitted together. I begged them to help, and they took me in. Berine the silent and I... merged. You cannot tell him, Bel. He must not know.'*

'But why not?'

'Why not? Silly girl, it would tie him even more closely to a ghost. And we need him to live. That's why we chose you in the first place. To make him live.'

'Then help me. Please, help me to help him. All of you. This is your land too. Do you want to see it destroyed?'

'But it's a land we have given up,' says Favre. *'We sleep now, and dream. That is our place.'*

'And what happens when they come here? They will, you know. How priceless are you to them, last of your race, a hive mind that can see all and hear all? We've shared so much with you. Why won't you help us and help yourselves?'

'*You think we have not helped, Bel?*' Rhenna asks. '*We have saved your life, showed you the enemy in secret and gathered information? What can we four do abroad that is greater than what we already do in helping you?*'

Rhenna's right, but it isn't enough. I need more. So much more. 'I'm going to find him. I'm going to get him back. No matter what. I could have left – my family want me to leave. But I won't. Not without Con, do you understand?'

'*Leave us?*' Aeron sounds instantly suspicious and more than a little hostile. '*What do you mean leave?*'

So that upsets him, does it? Well, too bad.

'My family.' I stride towards his panel. 'My brother and the fleet are orbiting this world, just beyond the blockade. They say it isn't safe, that if the Gravians take me, Anthaeus is lost for sure. Con will sign anything and the Vairians will refuse to attack with me as the shield.' It's stupid. So stupid. If I was anyone other than a Vairian princess there wouldn't be an issue at all. If I was just a soldier, it would be my duty to stay and fight. But no... Bitterly, I clench my teeth and glare at Aeron through the misty panel. I can't see a face, not as such. All gleaming golden planes and angles. 'You just don't get it, do you?'

'*I do not understand.*'

Exactly my point.

'No... no of course you don't. So listen to me. I am going to find him, to rescue him. And I might not return. But I have a plan, and I need your help. Timing is everything. We have to take that planetary shield down to break the blockade and get to Con in the palace. And if you don't help... well then, it will be over. And you won't have to worry about me again.'

Chapter Twenty-Five

'It's an awfully big gamble,' says Thom, his tone sombre. 'But then you always were one to take risks.'

I don't answer. It isn't the first time I've heard something of that kind over the last couple of days of preparation. Jondar, Petra, Zander... oh yes, Zander had said so many things about irresponsibility and foolhardiness that would have been more effective if the words hadn't been equally fitting for a dozen things he'd done in his life for a lot less reason. Unlucky for him I know him too well. I check my flight gear once more, from top to toe, focusing intently on that, not on the accusing stares of my bodyguards who will have to follow in their own Dragonflies. Last of all I rest my hands on the knife belt. Ornate and beautiful it might be, but it's also a weapon and I need every weapon I have now.

'Be safe,' says Jondar. 'We'll meet you there.'

They'll move in units, small and insignificant as possible while overground, and using the tunnels as far as they are able. Positioning themselves. But I know I have to get to the paths leading to Limasyll first, to open them. The great gates are heavy beyond belief, carved and ornate, stone like the rest of the tunnels. They take hours to open, if they still open at all. I don't want to think about that option. Then, once in the palace grounds we'll have to find the shield generators. If we don't get the gates open, or if we don't bring the shields down, the others are all going to be sitting out in the open, ready for the Gravians to pick them off and there will be no support from the air. Speed matters most, but too much speed will kill us. Hence the Dragonflies, precious as they are, need to be pressed into service. And the best pilots must take them. Myself, Thom and Petra, naturally, and three survivors of the Anthaese Royal Flying corps, including Ellish, the pilot from the first time Con took me to visit the Rondet chamber. We will fly ahead, get to those gates and open them, or at least start them opening. Ground troops will follow, slower on foot, stealthier, and by the time they arrive the way will be clear. That's the plan. It should work.

It has to work.

I climb on board, key up my radio. 'Flight, this is One. Report in for coms check.'

'This is Queen's Wing Two,' says Thom, even though I specifically told him *not* to call it that. As I'm leader of the Wing he's meant to do as I say. But no such luck. This is Thom, after all and he can't resist. 'And this is still insane.'

I grin in spite of myself. He always has that effect. 'Thank you, Two.'

'Queen's Wing Three,' Petra's voice chimes in. Oh ancestors, they're both at it. 'You could charge him with insubordination. Excessive happiness isn't an excuse you know.'

My smile widens, grateful they can't see me. 'Duly noted, Three. I'll consider it. For both of you.' Ellish and the rest of my Wing follow orders as they check in, somewhat more sedately, perhaps wondering what on earth they've got themselves into now. But still, they carry on, all six accounted for and flight ready. No more mention of a Queen's Wing, thank the ancestors, though I can hear it lingering behind every transmission. The Queen's Wing it is, whether I like it or not.

I take off first and they follow, like a colony of bats deep beneath the ground, swooping through the caverns made by the native Anthaese ancients, their elaborate decoration and delicate structures blurring as we pass. As they leave the range of ambient light, and head into the deeper tunnels, I hit the lights, the beams illuminating the way ahead in an amber glow. The others follow suit, flying through the night. Behind us the engines make the familiar iridescent waves. I wonder if we'll do this again, if any of us are coming back. It isn't the way to think, not at times like this, but I can't help it. A morbid side, my father warned me, is the curse of our family. They said my mother had a premonition when she set out on her last flight. Family mythology, perhaps, and I wonder how anyone knew. It isn't the sort of thing my mother, or any warrior, would have confided in anyone, not even the love of their life. But my father had known. Perhaps it was hindsight. Perhaps it had been his premonition too. Or maybe just his guilt. It doesn't matter now and I need to stop dwelling on it.

Premonition or not, it won't change anything. But I offer up a prayer to the ancestors, to watch over my Wing, the Queen's Wing, to watch over us and bring us home safe. And, most importantly of all, to keep Con safe until I can do it myself.

'*Focus,*' Rhenna murmurs deep in my mind. '*Favre says you're making the others nervous.*'

'Yes, Maestra,' I reply, all obedience and Rhenna gives one of her purrs. Do the others feel it too? There's no way to tell. I can only hope and trust in the Rondet and my plan.

It is so much easier to trust someone else. I wish that Con was there, his mind and his intellect. Or Shae, with his skills and expertise. But all I have is myself. And it feels as if I'm flying on failing power, my ship disintegrating around me.

We leave the tunnels and shoot up into the air. The moons are rising, one full and bright, the other a dim sliver. More visibility than I would have liked. I kill my lights. Behind me, the others go dark in my shimmering wake.

Silent running. Vital to keep it so. But they know the route. We have to be fast. It's little more than a hop above ground. I count, the easiest and most reliable way to calm myself and cover the ground, and then I arc the Dragonfly down again.

'Now Rhenna,' I whisper.

For a moment doubt assails me again, as the ground rushes up towards me, dark and looking so very hard. If I hit it, I'll probably never know about it, that's one thing. But my Wing will follow me to their deaths too. *Please Rhenna*, I think, but I don't send out the thought. *Don't fail me now.*

The ground ruptures, folding in on itself and the next tunnel opens. I dive in, threading the needle at speed, and then remember to breathe again, as I hit the lights, illuminating the way ahead. It's narrower than I'd hoped, tight flying, but we can do it. We have to.

I gradually slow the pace. To my relief the tunnel opens out again, a wide though shallow space. Little margin for error still, but easier.

'*Here*,' Rhenna says at last. '*Set down here.*'

At my signal, the others follow me down. The craft alights, delicate as the insect that gave it the name. I close my eyes in thanks. So far so good. And no one hurt.

Scrambling out of the Dragonfly I press my hand to its side, wishing it well, hoping against hope that I'll see it again.

The gates are huge, the carvings decorating them depicting creatures flying high above Anthaeus. Dragons again. I smile and glance at my Dragonfly. Then I press my hand to them, running my fingers over the stone surface, tracing the picture.

'You see?' I say to Rhenna. 'Wings.'

'*It was so long ago. We don't remember.*' She sounds like a petulant child. She doesn't want to remember.

It's too much. Why won't they just trust me? It's like they don't want to know. 'Ancestors! I thought I was meant to be stubborn. Just show me how to open them and link the tunnels.'

'*I can do that much.*' She even sounds smug. She knows something I don't after all. Infuriating creature. '*I heard that too. But it does not matter.*'

The gates rumble open, so slowly it's painful to watch. Just a crack at first and I look down into darkness. Passages lead down in multiple directions, and just one goes forward. Just one in the direction of Limasyll. So where do all the others go?

The Rondet hide so many secrets.

Now is not the time to find out, even though we have to wait for the others to arrive. The last thing I need is to get lost. Time drags by as we wait. No one speaks. There's nothing to speak about. It seems to take forever, time Con doesn't have.

*

My army, such as it is, arrives hours later. Jondar looks grim, determined, but I'm aware that others are clearly wavering. Nerves, of course. They're used to fighting for survival, for provisions, used to ambushes and guerrilla tactics. An assault, even a surprise one, is an entirely different matter. They've walked a long way in the darkness, to an uncertain end.

And all they have at the finish is me there to lift their spirits. It works on many – I can see that on their faces – but not all.

'You should say something,' says Thom.

Oh no. Not this. But he's right. Someone needs to.

I stand there with my mouth open. My father would know what to say, naturally. Something stirring and encouraging. It's expected. But it isn't me. What can I say?

Then again, when did my father have time for speeches?

'I don't think that'll help somehow,' I tell him. 'I'll probably scare them off.'

Jondar steps forward, facing the now murmuring crowd. His voice rises around them, strong and sure, a voice they know and trust, but best of all, a voice that is one of their own. Matilde's brother. Of course it should be him addressing them now. 'You know why we're here. We are going to find our Anthaem, and take him back. If nothing else, we will die trying. Because without him, what will become of Anthaeus? He is part of our land, part of our souls, part of us. Belengaria and the Vairians are here to help us, but *we* must do this. We are Anthaese.'

I glance at Thom, who is beaming, his eyes only for the prince, and at Petra who nods.

'*You see?*' Rhenna giggles inside my mind. '*Only simple words are needed when the cause is true.*'

Or when people want to believe them.

Right now, I want to believe them most of all. Jondar looks at me, waiting expectantly. And I never thought I would be as grateful for his existence as I am right now.

'Bel?' he murmurs. And I know I have to say something.

Let's not have you make any speeches, Petra once said to me. I wish that were an option.

'This isn't about us. It's about Anthaeus. It's about Con. It's now or never. I'm not coming back without him.' I look out over a sea of faces, all gazing up at me. Words drain out of my brain and I don't know what else to say. Perhaps I don't need to say anything more? After all, Jondar said everything that needed saying. I hope they can see that I will do anything in my power to find Con and save him. To free them. 'Let's go,' I finish, and start down the tunnels towards Limasyll, aware of them following me. I just hope I'm doing the right thing and not leading them all to their deaths. There's only one way out of this and it will be hours still before we reach the capital. That's the type of speech I probably would have given. Just as well I'm tongue tied really. The darkness looks as if it might swallow us whole. And after a few moments, it does.

*

The sound works differently underground. So do our fears. This is different to the great underground city and though it takes me a while, I realise why. There are crystal panels in the walls, as smooth and polished as the ones in the chamber of the Rondet. Many of them. Endless in number.

But they're all dark and lifeless. Empty. A chill slithers down my spine. How many of the native Anthaese had lain here. Once upon a time. And what happened? Where did they go?

'Rhenna?' I whisper, not wanting anyone else to hear. 'What is this place?'

But Rhenna doesn't answer. Her voice has fallen silent. She leaves only a lingering echo of grief behind her. They are walking through catacombs, where her long dead ancestors lay entombed. And they're all gone.

Our footsteps echo behind us and ahead of us. They bounce off the walls and the high domed roof of the tunnel and the remaining silence turns oppressive but still we carry on. Another gateway opens before them when I approach, Rhenna anticipating my request now.

It's a relief to know she's still with me, even if she is as quiet as one of those empty tombs.

Up ahead, a light is growing, the pale moonlit glow on the opalescent walls filtering down to the depths of the crowded gardens in the heart of Limasyll. A hidden entrance. No one would look for it down here, covered by the press of plant life which escaped the fire, or perhaps they've dismissed it as an older part of the ruins. A folly or a grove. Useless to them. Up until now it had been a dead end. I signal need-lessly for silence – everyone's silent anyway – and we fan out, secreting ourselves in the foliage, waiting.

The generator glows like a fireworm. Even from the deepest part of the garden I can see it. They've no shielding, nothing to keep in the light of the reactor or protect anyone from it. They brought their own because they can't be bothered to work out the Anthaese system. It's contaminating the air around it and probably the remaining plants too, those not burned to a cinder. *First objective*, I tell myself, even though everything I know and trust says to get to Con. If we don't take that thing down it's pointless. It cuts us off from reinforcements and the air attack. It isn't far. They built it on one of the higher terraces, trusting the surrounding ruins of the palace to protect it. They've been rebuilding here too, steel and glass structures bolted onto the ancient stonework like vile parasites. I grind my teeth, itching to tear it all down or blow it sky high. I'll do it myself if I have to.

'Scale the walls?' Thom suggests.

I nod grimly. Someone has to do it. But if the alarm is raised before we get to the thing…

'I'll go,' Petra volunteers and before I can stop her, she's away, crossing the garden and scaling the wall. Thom shakes his head and sets off in pursuit. I start up myself but Jondar catches my arm. Stopping me. He reads my mind too well.

'They know what they're doing.' But he doesn't sound any happier about it than I am.

My bodyguards scale the terraces like the shadows of mountain goats, their hands and feet finding footholds where no one else would see even a crack in the pearlescent walls. A patrol passes on an upper level and I'm sure my pulse, pounding in my throat, will alert them. Thom melts back into the shadows beneath them and I can't see Petra at all above him. But then the Gravians move on, and my friend appears again, rolling over the final balustrade to land lightly, silhouetted against the generator's glow. Thom joins her moments later.

They vanish inside the shelter to the control unit. For a moment nothing happens and then they reappear, scrambling back down the way they had come, as silently as ever. But a lot more quickly.

The generator hums on.

'What happened?' I ask, as they arrive, breathless. Thom's grinning wildly but Petra looks more sombre.

'He's rigged it to explode,' she says. 'We don't have a lot of time.'

'If it had just switched off mysteriously it would be more suspicious. Besides, this way they can't just switch it back on.'

Petra narrows her eyes. 'Yes, because a bloody great explosion isn't suspicious in the least. I would have taken something away so they couldn't fix it, Thom.'

He makes a face. 'Do you know what bit to take?'

'Well the on switch for one thing—'

'Never mind,' I interrupt them. 'It's good. It's all good. It'll buy us time.'

'For Con,' says Jondar. 'We have to find him.'

'I saw a dungeon.' I think back to the moment when my mind had connected with his. If only I could do that now, but the Rondet aren't that strong it seems. I've stretched them too thin. The network between them… that's one thing. But who knows where Con is?

'Not here,' Jondar says. 'We don't have…' But then his eyes take on a distant look. I know it. He's talking to them. Great, they're talking to Jondar but not to me? They really are annoyed with me then. 'Favre suggests the ice house. It's the deepest known part of the palace and would… give the same impression.'

'Favre knows the palace, does he?'

'He knows a lot of things.'

I'll bet he does. Yes, I'm fishing and I don't care who realises. Favre could stand to share a lot more.

'Four of us.' I signal to Thom and Petra who fall in without a word. 'Let's get him. The rest of you hold fast. Be ready when the generator blows. That's your distraction. And Zander's signal.' I send out the thought '*Let him know, please Rhenna.*'

We move through the darkness without incident. The Gravian patrols concentrate on the walls, not the interior. They are safe here, after all, or so they think. They'll discover differently before the night is out. Even now, my people are getting into position, inside and outside, above and beneath. I press on, in search of Con.

We find the body impaled on a spike, a broken doll dangling from the upper terrace. For a moment, a terrible moment, I choke on bile. He's been dead some time. Weeks.

But it isn't Con.

'Kendal.' Jondar's voice is very faint. Thom appears beside him, a hand on his shoulder and he falls silent again. I watch him as he takes in the fate of his brother and smothers his feelings once more. Grief is for later.

Beneath the prince's corpse, the ice-house is empty except for the ghastly statue. I saw it, in my vision of him, and it's just as chilling now. She looms over us, open mouthed, hands reaching out.

I kick some shackles on the cold, damp floor and my foot uncovers a smear of blood.

'*He was here.*' Rhenna's voice sounds sickened. '*Oh, poor Conleith. He was here. Not long ago. I can read his emotions, his agony, on this air. The trail is fresh and… and painfully vivid. But it's scattered, fragmented. I'm not sure I can follow it.*' Rhenna sounds as though the thought of trying repels her, but she at least doesn't argue or say it isn't her place. Rhenna cares deeply for Con too. And so, I realise, do all the Rondet. More than I'd understood. He is special.

Special to me, special to his people, so special that Matilde chose to remain a ghost encased in crystal to see him safe. So special that I'm here, even now, risking everything.

Always reckless.

'It's okay, Rhenna. I can.'

I slip the little receiver from my pack and flick the switch. The signal is stronger than I had hoped and I follow it, grateful for the transmitter implanted in the Anthaem, fearful of where it might take me. My bracelet communicator has one of a similar type, but Con's lies somewhere beneath his skin and I can only pray the Gravians have not discovered that.

Is Matilde with him? I don't know.

I hope not, for her sake. And for Con's. But I don't know where else she would be.

Three Gravians stand guard on the first terrace, three who are quickly despatched. Petra and Thom are perfect soldiers. I'm lucky to have them. We creep on, towards the upper gallery of the grand ballroom which had once sparkled with lights, and rung with music and laughter. Where my memories of the disastrous masked ball linger on.

Now I hear a scream, shaking those memories to pieces. Broken, agonised. I know the voice, know the pain threaded through it but wish I didn't. I don't need the tracker any more.

It's Con.

Chapter Twenty-Six

I gesture rapidly to Jondar and the others, aware of the light which enters their eyes, the hope restored there, outweighing every immediate concern. He's alive. Thank every ancestor, Con is still alive. Fear is there too. They all heard the pain. He's only alive for now.

We drift through the shadows, taking up position and I have to force myself not to rush to his side. I'm not the only one. Every one of us hold ourselves back.

He's in restraints, kneeling in the centre of the gallery and surrounded by guards, Gravian and their Mechas. Dried blood cakes the side of his face, and he holds one arm awkwardly. There's a red mark across his chest, a fresh burn. I can smell charred flesh, his flesh, and I choke back a cry. His face is thin and strained but his eyes blaze defiance and it makes my heart swell. They'd underestimated him, everyone does. Perhaps even me.

'We'll have to see what will make you more amenable, your Majesty. You've withstood torture, and drugs most admirably. The priests are thrilled with the pain you offered up. But it's over now. You need to learn your place.'

I know that voice too, that sneering whine. I hate it. I hate it more every time I hear it. Choltus strides into view, tapping a silver-tipped crop against his polished boots. He wears a blood-red frock coat, over a white silk shirt the same colour as his skin. Every inch of him looks a gentleman, a diplomat, a prince, except his eyes. His eyes are hard and vicious.

Several guards file out to be replaced by Mechas. Damn. It's harder to deal with these half-men than the Gravians themselves. They take more killing. But with so many of them here, in the ballroom, the occupying forces surrounding the palace have to be stretched thin by now, which can only work in our favour, can't it? Not here, not now, but when the Anthaese and Vairian forces attack.

'Shall we try this instead?' Choltus asks. I wait, counting, trying to ignore the look of horror on Con's face at whatever the ambassador is showing him now.

'I'm told it's agonising. I suppose it must be to remove all that makes you human and replace it with… well, other equipment. Normally, of course, we'd use those already far gone, battle fallen, already given up to pain. Or drug the subjects until they know no more. Normally.'

Something clanks and the air fills with a strangely metallic moan, a hum of the machinery with which my almost-husband has such affinity. The atmosphere crisps and the hairs on the back of my neck stand up. It's bad. Whatever it is. I sense it. I see it on his face.

'You can't do this,' Con gasps.

'Oh, but I can. This process is slow, but it is virtually undetectable to the naked eye. You'll look just as you do now, with barely a trace of scarring and you'll be so much more useful when you can follow orders. Like Lady Elara. She screamed for days. I feared she would lose her voice entirely, but we managed to engineer even that, to craft controls to save it and use it. Bring him.'

Two of the Mechas seize Con. He struggles, wounds forgotten, trying to tear himself free. Whatever he faces, it brings out the remaining fight in him.

I know why. I've been told about that sound, the smell of it, the way it alters even the air. It's the stuff of horror stories, of nightmares. A Mecha machine.

Ancestors, they're going to use that machine to make a soulless Mecha out of him.

The Gravians laugh as Con is dragged forwards, fighting every inch of the way, but helpless against men who are more machine themselves now. The Mechas are strong, programmed to obey without qualm or question. They might have been Anthaese themselves, dragged to the machine in just such a way to have their humanity torn from them. But they don't look human any more. A quick and dirty transformation. Or maybe there was too much damage to begin with. Con won't have the same luxury. Hours, Choltus said. But once he's in there...

'*Rhenna, give the signal.*'

Jondar hears me, my mental command amplified by panic. '*We're ahead of time! The generator—*'

And someone else hears too.

Con jerks his head our way. 'No!'

Whether he yells it to me or to his captors I don't know, or care.

'*Make* it ready. We're out of time.'

I step out into the open, firing as I do.

Dozens of Mechas face me. Con gives a cry of dismay as he sees me, but I don't hesitate or allow him to distract me. I take out three, while Jondar and the others rush in to flank me, plasma fire lighting up the room. The whine of their charges makes the air sing.

The Mechas holding Con topple, pulling him down with them. He struggles free, still in chains, still hurt, but he doesn't stop. I carry on firing, keeping them down, stopping them pursuing him. Con doesn't falter, running through the weapons fire like a deer in flight through the forest, ducking, leaping, pell-mell towards me.

As he reaches me, his legs almost give out. He goes down on his knees and scrambles up again. 'Bel? What are you doing here? What are you—'

I shoot past him, and the Mecha advancing on us crumples. Gravian shouts ring out, one of them producing a communicator, yelling for reinforcements. I take him between the eyes.

Thom goes down in a heap, swearing, and Petra tries to lay down covering fire. 'Back!' she yells to Jondar. 'Get behind me and get back. Princess – back.'

The bodyguard tries to grab me while Jondar lifts Thom, helping him to stand on a leg wound. But we're facing too many.

'Get out of here!' Con tells me, but it's already too late.

'Point one,' Thom barks into his coms, ignoring his injury. 'Point two, ready.' He pushes Jondar to the nearest window. 'Jump.' But he doesn't give the prince a chance to hesitate or argue. He shoves him out with a hand on the small of his back. Petra follows, not giving him the opportunity to push her. He looks right at me. 'You next, Princess.'

The shot strikes him in the shoulder, another in his stomach and he folds, his mouth open in surprise.

His name on my lips, his name screaming out of me. 'Thom!' I'm still trying to fire and pull Con with me, knowing it is all lost. Everything is lost.

Thom falls through the window after the others and I'm trapped, pinned down.

A massive explosion shakes the building. Dust tumbles from the ceilings and crashes echo around us as fragile stonework topples. Already damaged from the explosion that took out the tower during the invasion, the walls of the palace begin to crumble. The generator. It's the bloody generator.

I pull Con against me as the room begins to collapse around us, trying to shield him.

The chaos, noise and weapons fire dies. I look up, coughing through the dust to see the Mechas all around us despite the rubble. It barely hinders them. Every weapon is still trained on me and Con.

'Ah, the would-be Queen.' Choltus applauds from behind the line of his own guards. Where he's been throughout the fighting I don't know. Hiding, I expect. He doesn't strike me as the leading from the front kind. He steps forward now, right in front of me. Like I'm not any kind of threat any more. Like he has nothing to fear. 'We've been looking everywhere for you.'

I don't hesitate. I fire off a shot, but it glances harmlessly off his personal shield. I see it now, the bronze, ornate ball hanging at his belt. My weapon stutters and fails, the last of its power drained. My luck has just been used up.

I have to get Con out. That's all that matters now. Revenge can wait for another day. I pull him against me, aware at the time that he's trying to protect me, to put himself between me and the ambassador.

'Leaving so soon?' Choltus jeers. 'And we've so much to catch up on. Your family, for example. Your cousins. Your friends. You remember your friends, don't you? How many of them have died for you now?'

I drop the gun and close my hands on the belt knives, sliding the side blades from the sheaths that hug my body. I don't hesitate. I launch myself at him, ready to kill him with my bare hands if needs be.

An impossibly strong grip seizes me, pulls me off course and quells my struggles without any effort at all. I writhe in those pitiless hands, trying to kick and twist free. But I can't.

It's one of the Mechas. Just a Mecha, but my heart judders to a halt in my chest. My body goes limp, helpless and the blades drop from my hands, clattering uselessly to the ground.

Half the face is metal and an ocular implant replaces one eye. The other is as clear a blue as it ever was. I can only stare at the maimed form, more machine than human, but still recognisable. Just.

I would always recognise him.

'*No*,' I whisper, my voice weak.

The Mecha drops me and I scramble backwards under his intense scrutiny. His blue eye is as impassive as any piece of robotics. He doesn't look away and neither do I. It isn't possible…

'Bel, get to the window,' Con yells. 'Get out.'

Get out? How?

I can't move. Not even when Con screams my name again. All I can do is stare at Shae's ruined features.

'It's not him!' Con's trying to help. He really is. But nothing is going to help. 'Not any more. It just looks like him.'

I can't think. Can't react. The world turns to diamonds around me, impenetrable, hardest of all substances. And it can't protect me. It can't stop the agony that assaults me on every front.

It's Shae.

They've made Shae into one of their Mechas. He's still alive. Sort of. And though logic tells me that the Shae I knew is lost, I can see him there. In that brilliant blue tearless eye.

I'm falling, my legs turning liquid, my mind screaming.

The floor knocks the air from me but it doesn't matter. Nothing seems to matter any more.

Con calls my name. He gathers me in his arms, hampered by injuries and the manacles. But that doesn't stop him. His touch is a single brush of life against my battered soul.

'Are you hurt? Are you—?'

'It's Shae. Oh ancestors, Con, what did they do to him?'

It's the ambassador who answers. 'I'm more than happy to demonstrate. A fine example, isn't he? We kept enough of his mind to ensure he could counter your strategies. Most convenient. He was indeed useful but I think you bested him, Belengaria. You led us quite the dance, you clever girl. But not clever enough. Bring her.'

Shae, or what remains of him, and another Mecha seize me, their grip impossibly strong. Con is grabbed by another three of them and held there, struggling to get free.

'Let her go! You can't do this. You don't dare!'

Choltus strikes him full in the face with a clenched fist and Con sinks to stillness, dazed. 'Enough. Bring them to the ship. We're finally getting off this festering mudhole.'

Chapter Twenty-Seven

I desperately try to see something of Shae in the Mecha hauling me through the shattered corridors of Limasyll but he's gone. What remains is a shell, a hardwired machine that utilises his brain and his skills but has wiped the man from the equation.

But that doesn't seem to matter. I can't unsee him.

'Please, Shae, please, listen to me.' I can't help myself, even though I know it's hopeless.

We step out into the open air and I can hear battle. Overhead, ships whirl in the air, bright lines of weapons fire lighting up the sky. The Gravian shuttle whines into life even as we board. I'm flung down beside Con, and the Mecha that once was Shae stands over us, implacable and terrifying.

'Are you okay?' Con asks. 'Did he hurt you?'

Shae's covered in scars and metal implants. I can't take my eyes off him. The agony he must have endured as they put him back together. *Shae...*

'Bel, talk to me.'

'I... I'm fine. Con...'

I'm not. I'm really not. But I can't tell him that.

The ship roars into the sky, faster than I would have thought possible. Or maybe it just seems that way. The world has slowed to horror and pain. I can't think. All I want to do is scream and weep and tell myself to wake up.

Because this can't be real.

Because there's no waking from this.

The Gravian destroyer orbits the planet and it swallows us whole. I can see the lights of other ships, of battle, of the faltering, collapsing safeguards around them. And then we're inside, on the enemy ship, surrounded by bleak grey steel and nightmares. Even as we're hauled from the shuttle, I struggle to free myself but it's pointless. And the moment I see Shae again, I'm lost.

The room to which we're taken might have been a lab of some kind. Or a torture chamber. Con wraps his hand around mine, surprisingly warm and strong. I need that strength.

Choltus is waiting. He waves a hand nonchalantly and Con is dragged from me. When he fights, the Mecha punches him in the face, immediately putting an end to it. I jerk in rage and alarm as he goes down. But he drags himself back up again.

'Shall we begin the true negotiations, Anthaem?'

Con spits out blood. 'You're getting nothing from me. My people will never give up. And the Empire—'

But Choltus just smiles. 'Oh I think I am. Anthaeus isn't part of the Empire. The Empire can't act if you willingly cede this system to my people. They won't have any right to. You aren't beholden to the Empress, not really. In fact, she needs you more than you need her. Your people will stand down and obey you. I'm getting your signature on that treaty and I'll get a beautiful, new Mecha, in the form of the Vairian Princess, to do exactly what we tell her to. Be that torture you, assassinate her family, or even the Empress... anything really.' He laughs again, a high-pitched, grating laugh which makes me grind my teeth together.

'You can't,' I protest. 'You can't do this!'

If he sends me to kill the Empress, the whole Empire will turn on Vairian. They'll annihilate us all, warriors or not. If we're seen as a threat to the Empress, no quarter will be given, because even after fifteen years within the fold, they still see us as wolves. He knows that. He knows everything. He'll use the Empire to destroy my world, the world they couldn't conquer. He'll use *me* to make that happen…

Choltus marches towards me and seizes me by the throat. I grab one single breath before he tears me from Shae's grip and hefts me in the air, holding me there. I can't breathe. I can't—

'You need to learn your place, little bitch. Learn it and keep it. Your people let you run wild. Our women know better. Now, shall we begin?'

He drags me backwards, slamming my body into a waiting Mecha machine. Clamps snap shut around my arms and legs, a final band sliding around my throat so tightly that I can't breathe any more than I could with his hand around my throat.

'Let her go. Stop this!' Con screams. 'You win. Let her go.'

'No!' I shout, finding my voice from somewhere. He can't do this. He can't. Not now. Not for me. 'No, Con, please!'

Choltus ignores us, his hand sliding across the control panels. 'What'll we have? You can look just as you are. It hurts more, of course. Well, everything hurts. But this… this is excruciating, or so I'm told. Still, females have their vanities and are happy to suffer for them. Isn't that the case?'

I struggle and kick as best I can, trying to break my way free. I know what Con is going to do. I know and I can't let him do it. But there's no way to stop him. No way to stop either of them.

Choltus hits the switch and a thousand pinpricks of acid sink into my skin. My scream goes up a pitch, almost to the edge of hearing.

My brain tries to shut down, but the machine won't let it. The needles dig deeper.

The Mecha that was Shae watches me, his forehead creasing, skin stretching around the implants. It's more expression than I've seen in him since he appeared, but he doesn't move, doesn't do anything. I want to scream out to him for help, but there's no point. He's just a Mecha now. Elara… I remember Elara… she tried to help me. But Shae… Shae doesn't have any shadow of his own will left. He can't. If he did, if that was really a struggle I saw on his face, he'd do something to help me.

My vision blurs. My voice cracks And pain strangles it inside me.

Con surges up but the other Mechas pull him back before he can reach me.

'Stop! I'll sign it. I swear it. I'll sign anything. Let her go! Bel!'

The other Mechas pin him down, make him watch and my eyes fix on his. I've been so consumed with thoughts of Shae, but here's Con, giving up everything for me. Giving up a world. A planetary system. His own life and future. Everything.

No, Con. You mustn't. I try to send the thought to him, as another wave of agony breaks over me and my conscious thoughts became nothing but screams on the edge of hearing. Probes sink deeper into my body, fire in my veins. I reach out blindly with my mind, with my will, with the only thing I have left to wield. Even though I know we're off the planet, we're too far away, I reach for the hive mind. And scream.

The floor bucks violently, as if some great explosion rocks the ship. Choltus staggers back from the controls and the machine winds down with a sigh.

Drenched in sweat, heaving in breath after breath, I hang in its metal embrace, my skin and blood burning, my eyes streaming acid tears that sting my flesh as they fall.

'What is that?' Choltus snarls.

A Gravian guard speaks rapidly into his coms. 'We're under attack. The Vairians have broken through the line. We're taking heavy fire. The captain—'

'Tell him to take us to hyperspace at once.'

'He can't. He says... there's a hull breach. There's something... there's something else—'

All around us the ship howls and twists. We can hear screams and explosions, but it isn't the sound of a ship under attack. I know that sound. This ship is being torn apart.

Something huge slams into the other side of the metal wall. It buckles and groans. Again, a vast shape smashes against it and the metal begins to give, tearing, breaking. Something enormous punches its way through.

It is crystalline and terrible, from its strong jaws to the four outspread gossamer wings, the ends tipped with lethal looking blades.

Dragonfly, my aching mind screams. I know it, I've seen it before... In the broken tiles on the floor of the palace so far beneath me, in the tapestries and the carvings, in every Anthaese decoration. And here before me. A crystal dragonfly, the size of a tiger.

The Gravians scatter before it. My eardrums strain as it roars. Con collapses and the creature stands astride him, swiping at the Mechas still there. It devastates them, crushing them against the walls and floor. Multifaceted eyes gleam like tiny panels of stained glass.

'What is it?' Choltus cries, scrambling away, searching for a weapon.

'One of the ancient sleepers,' I manage, though why I answer him and whether he can hear me, I'm not sure. 'One of the native Anthaese.'

I need to hear it, to know that it's real. Who else would come so far to save us and stand guard over Con so ferociously? Who else would break all the rules to come to our aid? I want Choltus to know it too, to know that everything on the world below stood against him.

The creature roars again, a sound like stone cracking under pressure and the Mechas fire on it. Plasma fire bounces off its diamond hard sides. It's... no. *She*. She's a combination of insect, reptile and bird, a chimera that has no corresponding genus in our human science. Everything about her is fearsome and beautiful, as she still shelters Con and blocks them from me, circling warily. Her long tail lashes from side to side and she spreads her filigree lace wings, mantling those she guards like some kind of giant hawk.

'One of the...' Con gasps. He gazes up at the creature, his eyes wide. 'Who is it? Which...'

There's only one of them it can be. I want to tell him, but can't find the words. Which of them would come here alone, focused solely on protecting Con? I know the answer to that but can't share it with him. He'll never understand, or he'll blame himself. It can only be Matilde.

Choltus rushes for the door and the creature lurches towards him. But it's a feint. The Mecha that was Shae stands forward and he fires with pinpoint accuracy. Startled, Matilde rears away from the weapons fire and Choltus grabs me, the crop jabbing to my throat. The silver tip is a sharp blade.

Everything falls still. Too still.

'*Tell him to let you go,*' says Matilde. '*Tell him whatever you need to.*' She paces back and forth again, impatient, her eyes still gleaming sapphires. Her tail slices through the air, leaving gashes in the wall as she passes. '*Rhenna is coming now. When she is here together we will tear them to shreds.*'

'Let me go,' I whisper, my voice hoarse. 'And the creature will go. Fair's fair.'

Choltus grins without humour, showing all his teeth and tightens his grip. *'Fair's fair?* Since when was that true? It wasn't fair to my people, people of a dying world, who only wanted your water and resources. It wasn't fair to your royal family, who are dust in the wind. Fair's never fair, Princess. No, I think we're going to leave here together, you and me. And your beast is going to stay exactly where it is.'

He hits the door release and I wilt into his merciless grip. My body is too wrung out, the poisons in my system sapping my strength, leaving me without the ability to fight.

'Bel…' I can hear Con's voice so clearly in the bitter silence. 'Bel…'

'Trust her, Con. She'll take care of you.'

He looks up at the creature. 'Who is she?'

'Destroy it,' Choltus commands. Shae moves in a blur. He dives forward, rolling with unexpected grace and a grenade leaves his hand.

'Matilde, look out!' I scream.

The grenade rattles on the floor, rolling towards Con.

It only takes a moment. A terrible, endless moment. And I know… I know… Matilde won't let anything happen to Con.

She throws herself onto the explosive, and even her crystal body can't absorb so much destructive power. Con cries out, but the roar steals all sound. The detonation, the terrible shattering, the scream… Matilde's mental cry breaks like glass.

The silence that follows is cracked by a sob, by Con's voice crying out another woman's name. *'Matilde.'*

Sound thunders in on us. Outside I can hear battle, the whine of spaceships, shouted battle cries and death screams. And the roars of the Rondet as Matilde's death echoes through each of their minds.

'They're coming!' one of the guards shouts. 'Those things. More of them. What *are* they?'

I struggle free, my hands going to my waist, to the belt they had overlooked. The main knives slide free, curved like the fragments of her claws lying on the floor. I lunge at the ambassador, slicing through his shield, and deep into his shoulder and chest. But I miss his neck. He launches himself forward, hitting me full in the face with the back of his arm, and sending me sprawling onto the floor amid Matilde's shattered remains.

Con tries to reach me, crawling until his shaking hands cradle me. 'Was it her? How was it *her*? I heard *Matilde*. Bel? Answer me!'

The Rondet are screaming inside my head, and inside his as well. Screaming and aching, and raging. They are killing their enemies, slaughtering the Gravians wherever they find them, doing more damage than the vastly greater numbers of Vairian and Anthaese. Just three of them, furious in agony, wild with grief. I can feel them, their tangled emotions part of me, their pain my pain. Great wings beat the air like a hurricane.

The whine of plasma charging silences the two of us, drags our attention back to the room. I knot my fingers with Con's and look over my shoulder. Choltus stands by the door, clutching his side while blood pumps through fabric and fingers, but with his other hand holding the weapon aimed at my head.

'We underestimated you and the alliances you made, I see. But still, I can dispose of you both. One small vengeance to take home. The goddess will be pleased with this small thing.'

Con struggles to put himself in front of me. 'Let Bel be. This is our fight.'

'It's as much about her as you, Conleith. She's Vairian. The only race to defeat us. We took their royals in revenge and still they vex us. They are the teeth and claws of the Empire. Without them, what defences do they truly have? Weapons, yes, and riches to buy more. But no one to wield them. Not like the Vairians. The Empire doesn't care to fight, much like your own people. You're content to let the Vairians do it for you, encourage them and use them. Send them out like a pack of dogs to do your beck and call. And her family name is known to us. I want *her* most of all. And if I can't have her obedient, I'll have her dead.'

Everything about my world slows to a crawl. Each movement, each breath, each heartbeat dragging out in detail. He jerks his finger to fire. There's nothing I can do. I know that, with a painful stab of resignation. I'm going to die, here, on the floor even when escape is within our grasp.

A metallic whine breaks the silence and a line of silver slices through the air. It thuds into the ambassador's chest and another follows, embedding itself in his throat. Choltus stares at them, stupidly, as if trying to work out how they got there. With the weapon still in his hand, his finger jerks reflexively and he fires. Con and I duck, but he's shooting blind, above us, sparks raining from the metal ceiling. He falls, with the belt knives jutting from his body, still firing. Plasma fire saws through the Mecha who stands behind us, metal and flesh burning.

Shae!

He doesn't move for a moment, just looks at the two of us. If he knew us, there is no sign. I think his mouth moves, though whether to say something or to smile, I can't say. There's something like recognition in his eye, that remaining blue eye that's fixed on me and only on me, that knows me. He almost smiles once again, a smile as familiar to me as my own face in the mirror. And then he falls too, a lifeless body, held together by broken machinery.

Chapter Twenty-Eight

I don't move, can't move. Everything hurts. My body, my mind, my heart. Con holds me against him in the silence and we listen to the ship dying all around us.

'It's breaking up,' I whisper. 'We'll hit the atmosphere. We'll...'

We'll burn. That's what'll happen. We'll break up and burn.

Con lets me go and gets up, crossing to Choltus. He stands there for a moment, then kicks him to make sure he's really dead. After another pause he bends down, retrieving my knives first and then relieves the late ambassador of his weapons and anything else that might be of use. I've only ever seen him so business-like when tinkering with his inventions. He takes what he needs, pausing only to fiddle with something, bent over it with his back to me so I can't see what it is. It doesn't matter. Can't he see that? We're going to die.

'Con, we haven't a hope here—'

'Shhh...' Con pulls me to my feet, trying to protect me, even from this. And I had come to rescue *him*. Idiot that I am.

We stagger towards the corridor. It's bleak and grey, filling with smoke and noxious gases. There's nowhere to go from here either. Even if I could remember the way back to the hanger, even if there was a ship left to escape in... The lights flare and die around us. It's terribly still for a moment. Like a pause. Like the universe holding its breath.

The explosion tears the back of the great vessel away, throwing us both to the ground and for a moment I think that this is it. That we're dead. But, though the ship shrieks, tearing itself apart around us, it isn't over yet.

Fire has broken out behind us. I can feel the heat, smell the chemicals and the smoke. We'll suffocate here. We don't even get to die cleanly.

Through the *'ffftz'* of emergency containment defences, I can see the stars. I can see Anthaeus. It's a beautiful blue, white and green orb, shining in the darkness. You can't even see the damage the Gravians have done from up here. A sob catches in my throat. It's home. It's our home.

'Hold on,' says Con.

'What?'

Out among the stars, the ships whirl and dance. The red and blue flares burst and fade as Gravian vessels make the jump to hyperspace, fleeing now they are defeated, as they always do. But the ship around us is coming apart. I can feel it. It won't go anywhere but down.

Lifepods, such as there are on other ships, are few and far between here, an anathema to the Gravian way of life. Or rather death. There is no way off.

Except out.

Con gathers me against him. 'Ready?'

I nod. Better to go this way. Better to die among the stars than in a hulk of fiery metal, than to burn to death. Better to make that leap.

I intertwine my fingers with his and together we run for the end of the collapsing corridor. Decompression training takes over. Breathe out, empty the air from the lungs to avoid an embolism. It doesn't matter that we'll die seconds later with no air. Nothing matters. Together we leap into the void.

We fly.

Con hits something on his belt. The personal shield slides up around us, a clear barrier and oxygen floods in. Choltus' shield. I gasp, a snatched breath of relief and surprise and Con smiles at me, holding me close again as we float clear of the disintegrating ship.

Flying among the stars.

'I boosted its power. It won't last long. But I couldn't let you burn.'

Spinning into space is so much better, I suppose. But then I look down, towards the planet.

From beneath us a crystalline creature rises like a dragonfly from the atmosphere. She gleams as the light of the sun and the stars bounce off her. Great wings spread wide and her many lensed eyes pick us out amid the debris with the accuracy of a hawk. Rhenna gives a cry of joy and wraps herself around us.

*

The battle is over and even now, the remaining three Rondet circle overhead, ripping anything Gravian that flew from the sky, whether it's retreating or not. Their teeth and claws are all the weapons they need, their wings giving them speed. I know I must have blacked out. All I can remember is floating amid the stars and the fragments of the Gravian destroyer, and Rhenna coming to save us.

And Con holding me.

And Shae… dying for me. Again.

Rhenna brings us back to the palace, or what remains of it, settling in the gardens.

'Here! They're here!' It's Jondar's voice. He runs towards us, stumbling over himself in his haste. Behind him I see Petra and Thom, my bodyguards, miraculously still alive. Thom is wounded but he's still going, as determined as ever. Body armour, I remember. Thom always wore body armour.

I could kiss him for it. But I think both Con and Jondar would object.

Battered and patched up as they all are, we're much worse and they immediately take charge of us.

I see glimpses of Vairian flyers – transports, Falcons and even Wasps – zipping overhead. But mostly I stare at the remaining three members of the Rondet, sunlight glinting off their bodies like metal and precious stones. I can't stop watching them. They fly like dragonflies, like the creatures in my memory, their double wings flickering with such speed that they're just a blur. They shine, their colours iridescent and ever-changing. Did I help them take that form? Or had they always been that way, waiting to be awoken when they were needed?

'Report,' Con croaks the word.

'The day is ours,' Jondar tells him. 'They're running for hyperspace and the Imperial forces are in pursuit. And you need a medic. Both of you do.'

'Thom?' I interrupt them. 'What happened?'

'I'm fine, your Highness,' he tells me. 'Really. The armour took most of the impact and the leg's not bad.'

'He's made of rubber,' Petra tells me. 'Everything bounces off him.'

We're whisked away – half-dragged if the truth be told. I probably black out again. The pain smothers my consciousness and it's a blessed release. Con stays with me. I hear him shouting at anyone who tries to take him from me. It's not like him to shout. I hear him sobbing when we're alone. His hand never leaves mine.

I wake in a bedroom, with Con slumped on his knees beside my bed, his head and shoulders on the pillows. He still holds me, even with the lightest grip. He breathes fitfully and I know he hasn't even taken the time to see to his own wounds. His bandages have been done there, right beside me. He still wears the ragged remains of the clothes he'd been taken prisoner in. He hasn't even relinquished the metallic orb on his belt, the shield that saved us both. He looks so tired, so young. Far too young to be so worn.

'Con?'

He stirs, and lifts his face suddenly, dragging in a great gasp of air. The fear on his face is a stark reminder. The marks of torture and depredation are still on him. The ghosts haunting his eyes are far worse. I want to ask what they did to him, but I can't, not yet. He struggles to get control over himself.

'Was it her?' he asks, his voice rough and broken. I'm still reluctant to tell him, but he knows. He's too clever, my Con. Too clever for his own good. 'How?'

'She wanted to watch over you and the Rondet took her in, made her part of the fourth. And when we were in danger...'

'She's dead, isn't she? Really dead, this time. I heard them screaming. All of them. I hear them now.' I don't know what to say so I hold him, wrapping my arms around him and pulling him as close as I can. 'They're weeping. I don't think they'll ever stop weeping.'

'Come here,' I say and draw him up on to the bed beside me. We curl together as best we can, holding each other carefully. It hurts. But that doesn't matter.

Time passes. We lie there in silence. I listen to his breath, willing it to even out, to calm. Medics come and both of us are examined and given healing draughts and our dressings changed. But all the same, we don't pull apart.

I won't leave him. Not again. I think he feels the same. I hope. He has to. I can't be so wrong as all that, can I? I refuse to leave him.

Not after everything we've been through. I can't. I don't need to be a queen, or a princess or anything else. It doesn't matter. I just need him.

I couldn't let him go now. Not after everything. I've lost too much.

'It was Shae,' I say at last. 'He was a Mecha and he saved me. He remembered me. Mechas aren't meant to do that.'

'No,' Con agrees. 'They aren't.' He reaches out and brushes the tears from my cheekbone. I hadn't even been aware that I was crying. His fingers linger there, as if examining my skin. I can feel his touch tingling against me. Such a familiar, welcome sensation now.

'How then?'

'How did Matilde—'

'*I don't know.* Oh ancestors, Con... I never meant for either of them—'

He kisses me, fierce and determined, silencing me.

'I prayed you'd come,' he says. 'I prayed and I dreaded it. Because I knew you would. And I thought... when I saw Shae, I thought...'

'That he'd kill me?'

'No,' he replies, suddenly firm. 'No, I never thought that.'

'There was no saving him. He was a Mecha. Everything he was should have been scoured away. And yet, he still saved me.'

'I wouldn't expect anything else from him, in any form.'

I thread my fingers more intimately through his and tighten my grip. I kiss him again, but I'm tired now. My eyes slip closed...

I must have slept again. Maybe it's the medicines they keep feeding me. Maybe the exhaustion is finally too strong to fight.

Sometime later, there's more shouting outside. Not battle this time, at least not a military one. Someone profoundly unwise is trying to make

Jondar and Petra give way to let them in. And not exactly winning, but not giving up either. But then, stubbornness *is* a family trait.

I can't find words, but I know what's coming. I can't avoid it. Can't even get away now. Oh ancestors, this is a new nightmare.

Con scrambles to his feet, smoothing himself down. A defensive gesture, I realise now, arming himself for combat in his own way. Words, diplomacy and that ingenious brain, that's what he'll try to use. Against this foe, however, they'll have no effect. I pull him back against me. I'll protect him. He can no more stand than I can right now but he does it anyway. Strain shows on his now bloodless face. But he doesn't sit back down. Stubbornness doesn't just run in my family.

'You're the Anthaem,' I remind him, threading my fingers through his behind his back. 'This is your world.'

'Yes, but he's your—'

'Where is she?' Zander shouts as he throws the doors open and strides into the room. 'Where's my sister?'

I push myself up on one elbow, because it's all I can manage right now.

'Here. And you're making too much noise. People are recovering.'

'I thought you were dead, you stupid girl,' he snarls. 'And shouldn't you put that boy down?'

I hold on to Con, giving my brother my most obstinate look. Con just stares at Zander, without saying a word, but he doesn't move either. I smile slowly, with growing confidence. Con isn't going anywhere.

'He is my promised husband, Zander. And since I almost lost him already, I'm not letting him out of my sight.'

'Sentimental,' snorts my brother. 'Very well. They'll make songs of you, no doubt. You, who woke crystal dragons to rescue the Anthaem. Who leaped into the vacuum of space and lived. The Bloody Bride, wasn't it?' I wince at the hated title. It sounds so strange in his lips. He grins at me, clearly delighted. 'Apt. I like it. They love it at home, by the way. Oh, the adulation we'll have to live with. It's going to be sickening. And now, the Vairian Queen.'

'I'm not the queen.'

Con clears his throat at last. 'You are in all but name. And that's something we can remedy as soon as you're ready. If you... if you want, I mean. I've heard them talking while you slept, Bel. But then, we knew it weeks ago, back when we hid in the woods. You're their heroine, an inspiration, and they would do anything for you. I think you've won my people more completely than I ever could.'

I can't think of an answer. Listening to him speak, I think my heart will fill to overflowing. It aches with the love in his words. Tears sting at my eyes again, but not tears of pain this time. There's no pain left in me.

'Well, poetry seems to be the tender here all of a sudden.' Zander laughs. 'But my sister needs to think about her future. Our father and the Empress had an agreement to defend this world, and it is fulfilled. Without a marriage. Bel is within her rights to return home.'

I jerk back in alarm, staring at him. 'Leave Anthaeus?'

'That's usually what "return home" means, little sister. Although we can wait until there's time to wash at least.' He has the nerve to wrinkle up his nose. Zander, who I've seen covered in the ancestors knew what after a night out with his Wing, has the bloody nerve to...

But then Zander pauses, leaning in close to peer at me. 'What have you done to your skin? Is that gold?'

My hand flies up to my cheekbone, where Con had touched me earlier, where Zander stares now. Con's fingers closed over mine again and he smiles so gently, understanding. And I know then, know it without having to look, I have that same trace of gilded scales that he wears. He already knew.

'A side effect of prolonged contact with the Rondet. They leave little marks on you. It's beautiful. But it'll fade, if you go.'

Go? Now?

'I'm not planning on going *anywhere*,' I snarl with all the rage of Rhenna or Matilde at their angriest.

Zander shakes his head. 'Ferocious as a dragon too. Maybe their company has rubbed off on you in more ways than one.'

'And they aren't dragons, you moron. They're the native Anthaese. Dragons are mythical. These are completely different. They're real. Have you even looked at them?'

My brother tilts his head to one side, looking not at me but at Con. 'Really, Anthaem? Do you see what you're letting yourself in for? And I'm just her brother. I'm giving you the perfect escape plan, man. You'll have it much worse.'

'Crown Prince Lysander?' Con clears his throat, formal and solemn. 'I believe it would be an honour.'

I try to struggle off the bed, feeling outnumbered and not at all liking it. 'What?'

Con takes both of my hands in his own and guides me back to lie down again. I would protest, but my body is not cooperating. 'I can only offer you a shattered land in need of rebuilding. I can only offer you a broken Anthaem, in need of healing.' And he knelt before me. 'Say you'll stay here and be my queen.'

There's just one answer I could give. All I would have wished since I came here has changed. I lost Shae. I'd never really had him to begin with. Nothing is taking Con from me. Not even my own doubts. My choice is made. Perhaps it has been since I first went to the aid of the engineer in the bowels of a dying ship.

'Yes.' I press my lips to his, not caring about brothers, the will of the Empress, nobility, or anything else. His kiss is all that matters, his arms around me, his touch and the promise of a life together.

Epilogue

The breeze ripples through the new leaves on the trees, bringing a fall of blossoms swirling around the gardens. I can hear the sound of the building crews, hammers on stone and metal, the whine of drills, and the soft hum of the replication units. They're winding down for the night and they'd want to be – it's getting late and Jondar will have a fit if it interferes with his plans. Lights, strung up between the terraces above mirror the stars which are just emerging from the purpling sky.

The lake looks silver in the evening light. We've cleared back the entrances to the underground tunnels and about a hundred archaeologists from right across the system have applied to study the finds. Favre doesn't approve. Aeron is fascinated. Rhenna seems more concerned with flying as far as she can across Anthaeus.

'That's your influence,' says Con, when I bring it up. Perhaps it is.

We have other priorities right now, of course. The city is still mostly in ruins. Three months after the overthrow of the Gravians, there are still those who refuse to come out of hiding. Many of them have chosen to stay permanently in the underground city, and I can't say I blame them. It's beautiful down there, but most of all, it's safe. Anthaeus will take years to recover, both mentally and physically. An expeditionary force sent to Kelta returned the worst news. The moon is dead. Not a single survivor remained.

At the foot of the meandering pathway, at the top of the lake, we've built a shrine. A wall of fluttering pieces of paper, some printed with pictures, some handwritten and drawn, keepsakes and memories, interwoven with vines and flowers. The candles are lit each night, laid out like stars. When they melt down, another is placed on top of the wax and the colours bleed together.

All the lost faces look down on us.

I light my candles, as does he, in silence, in our own space, in our own time. I set tiny flames flickering for those I lost. For Nerysse, for Dan and Jessam, for Elara, for Devra the pilot.

And for Shae. The picture I found of him on file doesn't do him justice. It looks like it was taken for an ID card. I should ask someone to paint his portrait, but it would have to be someone who knew him. And there aren't many of us left.

I stand back, staring up at all those faces, not just my lost friends. Con comes close, wrapping me in his warm arms and I lean back against him. He tucks his chin on the top of my head.

'We should go,' I tell him. 'There's a wedding to prepare for.'

'We have ages yet. They can wait for us.'

I smile. The thought of Jondar pacing back and forth, waiting for us… it seems cruel.

'If we don't go soon, Thom will come and get us himself.' It's not fair to keep your friends waiting on their wedding day, even if you are the Anthaem. I shake my head. 'Come on.' And still holding his hand, I move to lead him away, to start back up the many steps through the gardens that are only just stirring back to life.

Three young woman are heading our way and they hesitate when they see us, sweeping into curtsies.

'Majesties, we're sorry,' one of them eventually stammers. 'We didn't mean to interrupt.' One look at their faces tells me what they're thinking and I almost laugh out loud. Even after all they've been through there's a certain prudishness to the Anthaese. It doesn't bother me any more. In fact there's something endearing about it. How can you not love a world full of people like them?

And Con? He blushes like a child. Really blushes.

'It's fine,' I tell them. 'We're just leaving. And this is a place for everyone, not just us. You know that.'

I glance back at the wall. I can see Matilde's face too, the tattered remains of that beautiful portrait I had once found Con standing in front of like a devotee. He must have found it in the ruins. How like him, to want to honour her, to put her here amongst her people, our people. Our lost loves gaze down on us, but it's not the same. The love I feel now is a different kind of love.

'Bel.' He lifts my hand to his mouth, kisses my fingers and I can't help but look back at him, to gaze into those green and perfect eyes. There's an uncertainty in them, concern. For a moment I don't understand. 'If you need more time…'

I kiss him. Sometimes it's the only way to shut him up, sometimes I just do it because I can. I pull him into my arms and push myself up on my toes so I can capture his mouth with mine. I pour my heart into that kiss and he slowly melts against me, relishing each moment, each movement.

After the longest time – with the girls whispering and stifling embarrassed, breathless giggles – I pull back, just a little, and look into his eyes. 'I'm sure, Con. I've never in my life been so sure of anything else. Let's go.'

A Letter from Jessica

Thank you so much for reading *The Queen's Wing*. I hope you enjoyed it as much as I liked writing it! If you'd like to keep up-to-date with all of my latest releases, you can sign up at the following link. Your email address will never be shared and you can unsubscribe at any time.

www.bookouture.com/jessica-thorne

Most books grow from a variety of seeds, all sorts of ideas and stories which meld together to create something new. I read a fascinating book about medieval queens (*Queens Consort* by Lisa Hilton). I loved *Star Wars* from the first moment I saw it (a long time ago…). I love the steampunk aesthetic and I adore a love story. On holidays, I visited various chateaux in the Loire Valley, and medieval citadels like Carcassonne and Mont Saint Michel. It wasn't exactly research, but it was, in the way that everything is research. My family puts up with a lot.

From *A Princess of Mars* to *Jupiter Ascending*, space opera and planetary romance are full of excitement, adventure, lavish settings, and wonder.

And who doesn't fall in love with a kickass princess like Leia whose place is definitely in the revolution. And when Han says 'I know'.

As for the wedding gown… I watch a LOT of *Say Yes To The Dress*.

If you have time, I'd love it if you were able to let me know what you thought of the book and **write a review of *The Queen's Wing*.** Feedback is really useful and also makes a huge difference in helping new readers discover one of my books for the first time.

Alternatively, if you'd like to contact me personally, you can reach me via my Website, Facebook page, Twitter or Instagram. I love hearing from readers, and always reply.

Again, thank you so much for deciding to spend some time reading *The Queen's Wing*. I'm looking forward to sharing my next book with you very soon.

With all best wishes,
Jessica

         www.rflong.com/jessicathorne

         www.facebook.com/JessThorneBooks

         @JessThorneBooks

Glossary

Anthaem – Ruler of Anthaeus, selected from among his or her people by the Rondet, noted for the ingenious technology, peaceful nature and great beauty

Anthaese – The people of Anthaeus, human colonists who left the expanding Empire to settle there

Anthaeus – A colony world ruled by the Anthaem, independent of the Empire. It was previously home to the Rondet and a great deal of their buildings and marks of civilisation remain

Camarth – An Imperial world, noted for its religious nature

Cuore – Central world of the Empire, seat of the Empress

Duneen – Rural area near Elveden on the planet Vairian

Elveden – Bel's home, now the new royal capital of Vairian

Falcons – Vairian flying machines designed specifically for combat

Firstworld – The original world from which all colonists set out

Gravia – Homeworld of the Gravians

Gravians – Ancient enemies of the Vairians, an alien race who worship a death goddess. Their dying world means they need to seek out other worlds to exploit

Higher Cape – The former royal capital of Vairian

Kelta – The moon of Anthaeus, source of powerful energy crystals which are mined there. Currently occupied by Gravians and the source of a bitter dispute

Limasyll – Capital of Anthaeus, mostly built by the Rondet and adopted by the Anthaese when they colonised the planet. Known for its beauty, the citadel which houses the palace and the elaborate gardens

Maestre – Honorary title of male member of the Rondet

Maestra – Honorary title of female member of the Rondet

Mechas – Human-machines, created by the Gravians by grafting technology onto the dead to fight as cannon fodder in their many wars

Melia – An imperial world, known for food and wine

Montserratt – A region of Anthaeus

Rondet – Ancient beings who guide the Anthaem as a council

Vairian – Bel's homeworld, independent of the Empire but closely aligned to it through a military alliance which sees Vairians as the military might of the Empire

Verdeyne – An imperial world, famous for fashion and the production of silk

Wasp – Vairian flying machines

Acknowledgements

Many thanks to all the wonderful people who have helped and supported me while I wrote *The Queen's Wing*. A special thank you to everyone who critiqued for me.

I'd like to thank my marvellous ladies of the Romantic Novelists Association Naughty Kitchen – Janet Gover, Kate Johnson, Alison May, Imogen Howson, Annie O'Neil and Rhoda Baxter– and C.E. Murphy, Susan Connolly, and Sarah Rees Brennan, all of whom offer continual support, patience and inspiration.

And of course, thanks to my agent Sallyanne Sweeney, and Kathryn, Maisie and all at Bookouture.

But most of all thanks to and for my husband Pat, who is always my hero, and my kids, Diarmuid and Emily, who thrived on burnt pizza (which encouraged them to learn to cook).

Keep reading for an exclusive extract from Jessica Thorne's next book, a follow-up to *The Queen's Wing*!

One golden Anthaese afternoon, there's a knock on the door of my office. I have an office now. Someone insisted. One day I will find out who and then they'll regret it.

'Enter,' I snap, pushing the tablet back from me and locking the screen. To my surprise, when the door opens it's Bel.

'Petra?' Just Bel, on her own, which is unusual. She's wearing her knife belt – a habit of which I approve. The slipping away from the guards I assign to keep her safe is a lot less endearing.

I get to my feet and give a bow but she rolls her eyes. 'Oh stop it.'

'What can I do for you, your Majesty?'

I should be reading reports but sometimes it's hard to concentrate in my little office where the windows look out over Limasyll. It's not everyone who gets to watch a new world being built out of the ruins of the old.

She slips inside, closes the door behind her and takes a seat by the window. 'I have a favour to ask.'

As if I could deny her anything. 'Of course. Just ask.'

She doesn't though. Not at first. Her attention is captured by the view.

Negotiations with the Empire stalled. The Anthaese don't actually need them now they have the Vairian alliance and the Rondet. The world is blossoming and the wounds are slowly being healed. They aren't ready to hand over everything to a distant Empire. The Empress seems content – for now, anyway – to allow my new homeworld to be her hand here. I don't think she realises how completely Anthaeus tends to make those who come here its own. Spend any time on this world and it draws you in, and gives you a new home.

Bel and Con, beautiful as night and day, complementing each other in all things, rule a court filled with wonders. His inventions are changing the galaxy and her courage is the ground on which he builds. Their people adore her like a living saint, as much as they did Matilde, an idea which makes her blush and laugh at the same time. But you can see how much it means to her. How much she loves them back.

Eventually she lets out a heavy sigh. 'You aren't going to like it.'

I sit in the matching chair. It's a nice space, relaxing. I don't know who decided I needed it but I do. Sometimes, just to know I'm not trapped behind that desk. 'Bel, I'm at your command. You know that.'

It must be to do with the wedding. The Wedding, which is being planned once again, but this time it's a formality, more like a celebration for the new Anthaeus and its restored freedom. A statement of their victory. It has to be perfect. Jondar will see to that, and Thom is almost as bad as he is.

And as for them, Thom and Jondar were handfasted in a traditional Vairian ceremony combined with a full Anthaese marriage. It was horribly complicated, overly elaborate and a lavish affair but they loved every minute of it. I pointed out that perhaps they should have let Bel and Con have their wedding first but Thom told me it would take too long and he wouldn't wait. So that was that.

We've been building up the military – a people who almost lost everything will not treat freedom so lightly again. I've never known troops work so hard and with such zeal. They're ingenious too, but then, their ruler is an engineer to his core. I think one day they will try even the Vairian military.

So here I am and here I stay, serving my princess, leading my troops, rebuilding a world anew. For now anyway. I'm not a soldier any more but a General, which just means more paperwork and less time. When the interstellar networks tell the story of the defence of Anthaeus, they speak of heroism and valour. Who wants to hear of death and agony, of sacrifice and destruction?

Bel laces her fingers together, a sure sign that she's nervous. So it really *is* something I won't like. To be honest, I'm intrigued.

'I'd rather not make it a command, Petra. It's difficult and it's not something I'd ask lightly.'

It's sounding worse with every second that drags by. I'm imagining ballgowns, tulle and so much lace. Probably in a very bright colour that definitely isn't my preferred black.

'What is it, Bel?'

She bites on her lower lip and looks guilty. It's really bad then. Worse than ballgowns. 'Zander's coming to the wedding.'

Oh.

I knew he was coming to the wedding. Of course I knew. Logically. He was a guest when it was originally planned. But I didn't really dwell on it. There has been so much else to worry about…

I desperately try to find something polite to say instead of what I'm thinking. He's her brother, after all. Ballgowns would be easy in comparison. 'Of course he is. Crown Prince Lysander is—'

'Stop it. I need you to look after him. He has a habit of getting himself into trouble. And I know this might be awkward but…'

She knows. Of course she knows. She finds out everything. She looks so little and helpless and suddenly she has you in a headlock with a knife at your throat and a gun in your back. Not that she needs both.

Zander and me. There's a history. Not just my refusing to follow his orders when they conflicted with my duty to her. But so much more. Back at home, all through training and on a hundred missions…

'I'm at your service, your Majesty,' I tell her, because what else can I say? She's my queen and if she wants me to babysit her big brother, well then. I'll babysit.

Zander and me.

This is going to be a disaster.

Printed in Great Britain
by Amazon

54542208R00218